About the Author

Since her first novel, *From Doon with Death*, published in 1964, Ruth Rendell has won many awards, including the Crime Writer's Association Gold Dagger for 1976's best crime novel with *A Demon In My View*, and the Arts Council National Book Award, genre fiction, for *The Lake of Darkness* in 1980.

In 1985 Ruth Rendell received the Silver Dagger for *The Tree of Hands*, and in 1987, writing as Barbara Vine, won her third Edgar from the Mystery Writers of America for *A Dark-Adapted Eye*.

She won the Gold Dagger for *Live Flesh* in 1986, for *King Solomon's Carpet* in 1991 and, as Barbara Vine, a Gold Dagger in 1987 for *A Fatal Inversion*.

Ruth Rendell won the *Sunday Times* Literary Award in 1990, and in 1991 she was awarded the Crime Writer's Association Cartier Diamond Dagger for outstanding contributions to the genre. In 1996 she was awarded the CBE, and in 1997 was made a Life Peer.

Her books have been translated into twenty-five languages and are also published to great acclaim in the United States.

Ruth Rendell has a son and two grandsons, and lives in London

By Ruth Rendell

RUTH RENDELL

MURDER BEING ONCE DONE

SHAKE HANDS FOR EVER

arrow books

This edition published by Arrow Books in 2005

Arrow Books
The Random House Group Limited
20 Vauxhall Bridge Road, London SW1V 2SA

Random House Australia (Pty) Limited
20 Alfred Street, Milsons Point, Sydney
New South Wales 2061, Australia

Random House New Zealand Limited
18 Poland Road, Glenfield,
Auckland 10, New Zealand

Random House (Pty) Limited
Endulini, 5a Jubilee Road Parktown 2193, South Africa

The Random House Group Limited Reg. No. 954009

www.randomhouse.co.uk

A CIP catalogue record for this book
is available from the British Library

Papers used by Random House
are natural, recyclable products made from wood grown in
sustainable forests. The manufacturing processes conform to
the environmental regulations of the country of origin

ISBN 0 09 190744 6

Printed and bound in Great Britain by
Cox & Wyman Ltd, Reading, Berkshire

RUTH RENDELL

MURDER BEING ONCE DONE

arrow books

For Frits and Nelly Twiss

The chapter heading quotations are taken from
Sir Thomas More's *Utopia*
in the Ralph Robinson translation of 1551

1

The sick ... they see to with great affection, and let nothing at all pass concerning either physic or good diet whereby they may be restored to their health.

WHEN Wexford came downstairs in the morning his nephew had already left for work and the women, with the fiendish gusto of amateur dieticians, were preparing a convalescent's breakfast. It had been like that every day since he arrived in London. They kept him in bed till ten; they ran his bath for him; one of them waited for him at the foot of the stairs, holding out a hand in case he fell, a lunatic smile of encouragement on her face.

The other—this morning it was his nephew's wife, Denise—presided over the meagre spread on the dining-room table. Wexford viewed it grimly: two circular biscuits apparently composed of sawdust and glue, a pat of unsaturated fat, half a sugarless grapefruit, black coffee and, crowning horror, a glass of wobbly pallid substance he took to be yoghurt. His own wife, trotting behind him from her post as staircase attendant, proffered two white pills and a glass of water.

'This diet,' he said, 'is going to be the death of me.'

'Oh, it's not so bad. Imagine if you were diabetic as well.'

'Who,' quoted Wexford, 'can hold a fire in his hand by thinking on the frosty Caucasus?'

He swallowed the pills and, having shown his contempt for the yoghurt by covering it with his napkin, began to eat sour grapefruit under their solicitous eyes.

7

'Where are you going for your walk this morning, Uncle Reg?'

He had been to look at Carlyle's house; he had explored the King's Road, eyeing with equal amazement the shops and the people who shopped in them; he had stood at the entrance to Stamford Bridge football ground and actually seen Alan Hudson; he had traversed every exquisite little Chelsea square, admired the grandeur of The Boltons and the quaint corners of Walham Green; on aching feet he had tramped through the Chenil Galleries and the antique market. They liked him to walk. In the afternoons they encouraged him to go with them in taxis and tube trains to the Natural History Museum and Brompton Oratory and Harrods. As long as he didn't think too much or tax his brain by asking a lot of questions, or stay up late or try to go into pubs, they jollied him along with a kind of humouring indulgence.

'Where am I going this morning?' he said. 'Maybe down to the Embankment.'

'Oh, yes, do. What a good idea!'

'I thought I'd have a look at that statue.'

'St Thomas More,' said Denise, who was a Catholic.

'Sir Thomas,' said Wexford, who wasn't.

'St Thomas, Uncle Reg.' Denise whisked away the unsaturated fat before Wexford could eat too much of it. 'And this afternoon, if it isn't too cold, we'll all go and look at Peter Pan in Kensington Gardens.'

But it was cold, bitingly cold and rather foggy. He was glad of the scarf his wife had wrapped round his neck, although he would have preferred her not to have gazed so piteously into his eyes while doing so, as if she feared the next time she saw him he would be on a mortuary slab. He didn't feel ill, only bored. There weren't even very many people about this morning to divert him with their flowing hair, beads, medieval ironmongery, flower-painted boots and shaggy coats matching shaggy Afghan hounds. The teeming young, who usually drifted past him incuriously, were this morning

8

congregated in the little cafés with names like Friendly Frodo and The Love Conception.

Theresa Street, where his nephew's house was, lay on the borders of fashionable Chelsea, outside them if you hold that the King's Road ends at Beaufort Street. Wexford was beginning to pick up these bits of with-it lore. He had to have something to keep his mind going. He crossed the King's Road by the World's End and made his way towards the river.

It was lead-coloured this morning, the 29th of February. Fog robbed the Embankment of colour and even the Albert Bridge, whose blue and white slenderness he liked, had lost its Wedgwood look and loomed out of the mist as a sepia skeleton. He walked down the bridge and then back and across the road, blinking his eye and rubbing it. There was nothing in his eye but the small blind spot, no immovable grain of dust. It only felt that way and always would now, he supposed.

The seated statue which confronted him returned his gaze with darkling kindliness. It seemed preoccupied with affairs of state, affairs of grace and matters utopian. What with his eye and the fog, he had to approach more closely to be sure that it was, in fact, a coloured statue, not naked bronze or stone, but tinted black and gold.

He had never seen it before, but he had, of course, seen pictures of the philosopher, statesman and martyr, notably the Holbein drawing of Sir Thomas and his family. Until now, however, the close resemblance of the reproduced face to a known and living face had not struck him. Only replace that saintly gravity with an impish gleam, he thought, those mild resigned lips with the curve of irony, and it was Dr Crocker to the life.

Feeling like Ahab in Naboth's vineyard, Wexford addressed the statue aloud.

'Hast thou found me, O mine enemy?'

Sir Thomas continued to reflect on an ideal state or perhaps on the perils of Reformation. His face, possibly by a trick of the drifting mist, seemed to have grown even more grave, not to say comminatory. Now it wore precisely the expression Crocker's had worn that Sunday in Kingsmarkham when he had diagnosed a thrombosis in his friend's eye.

'God knows, Reg, I warned you often enough. I told you to lose weight, I told you to take things easier, and how many times have I told you to stay off the booze?'

'All right. What now? Will I have another?'

'If you do, it may be your brain the clot touches, not your eye. You'd better get away somewhere for a complete rest. I suggest a month away.'

'I can't go away for a month!'

'Why not? Nobody's indispensable.'

'Oh, yes, they are. What about Winston Churchill? What about Nelson?'

'The trouble with you, apart from high blood pressure, is delusions of grandeur. Take Dora away to the seaside.'

'In *February*? Anyway, I hate the sea. And I can't go away to the country. I live in the country.'

The doctor took his sphygmomanometer out of his bag and, silently rolling up Wexford's sleeve, bound the instrument to his arm. 'Perhaps the best thing,' said Crocker, without revealing his findings, 'will be to send you to my brother's health farm in Norfolk.'

'God! What would I do with myself all day?'

'By the time,' said Crocker dreamily, 'you've had nothing but orange juice and sauna baths for three days you won't have the strength to do anything. The last patient I sent there was too weak to lift the phone and call his wife. He'd only been married a month and he was very much in love.'

Wexford gave the doctor a lowering cowed glance. 'May God protect me from my friends. I'll tell you what, I'll go to London. How would that do? My nephew's always asking us. You know the one I mean, my sister's boy, Howard, the superintendent with the Met. He's got a house in Chelsea.'

'All right. But no late nights, Reg. No participation in

swinging London. No alcohol. I'm giving you a diet sheet one thousand calories a day. It sounds a lot, but, believe me, it ain't.'

'It's starvation,' said Wexford to the statue.

He had started to shiver, standing there and brooding. Time to get back for the pre-lunch rest and glass of tomato juice they made him have. One thing, he wasn't joining any Peter Pan expedition afterwards. He didn't believe in fairies and one statue a day was enough. A bus ride, maybe. But not on that one he could see trundling up Cremorne Road and ultimately bound for Kenbourne Vale. Howard had made it quite plain in his negative gracious way that that was one district of London in which his uncle wouldn't be welcome.

'And don't get any ideas about talking shop with that nephew of yours,' had been Crocker's parting words. 'You've got to get away from all that for a bit. Where did you say his manor is, Kenbourne Vale?'

Wexford nodded. 'Tough sort of place, I'm told.'

'They don't come any tougher. I trained there at St Biddulph's.' As always when speaking to the green rustic of his years in the metropolis, Crocker wore his Mr Worldly Wiseman expression and his voice became gently patronising. 'There's an enormous cemetery, bigger than Kensal Green and more bizarre than Brompton, with vast tombs and a few minor royals buried there, and the geriatric wards of the hospital overlook the cemetery just to show the poor old things what their next stop'll be. Apart from that, the place is miles of mouldering terraces containing two classes of persons: *Threepenny Opera* crooks and the undeserving poor.'

'I daresay,' said Wexford, getting his own back, 'it's changed in the intervening thirty years.'

'Nothing to interest you, anyway,' the doctor snapped. 'I don't want you poking your nose into Kenbourne Vale's crime, so you can turn a deaf ear to your nephew's invitations.'

Invitations! Wexford laughed bitterly to himself. Much chance he had of turning a deaf ear when Howard, in the ten

11

days since his uncle's arrival, hadn't spoken a single word even to indicate that he was a policeman, let alone suggested a visit to the Yard or an introduction to his inspector. Not that he was neglectful. Howard was courtesy itself, the most considerate of hosts, and, when it came to conversation, quite deferential in matters, for instance, of literature, in spite of his Cambridge First. Only on the subject nearest to his uncle's heart (and, presumably, to his own) was he discouragingly silent.

It was obvious why. Detective superintendents, holding high office in a London crime squad, are above talking shop with detective chief inspectors from Sussex. Men who have inherited houses in Chelsea will not condescend very far with men who occupy three-bedroom villas in the provinces. It was the way of the world.

Howard was a snob. A kind, attentive thoughtful snob, but a snob just the same. And that was why, that above all, Wexford wished he had gone to the seaside or the health farm. As he turned into Theresa Street he wondered if he could stand another evening in Denise's elegant drawing room, the women chatting clothes and cooking, while he and Howard exchanged small talk on the weather and the sights of London, interspersed with bits of Eliot.

'You must try and see some City churches while you're here.'

'St Magnus Martyr, white and gold?'

'St Mary Woolnoth, who tolls the hours with a dead sound on the final stroke of nine!'

Nearly another fortnight of it.

They wouldn't go to Peter Pan without him. Some other day, they said, resigning themselves without too much anguish to attending Harvey Nichols' fashion show instead. He swallowed his pills, ate his poached fish and fruit salad, and watched them leave the house, each suitably attired as befitted thirty years and fifty-five, Denise in purple velvet, feathers and a picture hat, Dora in the ranch mink he had bought her for

12

their silver wedding. They got on fine, those two. As well as their joint determination to treat him like a retarded six-year-old with a congenital disease, they seemed to have every female taste in common.

Everybody got on fine but him: Crocker with his twenty-eight-inch waistline; Mike Burden in Kingsmarkham police station getting the feel of his, Wexford's, mantle on his shoulders and liking it; Howard departing every day for his secret hush-hush job which might have been in Whitehall rather than Kenbourne Vale nick, for all he told his uncle to the contrary.

Self-pity never got anyone anywhere. He mustn't look on it as a holiday but as a rest cure. It was time to forget all those pleasant visions he had had in the train to Victoria, the pictures of himself helping Howard with his enquiries, even giving—he blushed to recall it—a few little words of advice. Crocker had been right. He did have delusions of grandeur.

They had been knocked on the head here all right. The house itself was enough to cut any provincial down to size. It wasn't a big house, but then, nor is the Taj Mahal very big. What worried him and made him tread like a cat burglar were the exquisite appointments of the place: the fragile furniture, the pieces of Chinese porcelain balanced on tiny tables, the screens he was always nearly knocking over, Denise's flower arrangements. Weird, exotic, heterogeneous, they troubled him as almost daily a fresh confection appeared. He could never be sure whether a rosebud was intended to lie in that negligent fashion on the marble surface of a table or whether it had been inadvertently dislodged from its fellows in the majolica bowl by his own clumsy hand.

The temperature of the house, as he put it to himself, exaggerating slightly, was that of a Greek beach at noon in August. If you had the figure for it you could have gone about quite happily in a bikini. He wondered why Denise, who had, didn't. And how did the flowers survive, the daffodils ill-at-ease among avocado-pear plants?

When he had had his hour's rest with his feet up he took

the two library tickets Denise had left him and walked down to Manresa Road. Anything to get out of that house. The beautiful, warm, dull silence of it depressed him.

Why shouldn't he go home?

Dora could stay on if she liked. He thought of home with an ache in his belly that was only partly due to hunger. Home. The green Sussex meadows, the pine forest, the High Street full of people he knew and who knew him, the police station and Mike glad to see him back; his own house, cold as an English house should be except in front of the one great roaring fire; proper food and proper bread and in the fridge the secret beer cans.

Might as well get out a couple of books, though. Something to read in the train, and he could send them back to Denise by post. He chose a novel, and then, because he now felt he knew the old boy and had actually had a sort of conversation with him, More's *Utopia*. After that he had nothing at all to do so he sat down for a long while in the library, not even opening the books but thinking about home.

It was nearly five when he left. He bought an evening paper more from habit than from any desire to read it. Suddenly he found he was tired with the staggering weariness of someone who had nothing to do but must somehow fill the hours between getting up and bedtime.

A long way back to Theresa Street on foot, too long. He hailed a taxi, sank into its seat and unfolded his paper.

From the middle of the front page the bony, almost cadaverous, face of his nephew stared back at him.

2

They set up a pillar of stone with the dead man's titles therein engraved.

THE women were still out. Fighting the soporific heat which had met him with a tropical blast as he entered the house, Wexford sat down, found his new glasses, and read the caption under the photograph. 'Detective Superintendent Howard Fortune, Kenbourne Vale C.I.D. chief, who is in charge of the case, arriving at Kenbourne Vale Cemetery where the girl's body was found.'

The cameraman had caught Howard leaving his car, and it was a full-face shot. Beneath it was another picture, macabre, compelling the eye. Wexford, refusing to be drawn, turned his attention to the newspaper's account of the case, its lead story. He read it slowly.

'The body of a girl was this morning discovered in a vault at Kenbourne Vale Cemetery, West London. It was later identified as that of Miss Loveday Morgan, aged about 20, of Garmisch Terrace, W.15.

'The discovery was made by Mr Edwin Tripper, of Kenbourne Lane, a cemetery attendant, when he went to give the vault its monthly inspection. Detective Superintendent Fortune said "This is definitely a case of foul play. I can say no more at present."

'Mr Tripper told me, "The vault is the property of the Monfort family who were once important people in Ken-

15

bourne. A sum of money has been set aside under a trust to keep the vault cared for but the lock on the vault door was broken many years ago.

' "This morning I went as I always do on the last Tuesday in the month to sweep out the vault and put flowers on the coffin of Mrs Viola Montfort. The door was tightly closed and jammed. I had to use tools to force it. When I got it open I went down the steps and saw the body of this girl lying between the coffins of Mrs Viola Montfort and Captain James Monfort.

' "It gave me a terrible shock. It was the last place you would expect to find a corpse".'

Wexford chuckled a little at that, but the photograph of the vault chilled him again. It was a monstrous mausoleum, erected apparently at the height of the Gothic revival. On its roof lay two vast slaughtered lions with, rampant and triumphant above them, the statue of a warrior, the whole executed in black iron. Perhaps one of the Montforts had been a big-game hunter. Beneath this set-piece, the door, worked all over with heroic frescoes, stood half open, disclosing impenetrable blackness. Ilexes, those trees beloved of cemetery architects, lowered their dusty evergreen over the vault and shrouded the warrior's head.

It was a good photograph. Both photographs were good, the one of Howard showing in his eyes that perspicacity and passionate determination every good police officer should have but which Wexford had never seen in his nephew. And never would either, he thought, laying down the paper with a sigh. He hadn't the heart to read the rest of the story. What was the betting Howard would come in for his dinner, kiss his wife, enquire what his aunt had bought and ask solicitously after his uncle's health as if nothing had happened? If anyone could ignore that evening paper, he would. It would be surreptitiously whisked away and the *status quo* would just go on and on.

But now it would be worse. Howard wouldn't really be able to pretend any longer and his continuing silence would prove what Wexford guessed already, that he thought his uncle an

16

old has-been, maybe just fit to catch a country shop-lifter or root out a band of thugs with a cock-fighting hide-out on the South Downs.

He must have fallen asleep and slept for a long time. When he awoke the paper had gone and Dora was sitting opposite him with his dinner on a tray, cold chicken, and more of those bloody biscuits and junket and two white pills.

'Where's Howard?'

'He's only just got in, darling. When he's finished his dinner he'll come in here and have his coffee with you.'

And talk about the weather?

It was, in fact, the weather on which he began.

'Most unfortunate we're having this cold spell just now, Reg.' He never called his uncle uncle and it might have caused raised eyebrows if he had, for Howard Fortune, at thirty-six, looked forty-five. People were inclined to deplore the age gap between him and his wife, not guessing it was only six years. He was exceptionally tall, extravagantly thin and his lean bony face was wrinkled, but when he smiled it became charming and almost good-looking. You could see they were uncle and nephew. The Wexford face was there, the same bone construction, though in the case of the younger man the bones were almost fleshless and in the older obscured under pouches and heavy jowls. Howard smiled now as he poured Wexford's coffee and placed it beside him.

'I see you've got *Utopia* there.'

It was not quite the remark expected of a man who has spent his day in the preliminary enquiries into murder. But Howard, in any case, didn't look the part. His silver-grey suit and lemon Beale and Inman shirt were certainly the garments he had put on that morning but they appeared as if fresh from the hands of a valet. His thin smooth fingers, handling the leather binding of More's classic, looked as if they had never handled anything harsher than old books. Having placed a cushion behind his uncle's head, he began to discourse on *Utopia*, on the 1551 Ralph Robinson translation, on More's friendship with Erasmus, occasionally pausing to insert such deferential courtesies as, 'which, of course, you already know, Reg'. He talked of other ideal societies in literature, of Andreae's *Christianopolis*, of Campanella's *City of the Sun* and of Butler's *Erèwhon*. He talked pleasantly and with erudition and sometimes he broke off to allow a comment from Wexford, but Wexford said nothing.

He was boiling with anger. The man was not merely a snob, he was monstrously cruel, a sadist. To sit there lecturing like a professor on idealist philosophy when his heart must be full of its opposite, when he knew his uncle had brought in not only *Utopia* but that Dystopia on which the newspaper had enlarged. And this was the same little boy whom he, Wexford, had taught to take fingerprints!

The telephone rang and, out in the hall, Denise answered it, but Wexford could see Howard was alert for the call. He watched his nephew's face sharpen and when Denise came in to tell her husband it was for him, he saw a silent signal pass between them, a miniscule shake of the head on Howard's part indicating that the call and all it implied must be kept secret from their guest. Of course, it was one of Howard's subordinates phoning to tell him of a new development. In spite of his mortification, Wexford was hungry to know what that development could be. He listened to the murmur of Howard's voice from the hall, but he couldn't distinguish the words. It was all he could do not to open the door, and then, when Howard returned, ask him baldly. But he knew what the answer would be.

'You don't want to bother your head with all that.'

He didn't wait for Howard to come back. He took *Utopia* and made for the stairs, calling a curt good night to Denise and nodding to his nephew as he passed him. Bed was the best place for an old fogey like him. He got between the sheets and put on his glasses. Then he opened the book. His eyes felt gravelly but surely it wasn't his eye playing him a trick like that . . .? He stared and slammed the book shut.

It was in Latin.

He dreamed a lot that night. He dreamed that Howard had relented and personally driven him to Kenbourne Vale Cemetery to view with him the Montfort vault, and when he awoke it seemed impossible to him that he could go home without ever having actually seen it. The murder would, for a short space, be a topic of conversation even in Kingsmarkham. How was he going to explain to Mike that he had been excluded from all concern in it? That he had stayed with the man in charge of the case and yet learned no more than the average newspaper reader? By lying? By saying he wasn't interested? His temperament revolted from that. By telling the truth, then, that Howard had refused to confide in him.

At ten he came downstairs to the usual pantomime. Shredded wheat and orange juice and Denise waiting at the bottom of the stairs today. Otherwise it was the same as all the other mornings.

Without his having told her, Dora had discovered *Utopia* was in Latin and the two of them were already planning to get him an English translation. Denise's sister-in-law worked in a bookshop and would get him a paperback; to make assurance doubly sure, she would herself go into the library and order the Ralph Robinson.

'You needn't go to all that trouble for me,' said Wexford.

'Where are you going for your walk this morning, Uncle Reg?'

'Victoria,' he said, not adding that he was going to enquire about trains and listening in silence while they gasped about walking that distance.

Of course, he wouldn't walk. There was probably a bus. The eleven, he thought, there were always dozens of elevens except when you wanted one. Today the eleven and the twenty-two seemed to be on strike, while buses going to Kenbourne Vale charged in packs across the King's Road and up Gunter Grove.

He had a terrible urge just to see that cemetery. Howard's men would have finished with it by now, and anyone could go into cemeteries if he wanted to. Then, when he got home,

19

he could at least describe the vault to Mike and say it was unfortunate he had to leave just at that point. Victoria station could wait. Why not phone, anyway?

The next bus said Kenbourne Lane station on its front. Wexford didn't like to ask for the cemetery in case the smiling West Indian conductor took him for another ghoulish sightseer—he was unsure of himself in London, a little of his decisive identity lost—so he said, 'All the way, please,' and settled back into his seat to pretend he was complying with that piece of hackneyed advice to tourists that the best way to see London is from the top of a bus.

Its route was up to Holland Park Avenue and then along Ladbroke Grove. Once the bus had turned into Elgin Crescent, Wexford lost his bearings. He wondered how he would know they had left North Kensington, or Notting Hill or wherever it was and entered Kenbourne Vale. The neighbourhood already fitted Crocker's description of miles of mouldering terraces, but thirty years had passed and there were tower blocks and council estates as well.

Then he saw a sign: *London Borough of Kenbourne. Copeland Hill.* All the plaques with street names on them, Copeland Terrace, Heidelberg Road, Bournemouth Grove, bore the postal direction West Fifteen.

Must be nearly there. His humiliation was giving way to excitement. The bus had lumbered round a kind of circus and entered Kenbourne Lane, a wide treeless thoroughfare, inclining upwards, a street of Asiatic food shops, squat Edwardian pubs, pawnbrokers' and small tobacconists'. He was wondering how he would find the cemetery when, as the bus came over the crown of the hill, there rose to the left of him an enormous pillared portico of yellow sandstone. Wrought-iron gates, as huge as the gates to some oriental walled city, stood open, dwarfing the workman who was touching up the black paint on their posts.

Wexford rang the bell and got off when the bus pulled in to a request stop. In this exposed place the sharp wind caught him and he turned up the collar of his coat. The heavy leaden

20

sky looked full of snow. There were no sightseers about, no police cars, and neither the workman nor some sort of attendant —Mr Tripper, perhaps?—who stood at the entrance to a lodge, said a word to him as he passed under the archway.

As soon as he was inside the cemetery, he remembered what Crocker had said about it being huge and bizarre. This was not an exaggeration, but the doctor had omitted to say that it was also, perhaps because of its size and because of staff shortages, hideously neglected. Wexford stood still and took in the sprawling wild panorama.

Immediately in front of him was one of those buildings all large cemeteries boast and whose use is in doubt. It was neither a chapel nor a crematorium, but it possibly housed offices for the staff and lavatories for the mourners. The style was that of St Peter's in Rome. Not, of course, so large, but large enough. Unluckily for the inhabitants of Kenbourne Vale, its architect had been no Bernini: the dome was too small, the pillars too thick and the whole edifice executed in the same yellow sandstone as the portico.

Of this material also were the two colonnades which branched out of the right-hand side of the St Peter's building like encircling arms and met some hundred yards distant at an arch which supported a winged victory. Between them and the outer walls, above which could be seen St Biddulph's Hospital, were deep strips of wilderness, a jungle of shrubs and trees, showing here and there protruding from the mass the weather-torn peaks of tombs.

In the space between the colonnades some attempt had been made to tidy the place. The shaggy grass was chopped off, the bushes pruned, to reveal grime-encrusted monuments, angels with swords, gun-carriages, broken columns, weeping Niobes, Egyptian obelisks and, immediately beside St Peter's, two tombs the size of small houses. Training his eyes, Wexford saw that one was that of the Princess Adelberta of Mecklenburgh-Strelitz, and the other of His Serene Highness the Grand Duke Waldemar of Retz.

The place was ridiculous, a grandiose necropolis, devouring land which might better have served Kenbourne Vale's homeless. It was also profoundly sinister. It was awe-inspiring. Never before, not in any mortuary or house of murder, had Wexford so tellingly felt the oppressive chill of death. The winged victory held back her plunging horses against a sky that was almost black, and under the arches of the colonnades lay wells of gloom. He felt that not for anything would he have walked between those arches and the pillars which fronted them to read the bronze plaques on their damp yellow walls. Not for renewed health and youth would he have spent a night in that place.

He had mounted the steps to view the cemetery and he had viewed it. Enough was enough. Luckily, the Montfort vault must lie between the wall and the colonnade. He guessed that because only there grew the ilexes, and he was foolishly relieved to know that he would not have to explore the inner area where the most monstrous and folly-like tombs stood and where the winged victory dominated everything like some sinister fallen angel.

But as soon as he had descended the steps and taken a path which led to the right-hand side of the cemetery he found that the depths were no less unpleasant than the heights. True, the winged victory and the colonnades were made invisible by the trees, but these in themselves, crowded together, untended and almost all of evergreen varieties, held their own kind of menace. They made the path very dark. Their trunks were hidden to shoulder height by ivy and thick brambly shrubs, and among these shrubs began to appear first the outlines of gravestones and then, as the path ran parallel with the outer wall, the shapes of larger and larger tombs.

Wexford tried to chuckle at some of the pompous inscriptions but his laughter stuck in his throat. The absurd was overpowered by the sinister, by the figures in bronze and sculped stone which, made furtive and hideous by encroaching moss and decades of fallen grime, lurked among the trailing tendrils and even, as the wind rustled between leathery leaves and broken masonary, seemed to move. Overhead, he could see only a narrow corridor of sky and that stormy, black and Turneresque. He walked on, looking straight ahead of him down the defile.

Just when he was beginning to feel that he had had about as much of this as flesh and blood could stand, he came upon the Montfort vault. It was the size of a small cottage and much nastier in reality than in the photograph. The cameraman had not been able to capture the mouldy smell that breathed out of the half-open door or render the peculiarly unpleasant effect of sour green moss creeping across the warrior's face and the paws of the dead lions.

Nor had the inscription appeared in the paper. It was unlike any other Wexford had seen in the cemetery, bearing no information about the dead who lay in the vault. The copper plate had turned bright green with verdigris, but the lettering, of some untarnishable metal—gold leaf?—stood out clear and stark.

'He who asks questions is a fool.
He who answers them is a greater fool.
What is truth? What man decides it shall be.
What is beauty? Beauty is in the eye of man.
What are right and wrong? Today one thing, another
    tomorrow.
Death only is real.
The last of the Montforts bids you read and pass on
Without comment.'

This epitaph—if epitaph it could be called—so interested Wexford that he took a scrap of paper and a pencil from his pocket and copied it down. Then he pushed open the door, expecting a creak, but there was no sound at all. Perhaps Mr Tripper had oiled the hinges. A creak would somehow have been reassuring. He realised suddenly that some of the awe and the disquiet he felt was due to the profound silence. Since entering the cemetery he had heard nothing but the crepitation of dead leaves beneath his feet and the rustle of the wind.

Inside the vault it was not quite dark. Utter darkness would have been less unpleasant. A little greyish light fell on to the flight of steps from a narrow vitrine in the rear wall. He went down the steps and found himself in a chamber about twelve feet square. The dead Montforts lay not in the coffins mentioned by Mr Tripper but in stone sarcophagi which rested on shelves. In the centre of the chamber was a marble basin absurdly like a birdbath and containing a dribble of water. He couldn't imagine what purpose it served. He approached the sarcophagi and saw that there were two rows of them with a narrow space between. It must have been there in that trough, on the damp stone floor, that Loveday Morgan's body had been found.

He shivered a little. The vault smelt of decay. Not surely of the dead Montforts, passed long ago to dust, but of rotted grave flowers and stagnant water and unventilated age. A nasty place. She had been twenty, he thought, and he hoped she had died quickly and not in here. What are right and wrong? Today one thing, another tomorrow. Death only is real.

He turned back towards the steps and, as he did so, he heard a sound above him, a footfall on the overgrown gravel path. Some attendant, no doubt. He set his foot on the bottom stair, looking up at the rectangle of dingy light between door and frame. And then, as he was about to speak and declare his presence, there appeared in the aperture, gaunt and severe, the face of his nephew.

3

*You conceive in your mind either none at all or else
a very false image and similitude of this thing.*

EVERYONE is familiar with the sensation of wanting the
earth to swallow him when he is caught in embarrassing
circumstances. And what more appropriate plot of earth than
this, thought Wexford, aghast. These acres, choked with the
dead, might surely receive one more. There was, however,
nothing for it but to mount the stairs and face the music.

Howard, peering down into semi-darkness, had not at first
recognised the intruder. When he did, when Wexford, awkwardly brushing cobwebs from his coat, emerged on to the
path, his face registered simple blank astonishment.

'Good God. Reg,' he said.

He looked his uncle up and down, then stared into the vault,
as if he thought himself the victim of some monstrous delu-
sion. Either this was not Wexford, but some Kenbournite disguised to resemble him, or else this was not Kenbourne Vale
cemetery. It took him a few moments to recover and then he
said:

'I thought you wanted a holiday from all this sort of thing.'

It was stupid to stand there like a schoolboy. In general,
embarrassment was foreign to Wexford and he brimmed over
with self-confidence. Now he told himself that he was catching
criminals when this man was chewing on a teething ring and
he said rather coldly, 'Did you? I can't imagine why.' Never

apologise, never explain. 'Don't let me keep you from your work. I've a bus to catch.'

Howard's eyes narrowed. 'No,' he said, 'you're not going like that.' He always spoke quietly, in measured tones. 'I won't have that. If you wanted to see the vault, why didn't you say last night? I'd have brought you with me this morning. If you wanted the inside stuff on the case, you only had to ask.'

Absurd as it was, undignified, to stand arguing in the bitter cold among toppled gravestones, Wexford couldn't leave it like that. All his resentment had boiled to the surface.

'Ask?' he shouted. 'Ask you when you've made a point of excluding me from everything to do with your work? When you and Denise have conspired to keep quiet about it like a couple of parents turning off the television in front of the child when the sexy play starts? I know when I'm not wanted. *Ask!*'

Howard's face had fallen glumly at the beginning of this speech, but now a faint smile twitched his lips. He felt in the pocket of his coat while Wexford leaned against the vault, his arms folded defiantly.

'Here, read that. It came two days before you did.' Reassured by the evidence he had produced, Howard spoke firmly now. 'Read it, Reg.'

Suspiciously Wexford took the letter. Without his glasses he could only just read it, but he could make out enough. The signature, 'Leonard Crocker', leered blackly at him. '. . . I am confident I can rely on your good sense . . . Your uncle, a close friend of mine and my patient . . . Nothing he wants more than to get completely away from everything connected with police work . . . Better not let him come into any contact with . . .'

'We thought we were acting for the best, Reg.'

'Close friend!' Wexford exploded. 'What business has he got interfering with me?' Usually litter-conscious, he forgot his principles and, screwing the letter into a ball, hurled it among the bushes and the crumbling masonry.

Howard burst out laughing. 'I spoke to my own doctor

about it,' he said, 'telling him what had been the matter with you and he said—you know how diplomatic they are—he said there were two opinions about it but he couldn't see that you'd come to any harm indulging—er, your usual tastes. Still, Denise insisted we abide by what your own doctor said. And we did think it was your wish.'

'I took you for a snob,' said his uncle. 'Rank and all that.'

'Did you? That never struck me.' Howard bit his lip. 'You don't know how I've longed for a real talk instead of literary chit-chat, especially now when I'm short of men and up to my eyes in it.' Frowning, still concerned, he said, 'You must be frozen. Here comes my sergeant, so we can get away from all these storeyed urns and animated busts.'

A thickset man of about forty was approaching them from the direction of St Peter's. He wore the cheerful and practical air of someone totally insensitive to atmosphere, to that of the cemetery and that which subsisted between the two other men. Howard introduced him as Sergeant Clements and presented the chief inspector without saying that Wexford was his uncle or attempting to account for his sudden and surely astonishing appearance at the scene of a crime.

In such august company the sergeant knew better than to ask questions, or perhaps he had read the Montfort injunction.

'Very pleased to meet you, sir.'

'My uncle,' said Howard, relenting a little, 'is on holiday. He comes from Sussex.'

'I daresay it's a change, sir. No green fields and cows and what-not round here.' He gave Wexford a respectful and somewhat indulgent smile before turning to the superintendent. 'I've had another talk with Tripper, sir, but I've got nothing more out of him.'

'Right. We'll go back to the car. Mr Wexford will be lunching with me, and over lunch I'm going to try to persuade him to give us the benefit of his brains.'

'We can certainly use them,' said the sergeant, and he fell back to allow the others to precede him out of the cemetery.

The Grand Duke was a little old pub Howard took him to on the corner of a mews in Kenbourne Lane.

'I didn't know there were places like this left in London,' Wexford said, appreciating the linenfold panelling, the settles and the old mullioned glass in the windows. It was like home, the kind of inn to be found in Pomfret or Stowerton.

'There aren't around here. Kenbourne's no Utopia. Would you believe, looking out of the window, that in an unpublished poem, Hood wrote:

' "O, to ride on the crest of a laden wain
Between primrose banks in Kenbourne Lane"?'

'What will you eat, Reg?'

'I'm not supposed to eat anything much.'

'Surely a little cold duck and some salad? The food's very good here.'

Wexford felt almost dizzy, but he mustn't allow himself to break out entirely. It was a triumph of communication over misunderstanding that he was here with Howard at all and about to get his teeth into some real police work again without getting them into duck as well. The spread on the food counter looked mouth-wateringly enticing. He chose the least calorific, thin sliced red beef and *ratatouille froide*, and settled back with a sigh of contentment. Even the tall glass of apple juice which Howard presented to him with the assurance that it was made out of Cox's Oranges from Suffolk couldn't cloud his pleasure.

Ever since his arrival in London he had felt that partial loss of identity which is common to everybody on holiday except the most seasoned of travellers. But instead of returning to him as he grew accustomed to the city, this ego of his, this essential Wexfordness, had seemed to continue its seeping away, until at last in the cemetery he had briefly but almost entirely lost his hold on it. That had been a frightening moment. Now, however, he felt more himself than he had done for days. This was like being with Mike at the Olive and Dove where, on so many satisfactory occasions, they had thrashed out some case over lunch, but now Howard was the instructor and he in Mike's role. He found he didn't mind this at all. He could even look with equanimity at Howard's lunch: a huge plateful of steak-and-kidney pudding, Jersey new potatoes and courgettes *au gratin*.

For the first five minutes they ate and drank and talked a little more about this misunderstanding of theirs, and then Howard, opening their discussion in the clearest and most direct way, pushed a snapshot across the table.

'This is the only photograph we have of her. Other may come to light, of course. It was in her handbag. Not very usual that, to carry photographs of oneself about on one. Perhaps she had some sentimental reason for it. Where and when it was taken we don't know.'

The snapshot was too pale and muzzy for reproduction in a newspaper. It showed a thin fair girl in a cotton frock and heavy unsuitable shoes. Her face was a pale blob and even her own mother, as Wexford put it to himself, wouldn't have recognised her. In the background were some dusty-looking shrubs, a section of wall with coping along the top of it and something that looked like a clothes post.

He handed it back and asked, 'Is Garmisch Terrace near here?'

'The backs of the houses overlook the cemetery but on the opposite side to where we were. It's a beastly place. Monstrous houses put up around 1870 for city merchants who couldn't run to fifteen hundred a year for a palace in Queen's Gate. They're mostly let off into rooms now, or flatlets as they're euphemistically called. She had a room. She'd lived there for about two months.'

'What did she do for a living?'

'She worked as a receptionist in a television rental place. The shop is called Sytansound and it's in Lammas Grove. That's the street which runs off to the left at Kenbourne Circus and also skirts the cemetery. Apparently she went to work by taking a short-cut through the cemetery. Why do you look like that?'

'I was thinking of passing through that place every day.'

'The local people are used to it. They don't notice it any more. You'd be surprised in the summer how many young housewives you see in there taking their babies for an afternoon's airing.'

Wexford said, 'When and how did she die?'

'Probably last Friday. I haven't had a full medical report yet, but she was strangled with her own silk scarf.'

'Last Friday and no one reported her missing?'

Howard shrugged. 'In Garmisch Terrace, Reg? Loveday Morgan wasn't living at home with her parents in some select suburb. They come and they go in Garmisch Terrace, they mind their own business, they don't ask questions. Wait till you hear Sergeant Clements on that subject.'

'How about boy friends?'

'She didn't have any, as far as we know. The body was identified by a girl called Peggy Pope who's the housekeeper at 22 Garmisch Terrace and she says Loveday had no friends. She came to Kenbourne Vale in January, but where she came from nobody seems to know. When she applied for the room she gave Mrs Pope an address in Fulham. We've checked on that. The street she named and the house she named are there all right but she never lived there. The owners of the house are a young married couple who have never let rooms. So we don't yet know where she came from and in a way we don't really know who she was.'

Having built up the suspense in a way Wexford recognised, for it was the way he had himself used on countless occasions, Howard went away to fetch cheese and biscuits. He returned with more apple juice for his uncle, who was feeling so contented that he drank it obediently.

'She lived in Garmisch Terrace by herself, very quietly,' Howard went on, 'and last Friday, February 25th, she went to work as usual, returning, as she occasionally did, during her lunchtime break. Mrs Pope supposed that she had gone back to work in the afternoon, but in fact, she didn't. She telephoned the manager of Sytansound to say she was sick and that was

30

the last anyone heard of her.' He paused. 'She may have gone straight into the cemetery; she may not. The cemetery gates are closed each day at six, and on Fridays they were closed at that time as usual. Clements sometimes cuts through on his way home. He did that on Friday, spoke to Tripper, and Tripper closed the gates behind him at six sharp. Needless to say, Clements saw nothing out of the way. His route took him nowhere near the Montfort vault.'

Wexford recognised this short pause as the cue for him to ask an intelligent question, and he asked one. 'How did you know who she was?'

'Her handbag was beside her in the vault, brimming with information. Her address was on a bill from a dry cleaner's and this snapshot was there too. Besides that, there was a sheet of notepaper with two telephone numbers on it.'

Wexford raised an enquiring eyebrow.

'You rang those numbers, of course?'

'Of course. That was among the first things we did. One was that of an hotel in Bayswater, a perfectly respectable, rather large, hotel. They told us they had advertised in a newspaper a vacancy for a receptionist and Loveday Morgan had replied to the advertisement. By phone. She didn't sound the sort of girl they wanted—too shy and awkward, they said— and she hadn't the necessary experience for the job.

'The other number was that of a West End company called Notbourne Properties who are particularly well known in Notting Hill and Kenbourne Vale. Hence their name. They also had advertised a job, this time for a telephone girl. Loveday applied and actually got as far as an interview. That interview was at the end of the week before last, but they didn't intend to take her on. Apparently, she was badly dressed and, anyway, she wasn't familiar with the particular phone system they use.'

'She wanted to change her job? Does anyone know why?'

'More money, I imagine. We may be able to get some more information about that and her general circumstances from this Mrs Pope.'

31

'That's the woman who identified her? The housekeeper?'

'Yes. Shall we wait and have coffee or would you like to go straight round to Garmisch Terrace?'

'Skip the coffee,' said Wexford.

4

A little farther beyond that all things begin by little
and little to wax pleasant; the air soft, temperate and
gentle covered with green grass.

GARMISCH TERRACE was straight and grey and forbid-
ding, a canyon whose sides were six-storey houses. All the
houses were alike, all joined together, flat-fronted but for
their protruding pillared porches, and, like the cemetery
building, their proportions were somehow wrong. It had been
an unhappy period for architecture, the time when they were
built, a period in which those designers who had not adopted
the new Gothic, were attempting to improve on the Georgian.

This would have mattered less if some effort had been made
to maintain these houses, but Wexford, looking at them with
a sinking heart, could not see a single freshly painted façade.
Their plaster was cracked and their pillars streaked where
water had run through dust. Rubbish clogged the basement
areas and these were separated from the pavement by broken
railings patched with wire netting. Instead of trees, parking
meters stood in a grey row, an avenue of them leading up the
cul-de-sac to where it ended in a red-brick church.

There were few people about, a turbaned Sikh lugging his
dustbin up area steps, an old woman wheeling a pram filled
apparently with jumble-sale spoils, a pregnant black girl
whose kingfisher-blue raincoat provided the only colour in the

33

street. The wind blew paper out of the Sikh's dustbin, whirling sheets of newsprint up into the grey sky. It teased at the girls woolly hair which, in a pathetic attempt to be accepted, to be in fashion, she was trying to grow long. Wexford wondered sadly about these coloured people who must have looked to a promised land and had found instead the bitter indecency of Garmisch Terrace.

'Would anyone live here from choice?' he said to Sergeant Clements, who, while Howard studied a report in the car, had attached himself to him as mentor, guide, and possibly protector.

'You may well ask, sir,' said the sergeant approvingly. His manner was not quite that of the schoolmaster addressing a promising pupil. Wexford's rank and age were recognised and respected, but he was made aware of the age-old advantage of the townsman over the greenhorn from the country. Clements' plump face, a face which seemed not to have changed much since he was a fat-cheeked, rosebud-mouthed schoolboy, wore an expression both smug and discontented. 'They like it, you see,' he explained. 'They like muck and living four to a room and chucking their gash about and prowling all night and sleeping all day.' He scowled at a young man and woman who, arm in arm, crossed the road and sat down on the pavement outside the church where they began to eat crisps out of a bag. 'They like dropping in on their friends at midnight and dossing down on the floor among the fag-ends because the last bus has gone. Ask 'em and most of 'em don't know where they live, here this week, there the next, catch as catch can and then move on. They don't live like you or me sir. They live like those little furry moles you have down in the country, always burrowing about in the dark.'

Wexford recognised in the sergeant a type of policeman which is all too common. Policemen see so much of the seamy side of life and, lacking the social worker's particular kind of training, many of them become crudely cynical instead of learning a merciful outlook. His own Mike Burden came

34

dangerously near sometimes to being such a one, but his intelligence saved him. Wexford didn't think much of the sergeant's intelligence, although he couldn't help rather liking him.

'Poverty and misery aren't encouragements to an orderly life,' he said, smiling to take the sting out of the admonition.

Clements didn't take this as a rebuke but shook his head at so much innocence.

'I was referring to the *young*, sir, the young layabouts like that pair over there. But you'll learn. A couple of weeks in Kenbourne Vale and you'll get your eyes opened. Why, when I first came here I thought hash was mutton stew and S.T.D. a dialling system.'

Perfectly aware of the significance of these terms, Wexford said nothing, but glanced towards the car. He was beginning to feel chilly and at a nod from Howard he moved under the porch of number 22. That a lecture, contrasting the manners of modern youth with the zeal, ambition and impeccable morality of Clements' contemporaries in his own young days, was imminent he felt sure, and he hoped to avoid. But the sergeant followed him, stamping his feet on the dirty step, and launched into the very diatribe Wexford most feared. For a couple of minutes he let him have his head and then he interrupted.

'About Loveday Morgan . . .'

'So-called,' said Clements darkly. 'That wasn't her real name. Now, I ask you, is it likely to be? We checked her at Somerset House. Plenty of Morgan girls but no Loveday Morgan. She just called herself that. Why? You may well ask. Girls call themselves all sorts of things these days. Now, let me give you an illustration of what I mean . . .'

But before he could, Howard had joined them and silenced him with an unusually cold look. There was a row of bells beside the front door with numbers instead of nameplates.

'The housekeeper lives in the basement,' said Howard, 'so we may as well try Flat One.' He rang the bell and a voice snapped what sounded like 'Teal' out of the entry phone.

'I beg your pardon?'

'This is Ivan Teal. Flat One. Who are you?'

'Detective Superintendent Fortune. I want Mrs Pope.'

'Ah,' said the voice. 'You want Flat Fifteen. The thing that works the door is broken. I'll come down.'

'Flats!' said the sergeant while they waited. 'That's a laugh. They aren't any of 'em flats. They're rooms with a tap and a gas meter, but our girl was paying seven quid a week for hers and there are only two loos in the whole dump. What a world!' He patted Wexford's shoulder. 'Brace yourself for what's coming now, sir. Whoever this Teal is he won't look human.'

But he did. The only shock Wexford felt was in confronting a man nearly as old as himself, a shortish, well-muscled man with thick grey hair worn rather long.

'Sorry to keep you waiting,' he said. 'It's a long way down.' He stared at the three men, unsmiling, insolent in a calculating way. It was a look Wexford had often seen on faces before, but they had almost always been young faces. Teal had, moreover, a smooth upper-class accent. He wore a spotlessly clean white sweater and smelt of Faberge's Aphrodisia. 'I suppose we're all going to be persecuted now.'

'We don't persecute people, Mr Teal.'

'No? You've changed then. You used to persecute me.'

Assuming that Howard had given him *carte blanche* to question possible witnesses if he chose, Wexford said, 'Did you know Loveday Morgan?'

'I know everybody here,' Teal said, 'the oldest inhabitants and the ships that pass in the night. I who have sat by Thebes below the wall . . .' He grinned suddenly. 'Flat One if you want me.'

He led them to the basement stairs and went off without saying any more.

'A curious old queen,' said Howard. 'Fifteen years in this hole . . . God! Come on, it's down here.'

The stairs were narrow and carpeted in a thin much-worn haircord. They led down to a largish lofty hall, long ago painted dark crimson, but this paint was peeling away, leaving white islands shaped like fantastic continents, so that the walls might have been maps of some other unknown world, a charted Utopia. Furniture, that looked too big to go up those stairs although it must have come down them, a sideboard, a huge bookcase crammed with dusty volumes, filled most of the floor space. There were three closed doors, each with an overflowing dustbin on its threshold, and the place smelt of decaying rubbish.

Wexford had never seen anything like this before, but the interior of Flat Fifteen was less unfamiliar. It reminded him of certain Kingsmarkham cottages he had been in. Here was the same squalor that is always present when edibles and washables are thrown into juxtaposition, opened cans among dirty socks, and here in one of those battered prams was a baby with a food-stained face such as town and country alike produce. It was deplorable, of course, that this young girl and her child should have to live in a subterranean cavern, perpetually in artificial light; on the other hand, daylight would have revealed even more awfully the broken armchairs and the appalling carpet. In a way, this was a work of art, so carefully had some female relative of the landlord's repaired it. Wexford couldn't tell whether it was a blue carpet mended with crimson or a piece of red weaving incorporating patches of blue Axminster. The whole of it was coated with stains, ground-in food and the housekeeper's hair combings.

She alone of the room's contents could have stood up to the searching light of day. Her clothes were awful, as dirty and dilapidated as the chair coverings, and dust clung to her greasy black hair, but she was beautiful. She was easily the most beautiful woman he had seen since he came to London. Hers was the loveliness of those film stars he remembered from his youth in the days before actresses looked like ordinary women. In her exquisite face he saw something of a Carole Lombard, something of a Loretta Young. Sullen and dirty though she was, he could not take his eyes off her.

Howard and Clements seemed totally unaffected. No doubt

they were too young to have his memories. Perhaps they were too efficient to be swayed by beauty. And the girl's manner didn't match her looks. She sat on the arm of a chair, biting her nails and staring at them with a sulky frown.

'Just a few questions, please, Mrs Pope,' said Howard.

'Miss Pope. I'm not married.' Her voice was rough and low. 'What d'you want to know? I can't spare very long. I've got the bins to take up if Johnny doesn't come back.'

'Johnny?'

'My friend that I live with.' She cocked a thumb in the direction of the baby and said, 'Her father. He said he'd come back and help me when he'd got his Social Security, but he always makes himself bloody scarce on bin day. God, I don't know why I don't meet up with any ordinary people, nothing but layabouts.'

'Loveday Morgan wasn't a layabout.'

'She had a job, if that's what you mean.' The baby had begun to grizzle. Peggy Pope picked up a dummy from the floor, wiped it on her cardigan and thrust it into the child's mouth. 'God knows how she kept it, she was so *thick*. She couldn't make her meter work and had to come to me to know where to buy a light bulb. When she first came here I even had to show her how to make a phone call. Oh, they all impose on me, but never the way she did. And then she had the nerve to try and get Johnny away from me.'

'Really?' said Howard encouragingly. 'I think you should tell us that, Mrs Pope.'

'*Miss* Pope. Look, I've got to get the bins up. Anyway, there wasn't anything in it, not on Johnny's side. Loveday was so bloody obvious about it, always coming down here to chat him up when I was out, and it got worse the last couple of weeks. I'd come back and find her sitting here, staring at Johnny, or making out she was fond of the baby. I asked him what she was up to. What d'you talk about, for God's sake? I said. Nothing, he said. She'd hardly opened her mouth. She was such a bloody miserable sort of girl.' Peggy Pope sighed as

38

if she, the soul of wit and gaiety, had a right to similarly exuberant companions.

'Do you know why she was miserable?'

'It's money with most of them. That's all they talk about, as though I was rolling in it. She asked me if I could find her a cheaper room, but I said, No, I couldn't. We don't have any flats less than seven a week. I thought she was going to cry. Christ, I thought, why don't you grow up?'

Howard said, 'May we come to last Friday, Mrs Pope?'

'*Miss* Pope. When I want to be *Mrs* I'll find a man who's got a job and can get me something better than a hole in the ground to live in, I can tell you. I don't know anything about last Friday. I saw her come in about ten past one and go off again about ten to two. Oh, and she made a phone call. I don't know any more about it.'

Wexford caught Howard's eye and leant forward. 'Miss Pope,' he said, 'we want you to tell us about that in much greater detail. Tell us exactly what you were doing, where you saw her, what she said, everything.'

'O.K., I'll try.' Peggy Pope pulled her thumbnail out of her mouth and looked at it with distaste. 'But when I've done you'll have to let me get shifting those bins.'

The room was rather cold. She kicked down the upper switch on an electric fire and a second bar began to heat. It was evidently seldom used, for as it glowed red a smell of burning dust came from it.

'It was just after one, maybe ten past,' she began. 'Johnny was out somewhere as usual, looking for work, he said, but I reckon he was in the Grand Duke. I was in the hall giving it a bit of a sweep up and Loveday came in. She said hallo or something, and I said hallo, and she went straight upstairs. I was getting out the vacuum when she came down again and said had I got change for ten pence because she wanted two pence to make a phone call. She must have known I don't carry money about when I'm cleaning the place, but, anyway, I said I'd see and I came down here and got my bag. I hadn't got change, but I'd got one two-pence piece so I gave her that and she went into the phone box.'

'Where's that?'

'Under the stairs. You passed it when you came down.'

'Do you know whom she was phoning?'

She warmed her bitten fingers at the fire and creased her beautiful face into a ferocious scowl. 'How would I? There's a door on the box. She didn't say I'm going to give my mother a tinkle or ring my boy friend, if that's what you mean. Loveday never said much. I'll give her that, she wasn't talkative. Well, she came out and went upstairs again and then I went down to see if the baby was O.K., and when I came up with the pram to take the washing to the launderette she was just going out through the front door, all got up in a green trouser suit. I noticed because it was the only decent thing she had. She didn't say anything. And now can I get on with my work?'

Howard nodded, and he and Clements, thanking her briefly, made for the stairs. Wexford lingered. He watched the girl—she was round-shouldered and rather thin—lift one of the smelly bins and then he said, 'I'll give you a hand.'

She seemed astonished. The world she lived in had unfitted her for accepting help graciously, and she shrugged, making her mouth into an ugly shape.

'They should employ a man to do this.'

'Maybe, but they don't. What man would practically run this dump and do all the dirty work for eight quid a week and that room? Would *you*?'

'Not if I could help it. Can't you get a better job?'

'Look, chum, there's the kid. I've got to have a job where I can look after her. Don't you worry yourself about me. Some day my prince will come and then I'll be off out of here, leaving the bins to Johnny.' She smiled for the first time, a transcending, glorious smile, evoking for him old dark cinemas and shining screens. 'Thanks very much. That's the lot.'

'You're welcome,' said Wexford.

The unaccustomed effort had brought the blood beating to his head. It had been a silly thing to do and the pounding inside his temples unnerved him. Howard and the sergeant were nowhere to be seen, so, to clear his head while he waited for them, he walked down to the open end of Garmisch Terrace. A thin drizzle had begun to fall. He found himself in something which at home would have passed for a high street. It was a shabby shopping centre with, sandwiched between a pub and a hairdresser's, a little cheap boutique called *Loveday*. So that was where she had found the name. She had possessed some other, duller perhaps but identifying, distressing even, which she had wished to conceal. . . .

'Been having a breath of fresh air, sir?' said the sergeant when he rejoined them. 'Or what passes for it round here. By gum, but those bins stank to high heaven!'

Howard grinned. 'We'll take the sergeant back to the station and then I want to show you something different. You mustn't run away with the idea that the whole of Kenbourne is like these rat holes.'

They dropped Clements at the police station, a blackened pile in Kenbourne Vale High Street whose blue lamp swung from the centre of an arch above an imposing flight of steps. Then Howard, driving the car himself, swung into a hinterland of slums, winding streets with corner shops and pubs and patches of waste ground, once green centres of garden squares, but now wired-in like hard tennis courts and littered with broken bicycles and oil-drums.

'Clements lives up there.' Howard pointed upwards, apparently through the roof of the car, and, twisting round to peer out of the window, Wexford saw a tower block of flats, a dizzy thirty storeys. 'Quite a view, I believe. He can see the river and a good deal of the Thames Estuary on a clear day.'

Now the towers grew thickly around them, a copse of monoliths sprouting out of a shabby and battered jungle. Wexford was wondering if this was the contrast he had expected to admire when a bend in the road brought them suddenly to a clear open space. The change was almost shocking. A second before he had been in one of the drabbest regions he had ever set eyes on, and now, as if a scene had been rapidly shifted on a stage, he saw a green triangle, plane trees, a scattering of Georgian houses. Such, he supposed, was London, ever variable, constantly surprising.

Howard pulled up in front of the largest of these houses, cream-painted, with long gleaming windows and fluted columns supporting the porch canopy. There were flower-beds and on each side of the house carefully planned layouts of cypresses and pruned kanzans. A notice fixed to the wall read: *Vale Park. Strictly Private. Parking for Residents only. By order of Notbourne Properties Ltd.*

'The old Montfort house,' said Howard, 'owned by the company to whom Loveday applied for a job.'

'The paths of glory,' said his uncle, 'lead but to the grave. What became of the Montforts, apart from the grave?'

'I don't know. The man to tell you would be Stephen Dearborn, the chairman of Notbourne Properties. He's supposed to be a great authority on Kenbourne Vale and its history. The company have bought up a lot of places in Kenbourne and they've done a good job smartening them up.'

It was unfortunate, Wexford thought, that they hadn't operated on Kenbourne Vale police station. It was in acute need of renovation, of pale paint to modify the gloom of bottle-green walls, mahogany woodwork and dark passages. One of these vaulted corridors led to Howard's own office, a vast chamber with a plum-red carpet, metal filing cabinets and a view of a brewery. The single bright feature of the room was human and female, a girl with a copper beech hair and surely the longest legs in London.

She looked up from the file she was studying as they entered and said, 'Mrs Fortune's been on the phone for you, sir. She said please would you call her back as it's very urgent.'

'Urgent, Pamela? What's wrong?' Howard moved to the phone.

'Apparently your . . .' The girl hesitated. 'Your uncle that's

42

staying with you is missing. He went out five hours ago and he hasn't come back. Mrs Fortune sounded very worried.'

'My God,' said Wexford. 'I was going to Victoria station. I shall be in terribly deep water.'

'You and me both,' said Howard, and then they began to laugh.

5

They gladly hear also the young men, yea, and purposely provoke them to talk . . .

'AUNT DORA,' said Denise icily, 'is lying down. When her headache is better we're going over to my brother's to play bridge.'

Wexford made a further attempt to placate her. 'I'm very sorry about all this, my dear. I didn't mean to upset you, but it went right out of my head.'

'Please don't worry about me. It's Aunt Dora who's upset.'

'Men must work and women must weep,' said Howard rather unkindly. 'Now, where's my dinner and his snack?'

'I'm afraid I didn't prepare anything special for Uncle Reg. You see, we thought that since he seems to be disregarding all his doctor's warnings . . .'

'You'd punish him by giving him a proper meal? Poor old Reg. It looks as if we shall have to deal with you as More dealt with the children in Utopia, by letting them stand and be fed from the master's plate.'

Dora's manner, when she came down, was injured and distrait, but the chief inspector had been married for thirty years and had seldom permitted petticoat government.

Observing the determined gleam in his eye, she contented herself with a piteous, 'Oh, darling, how *could* you?' before sallying forth to her bridge game.

'Let's go into my study,' Howard said when they had finished their pilaf. 'I want to talk to you about that phone call.'

The study was a lot pleasanter than Howard's office in Kenbourne Vale and its appointments less vulnerable than those in the feminine-dominated part of the house. Wexford took his seat by a window through which could be seen, by way of a narrow opening between house backs, the flash of lights passing eternally down the King's Road. He was not yet used to living in a place where it never grew dark and where all night the sky held a plum-red glow.

'You look much better, Reg,' Howard said, smiling. 'May I say that ten years have fallen away from you in the space of one afternoon?'

'I daresay. One doesn't like to take a back seat, to live vicariously.' Wexford sighed. 'The tragedy of growing old is not that one is old but that one is young.'

'I've always thought *Dorian Gray* a very silly book and that epigram one of its few redeeming features. *And* it comes nearly on the last page.'

'Literary chit-chat, Howard?'

His nephew laughed. 'Not another word,' he said. 'Now that phone call Loveday made from Garmisch Terrace . . .'

'It was to Sytansound, wasn't it? You said she phoned Sytansound to say she was sick.'

'So she did, but that call was made at two o'clock and the one from Garmisch Terrace at one-fifteen. Whom did she phone?'

'Her mother? An old aunt? A girl friend? Perhaps she was replying to one of those advertisements.' When Howard shook his head at that, Wexford said, 'You're sure the call to Sytansound wasn't made earlier?'

'The manager took it, a man called Gold, and he's positive Loveday didn't phone before two. She was due back at two and he was beginning to wonder where she was when the phone rang.'

'She made one call from home but the other from a call box outside? Why?'

'Oh, surely because she had no more change. Don't you remember the Pope woman said Loveday asked her for change but all she had was one two-pence piece? Loveday must have got change outside, bought some cigarettes or a bar of chocolate and then gone into a phone box.'

'Yes, the first call was the decisive one, the important one On the outcome of that depended whether she returned to work or not. It was made to her killer.' Wexford rubbed his eye, caught himself doing it and relaxed. It was easy to relax now that he was being admitted to the secret sanctum of Howard's house and, better than that, the sanctum of his thoughts. 'Tell me about the Sytansound people,' he said.

Believing that the passing lights troubled his uncle, Howard drew the curtains and began. 'Gold is a man of sixty,' he said. 'He has a flat over the shop and he was in the shop all Friday afternoon. At five-thirty he switched the phone over to the answering service and went upstairs where he remained all the evening. That's well corroborated. Also at Sytansound are two reps and two engineers. The two reps and one of the engineers are married and live out of Kenbourne. The other is a boy of twenty-one. Their movements are being checked, but, if we're assuming that whoever received that phone call is Loveday's killer, it wasn't any of the older ones. They were all in the Lammas Arms from one till ten to two and none left the table to take a phone call. The twenty-one-year-old was putting a new valve in a television set at a house in Copeland Road. It may be worth checking as to whether anyone phoned that house while he was there, although it seems unlikely. As far as we know, Loveday had hardly ever spoken to the reps and the engineers. Listen, this is from Gold's statement.'

Howard had brought his briefcase into the study with him. He opened it and sorted out one sheet of paper from a small stack. ' "She was very quiet and polite. She was popular with the customers because she was always polite and patient. You would not call her the kind of girl who would ever stick up for herself. She was old-fashioned. When she first came she

46

wore no make-up and I had to ask her to." Apparently, he also asked her to turn her skirts up a bit and not to wear the same clothes every day.'

'What wages did he pay her?'

'Twelve pounds a week. Not much, was it, when you remember she was paying seven for her room? But the job was quite unskilled. All she had to do was show people two or three types of television set and ask for their names and addresses. The reps deal with the rental forms and take the money.'

Wexford bit his lip. It troubled him to think of this quiet polite girl, a child to him, living among the Peggy Popes of this world and paying more than half her wages for a room in Garmisch Terrace. He wondered how she had filled her evenings when, after walking from work through the gloomy defiles of the cemetery, she let herself into a cell perhaps twelve feet by twelve, a private vault for the living. No friends, no money to spend, no kind lover, no nice clothes . . .

'What was in her room?' he asked.

'Very little. A couple of sweaters, a pair of jeans, one dress, a topcoat. I don't think I've ever been in a room occupied by a girl and found so little evidence that a girl had ever occupied it. What little sticks of make-up she had were in her handbag. There was a cake of soap in the room, a bottle of shampoo, two or three women's magazines and a Bible.'

'A *Bible*?'

Howard shrugged. 'It may not have been hers, Reg. There was no name in it and the room was furnished—so-called, as Clements would say. It's possible the Bible was left behind by a previous tenant or that it just drifted there from some hoard of old books. There was a bookcase in the basement, if you noticed. Peggy Pope didn't know if it was hers or whose it was.'

'Will you try to find her parents?'

'We *are* trying. Of course, we haven't a proper photograph but all the newspapers have carried detailed descriptions. They must show themselves in the next couple of days if they're still alive, and why shouldn't they be? They wouldn't have to be more than in their forties.'

Wexford said carefully, 'Would you mind if tomorrow I sort of poke about a bit at Garmisch Terrace, talk to people and so on?'

'Poke about all you like,' Howard said affectionately. 'I need your help, Reg.'

Wexford was up by seven-thirty, bent on leaving by car with Howard, and this defiance sent both women into a flurry. Dora had only just come downstairs and there had been no time to prepare a special breakfast for him.

'Just boil me an egg, my dear,' he said airily to Denise, 'and I'll have a cup of coffee.'

'If you hadn't worried us nearly to death yesterday, we'd have gone out and bought you some of that Austrian cereal with the dried fruit and the extra vitimins.'

Wexford shuddered and helped himself surreptitiously to a slice of white bread.

'Your pills,' said his wife, trying to sound cold. 'Oh, Reg,' she wailed suddenly, 'carry them with you and please, please, don't forget to take them!'

'I won't,' said Wexford, pocketing the bottle.

The rush-hour traffic was heavy and nearly forty minutes elapsed before Howard dropped him outside 22 Garmisch Terrace. The pavements were wet and darkly glittering. As he slammed the car door, he saw a black-caped figure come out of the church and scurry off towards the shops.

The only living creature visible, apart from a cat peering through a grating into sewer depths, was a young man who sat on the top step of number 22, reading a copy of *The Stage*.

'The entry phone doesn't work,' he said as Wexford approached.

'I know.'

'I'll let you in if you like,' said the young man with the lazy indifference of the Frog Footman. He looked, if no means of entering had been available, capable of sitting there until tomorrow. But he had a key, or said he had, and he proceeded to search for it through the pockets of a smelly Afghan jacket. In fashionable usage, Wexford decided, he would be termed one of the Beautiful People, and if like went to like, this must be Johnny.

'I believe you were friendly with the dead girl,' he said.

'Don't know about friendly. I sort of knew her. You the police?'

Wexford nodded. 'You're called Johnny. What's your other name?'

'Lamont.' Johnny wasn't disposed to be talkative. He found his key and let them into the hall where he stood gazing rather moodily at the chief inspector, a lock of dark chestnut hair falling over his brow. He was certainly very handsome with the look of an unkempt and undernourished Byron.

'Who was she friendly with in this house?'

'Don't know,' said Johnny. 'She said she hadn't any friends.' He seemed even more gloomy and indifferent than Peggy Pope and a good deal less communicative. 'She never spoke to anyone here but Peggy and me.' With a kind of lugubrious satisfaction he added: 'No one here can tell you anything. Besides, they'll all be at work by now.' He shrugged heavily, stuffed his magazine into his pocket and shambled off towards the basement stairs.

Wexford took the upward flight. Johnny had been correct in his assumption that most of the tenants would be out at work. He had expected the door of Loveday's room to be sealed up, but it stood ajar. Two plain-clothes men and one in uniform stood by the small sash window talking in low voices. Wexford paused and looked curiously into the room. It was very small and very bare, containing only a narrow bed, a chest of drawers and a bentwood chair. One corner, curtained off with a strip of thin yellow cretonne, provided storage space for clothes. The view from the window was of a plain and uncompromising brick wall, the side evidently of a deep well between this house and the one next door. The well acted as a sounding box, and the cooing of a pigeon perched somewhere higher up came to Wexford's ears as a raucous and hollow bray.

One of the men, seeing him and taking him for a sightseer, stepped briskly over and slammed the door. He went on up. On the third floor he found two tenants at home, an Indian whose room smelt of curry and joss-sticks and a girl who said she worked in a nightclub. Neither had ever spoken to Loveday Morgan but they remembered her as self-effacing, quiet and sad. Somewhat breathless by now, he reached the top of the fourth flight, where he encountered Peggy Pope, a pile of bed-linen in her arms, talking to a girl with a plain but vivacious face.

'Oh, it's you,' said Peggy. 'Who let you in?'

'Your friend Johnny.'

'Oh God, he's supposed to be down the Labour. He'll just lie about in bed now till the pubs open. I don't know what's got into him lately, he's going to pieces.'

The other girl giggled.

'Did you know Loveday Morgan?' Wexford asked her sharply.

'I said hallo to her once or twice. She wasn't my sort. The only time I really talked to her was to ask her to a party I was giving. That's right, isn't it, Peggy?'

'I reckon.' Peggy turned dourly to Wexford. 'She has a party every Saturday night and a bloody awful row they make. Sets my kid off screaming half the night.'

'Come off it, Peggy. You know you and Johnny have a great time at my parties.'

'Did Loveday accept your invitation?' Wexford asked.

'Of course not. She looked quite shocked like as if I'd asked her to an orgy. Mind you, she was very nice about it. She said not to worry about the noise. She liked to hear people enjoying themselves, but I thought, well, you're more like an old aunt than a kid of twenty.'

'She'd got no life in her at all,' said Peggy with a heavy sigh.

50

At the top of the last flight Wexford had much the same sensation as he had received when coming from the dingy wastes of Kenbourne into the light and space which surrounded the Montfort house. The arch at the head of the stairs had been filled in with a glass door set in a frame of polished wood and from this frame, hooked to white trellis, hung a display of house plants. These were so well arranged and well tended as to have satisfied even Denise.

The air smelt cleaner, fresher. Wexford stood still for a moment, getting his breath back, and then he put his finger to the bell above a small plaque which read: *'Chez* Teal.'

6

*There be divers kinds of religion not only in sundry
parts of the island, but also in divers places of every
city*

'I THOUGHT you'd turn up sooner or later,' said Ivan Teal.
The look he gave Wexford was not the insolent stare
of the previous day, but slightly mocking, containing a kind
of intense inner amusement. 'Come in. You seem rather out of
breath. Perhaps you've been afraid to breathe in case you
might inhale something nasty? The stairs do smell, don't they?
There must be some very unusual germs lurking in those
cracks. I'm sure they'd be a source of fascination to a
bacteriologist.' He closed the door and continued to talk in the
same light indulgent tone. 'You may wonder why I live here.
In point of fact, it has its advantages. The view, for instance,
and I have plenty of space for a low rent. Besides, I'm sure
you'll agree I've made the flat rather nice.'

It would have seemed nice in any surroundings. Here it was
like a jewel in a pigsty. Apart from being spotlessly clean, the
flat was decorated with an artist's taste in intense clear
colours, the carpets deep, the walls hung here and there with
abstract paintings. Wexford walked ahead of Teal into a long
lounge running the length of the back of the house. The small
sash windows had been removed and replaced by a fifteen-
foot-long sheet of plate glass through which could be seen,
starkly and almost indecently, the full windswept panorama of
Kenbourne Cemetery. He stepped back, disconcerted, and saw

Teal's lips twitch.

'Our guest thinks we have an unhealthy taste for the macabre,' he said. 'Perhaps, child, we should get some pretty little lace curtains.'

Wexford had been so drawn to the window that he had not noticed the boy who knelt on the floor beside a wall-length well-stocked bookcase. As Teal addressed him, he got up and stood awkwardly, fidgeting with the girdle of his towelling dressing gown. He was perhaps twenty-two, slim, fair, with huge rather dull eyes.

'Let me introduce Philip Chell, the other consenting adult in this establishment.' Teal's twitching mouth broke into a grin. 'You've no idea what a pleasure it is to say that openly to a policeman.'

'Oh, Ivan!' said the boy.

'Oh, *Ivan*!' Teal mocked. 'There's nothing to be afraid of. We're doing nothing wrong. At your age you can surely hardly remember when it *was* wrong.' Still smiling, but rather less pleasantly, he said to Wexford, 'Unlike me who have suffered much from policemen.' He shrugged in the boy's direction. 'We must let bygones be bygones and give him some coffee. Go and get it, child.'

Philip Chell went with a sulky flounce.

Teal stared out at the cemetery, his head slightly on one side. 'I'm badly hung-up about it, aren't I? Shall I tell you a joke? It's quite proper, though you might not think so from the way it starts.' He turned his pale grey insolent eyes full on Wexford's face. 'Three men, an Englishman, a Frenchman and a Russian. Each tells the others what gives him the greatest pleasure. The Englishman says cricket on the village green on a fine Saturday afternoon in June. A bowl of bouillabaisse made by *une vraie Marseillaise*, says the Frenchman. It is night, says the Russian, I am in my flat. There comes a knock at my door the secret police are outside, soft hats, raincoats concealing guns. And my greatest pleasure comes when they ask for Ivan Ivanovitch and I can tell them that Ivan Ivanovitch lives next door.'

Wexford laughed.

'But you see, my friend, I wasn't able to say that, for Ivan lived here. And on two occasions I had to go with them.' His voice changed and he said lightly. 'Now my pleasure is to have policemen in for coffee. You know, one advantage the straight has over the gay is that he has a woman in the house and women are better at chores. That boy's hopeless. Make yourself at home while I go and rescue him.'

The bookshelves contained Proust, Gide and Wilde, as he might have expected, and a lot more he didn't expect. If Teal had read all these books Teal was well read. He reached for a calf-bound volume and, as he did so, its owner's voice said at his elbow:

'John Addington Symonds? Isn't he rather old-hat? Poor fellow. Swinburne called him Mr Soddington Symonds, you know.'

'I didn't know,' said Wexford, laughing, 'and I don't want Symonds. I see you've Robinson's translation of *Utopia*.'

'Borrow it.' Teal took the book down and handed it to Wexford. 'Do you take cream with your coffee? No? My friend has retired to the bedroom. I think he's afraid I'm going to make all sorts of revelations to you.'

'I hope you are, Mr Teal, though not of a kind that would embarrass Mr Chell. I want you to talk to me about Loveday Morgan.'

Teal placed himself on the window-seat, resting one arm along the sill. Sitting down, Wexford couldn't see the cemetery. Teal's face, one of those polished brown faces, both youthless and ageless, was framed against the milky sky. 'I knew her only very slightly,' he said. 'She was a strange repressed child. She had that look about her of a person who had been brought up by strict old-fashioned parents. Once or twice on Sunday mornings I saw her go off to church, go creeping off as if she were doing something both wrong and irresistible.'

'To *church*?' Suddenly he remembered the Bible. It had been hers then, after all.

'Why not?' exclaimed Teal, his voice loud and impatient.

'Some people still go to church even in these enlightened times.'

'Which church?'

'That one up at the end of the street, of course. I wouldn't have known she was going to church if she'd been trotting off to St Paul's, would I?'

'You needn't get so heated,' Wexford said mildly. 'Is that place C. of E.? No, I shouldn't think so.'

'They call themselves the Children of the Revelation. They're rather like Exclusives or Plymouth Brethren. There's this chapel—temple, they call it—and another one up north somewhere and one in South London. Surely you as a policeman remember the fuss a year or two back when one of their ministers was up in court for some sort of indecency. Poor sod. It was in all the papers.' He added reflectively, 'It always is.'

'Was Loveday a—er, Child of the Revelation?'

'Hardly. She worked in a television shop, and to them television, newspapers and films are synonymous with sin. She probably went there because it was the nearest church and she wanted some comfort. I never discussed it with her.'

'What did you discuss with her, Mr Teal?'

'I'm coming to that. More coffee?' He refilled Wexford's cup and stretched out his legs, yawning. 'She was a quiet, sad sort of a girl as I daresay you've gathered. I don't think I'd ever seen her smile or look cheerful until one day about a fortnight ago. It was February the 14th, if that's any help to you. I remember'—he smiled sourly—'because that idiot child Philip had seen fit to send me a Valentine and we had a row about it. Sentimental nonsense! Well, instead of going out with him as we'd arranged, I was going for a quiet drink on my own to the Queen's Arms when I met Loveday coming along Queen's Lane—that's the street at the bottom here, in case you didn't know—looking as if she'd come into a fortune. It was just before six and she was on her way home from work. I'd never seen her looking the way she looked that evening. She was almost laughing, like a child laughs, you know, from joy.'

Wexford nodded. 'Go on.'

'She almost bumped into me. She didn't know where she was going. I asked her if she was all right and she stopped smiling and gave me a rather a stunned look. For a moment I thought she was going to faint. "Are you all right?" I said again. "I don't know," she said. "I feel funny. I don't know what I feel, Mr Teal. I'd like to sit down." Anyway, the upshot of it was I took her into the Queen's Arms and bought her a brandy. She was rather reluctant about that, but she didn't seem to have much resistance left. I don't think she'd ever had brandy before. The colour came back into her face, what colour she ever had, and I thought she'd open her heart to me.'

'But she didn't?'

'No. She looked as if she wanted to. She couldn't. Years of repression had made it impossible for her to confide in anyone. Instead she began asking me about Johnny and Peggy Pope. Were they trustworthy? Did I think Johnny would stay with Peggy? I couldn't tell her. They've only been here four months, not much longer than Loveday herself. I asked her in what way trustworthy, but she only said, "I don't know." Then I brought her back here and the only other time I ever spoke to her was last week when she asked me about Johnny and Peggy again. She wanted to know if they were very poor.'

'Strange question. She couldn't have helped them financially.'

'Certainly not. She hadn't any money.'

'What does Lamont do for a living?'

'Peggy told me he's a bricklayer by trade but that kind of work spoils the hands, if you please, and our Johnny has ambitions to act. He did a bit of modelling once and since then he's had some very grandiose ideas about his future. He's scared Peggy'll leave him and take the baby, but not scared enough apparently to settle down to a job of work. I imagine Loveday was a bit in love with him but he wouldn't have looked at her. Peggy's quite dazzlingly beautiful, don't you think, in spite of the dirt?'

Wexford agreed, thanking Teal for the coffee and the information, although it had let in little daylight.

The bedroom door moved slightly as they came out into the hall.

'She had no friends, no callers?' Wexford asked.

'I wouldn't know.' Teal eyed the door narrowly, then flung it open. 'Come out of there, child! There's no need to eavesdrop.'

'I wasn't eavesdropping, Ivan.' In the interim the boy had dressed himself in a scarlet sweater and velvet trousers. He looked pretty and he smelt of toilet water. 'I *do* live here,' he said sulkily. 'You shouldn't shut me up.'

'Perhaps Mr Chell can help us.' Wexford did his best not to laugh.

'As a matter of fact, maybe I can.' Chell turned a coquettish shoulder in Teal's direction and gave the chief inspector a winning smile. 'I saw a girl looking for Loveday.'

'When was that, Mr Chell?'

'Oh, I don't know. Not very long ago. She was young. She came in a car, a red Mini. I was going out and this girl was standing on the step, looking at the bells. She said she'd rung at Flat Eight but the young lady seemed to be out. Funny thing for one girl to say about another, wasn't it? The young lady? Then Loveday came along the street and said hallo to her and took her upstairs with her.'

Teal looked piqued. He seemed put out because Chell had told Wexford so much and he had told him so little. 'Well, describe this girl, child,' he said pettishly. 'Describe her. You see, Mr Wexford, that here we have a close observer who looks quite through the deeds of men.'

Wexford ignored him. 'What was she like?'

'Not exactly "with it", if you know what I mean.' The boy giggled. 'She'd got short hair and she was wearing a sort of dark blue coat Oh, and *gloves*,' he added as if these last were part of some almost unheard-of tribal paraphernalia.

'A full and detailed portrait,' sneered Teal. 'Never mind what colour her eyes were or if she were five feet or six feet tall. She wore *gloves*. Now all you have to do is find a conventional young lady who wears gloves and there's your murderer. Hey presto! Run along, now, back to your mirror. Be good, sweet child, and let who will be clever!'

It wasn't until Wexford was out in the street that he realised he had left *Utopia* lying on Teal's table. Let it stay there. He didn't relish the thought of climbing all those stairs again to fetch it and perhaps intruding into the monumental row he guessed had broken out between the two men. Instead, he walked to the limit of the cul-de-sac where two stumpy stone posts sprouted out of the pavement and eyed the strange ugly church.

Like Peggy Pope's clothes, every item which went to make up this unprepossessing whole seemed chosen with a deliberate eye to the hideous. What manner of man, or group of men, he asked himself, had designed this building and seen it as fit for the worship of their God? It was hard to say when it had been built. There was no trace of the Classical or the Gothic in its architecture, no analogy with any familiar style of construction. It was squat, shabby and mean. Perhaps in some seamy depths at its rear there were windows, but here at the front there was only a single circle of red glass not much bigger than a bicycle wheel, set under a rounded gable of port-coloured brick. Scattered over the whole façade was a noughts and crosses pattern of black and ochre bricks among the red.

The door was small and such as might have been attached to a garden shed. Wexford tried it but it was locked. He stooped down to read the granite tablet by this door: *Temple of the Revelation. The Elect shall be Saved.*

The hand which descended with a sharp blow on his shoulder made him wheel round.

'Go away,' said the bearded man in black. 'No trespassers here.'

'Kindly take your hand off my coat,' Wexford snapped.

Perhaps unused to any kind of challenge, the man did as he was told. He glared at Wexford, his eyes pale and fanatical. 'I don't know you.'

'That doesn't give you the right to assault me. I know you. You're the minister of this lot.'

'The Shepherd. What do you want?'

'I'm a police officer investigating the murder of Miss Loveday Morgan.'

The Shepherd thrust his hands inside his black cloak. 'Murder? I know nothing of murder. We don't read newspapers. We keep ourselves apart.'

'Very Christian, I'm sure,' said Wexford. 'This girl came to your church. You knew her.'

'No.' The Shepherd shook his head vehemently. He looked angry and affronted. 'I have been away ill and someone else was in charge of my flock. Maybe she slipped in past him. Maybe, in his ignorance, he took her for one of the five hundred.'

'The five hundred?'

'Such is our number, the number of the elect on the face of the Earth. We make no converts. To be one of the Children you must be born to parents who are both Children, and thus the number swells and with death declines. Five hundred,' he said adding less loftily, 'give or take a little.' Gathering the heavy dull folds of his robe around him,' he muttered, 'I have work to do. Good day to you,' and marched off towards Queen's Lane.

Wexford made his way to the northern gate of the cemetery. The ground at this end was devoted to Catholic graves. A funeral had evidently taken place on the previous day and the flowers brought by mourners were wilting in the March wind. He took an unfamiliar path which led him between tombs whose occupants had been of the Greek Orthodox faith, and he noted an epitaph on a Russian princess. Her name and patronymic reminded him of Tolstoy's novels with their lists of *dramatis personae*, and he was trying to decipher the Cyrillic script when a shadow fell across the tomb and a voice said:

'Tatiana Alexandrovna Kratov.'

For the second time that day he had been surprised while

reading an inscription. Who was it now? Another churlish priest, bent on correcting him and reproving his ignorance? This time he turned round slowly to meet the eyes of a big man in a sheepskin jacket who stood, smiling cheerfully at him, his hands in his pockets.

'Do you know who she was?' Wexford asked, 'and how she came to be buried here?'

The man nodded. 'There's not much I don't know about this cemetery,' he said, 'or Kenbourne itself, for that matter.' A kind of boyish enthusiasm took the arrogance from his next words. 'I'm an expert on Kenbourne Vale, a walking mine of information.' He tapped the side of his head. 'There are unwritten history and geography books in here.'

'Then you must be . . .' What was the name Howard had given him? 'You're Notbourne Properties,' he said absurdly.

'The chairman.' Wexford's hand was taken in a strong grip. 'Stephen Dearborn. How do you do?'

7

He thinketh himself so wise that he will not allow another man's counsel.

THEY had emerged into a windswept clearing, and now that he examined him more closely, Wexford saw that his new acquaintance was a man of substance. Dearborn's suit had come from a price range to which Wexford could never aspire, his shoes looked hand-made, and the strap of his watch was a broad band of gold links.'

'You're a stranger here, are you?' Dearborn asked him.

'I'm on holiday.'

'And you thought you'd like to visit the scene of a recent crime?'

Dearborn's voice was still friendly and pleasant, but Wexford thought he detected in it that note of distaste that was sometimes present in his own when he spoke to ghoulish sightseers. 'I know about the murder, of course,' he said, 'but the cemetery is fascinating enough in itself.'

'You wouldn't agree with those people who are in favour of deconsecrating the place and using it for building land?'

'I didn't know there was any such move on foot.' Wexford saw that now the other man was frowning. 'You're opposed to building?' he asked. 'To renovating the place?'

'Not at all,' Dearborn said energetically. 'I've been largely responsible for improving Kenbourne Vale. I don't know how much of the district you've seen, but the conversions in Cope-

61

land Square, for instance, they're my work. And the old Mont-fort house. My company's aim is to retrieve as much as possible of the Georgian and early Victorian from the wanton demolition that goes on. What I don't want to see is every place of interest like this cemetery levelled to make . . .' He spread out his arms and went on more hotly, '. . . characterless concrete jungles!'

'You live in Kenbourne Vale?' Wexford asked as together they followed the path to St Peter's and the main gates.

'I was born here. I love every inch of the place, but I live in Chelsea. Laysbrook Place. Kenbourne Vale wouldn't suit my wife. It will one day when I've done with it. I want to make this the new Hampstead, the successor to fashionable Chelsea. And I can, I can!' Again Dearborn swept out an arm, striking an ilex branch and sending dust-filled raindrops flying. 'I want to show people what's really here, hidden under the muck of a century, the beautiful façades, the grand squares. I'd show you over the cemetery now, only I don't suppose you've got the time and—well, it rather . . . I don't feel . . .'

'The murder,' said Wexford intuitively, 'has temporarily spoiled it for you?'

'In a way, yes. Yes, it has.' He gave Wexford a look of approval: 'Clever of you to guess that. You see, the odd thing is that that very girl came to me for a job. I interviewed her myself. Putting her body in that tomb seemed a sort of desecration to me.' He shrugged. 'Let's not talk about it. What d'you think of this building, now?' he went on, pointing towards the sandstone dome. 'Eighteen-fifty-five and not a trace of the Gothic, but by then they had lost the art of emulating the Classical and were experimenting with Byzantine. Look at the length of those columns . . .' Laying a large hand on Wexford's arm, he plunged into a lecture on architectural styles, laced with obscure terms and words which to Wexford were almost meaningless. His listener's faint bewilderment communicated itself to him and he stopped suddenly, saying, 'I'm boring you.'

'No, you're not. It's just that I'm afraid I'm rather ignorant. I find the district fascinating.'

'Do you?' The chairman of Notbourne Properties was evidently unused to an appreciative audience. 'I'll tell you what,' he said eagerly. 'Why don't you drop round and see us one night? Laysbrook House. I could show you maps of this place as it was a hundred and fifty years ago. I've got deeds of some of these old houses that would really interest you. What do you think?'

'I'd like that very much.'

'Let's see. It's Thursday now. Why not Saturday night? Come about half-past eight and we'll have a drink and go over the maps together. Now, can I give you a lift anywhere?'

But Wexford refused this invitation. The man had been kind and expansive to him. To confess now that he was a policeman, bound for Kenbourne Vale police station, might make Dearborn see him in the guise of a spy.

Instead of returning to the station, however, he turned eastwards along Lammas Grove in search of Sytansound. The police car parked outside told him where it was before he could read the shop sign. Sergeant Clements was at the wheel. He welcomed the chief inspector with a cheery, 'Had your lunch yet, sir?'

'I thought I might try your canteen,' Wexford said, getting in beside him. 'Would you recommend it?'

'I usually pop home if I can. I only live round the corner. I like to see the boy when I get the chance. He's in bed by the time I get home at night.'

'Your son?'

Clement's didn't reply at once. He was watching a boy unload something from a Sytansound van, but it seemed to Wexford that this was a simulated preoccupation, and he repeated his question. The sergeant turned back to face him. The strong colour in his cheeks had deepened to crimson and he cleared his throat.

'As a matter of fact,' he said, 'we're adopting him. We've

got him on three months probation, but the mother's signed the consent and we're due to get the order next week, a week tomorrow.' He slid his hands slowly around the wheel. 'If the mother changed her mind now I reckon it'd about kill my wife.'

Embarrassment and uncertainty had been transferred from one to the other, but there was nothing that Wexford could do about it now. 'Surely, if she's consented . . . ?'

'Well, sir, yes. That's what I keep telling my wife. We're ninety-nine per cent there. It's all been done through the proper channels, but natural mothers have been known to change their minds at the last minute and the court will always go with the mother even if she's given her consent in writing.'

'Do you know the mother?'

'No, sir. And she doesn't know us. We're just a serial number to her. It's done through what's called a guardian *ad litem*, she's a probation officer really. When the time comes the wife and I will go along to the court and the wife'll sit there with the boy on her lap—nice touch that, isn't it?—and the order'll be made and then—then he'll be ours for ever. Just as if he was our own.' Clements' voice grew thick and his lips trembled. 'But you can't help having just that one per cent chance in mind that something may go wrong.'

Wexford was beginning to feel sorry that he had ever opened the subject. The steering wheel which Clements' hands had gripped was wet with sweat and he could see a pulse drumming in his left temple. When he had spoken those last words he had looked near to actual tears.

'I take it Mr Fortune's inside the shop?' he said in an effort to change the subject. 'Who's the boy with the van?'

'That's Brian Gregson, sir. You've heard of him, I daresay. The one with the good friends all burning to give him an alibi.' Clements was calmer now as his attention was diverted from his personal problems back to the case. 'He's one of Sytansound's engineers, the only young unmarried one.'

Wexford remembered now that Howard had mentioned Gregson, but only in passing and not by name. 'What's this about an alibi?' he asked. 'And why should he need one?'

'He's just about the only man who ever associated with Love-day Morgan so-called. Tripper—that's the cemetery bloke—saw him giving her a lift home one night in his van. And one of the reps says Gregson used to chat her up in the shop some-times.'

'A bit thin, isn't it?' Wexford objected.

'Well, his alibi for that Friday night is thin, too, sir. He *says* he was in the Psyche Club in Notting Hill—that's a sort of drinking place, sir. God knows what else goes on there—and four villains say he was with them there from seven till eleven. But three of them have got form. You couldn't trust them an inch. Look at him, sir. Wouldn't you reckon he'd got some-thing to hide?'

He was a slight fair youth who seemed younger than the twenty-one years Howard had attributed to him and whose thin schoolboy arms looked too frail to support the boxes he was carrying from the van into the shop. Wexford thought he had the air of someone who believes that if he bustles away at his job, giving the impression of a rapt involvement, he may pass unnoticed and escape the interference of authority. Whether or not this was the hope that spurred him to trot in and out so busily with his loads, his work was destined to be inter-rupted. As he again approached the rear of the van, deter-mindedly keeping his eyes from wandering towards the police car, a ginger-headed, sharp-faced man came out of Sytansound, beckoned to him and called out:

'Gregson! Here a minute!'

'That's Inspector Baker, sir,' said Clements. 'He'll put him through the mill all right, tell him a thing or two like his father should have done years ago.'

Wexford sighed to himself, for he sensed what was coming and knew that, short of getting out of the car, he was power-less to stop it.

'Vicious, like all the young today,' said Clements. 'Take these girls that have illegits, they've got no more idea of their responsibilities than—than rabbits.' He brought this last word out on a note of triumphant serendipity, perhaps believing that the chief inspector with his rustic background would be familiar with the behaviour of small mammals.

'They can't look after them,' he went on. 'You should have seen our boy when he first came to us, thin, white, his nose always running. I don't believe he'd been out in the fresh air since he was born. It isn't fair!' Clements' voice rose passionately. 'They don't want them, they'd have abortions only they leave it too late, while a decent, clean-living woman, a religious woman, like my wife has miscarriage after miscarriage and eats her heart out for years. I'd jail the lot of them, I'd...'

'Come now, Sergeant...' Wexford hardly knew what to say to calm him. He sought about in his mind for consoling platitudes, but before he could utter a single one the car door had opened and Howard was introducing him to Inspector Baker.

It was apparent from the moment that they sat down in the Grand Duke that Inspector Baker was one of those men who, like certain eager philosophers and scientists, form a theory and then force the facts to fit it. Anything which disturbs the pattern, however relevant, must be rejected, while insignificant data are grossly magnified. Wexford reflected on this in silence, saying nothing, for the inspector's conclusions had not been addressed to him. After the obligatory handshake and the mutterings of a few insincere words, Baker had done his best to exclude him from the discussion, adroitly managing to seat him at the foot of their table while he and Howard faced each other at the opposite end.

Clearly Gregson was Baker's candidate for the Morgan murder, an assumption he based on the man's record—a single conviction for robbery—the man's friends, and what he called the man's friendship with Loveday.

'He hung around her in the shop, sir. He gave her lifts in that van of his.'

'We know he gave her *a* lift,' said Howard.

Baker had a harsh unpleasant voice, the bad grammar of his childhood's cockney all vanished now, but the intonation remaining. He made everything he said sound bitter. 'We can't expect to find witnesses to every time they were together. They were the only young people in that shop. You can't tell me a girl like Morgan wouldn't have encouraged his attentions.'

Wexford looked down at his plate. He never liked to hear women referred to by their surnames without Christian name or style, not even when they were prostitutes, not even when they were criminals. Loveday had been neither. He glanced up as Howard said, 'What about the motive?'

Baker shrugged. 'Morgan encouraged him and then gave him the cold shoulder.'

Wexford hadn't meant to interrupt, but he couldn't help himself. 'In a *cemetery*?'

The inspector acted exactly like a Victorian parent whose discourse at the luncheon table had been interrupted by a child, one of those beings who were to be seen but not heard. But he looked as if he would have preferred not to see Wexford as well. He turned on him a reproving and penetrating stare, and asked him to repeat what he had said.

Wexford did so. 'Do people want to make love in cemeteries?'

For a moment it seemed as if Baker was going to do a Clements and say that 'they' would do anything anywhere. He appeared displeased by Wexford's mention of love-making, but he didn't refer to it directly. 'No doubt you have a better suggestion,' he said.

'Well, I have some questions,' Wexford said tentatively. 'I understand that the cemetery closes at six. What was Gregson doing all the afternoon?'

Howard, who seemed distressed by Baker's attitude, making up for it by a particularly delicate courtesy to his uncle, attending to his wants at the table and refilling his glass from the bottle of apple juice, said quickly, 'He was with Mrs Kirby in Copeland Road until about one-thirty, then back at Sytansound. After that he went to a house in Monmouth Street—

67

that's near Vale Park, Reg—and then he had a long repair job in Queen's Lane that took him until five-thirty, after which he went home to his parents' house in Shepherd's Bush.'

'Then I don't quite see . . .'

Baker had been crumbling a roll of bread into pellets with the air of a man preoccupied by his own thoughts. He raised his head and said in a way that is usually described as patient but in fact is a scarcely disguised exasperation, 'That the cemetery closes at six doesn't mean that no one can get in or out. There are breaches in the walls, quite a bad one at the end of Lammas Road, and vandals are always making them worse. The whole damned place ought to be ploughed up and built on.' Having given vent to his statement, utterly in opposition to Stephen Dearborn's views, he sipped his gin and gave a little cough. 'But that's by the way. You must admit, Mr Wexford, that you don't know this district like we do, and a morning's sightseeing isn't going to teach it to you.'

'Come, Michael,' Howard said uneasily. 'Mr. Wexford's anxious to learn. That's why he asked.'

Wexford was distressed to hear that his new acquaintance—his antagonist rather—shared Burden's Christian name. It reminded him bitterly how different his own inspector's response would have been. But he said nothing. Baker hardly seemed to have noticed Howard's mild reproof beyond giving a faint shrug. 'Gregson could have got in and out of the cemetery,' he said, 'as easily as you can swallow whatever that stuff is in your glass there.'

Wexford took a sip of the 'stuff' and tried again, determined not to let Howard see him show signs of offence. 'Have you a medical report yet?'

'We'll come to that in a minute. Gregson met her in Queen's Lane at half past five and they went to a secluded spot in the cemetery. She became frightened, screamed perhaps, and he strangled her to silence her.'

Why hadn't they gone to her room? Wexford asked himself. Why not to her room in that house where no questions were asked? And why had she taken the afternoon off if she didn't intend to meet Gregson until after work? These were questions he might ask Howard when they were alone together but not now. He saw that Baker was a man whose idea of a discussion was that he should be invited to state his views while the other so-called participants admired, agreed and encouraged him. Having given his own limited reconstruction of the case, he had turned to Howard once more and was attempting to discuss with him in an almost inaudible tone the findings of the medical report.

But Howard was determined not to exclude his uncle. Aware that Wexford had a small reputation as an investigator into quirks of character, he pressed Wexford to tell them about his morning's work.

'She was a very innocent girl,' Wexford began. He felt he was on safe ground here, for Baker could hardly claim to be as conversant with the personality of the dead girl as he was with the geography of Kenbourne Vale. 'She was very shy,' he said, 'afraid to go to parties, and very likely she'd only once in her life been into a public house.' He was pleased to see a smile of what might have been approval on Baker's face. It encouraged him to be bolder, to ask a question which might seem to reflect on the inspector's theory. 'Would a girl like that lead a man on, go alone with a comparative stranger into a lonely place? She'd be too frightened.'

Baker went on smiling tightly.

'There was another point that struck me ...'

'Let's have it, Reg. It may be helpful.'

'Tuesday was February the 29th. I've been wondering if he put her in the Montfort vault because he knew it was only visited on the last Tuesday of the month and that Tuesday, he thought, had already gone by.'

Baker looked incredulous, but Howard's eyes narrowed. 'You mean he *forgot* that this year, Leap Year, there was an extra Tuesday in the month?'

'It's a possibility, isn't it? I don't think a boy like Gregson would know about the vault and the trust. I was thinking that the man who killed her did know and that he might have put her in there because Loveday knew something he didn't want revealed before a few weeks had passed by.'

'Interesting,' said Howard. 'How does that strike you, Michael?'

The man who was not Burden, who shared with Burden only a Christian name and a certain sharp-featured fairness, raised his eyebrows and drawled, 'To your—er, uncle's other point, sir?' It was clever the hesitation he managed before saying 'uncle's', just sufficiently emphasising the nepotism. But he had gone a little too far. His remark brought a frown to Howard's usually gentle face and set him tapping his fingers against his wineglass. And Baker understood that he was admonished. He shrugged, smiled and spoke with cool courtesy.

'You called Morgan innocent and shy, Mr Wexford, but I'm sure you know how deceptive appearances can be. Post-mortem findings, on the other hand, aren't deceptive. Would it surprise you to hear that, according to the medical report, she gave birth to a child during the past year?'

8

Away they trudge, I say, out of their known and accustomed houses, finding no place to rest in.

AFTER Howard's kindness and the cheerful, matter-of-fact welcome he had received from other members of Howard's force, Wexford felt Baker's antagonism almost painfully. He was curiously disheartened. His first day here—his first day anywhere, come to that—as a private investigator had begun so promisingly. Baker's intervention had been like a dark cloud putting out the sun.

He knew that if he had been fit and quite well, if his confidence hadn't been shaken by his tough old body suddenly betraying him, he would have taken this small reverse in his stride. He wasn't, after all, a child to be put off playing his favourite game because another stronger and healthier child had come along and tried to show him how the bricks ought to be stacked. But now within himself he felt almost childlike, his bold adult identity once more disturbed. And when he looked back on his morning's work, it seemed amateurish. The appalling thought that Howard had sent him off on a little hunt of his own simply to occupy him and keep him happy couldn't be resisted.

Nor was he much comforted by the private office which Howard had set aside for his use and to which Detective Constable Dinehart had just conducted him. Like all the rooms Wexford had seen in this police station, it was dark, gloomy and with an enormously high ceiling. This one had a bit of greyish carpet, chairs covered in slippery brown leather, and the view from the window was a full frontal one of Kenbourne gasworks. He couldn't help thinking nostalgically of his own office in Kingsmarkham which was bright and modern, and, looking at the pitch pine, pitted monstrosity in front of him, of his beloved rosewood desk, damson-red and always laden with his own particular clutter.

Sitting down, he asked himself sharply what was the matter with him. Howard's house was too grand for him, this place too shabby. What did he expect? That London would be a Utopian Kingsmarkham and that all these London coppers were going to roll out the red carpet for him?

He stared at the gasometer, wondering how he was going to pass the afternoon. 'Poke about all you like,' Howard had said, but where was he to poke about and how much authority had he got? He was considering whether it would be pushing or against protocol for him to seek Howard out when his nephew tapped on the door and came in.

Howard looked tired. His was a face which easily showed wear and tear. The grey eyes had lost their brightness and the skin under them was puffy.

'How d'you like your office?'

'It's fine, thanks.'

'Horrible outlook, I'm afraid, but it's either that or the brewery or the bus station. I want to apologise for Baker.'

'Come off it, Howard,' said Wexford.

'No. His treatment of you was rude but not indefensible. One has to make allowances for Baker. He's been under a good deal of strain lately. He married a girl half his age. She became pregnant, which made him very happy until she told him the child was another man's and she was leaving him for that other man. Since then he's lost his confidence, distrusts people and is chronically afraid of not being up to the job.'

'I see. It's a nasty story.'

They were both silent for a moment. Wexford found himself hoping desperately that Howard wouldn't go away again, leaving him alone with the gasworks and his depressing thoughts. To keep him there a little longer, he said, 'About this child of Loveday Morgan's . . .'

'That's really why I came to talk to you,' Howard said. 'I don't know what to think. I don't even know if it's significant in this case, and I need to talk it over with someone. With you.'

Wexford felt himself relax with relief. His nephew sounded sincere. Perhaps, after all . . . 'The child may be with his or her grandparents,' he said, and as he spoke he felt the case beginning to drive self-pitying thoughts from his mind. 'You've still heard nothing of them?'

'We're doing everything possible to trace them. For one thing, they'll have to be found before she can be buried, but I'm beginning to think they must be dead. Oh, I know that these days girls are always having differences with their parents and leaving home, but often that only makes the parents more anxious about them. What sort of people who have a missing, or at least absent, blonde twenty-year-old daughter, could read all the newspaper stories there have been these past few days and not get in touch with us?'

'Very simple unimaginative people, perhaps, Howard. Or people who just don't connect their daughter with Loveday Morgan because that isn't her real name and they don't know that their daughter was living in Kenbourne Vale.'

Howard shrugged. 'It's as if she dropped out of the blue, Reg, arrived in Kenbourne Vale two months ago without a history. Let me put you a bit more fully into the picture. Now, as you know, although we don't have absolute cards of identity as certain European nationals do, everyone has a medical card and a National Insurance number. There was no medical card in Loveday Morgan's room and she was on none of the local doctor's lists. It's inconceivable that she should have been the private patient of any doctor, but maybe she was so healthy that she didn't need medical attention. But she had a *child*, Reg. Where? Who attended her at the birth?

'When she first went to Sytansound, Gold asked her for her National Insurance card. She told him she hadn't got one and he sent her along to the Social Security people to get a card which she did in the name of Loveday Morgan.'

'Stop a minute, Howard,' said his uncle. 'That means that she had never worked before. A working-class girl of twenty who had never worked . . .'

'She may, of course, have worked before and had a card in her real name. They don't ask for your birth certificate, you know, only your name and where you were born and so on. I really don't think there's anything to stop anyone from getting half a dozen cards and fraudulently claiming sickness benefit and unemployment money, only that one day they'd catch up with you. Of couse, there are certain jobs you can do where you needn't have a card at all. Most charwomen don't. Prostitutes don't. Nor do those who make their living by crime or drug pushing. But surely Loveday Morgan wasn't any of those things?'

Wexford shook his head. 'She seems the last girl in the world who would have had an illegitimate child.'

'You know what they say, it's the good girls who have the babies. Now, as well as her parents, we're trying to trace her child. It isn't fostered in Kenbourne Vale, we've established that. It could be anywhere. D'you know what I find hardest of all to understand, Reg?'

Wexford looked enquiring.

'I can see that she might have had reasons for wanting to cover her tracks, for wanting to be anonymous. She may, for instance, have had possessive parents who tried to deny her a life of her own. She may have been hiding from some man who threatened her—a point that, I must remember that. But what I can't fathom at all is why she had apparently been *doing this for years*. It almost looks as if years ago she avoided going to a doctor or getting a National Insurance card so that one day, *now*, when she came to die by violence, she would appear to have had a life of no more than two months duration, to have dropped from another planet.'

'What about this Fulham address?' Wexford asked.

'The one she gave Peggy Pope? It's a house in Belgrade

Road, as I told you, but she was never there.'

'The owners of the house . . . ?'

'I suppose they could be lying, playing some deep game of their own, but all the neighbours aren't. I expect Loveday went along Belgrade Road in a bus one day and the name stuck in her mind. I realise, of course, that when you give a false address, unless you simply make up a name, the address you give is that of a street you've either seen or heard of in some connection that causes it to remain in your memory. But the mind is so complex, Reg, and she isn't alive to be psycho-analysed. If she were, we wouldn't be doing this, talking this way.'

'I was thinking that she might have known someone in this Belgrade Road.'

'You mean we ought to do a house to house on the chance of that?'

'Well, *I* could,' said Wexford.

He weighed himself before he went to bed and found that he had lost five pounds. But instead of being cheered by this in the morning he awoke depressed. It was raining. Like a humble trainee, he was going to have to plod round Fulham in the rain. And where, anyway, *was* Fulham?

Denise had stuck a rather alarming flower arrangement on the landing, a confection which was to floral decoration as Dali is to painting. A branch of holly grabbed him as he started to go downstairs and when he freed himself his hand came into disagreeable contact with a spider plant.

'Where's Fulham?' he asked as he ate his sugarless grape-fruit. 'Not miles away I hope.'

Denise said, 'It's just down the road.' She added mournfully, 'Some people call *this* Fulham.'

She didn't ask why he wanted to know. She and Dora thought he was going for his favourite Embankment walk, not understanding that he hated the river when it was shivering and prickly with rain. By now it was falling steadily, not country rain which washes and freshens and brings with it a green scent, but London rain, dirty and soot-smelling. He went

75

westwards, crossed Stamford Bridge and past the gates to the football ground. By the station, fans were buying Chelsea scarves and badges in the sports souvenir shops. Young couples stared disconsolately at secondhand furniture, battered three-piece suites growing damp on the pavement. In North End Road traffic crawled between the stalls, splashing shoppers. But it was more the sort of thing he was used to, a bit like Stowerton really. Here was none of the jaded and somehow sinister sophistication of Kenbourne Vale. The side streets looked suburban. They had gardens and whole families lived in them. Housewives shopped here with proper shopping baskets and almost everyone he passed seemed to belong to an order of society with which he was familiar.

He laughed at himself for being like a conventional old fuddy-duddy, and then he saw Belgrade Road ahead of him, debouching at a right angle from the main street. The houses were three storeys tall, sixty or seventy years old, terraced. At the end, as in Garmisch Terrace, was a church, but grey and spired and as a church should be. He furled the umbrella he was carrying and began on his house to house.

There were a hundred and two houses in Belgrade Road. He went first to the one where Loveday said she had lived, a cared-for house which had recently been painted. Even the brickwork had been painted, and it was a curious colour to choose for an English house in a grimy street, a bright rose-pink. Number seventy. It had a name too, Rosebank, printed in white on pink, the sign swinging in the rain. Had she chosen it for the number? For the name? Had she even seen it?

A couple lived there, Howard had said, and it was a young woman who answered his ring. It made him feel rather awkward asking about a girl with fair hair, quiet and reserved, a girl who might have had a baby with her, for this woman was also a blonde and she carried a young child supported on her hip.

'They came and asked me before,' she said. 'I told them we never let rooms or a flat.' She added proudly, 'We live in the *whole* house.'

He tried the immediate neighbours, worked back to the main street from which this one turned, then up towards the church, down the other side. A lot of people in Belgrade Road let rooms and he talked to half a dozen landladies who sent him off to other landladies. At one point he thought he was getting somewhere. A West Indian hospital orderly who worked nights but showed no dismay at being awakened from his sleep, remembered young Mrs Maitland who had lived on the top floor of number 59 and whose husband had abandoned her and her baby in December. She had moved away a couple of weeks later.

Wexford went back to 59 where he had previously met with ungraciousness on the part of the owner, and met this time with pugnacity. 'I told you my daughter was living here. How many more times, I should like to know? Will you go away and let me get on with my cooking? She left in December and she's living up Shepherd's Bush way. I saw her last night and she wasn't dead then. Does that satisfy you?'

Disheartened, he went on. There was no point in giving her name. He was sure she hadn't called herself Loveday Morgan until she went to live in Garmisch Terrace. All he could do was repeat the description and enquire about anyone known to have moved away at the end of the previous year. The rain fell more heavily. What a stupid invention an umbrella was, almost useless for a job like this! But he put it up again, tilting it backwards while he stood under the dripping porches.

Facing the rose-pink house and on the corner of the only side street to run out of Belgrade Road was a little shop, a general store, very like those to be found in the villages near Kingsmarkham. Wexford marvelled to see such a place here, only a hundred yards from a big shopping centre, and marvelled still more to see that it was doing a thriving trade. There was just one assistant serving the queue, a shabby little woman with a mole on the side of her nose, and he made his enquiries of her briefly, anxious not to keep her from her work. She had a curious flat voice, free from cockney, and she was patient with him, but neither she nor the woman shopper behind him

77

—a resident of the side street—could recall anyone answering his description who had moved away in December.

About twenty houses remained to be visited. He visited them all, feeling very cold now and wondering how he was going to explain to Dora that he had got soaked to the skin. Between them all they were turning him into a hypochondriac, he thought, and he began to feel nervous, asking himself what all this tramping about and getting wet might be doing to his health. Crocker would have a fit if he could see him now, water running from his hair down the back of his neck as he emerged from the last house. Well, Crocker didn't know everything, and for the rest of the day and all tomorrow until the evening he would take it easy.

He paused and, turning back, surveyed the whole length of the street once more. Through the falling silvery rain, under the massy clouds which were streaming across the sky from behind the grey church spire, Belgrade Road looked utterly commonplace. Nothing but the church and the pink house distinguished it from a sister street which ran from the main highway in the opposite direction, and this latter was, if anything, more interesting and memorable. Buses used it and on a sunny day both sides of it would catch the full sun for hours. Why, then had Loveday Morgan chosen Belgrade Road?

He tried to imagine himself giving a false address in London. What street would *he* choose? Not one that he had stayed in or knew well, for that might lead to discovery. Say Lammas Grove, West Fifteen? Number 43, for instance. Immediately he asked himself why, and reasoned that he had picked the street because he had sat outside Sytansound there with Sergeant Clements, the number was just a number that had come to him. . . .

So that was how it was done. That was the way Howard had inferred that it was done, and he had been right again. Obviously, then, it was hopeless to try to trace Loveday by these means. He must approach the matter from other angles.

9

In them they have . . . all manner of fruit, herbs and
flowers, so pleasant, so well furnished, and so finely
kept, that I never saw thing more fruitful nor better
trimmed in any place.

GOING out in the evening was one of the excesses on
which Crocker had placed a strict ban. If Wexford's
faith in the doctor had been shaken, his wife's had not. She
could only be consoled by his promise to take a taxi to Laysbrook Place, to abstain from strong drink and not to stay out
too long.

He was looking forward to this visit. A little judicious
questioning might elicit from Dearborn more information
about the cemetery. Was it, for instance, as easy to get in and
out after the gates were closed as Baker had insisted? Before
Tripper and his fellows went home at night did they make
any sort of search of the place? Or must Loveday have been
killed before six? If this was so, Gregson, occupied at work,
would be exonerated. And might Dearborn not also know
something of Loveday herself? He had interviewed her. It was
possible that, at that interview, she had told him something
of her past history.

Laysbrook Place was one of those country corners of
London in which the air smells sweeter, birds sometimes sing
and other trees grow apart from planes. An arch, hung with
a brown creeper Wexford thought was wistaria, concealed most
of the little street from Laysbrook Square. He walked under
it, light falling about him from two lamps on brackets, and

saw ahead of him a single house such as might have stood in Kingsmarkham High Street. It wasn't an old house but old bricks and timber had been used in its construction, and it was like no London house Wexford had seen. For one thing, it was rather low and sprawling with gables and lattice windows; for another, it had a real garden with apple trees in it and shrubs that were probably lilac. Now, in early March, forsythia blazed yellow and luminous through the lamplit dark and, as he opened the gate, he saw snowdrops in drifts as thick and white as real snow.

The front door opened before he reached it and Stephen Dearborn came down the steps.

'What a lovely place,' Wexford said.

'You'd agree with my wife, then, that it's an improvement on Kenbourne?'

Wexford smiled, sighing a little to himself, for he had been so piercingly reminded of the country. He was suddenly conscious of the peace and the silence. Not even in Howard's house had he been able to escape from the ceaseless sound of traffic, but there was nothing more to be heard than a faint throbbing, what Londoners call the 'hum', ever present in the city and its suburbs but sometimes so remote as to seem like a sound in one's own head.

'My wife's upstairs with our daughter,' Dearborn said. 'She wouldn't go to sleep and it's no good my staying with her. I just want to cuddle her and play with her all the time.'

It was warm inside but airy, enough heat turned on to take off the March chill without making one gasp. The house was very obviously the residence of a rich man, but Wexford couldn't see any sign of pretentiousness or evidence that money had been spent with an eye to impress. It wasn't even very tidy. There was a scattering of crumbs under a tea-table and an ivory teething ring lay on a blanket in the middle of the carpet.

'What will you drink?'

Wexford was getting tired of drawing attention to his illness and his diet. 'Have you any beer?' he asked.

'Sure we have. I couldn't get through the weekend without it after all those shorts I have to consume the rest of the time. I drink it from the can, as a matter of fact.' Dearborn gave a sudden boyish smile. 'We'd better have glasses or my wife will kill me after you've gone.'

The beer was kept in a refrigerator with a wood veneered door which Wexford had at first glance taken for a glass cabinet. 'My favourite toy,' said Dearborn. 'When Alexandra gets a bit older I shall always keep it full of ice cream and cans of coke.' Still smiling, he filled their glasses. 'I've come to fatherhood rather late in life, Mr Wexford—I was forty-three last Tuesday—and my wife says it's made me soppy. I'd like to get the moon and stars for my daughter, but, as this is impossible, she shall have all the good things of this world instead.'

'You're not afraid of spoiling her?'

'I'm afraid of many things, Mr Wexford.' The smile died away and he became intensely serious. 'Of being too indulgent and too possessive among other things. I tell myself that she's not mine, that she belongs to herself. It's not easy being a parent.'

'No, it's not easy. And it's as well people don't know it, for if they did, maybe they wouldn't dare have children.'

Dearborn shook his head. 'I could never feel like that. I'm a fortunate man. I've been lucky in marriage. And you know what they say, happy is the man who can make a living from his hobby. But, for all that, I didn't know what real happiness was till I got Alexandra. If I lost her I'd—I'd kill myself.'

'Oh, come, you mustn't say that.'

'It's true. I mean it. You don't believe me?'

But Wexford, who had many times heard men make similar threats without taking them very seriously, did believe him. There was a kind of earnest desperation in the man's whole manner, and he was relieved when the tension was slackened by the entry of Mrs Dearborn.

She told him she was glad to see him. 'As long as you don't

encourage Stephen to cart us all off to some slum,' she said. 'He gets tired of places he can't improve.'

'It would be hard to improve on Laysbrook House,' said Wexford politely.

She was not at all beautiful and she had made no attempt to look younger than her forty years. Her walnut-brown hair was threaded with grey, her neck ringed with lines. He wondered what constituted her appeal. Was it the willowy ease with which she moved—for she was very slim—or the play of her long fine hands or her extreme femininity? The last, he thought. Her nails were varnished, her skirt short, she was even now taking a cigarette from a cedarwood box, but for all that she had all the old-fashioned womanly grace of a lady out of one of Trollope's novels, a squire's lady, a chatelaine.

That Dearborn was in love with her was immediately apparent from the way his eyes followed her to her chair and lingered on her, watching her settle herself and smooth her skirt over her crossed legs. It was almost as if those briefly caressing hands had for a moment become his own and, vicariously, he felt under them the smoothness of silk and flesh.

Wexford was wondering how to broach the subject of Kenbourne cemetery when Dearborn announced that it was time to get the maps out.

'Dull for you, darling,' he said. 'You've heard it all so many times before.'

'I can bear it. I shall knit.'

'Yes, do. I like to see you knitting. It's a funny thing, Mr Wexford, the qualities women think will attract us and the qualities which really do. I could watch Miss World doing a striptease and it would leave me cold, but let me see a woman in a clean white apron rolling pastry and I'd be in love with her before she could close the kitchen door.'

Mrs Dearborn laughed. 'That's true,' she said. 'You were.'

So that's the way they came together, Wexford thought. It really happened and not too long ago either. It must have been like a Dutch interior, the man visiting the house as a guest for the first time, the kitchen door half open and behind

82

it this brown-haired woman with the sweet face looking up, startled from her cooking, shy at being caught in her apron and with flour on her arms.

Mrs Dearborn seemed to sense what was going on in his mind, for her eyes met his fleetingly and she pursed her lips, suppressing a smile. Then she lifted from a bag a mass of wool and half-completed work, as white and fluffy as flour, and began to knit.

To watch her was curiously soothing. Every harassed businessman, he thought, should have a tank of tropical fish at one end of his office and a woman knitting at the other. Tired now, he could have watched her all the evening, but he had to turn his attention to the maps, photographs and the old deeds which Dearborn had brought into the room and spread in front of them.

The enthusiasm of the crusader had taken hold of Dearborn and as he talked a light came into his eyes. This was Kenbourne as it had been in the time of the fourth George; here had stood the manor house which a royal duke had rented for his actress mistress; on the south side of Lammas Grove had stood a row of magnificent elms. Why shouldn't the land be cleared and fresh trees planted? Why not make all this waste stretch here into playing fields? There was no need for Wexford to ask about the cemetery. Before he could interrupt he was told its acreage, the history of every interesting person buried there, and informed that the state of the walls on the eastern side was so bad that soon vandals would be able to enter and plunder at will.

A point to Baker. Wexford tried to relax and make himself receptive, but he felt overwhelmed. He was experiencing a sensation he had often had before when lectured by someone with an obsession. It is all too much. It should be done in easy stages, but the obsessed cannot see this. Night and day he has lived with his passion and when he comes to enlighten the tyro, he is unable, because he has not been trained in teaching, to sketch in a simple background, awaken interest and postpone the complex details until another occas-

ion. Unrelated facts, historical anecdotes, instances of icono-
clasm came tumbling from Dearborn's lips. He found maps to
confirm this, deeds to verify that, until Wexford's head began
to spin.

It was a relief when the time came for his glass to be re-
filled and he could lean back briefly to exchange a smile with
Mrs Dearborn. But when he looked in her direction, expecting
to be calmed by the sight of those rhythmically moving fingers,
he saw that her work lay in her lap, her eyes were fixed in a
dead stare on a distant part of the room, and she was com-
pulsively picking at the piping on the arm of her chair.

The piping had been so badly frayed that the cord beneath
was fully exposed on both arms. This was not the result of
one evening of nervous tension but surely of many. And when
he glanced at the other five or six chairs in the room and at
the sofa, he saw that all, though otherwise immaculate, were
in the same state. Loops of cord showed on every arm, protruding from feathery rags.

The sight upset him, for it seemed to destroy the picture
he had of this couple's serene happiness. He felt a sudden tension. At the drinks tray Dearborn stood watching his wife, his
face compassionate yet very slightly exasperated.

No one spoke. Into the silence the telephone rang shatter-
ingly, making them jump but none of them as violently as Mrs
Dearborn. She was out of her chair on the second ring, her
sharp 'I'll get it!' almost a cry. Her grace had gone. She was
like a medium who, awakened from a strange and transcending communion, must gather together the threads that hold her
to reality and, in gathering them, suffers intolerable mental
stress.

The telephone was at the far end of the room, on a table
under the point on which Mrs Dearborn's eyes had long been
fixed. She took the receiver and said hallo, clearing her throat
so that she could repeat the word in a voice above a whisper.
That she wanted the call and was not afraid of it was apparent; that the wrong person had called showed in the sudden sagging of her shoulders.

'That's all right,' she said into the mouthpiece, and then to her husband, 'Only a wrong number.'

'We get so many,' Dearborn said, as if apologising for a fault of his own. 'You're tired, Melanie. Let me give you a drink.'

'Yes,' she said. 'Yes, thanks.' She pushed a lock of hair from her forehead and Wexford saw how thin her wrists were. 'It's my daughter,' she said, the good hostess who knows that there must be no subterfuge before guests. 'I get so worried about her. Children are an anxiety these days, aren't they? You never know what trouble they may be in. But I won't bore you.' She took the whisky her husband handed her. 'Thank you, darling.' She sighed.

Husband and wife stood facing each other, hands briefly locked. Wexford was even more in the dark than before. What had she meant about her daughter, about not knowing what trouble she might be in? A baby young enough to use a teething ring, a baby its mother had left upstairs an hour before, was surely peacefully sleeping in its cot. Unless she was expecting a doctor to phone her because the child had been ill...

He drank his second glass of beer with a feeling of guilt. The unfamiliar alcohol made him feel lethargic and light-headed and he was glad when Dearborn packed up his papers and said that was enough for one night.

'You must come again. Or, better than that, I'll take you on a tour round some of the places we've talked about. I take Alexandra to Kenbourne Vale.' He spoke quite seriously. 'She's not really old enough yet to understand, but you can see in her eyes she's beginning to take an interest. She's a very intelligent child. Are you in London for long?'

'Only till next Saturday, I'm afraid. Then it's back to Sussex and work.'

'What sort of work?' Mrs Dearborn asked.

'I'm a policeman.'

'How interesting. Not an ordinary policeman, I'm sure.'

'A detective chief inspector.'

Her face sharpened. She looked at her husband, then away. Dearborn might have been expected to refer to the murder, but he didn't. 'That puts paid to our tour,' he said. 'You're going home and I've got an architect's convention in Yorkshire at the end of next week. Next time you come to London, maybe?'

Wexford nodded, but all further conversation was cut short by a wailing cry from upstairs. The adored, troublesome, precocious, super-intelligent infant was once more awake.

Melanie Dearborn, who had been so electrified by the telephone bell, behaved now like a woman who had reared six children. With a 'That's Alexandra off again,' she rose casually from her chair. It was Dearborn who made the fuss. Was the child ill? Should they call a doctor? He hadn't liked the rash on her face, although his wife had said it was only teething.

Wexford took advantage of this small crisis to leave them, furnishing them with Howard's telephone number and thanking them for a pleasant evening. Mrs Dearborn saw him out. Her husband was already upstairs, calling to the baby that Daddy was coming, that Daddy would make everything all right.

10

For as love is oftentimes won with beauty, so it is not kept, preserved and continued but by virtue and obedience.

WHILE Wexford was with the Dearborns and Howard at home playing bridge a burglary took place in Kenbourne Vale. It was one of a series, all break-ins involving the theft of silver or jewellery and cash and all occurring on Friday or Saturday nights.

'Your friend's answerable for some of this,' said Howard on Monday morning.'

'Dearborn?' Wexford queried.

'Kenbourne's coming up, you see, Reg. I'm all for improving the place, converting some of these old slums and so on, but there's no doubt that when you bring money in you bring crime too. Ten years ago there was scarcely a Kenbournite, excepting the shopkeepers, with anything worth pinching. Now, in the better parts, we've got company directors with heirlooms and safes a child could open. None of the break-ins have been in places owned by Notbourne Properties yet, but unless I'm much mistaken they'll go for Vale Park next.'

'Any idea who "they" are?'

'One always has. You know that,' Howard said bitterly. 'I spent most of yesterday questioning a man called Winter who has, of course, a beautiful unbreakable alibi. And who do you think is supplying it for him? None other than our old friend Harry Slade.'

Wexford looked puzzled. 'Not an old friend of mine.'

'Sorry, Reg. Haven't we put you in the picture? Harry Slade is one of the men who says Gregson was with him in the Psyche Club on the night of Friday, February 25th. He hasn't got a record but I'm beginning to think he's a professional alibi provider.'

'But surely . . . ?'

'Surely his word counts for nothing? Not to a judge, Reg. Here's a blameless citizen, a milkman of all things, pure as the goods he purveys, who says Winter spent Saturday night with himself, his dear old mother and his typist fiancée, playing Monopoly—again of all things—in mother's flat.'

'At least it gives you another lever against Gregson,' Wexford said as Baker entered the room. He spoke placatingly, for he pitied any man who feared he was losing his grip, but Baker eyed him with frosty politeness. He had the face of a cheetah, Wexford thought, all nose and little sharp mouth, the forehead receding and the gingery hair growing down his cheeks in sideburns.

'If you're going to Sytansound now, Michael,' said Howard, 'you might take my uncle with you.'

'Nothing would please me more, sir,' said Baker, 'but I'm taking Sergeant Nolan as it is, and I've promised to show young Dinehart the ropes. Won't it be rather using a sledgehammer to swat a fly?'

Wexford found it hard to keep his temper, to smile and pretend for Howard's benefit that he was happy to be the onlooker who is said to see most of the game. He reminded himself of Baker's unhappy history, the cruel young wife and the child who was not his. *Tout comprendre, c'est tout pardonner.* But what was he going to do with himself for the rest of the day? Gossip with Howard and distract him from his work? Potter about Kenbourne? He was beginning to understand just what Howard's kind act of opting him on to his force in an honorary capacity amounted to. He did no harm, he appeared to amuse himself, he supplied ideas for experts to demolish; he was like, he thought, a workman whose usefulness is at end, who should really be made redundant, but for whom a kindly boss finds a job which could more efficiently be done by a computer if it even needed to be done at all.

He might as well go home and take Dora to the pictures. In the entrance hall he met Sergeant Clements.

'Have a good weekend, sir?'

'Very pleasant, thank you. How's that boy of yours?'

'He's grand, sir. Had the wife up in the night, the little beggar, yelling his head off, but when she went in to him all he wanted was to play. The way he laughs! He's starting to crawl. He'll walk before he's a year old.'

These fathers! 'What are you going to call him?'

'Well, sir, I think his mother must have been one of the romantic kind, fond of fancy names. She called him Barnabas, but the wife and I, we like something plainer, so we've settled for James after my old dad. As soon as we've got that adoption order out of the way we'll have a proper christening.'

'Only four days to go, isn't it?'

Clements nodded. His cheerfulness had suddenly evaporated at the reminder of the short time—the agonisingly short, agonisingly long time—which separated probationary fatherhood from the real thing. Or denied him fatherhood altogether? Looking at the man's red weathered face which, for all his vaunted worldly wisdom, remained immature and schoolboyish, Wexford thought of the coming Friday with a small shiver of dread. Suppose this young woman, this romantic girl who had named her child fancifully, changed her mind again and came into the court to claim him? What would life be like then for Clements and his good patient wife, alone and desolate on top of their tower? It was fine and just, this law which gave prime consideration to the natural mother and her child, but it was a cruel law for the sterile who waited and longed and prayed.

'You've shown such an interest in our boy, sir,' Clements

89

said, smiling again, 'that the wife and I were wondering if you'd come along one day and have a bite of lunch with us and—well, see young James. Say tomorrow or Wednesday? We'd take it as an honour.'

Wexford was touched. 'Tomorrow will be fine,' he said, reflecting that it would be a way of passing the time. On an impulse, he patted the sergeant's shoulder.

Denise and Dora had just finished their lunch. Neither expressed surprise at seeing him or shock that he was still alive. There was a look in his wife's eyes that he had not seen there for many years.

'What have you been up to, Uncle Reg?' asked Denise, for the first time in their acquaintance eyeing him as a man rather than as an ancient invalid.

'Me?' said Wexford ungrammatically. 'What d'you mean?' It was odd, he thought, how guilty the innocent can be made to feel. Certainly the telegram: Fly at once, all is discovered, would send half the population packing their bags and making for the nearest airport. 'What d'you mean, "up to"?'

'Well, a woman's been phoning for you, a Melanie something. I didn't catch the last name. She said, could you go round and see her and in the daytime, please, *when her husband is out*. You're to phone her back and she says you know the number.'

Wexford was puzzled, but he burst out laughing just the same.

'Who is she, Reg?' said Dora, not quite believing she was deceived, but not entirely happy either.

'Melanie?' he said airily. 'Oh, *Melanie* Just a woman I'm having a red-hot affair with. You know all those times you thought I was over at Kenbourne with Howard? Well, actually I was with her. There's many a good tune played on an old fiddle, my dear.' He stopped, caught his wife's eye. It was admonitory, yet faintly distressed. 'Dora!' he said. 'Look at me. Look at *me*. What woman in her right mind would want *me*?'

'I would.'

'Oh, *you*.' He was oddly moved. He kissed her lightly. 'That's the blindness of love,' he said. 'Excuse me. I'll just give my mistress a tinkle.'

Dearborn was in the phone book, Stephen T., with some letters after it that Wexford thought indicated architectural qualifications. He dialled and Melanie Dearborn answered on the second ring. Did she always? Had she been sitting by the phone to jump out of her skin when it rang?

'I'm very sorry to trouble you Mr Wexford. I—I . . . Would it be a great imposition to ask you if you could come over here and see me?'

'Now, Mrs Dearborn?'

'Well, yes, please. Now.'

'Can you give me some idea what it's about?'

'May I leave that until I see you?'

Much intrigued, Wexford said, 'Give me ten minutes,' and rang off. He explained to Denise and Dora, or rather gave them what explanation he could, for he had no more idea than they as to why Melanie Dearborn wanted to see him in her husband's absence. Could it be that she was genuinely worried about Dearborn's obsession with the transformation of Kenbourne Vale because his passion led him to neglect her or his business? Or was it anxiety over some aspect of Alexandra's welfare that distressed her? Neither of these answers seemed probable.

'The library have got your book in, Uncle Reg,' said Denise. 'You can call in for it on your way back.'

As he picked up the blue card and left the house, he came to the conclusion that Mrs Dearborn had sent for him because he was a policeman.

The cab came to a halt at a double white line, and on the major road a red Mini passed them, coming from the direction of Laysbrook Square. Wexford caught only a quick glimpse of its driver, a young woman in a dark coat. Her gloved hands rang a bell in his mind but summoned nothing from its recesses, and he forgot the gloved girl when the taxi brought him under the mews arch and he saw Melanie Dear-born waiting for him on the steps of Laysbrook House.

Wexford achieved a calm and, he hoped, reassuring smile for her, but she did not smile back. She clasped his hand in both hers and began to let forth a stream of apologies for disturbing someone who was only a slight acquaintance.

His guess had been right. 'It's because you're a policeman,' she said when they were inside. 'Or rather, because you're a detective, but not exactly working at the moment, if you know what I mean.'

Wexford didn't.

'You can tell me what I ought to do,' she said, dropping into a chair and immediately applying both hands to the piping cords.

'I'm not so sure of that,' he demurred. She was such a nice woman and so obviously distressed that he allowed himself advice that should only have come from an intimate friend. 'Try to relax,' he said. 'Your hands . . . Let me give you a cigarette.'

She nodded, pulling her hands away from the chair arms and clutching one in the other. 'You're a soothing sort of person, aren't you?' she said as he lit her cigarette. 'I feel a bit better.'

'That's good. What's it all about?'

'My daughter,' said Melanie Dearborn. 'She's missing. I don't know where she is. Ought I to report her as a missing person?'

Wexford stared. 'The *baby*? You mean someone has taken the *baby*?'

'Oh, no, no, of course not! Alexandra is upstairs. I mean my elder daughter, Louise. She's twenty-one.' It was pathetic the way she waited shyly for the gallant thing to be said. Wexford couldn't say it. Today Mrs Dearborn looked amply old enough to be the mother of a grown-up daughter. But Dearborn—was he the father? He could have sworn this pair hadn't been married more than three or four years. 'She's not Stephen's,' said Mrs Dearborn. 'I was married before. I was only nineteen when Louise was born and my first husband died when she was ten.'

'What makes you think she's missing? Does she usually live here?'

'No. She never has. She and Stephen don't get on, but I don't really know why not. They used to and it was actually through Isa—she calls herself that—that I first met Stephen. I suppose she resented my marrying again.'

An old story. The mother and daughter close, the interloping lover who leaves the daughter out in the cold.

'We got married three years ago,' she said. 'Isa was still at school, waiting to do her A Levels. She already had a provisional place at Cambridge, but when she heard we were going to get married she threw all that up and went off to share a flat with another girl.' Mrs Dearborn's fingers had returned to the compulsive fraying of the cords while her cigarette burnt itself out on the rim of the ashtray. 'She has an allowance under her father's will, a thousand a year. I don't know if she ever worked.'

'You never hear from her?'

'Oh, yes, we made up our quarrel in a sort of way. We were never like we used to be. She was always reserved and she became terribly secretive. I suppose that was my fault. I don't want to go in for a display of self-pity, Mr Wexford, but I had rather a lot to bear in my first marriage and then widowhood wasn't easy. I rather taught Isa to keep—well, a stiff upper lip, and not show her feelings.'

Wexford nodded. 'But she kept in touch with you by phone or by letter?'

'She'd phone me from time to time but she would never come here and she refused to tell me where she was living after she had left the flat she shared with the other girl. She phoned from call boxes. It made me very unhappy and Stephen saw it and then—then he got some private detective to find out where she was. Oh, it was so terrible! Isa swore she'd never speak to me again. She said I'd ruined her life. After that I tried not to let Stephen know I was worried about

93

her and that's why I asked you to come here while—while he was out.'

'When did you last hear from her?'

She crushed out the smouldering cigarette stub and lit another. 'I'd better tell you a bit more about it all. After Stephen ran her to earth like that she phoned me to tell me I'd ruined her life, I didn't hear a word for months. Then, about a year ago, she started phoning quite regularly again, but she wouldn't say where she was living and she always sounded unhappy.'

'You must have commented on that?'

'Of course I did. She'd always said, "Oh, it's nothing. The world's not a very jolly place, is it? You taught me that and it's true." Mr Wexford, you don't know her. You don't know how impossible it is to question her. She just says, "Let's leave that, shall we?" I wanted her to come and see me at Christmas to tell her about . . .'

He raised his eyebrows a fraction. 'Excuse me, if I don't tell you what that something was. It can't have anything to do with Isa being missing. Anyway, I begged her to come and she did come. She came on Boxing Day. That was the first time I'd seen my daughter for nearly three years. And after that she came again, two or three times, but always when Stephen was out.'

'She saw him on Boxing Day'?

Melanie Dearborn shook her head. 'No, he spent the day with his mother. She's in a nursing home. Isa looked very thin and pale. It frightened me. She was never vivacious, if you know what I mean, but all the life seemed to have gone out of her. But she began to phone me regularly, about once a week. The last time I heard from her—that was what you wanted to know, wasn't it?—the last time was Friday a week ago. Friday, February 25th.'

Wexford felt the blood go from his face. He hoped it didn't show. 'She phoned you last Friday week?'

'Yes, at lunchtime. She knows Stephen's never in for lunch and she always phoned at about one-fifteen.'

11

*Other rocks there be lying hid under the water, which
therefore be dangerous.*

WEXFORD sat quite still. He knew that her observant eyes
would detect any unease that he might show. He could
hear a clock ticking in the room, a sound he had not previously noticed Mrs Dearborn's fingers made a rending noise
as they tore another half-inch of piping out of the chair. Picking feverishly, she went on talking.

'Isa sounded tremendously happy. There was a note in her
voice I hadn't heard there since she was a little girl. She
actually asked me how I was and how Alexandra was. Then
she said she thought she'd soon have some news that would
please me. Of course I asked her what news and she said she
thought that could wait for a week or two, but she'd phone
me again in a few days. Well, I couldn't bear to leave things
like that, and I was begging her to tell me when the pips went
on the phone. I said to give me her number and I'd call her
back, but before she could they'd cut us off.'

It all fitted. It fitted horribly. 'She didn't phone you again?'
he said, knowing what the answer would be.

'No, it was a terrible let-down. I went almost mad with—
well, curiosity, I suppose you'd call it and I forgot all about
not chasing her and I tried to phone Stephen to get him to
find her again if he could. . . . But he was out all that afternoon and when he did come home I'd cooled off and I
thought I'd just wait until she phoned again. But she hasn't
phoned since.'

'What are you afraid of?'

'Of her happiness.' She laughed a little shrilly. 'Doesn't that sound absurd? I keep asking myself if happiness hasn't made her do something reckless, take some awful risk.' With a shiver, she said. 'What shall I do? Tell me what to do.'

Come to Kenbourne Vale with me and identify a body. He couldn't say that. If this had been Kingsmarkham and he in charge of the Morgan case, he would have said something like that but in the gentlest possible, the most roundabout way. He wasn't in Kingsmarkham and before he did anything he would have to talk to Howard, perhaps find out more before he did even that.

Melanie Dearborn had suffered a lot in her forty years. If his present assumption was correct, all the pain she had ever been through would be nothing compared with the anguish she was going to have to bear. He wouldn't wish it on his worst enemy. And this woman wasn't that. He liked her; he liked her femininity and her concern and her good manners.

What harm would it do to comfort her and let things slide for a bit? He had no duty here. He was on holiday.

'It's only just over a week, Mrs Dearborn,' he said. 'Remember there was a time when you didn't hear from Isa for months.'

'That's true.'

'If I may, I'll call on you again on Wednesday and if you still haven't heard by then, we'll report your daughter as a missing person.'

'You really think I'm making a mountain out of a molehill?'

'I do,' he lied. So what? He could be wrong, couldn't he? Isa—what was her other name?—could be alive and well and junketing about Europe with some boy for all he knew. Something like this had happened to him once before. He had *known* the girl was dead, all the evidence had pointed to it, and then she had turned up, all tanned and smiling from a holiday in Italy with a poet.'

'What's your daughter's surname?' he asked.

'Sampson,' said Mrs Dearborn. 'Louise Sampson, or Isa or Lulu or whatever she's calling herself at present.'

Or Loveday? Don't, he wanted to cry—he who had always rejoiced at positive identifications—don't make the thing worse for me, more definite.

'I must go.'

'How?' she asked. 'Taxi? Bus?'

'One of those,' he smiled.

'Let me drive you. You've been so kind, giving up your holiday time to me, and I've got to go shopping.'

They argued. Mrs Dearborn won. She went upstairs to fetch the baby and when she reappeared at the head of the stairs, Wexford went up to help her with the carry cot. Her head resting on a pale pink pillow, the child Alexandra stared up at him with large, calm blue eyes. She was rather a fat baby, exquisitely clean and dressed in an expensive-looking, one-piece garment of pink angora.

Mrs Dearborn tucked a white fur rug round her. 'My husband's latest extravagance,' she said. 'He buys presents for this child practically every day. She's got far more clothes than I have.'

'Hallo,' said Wexford to the baby. 'Hallo, Alexandra.' She behaved after the manner of her kind by first wrinkling her face threateningly, then allowing it to dissolve into a delightful smile of friendliness and trust. 'She's beautiful,' he said sincerely.

Mrs Dearborn made no reply to this. She was groping under coats on the hallstand. 'I'm looking for a scarf,' she said half to him, half to herself, 'a blue silk one I'm rather fond of. Heaven knows where it's got to. Come to think of it, I haven't seen it for weeks. I wonder if Stephen could have given it to the cleaning woman I had before this one? When she left he insisted on giving her masses of clothes. He's such an impulsive man.' The baby began to whimper. 'Oh, Alexandra, don't *start*. She's like a dog,' said Mrs Dearborn rather crossly, 'Once she knows she's going out she won't let

97

you rest till you're up and away. I may as well borrow Stephen's coat. My fur's at the cleaners and it's so cold, isn't it?'

She enveloped herself in Dearborn's sheepskin jacket which was much too big for her and they ran to the car through a sudden downpour. Child and cot were dumped on the back seat as if they were luggage to be safely stowed and then forgotten. Wexford was rather surprised. He had judged Mrs Dearborn as a strongly maternal woman, wrapped up in her husband and her daughters. She wasn't too old to have a baby, but perhaps she was too old to enjoy caring for one. And yet she was no older than the sergeant's wife who even enjoyed playing with her baby when he woke her in the night. It must be her worry over Louise which all-consuming, withdrew her from the rest of her family.

'Tell me the name of the friend Isa shared a flat with,' he said.

'Verity Bate. They were at school together and Verity went to train as a teacher at St Mark and St John.'

'I take it that that's in London?'

'We're not half a mile from it now,' said Mrs Dearborn. 'It's quite near where you're staying, in King's Road. I'll show you. She'll be in her last year now, but I don't know if she's still in the flat. It's near Holland Park and I did try ringing the number, but I didn't get any reply.'

By now they had crossed the King's Road and were going nothwards. On the back seat Alexandra was making soft gurgling sounds. Wexford looked over his shoulder and saw that she was watching the rain slapping against the window, reaching out a fat hand as if she thought she could catch the bright glittering drops. They came into the Fulham Road by way of Sydney Street, and when they had passed the cinema and entered that part of the road which is as narrow as a country lane, Mrs Dearborn asked him if he would mind a few minutes delay.

'I always buy my bread and cakes here,' she said. 'Could you bear if if I left you with Alexandra?'

Wexford said he could bear it very happily. She parked the car by a meter in Gilston Road, exclaiming with satisfaction because its last occupant had left ten minutes still to run, and walked off to the cake shop without a parting word to the baby. Wexford turned to talk to her. She didn't seem at all put out at being left alone with a stranger, but put up her hands to explore his face. The rain drummed on the car roof and Alexandra laughed, kicking off the white rug.

Playing with the baby passed the time so pleasantly that Wexford almost forgot Mrs Dearborn and he was surprised when he saw that ten minutes had gone by. Alexandra had temporarily lost interest in him and was chewing her rug. He looked out of the window and saw Mrs Dearborn, deep in conversation with another woman under whose umbrella they were both sheltering. She caught his eye, mouthed, 'Just coming,' and then the two women approached the car.

Mrs Dearborn seemed to be pointing out the baby to her friend, if friend she was. From what he could see of her through the streaming rain as she pressed her face against the rear window, Wexford thought her an unlikely sort of acquaintance for a company chairman's wife. Her umbrella was a man's, of cheap uncompromising black, her shabby coat black, and underneath it she wore what looked like an overall. An old felt hat, jammed hard down on her head, partly hid her face but couldn't conceal the disfiguring mole between cheek and left nostril. He fancied he had seen her somewhere before.

Just as he was wondering how long they could bear standing there and gossiping in a downpour which had become a tempest, the woman in black moved off and Mrs Dearborn jumped into the car, slicking back her wet hair with her wet hands.

'I'm so sorry to have kept you. You must be wishing you'd taken that taxi. But you know how it is when you run into people and there's a very . . .' She stopped quite suddenly. 'Now, let's get you home,' she said.

'You were going to show me St Mark and St John.'

'Oh, yes. Can you see that sort of round building right down there to the left? Just before you get to Stamford Bridge? That's St Mark's library. The college grounds go right through to the King's Road. Are you going to talk to Verity?'

'I expect so,' Wexford said. 'At any rate, she can tell me where Isa went after she left her.'

'I can do that,' Melanie Dearborn said quickly. 'Don't forget that's where Stephen found her. It's in Earls Court. I'll write down the phone number. I'd phone it myself, I'd try to talk to Verity, only . . .' She hesitated and added rather sadly, 'None of her friends would tell *me* anything.'

Outside the house in Theresa Street they stopped and Mrs Dearborn wrote the number down for him. For half an hour her thoughts had been distracted from her daughter, but now he noticed that the hand which held the pen was shaking. She looked up at him, nervous again, her brow furrowed with anxiety.

'Are you really going to try and trace her for me? I'm a bit —I remember what happened when Stephen . . .'

'I'll be discreet,' Wexford promised, and then he said good-bye, adding that he would see her without fail on Wednesday.

The house was empty. Denise had left him a note, propped against a crystal vase of freesias, to say that they had gone out to buy a blackberry poncho. He wasn't sure whether this was something to wear or something to eat.

He phoned the Holland Park number, but no one answered. Now for girl number two, the witness perhaps to Dearborn's clumsy and tactless trapping.

A young man's voice said hallo.

'Who occupied the flat before you?' Wexford asked when he had explained who he was.

'Don't know. I've been here four years.'

'Four years? Louise Sampson was living there a couple of years ago.'

'That's right. With me. Lulu and I lived here together for— Oh, four or five months.'

'I see.' This little piece of information was doubtless one which Dearborn had thought it wise to keep from his wife. 'Can I come and see you, Mr . . . ?'

'Adams. You can come if you like. Not today, though. Say tomorrow, about seven?'

Wexford put the phone down and looked at his watch. Just gone five. The rain had dwindled to drizzle. What time did these college classes end for the day? With any luck, Verity Bate might just be leaving now or, better still, living in hall for her final year.

He found the big gates of the college its students call Marjohn's without difficulty. There were a few boys and girls about on the forecourt, embryo teachers, who gave him the kind of glances his generation—but not he—reserved for them, the looks which ask, Why are you wearing those curious clothes, that hairstyle, that outlandish air? He was convinced that no one in the King's Road wore his kind of clothes or was as old as he. He went rather tentatively into the porter's lodge and asked where he could find Miss Verity Bate.

'You've just missed her. She came in to see if there were any letters for her and then she went off home. Are you her dad?'

Wexford felt rather flattered. Suppose he had been asked if he were the girl's grandfather? 'I'll leave a note for her,' he said.

Before he went any further he really ought to tell Howard. His nephew had a force at his command, a force who could trace Louise Sampson in a matter of hours, match her with Loveday Morgan, or else show the two girls to be—two girls. But how much more satisfying it would be if he on his own could present Howard with a *fait accompli*, the checking and tracing all done. . . .

12

*The truth shall sooner come to light . . . whiles he
helpeth and beareth out simple wits against the false
and malicious circumventions of crafty children.*

'ANOTHER one of your women on the phone,' said Denise
rather nastily.

Wexford was just finishing his breakfast. He felt relieved that
Howard, who had gone to the study to fetch his briefcase, and
Dora, who was making beds, hadn't heard the remark. He
went to the phone and a girl's voice, breathless with curiosity,
said this was Verity Bate.

It was only eight-fifteen. 'You didn't waste any time, Miss
Bate.'

'I had to go back to Marjohn's last evening to fetch
something and I saw your message.' The girl went on smugly,
'I realised it must be very important and, as I've got a social
conscience, I felt I should get in touch with you as soon as
possible.'

Couldn't wait to know what it's all about, more like,
thought Wexford. 'I'm trying to trace someone you used to
know.'

'Really? Who? I mean, who can you possibly . . . ?'

'When and where can we meet, Miss Bate?'

'Well, I've got this class till eleven-thirty. I *wish* you'd tell
me who it is.' She didn't express any doubts as to his
identity, his authority. He might have been a criminal lunatic

bent on decoying her away. 'You could come to my flat . . . No, I've got a better idea. I'll meet you at a quarter to twelve in Violet's Voice, that's a coffee place opposite Marjohn's.'

Howard made no comment, asked no questions, when he said he wouldn't be in until after his lunch with Sergeant and Mrs Clements. Perhaps he was glad to be relieved of his uncle's company for the morning or perhaps he guessed that Wexford was pursuing a private line of enquiry, in current parlance, doing his own thing.

He got to Violet's Voice ten minutes before time. It was a small dark café, almost empty. The ceiling, floor and furniture were all of the same deep purple, the walls painted in drug-vision swirls of violet and lavender and silver and black. Wexford sat down and ordered tea which was brought in a glass with lemon and mint floating about in it. From the window he could see St Mark's gates, and before he had begun to drink his tea he saw a diminutive girl with long red hair come out of these gates and cross the road. She was early too.

She came unhesitatingly up to his table and said loudly, 'It's about Lou Sampson, isn't it? I've thought and thought and it must be Lou.'

He got to his feet. 'Miss Bate? Sit down and let me get you something to drink. What makes you so sure it's Louise?'

'She *would* disappear. I mean, if there's anyone I know who'd be likely to get in trouble or have the police looking for her, it's Lou.' Verity Bate sat down and stuck her elbows on the table. 'Thanks, I'll have a coffee.' She had an aggressive, rather theatrical manner, her voice pitched so that everyone in the café could hear her. 'I haven't the faintest idea where Lou is, and I wouldn't tell you if I had. I suppose it's Mrs Sampson tracking her down again. Mrs Dearborn, I should say. One thing about that woman, she never gives up.'

'You don't like Mrs Dearborn?'

The girl was very young, very strict and very intolerant. 'I don't like deceit. If my mother did to me what she did to Lou I'd never speak to her again.'

'I'd like to hear about that,' said Wexford.

'I'm going to tell you. It's no secret, anyway.' Verity Bate was silent for a moment and then she said very seriously, 'You do understand, don't you, that even if I knew where Lou was, I wouldn't tell you? I don't know, but if I did I wouldn't tell you!'

Equally seriously, Wexford said, 'I appreciate that, Miss Bate. Your principles do you credit. Let me get this quite straight. You don't know where Louise is, you've no idea, and you won't tell me because it's against your principles.'

She looked at him uncertainly. 'That's right. I wouldn't help Mrs Samp—Dearborn or *him*.'

'Mr Dearborn?'

Her white skin took a flush easily and now it burned fiery red, earnest and indignant. 'He was my dad's best friend. They were in partnership. Nobody ought ever to *speak to him again*. Don't you think the world would be a lot better place if we just refused to speak to people who behave badly? Then they'd learn bloody awful behaviour doesn't pay because society won't tolerate it. Don't you agree with me?'

She was more like fifteen than twenty-one. 'We all behave badly, Miss Bate.'

'Oh, you're just like my father! You're resigned. It's because you old people compromise that we're in the mess we're —well, in. Now I say that we ought to stop sending people to prison for stealing things and start sending people to prison who destroy other people's lives. Like Stephen Bloody Dearborn.'

Wexford sighed. What a little talker she was! 'He seems quite a pleasant man to me,' he said. 'I gather Louise didn't like him much, though.'

'*Like him*?' Verity Bate pushed back her hair and thrust her face forward until little sharp nose and large blue eyes were perhaps six inches from him. 'Like him? You don't know anything, do you? Lou worshipped that man. She was just so crazy about Stephen Dearborn it wasn't true!'

This statement had the effect on him she had evidently hoped for. He was profoundly surprised, and yet, when he considered it, he wondered why he hadn't arrived at the truth himself. That it was the truth, he had no doubt. No normal clever girl leaves school at a crucial stage in her school career, throws up a university place and cuts herself off almost entirely from her mother just because her mother has made a proper and entirely suitable marriage with a man to whom the girl herself has introduced her.

'She was in love with him?' he asked.

Of course she was!' Verity Bate shook her head until her face was entirely canopied in red hair, but whether this was in continuing wonder at her own revelation or at Wexford's obtuseness, he couldn't tell. The hair flew back, driven by a sharp toss. 'I'd better tell you the whole story and mine will be an unbiassed account, at any rate. It's no use you talking to Stephen Dearborn, he's such a liar. He'd only say he never thought of Lou in that way because that's what he said to my dad. Ooh, he's *disgusting*!'

'This—er, unbiassed account of yours, Miss Bate?'

'Yes, well, we were at school together, Lou and I, in Wimbledon. That's where my parents live, and Lou and Mrs Sampson lived in the next street. Stephen Dearborn was living up in ghastly Kenbourne Vale and Dad used to bring him home sometimes on account of him being what dad called a poor lonely widower.'

'He was married before, then?'

'His wife died and their baby died. That was all centuries ago. Stephen was supposed to be fond of kids and he used to take me out. Tower of London, Changing of the Guard, that sort of crap. Oh, and he dragged me around Kenbourne Vale too, showing me a lot of boring old architecture. It's a wonder I didn't catch something awful in that slum. When I got friendly with Lou, he took us both.'

'How old were you?'

'Sixteen, seventeen. I had to call him Uncle Steve. It makes me feel sick when I think of it, physically sick.' Her mouth turned down at the corners. 'Lou's not like me, you know. She keeps everything below surface, but it's all there, emotion welling and churning like a . . .' The childish voice dropped thrillingly. '. . . a cauldron! Anyway, we all went out together but I was the odd one. Stephen and Lou—well, it was like in the days when people had chaperones. I was their chaperone. And then one night when she was staying at my place she told me she was in love with him and did I think he loved her? It gave me quite a shock, Lou telling me anything about her personal life. I didn't know what to say, I didn't understand it. I mean, she was seventeen—maybe eighteen by then—and he was middle-aged. You can't imagine a girl of eighteen falling for a man of forty, can you?'

'It happens.'

'I think it's urky,' said Miss Bate with what looked like a genuine shudder. 'The next thing was she asked him back to her place. To meet,' she added darkly, 'her mother.'

Wexford had almost forgotten that the purpose of this talk had been to discover Louise Sampson's whereabouts. He was seeing the little cameo again, the stranger entering the house alone—because an unmannerly girl had left him to introduce himself—then, searching for the girl's mother, had come upon a half-open door and seen in a kitchen a woman in a white apron engaged in an age-old feminine task. The girl's strident voice jerked him out of his daydream.

'Lou and I were due to sit for our A's, but the week before they started Lou didn't come to school. I phoned her place and her mother said she wasn't well. Then one night my dad came in and said to Mummy, "What d'you think, Steve's going to marry the Sampson girl." Of course, I thought he meant Lou, but he didn't. Fancy calling a woman of thirty-seven a girl! Lou never took her A's. She was really ill, she had a sort of nervous breakdown '

'A case of *filia pulchra, mater pulchrior*,' said Wexford.

'I wouldn't know. I never did Latin. They sent Lou down to her grandmother and then they got married. I left school and started at Marjohn's and Daddy said he'd pay half the rent of a flat for me if I could find another girl to share and I was sort of looking for someone when Lou rang up from this grandmother's and said she'd never go to those two in Chelsea, and could she share with me?'

'How long did that last?'

'About a year. Lou was more shut in than ever. She was heartbroken. Her bloody mother used to phone and pretend to me it was all rubbish about Lou fancying Stephen. Anyway, Lou got fed up being hunted and she went off to share with someone in Battersea. I'm not telling you the address, mind you.'

'I wouldn't dream of asking you, Miss Bate.'

'After that we sort of lost touch.'

'You couldn't bear to see so much suffering, was that it?'

'Exactly.' She seemed relieved at so pat a solution which perhaps avoided for her the necessity of explaining that she hadn't bothered to phone and never wrote letters. 'Louise Sampson,' she said dramatically, 'went out of my life. Perhaps she's found happiness, perhaps not. I shall never know.' She lifted her chin and stared intensely in the direction of the coffee machine, showing to Wexford a delicate and faintly quivering profile. He wondered if she had attended all or some of the films shown at the Garbo season, a recent offering, according to Denise, of the Classic Cinema up the road. 'That's all I can tell you,' she said, 'but if I knew any more I wouldn't reveal a single word.'

Surely the sergeant's wife didn't go to all this trouble, a full dinner service, linen napkins, side plates and all, when her husband popped home alone for a bite to eat? Wexford was sure she didn't but he behaved as if all this ceremony was normal and even forgot his diet.

He was aware that further pomp was to attach to the entry of the child, delayed until after their coffee, not only for the sake of suspense but to prove Mrs Clements' ability to be a gracious hostess though a mother. It was touching, he thought, the way she kept stoically to the theme of their conversation—

107

inevitably, with her husband taking part, the general decadence of modern life—while listening surreptitiously for a squeak from the next room. At last, when Clements and Wexford had left the table and were standing at the picture window, contemplating Kenbourne Vale from twelve floors up, she re-entered the room with the baby in her arms.

'He's got two teeth,' she said, 'and not a bit of trouble cutting them.'

'A fine boy,' said Wexford. He took the child from her and talked to him as he had talked to Alexandra Dearborn, but James responded less happily and his shining dark eyes grew uneasy. An adopted child, Wexford thought, might well show signs of insecurity, handled as he must have been since leaving his true mother by stranger after stranger. 'He's a credit to you,' he said, and then to his shame he found his voice thick with an unlooked-for emotion. It was out of his power to say more.

But he had said enough, or his expression had told what he couldn't say. Mrs Clements beamed. 'I've waited fifteen years for this.'

Wexford handed the boy back. 'And now you've got fifteen years of hard labour.'

'Years and years of happiness, Mr Wexford.' The smile died. Her full, rather dull, face seemed on an instant to grow thinner. 'If—if they'll let me keep him.'

'She's signed an affidavit, hasn't she?' said the sergeant fiercely. 'She's promised to give him up.'

His wife gave him a wifely look, part compassion, part gentle reproof. 'You know you're as worried about it as I am, dear. He was more worried than me at first, Mr Wexford. He wanted to—well, find out who she was and give her some money. To sort of buy James, you see.'

'I don't know much about adoption,' said Wexford, 'but surely it's illegal for money to pass in the course of these transactions?'

'Of course it is,' said Clements huffily. He looked put out. 'I wasn't serious.' His next words rather belied this remark.

'I've always been a saver, I daresay I could have raised quite a bit one way and another, but I . . . You don't think I meant it, sir?'

Wexford smiled. 'It would be a bit too risky, wouldn't it?'

'Breaking the law, you mean, sir? You'd keep the child but you'd always have the fear of being found out hanging over you.'

Clements was never very quick on the uptake, Wexford thought. He said, 'But would you have the child?

'Of course you would, sir. You'd have brought it from the natural mother, in a manner of speaking, thought it doesn't sound very nice put that way. You'd offer her a thousand pounds, say, not to oppose the making of the order.'

'And suppose she took the money and agreed and opposed the order just the same? What redress would you have? None at all. You couldn't ask her to sign an agreement or enter into a contract as any such transaction in matters of adoption would be illegal.'

'I never thought of that. An unscrupulous sort of girl might even engineer it so that she could get hold of money to support her child.'

'She might indeed,' said Wexford.

13

But in Utopia every man is a cunning lawyer . . .

SHE too had had a baby . . . During the past year Loveday
Morgan had had a baby. If Loveday Morgan was Louise
Sampson, Louise had had that baby. A good reason, added to
the other good reasons, for not letting her mother see her until
Christmas when she might have been fully recovered from the
child's birth.

Now that birth must have been registered, but not, apparently,
to a mother called Morgan. Surely Louise wouldn't have
dared register the child in a false name? The penalties for
making false registrations were stated clearly enough, Wexford
knew, in every registrar's office. They were more than sufficient to daunt a young girl. She would have registered it in
her own name.

This, then, was what he just had to check on before he went
any further. This might mean he need go no further. But his
plan was doomed to postponement, for he was no sooner in
his own office when Howard phoned through to request his
presence at a house in Copland Road.

'Mrs Kirby?' Wexford said. 'Who's she?'

'Gregson was mending her television at lunchtime on February 25th. She's just phoned to say she's remembered something we ought to know.'

'You won't want me.'

But Howard did. He was very pressing. When Wexford

110

joined him at the car and noted the sullen presence of Inspector Baker, he saw it all. Tactful pressure had been brought to bear on Baker to include the chief inspector in this visit. A king-size sledge-hammer, indeed, to swat a fly, unless the fly itself had suddenly developed into a far larger insect. Evidently Baker didn't like it and not on these grounds alone. He gave Wexford a cold penetrating stare.

And Wexford himself was annoyed. He would have been far happier making his own private researches. Howard had arranged it to avoid hurting his uncle and Wexford was there to avoid hurting his nephew, but all they had succeeded in doing was to upset Baker thoroughly. The nape of his neck, prickly with ginger bristles, had crimsoned with anger.

Wexford wondered about his private life, the solitary existence he must lead somewhere, perhaps in a trim suburb in a neat semi-detached which he had furnished for the young wife who had deserted him. He could hardly imagine a greater humiliation for a middle-aged man than that which Baker had suffered. It would dig into the very roots of his manhood and shake what should, at his age, have been a well-adjusted personality.

He was sitting beside the driver, Wexford in the back with his nephew, and since they had left the station no one had uttered a word. Now Howard, trying to ease the tension, asked Baker when he would be moving from Wimbledon into the new flat he was buying in north-west London.

'Next month, I hope, sir,' Baker said shortly. He didn't turn his head and again the dark flush had appeared on his neck.

The mention of Wimbledon reminded Wexford of Verity Bate who had said that her parents and, at one time, the Sampsons had lived in that suburb. So it was there that the inspector's trouble had come upon him. Not discouraged, Howard pressed the point, but Wexford had the impression that Baker only replied because Howard was his superior officer. And when the superintendent spoke next of the week, terminating on February 27th, that Baker had taken off to consult with solicitor's and arrange with decorators, Baker's shrug was almost rude.

'I'm afraid you're one of those people who never take a proper holiday, Michael,' Howard said pleasantly. 'Even when you were supposed to be off you were hanging about Kenbourne Vale nearly every day. Is it such an attractive place?'

'Filthy hole,' Baker said abruptly. 'How anyone could live here beats me.'

From the tensing of the driver's shoulders, Wexford guessed that he was one of those who did. Here was another instance of the inspector putting people's backs up, literally this time. A gloomy silence fell. Howard deliberately avoided catching his uncle's eye and Wexford, embarrassed, looked out of the window.

It was a damp, raw day, and although it was still early afternoon, lights showed here and there behind long sash windows, making pale bright rectangles in the grey façades. The air itself seemed grey, not dense enough for fog but laden with a damp which blackened the pavements. Kenbourne Vale wore the colours of a snail shell, glimmering faintly in a snail's pallid, dull hues, under the ashen sky which seemed to have dropped and to lie low and sombrely over it. Church spires, a stadium, sprawling factories loomed before the car, took solid shape and then dissolved again as they passed. Only the new office blocks, strident columns of light, had a positive reality in the thickening gloom.

They entered Copeland Hill, that district which, nearly a week before, had been Wexford's gateway to his nephew's manor. Much had happened since then. He asked himself how he would have felt on that bus last week if he had known that today he would be riding in a police car with Howard, honorary yet treated by Howard with honour, to interrogate an important witness. The thought cheered him and, viewing Copeland Road with quickening interest, he resolved not to let Baker deter him or damp his ardour.

This was one of the streets which Dearborn had his eye on, and Wexford saw that a whole section of the left-hand terrace was undergoing renovation. Scaffolding covered it and men were painting the broad lofty expanse a rich cream colour so that the moulding above the windows was revealed as swags, bunches of grapes and lovers' knots. New railings of curled wrought iron rested against the scaffolding, ready to be fixed to the balconies.

The effect of this half-completed conversion was to make the neighbouring houses look even shabbier than they would otherwise have done. But neither the scars of decay nor the unmistakable signs that each was inhabited by a score of ill-assorted tenants rather than one prosperous family could quite ruin their stateliness. Garmisch Terrace was mean now and had been mean in the spirit of its conception; this place had a strange indestructible beauty because, like an old woman who had once been a pretty girl, its bones were good.

Mrs Kirby who occupied part of the ground floor of a house whose plaster front was scored all over with long river-like cracks, had also once been pretty in the Yorkshire of her girlhood. Her accent marked her as a native of the East Riding, and Wexford wondered what combination of circumstances had brought her to Kenbourne Vale. She was about sixty now. Apparently she owned a lease of the whole house, but lived in only three rooms of it which she kept as neat and sparkling as a pin.

He marvelled at her ordinariness. This place seemed curious to him, the broad street, the mansions like ornamented and windowed cliffs fascinating and wonderful, and he thought they must seem so to her too with her background. What did she think of the people in their exotic clothes, the black faces, the defiant boys and girls who lived in the warren above her head? She conducted her life as if she still lived in some Yorkshire cottage, it seemed, from the description she gave them in minute detail of the way she had spent February 25th. An early riser, she had got up at seven, cleaned the flat, chatted over the fence to a neighbour. Loquaciously, she took the three policemen round the shops with her, listed the dishes prepared for her lunch and came finally, while Baker tapped an impatient foot, to the arrival of Gregson sharp at twelve-thirty.

'Aye, it were half past twelve when he come. I know that on account of that's when I have my bit of dinner and I thought to myself, some folks have no consideration. I said to him, How long will you be? and he said half-an-hour so I put my plate in t'oven, not liking to have folks watch me eating.'

'When did the phone call come?' Howard asked.

'Must have been after one.' She pronounced the last word to rhyme with 'on'. 'Aye, because I recall thinking, you're taking a long half hour, lad. I heard t'phone ring and I answered it and this girl says, Can I speak to Mr Gregson. It's t'shop.'

'You're sure that's what was said, "the shop"?'

'Nay, I can't be sure. Might have been Sytansound or whatever they call theirselves. I called t'young lad and he talked to her, just said yes and no and good-bye. Then he finished t'job and off he went.'

'Be more precise about the time of the call, Mrs Kirby.'

She enjoyed being precise. Wexford could see, and see Howard also saw, that to her precision and accuracy were not the same thing. Her eyes flickered doubtfully. She wanted to impress, to earn praise, even if she did so through a precise inaccuracy.'

Baker said, 'If you thought it had been a long half hour Mrs Kirby, it must have been a while after one. Five or ten minutes.'

Wexford longed for the power to say like a judge to counsel, 'Don't lead, Mr Baker.'

The leading had done its work. 'Aye, about ten past,' said Mrs Kirby, and hopefully, 'Near a quarter past.'

Baker smiled in silent triumph. Smile on, thought Wexford. Loveday didn't phone Gregson, she phoned her mother. He spoke at last. Howard's encouraging glance permitted him a question. 'Did you recognise the girl's voice?'

'Nay, why would I?'

'Well, presumably you phoned the shop yourself to tell them your set wanted attention.'

'Aye, I did, and I phoned them last back end too, but I never talked to any girls. It was always that manager, that Gold.'

'Let him lie his way out of this one,' said Baker as they trooped into Sytansound where, on a dozen lambent screens, goblin puppets cavorted for the entertainment of the under-fives. Behind the desk which had been Loveday's was a fifty-year-old lady in boots and knee-breeches who swam out to them, followed by fat lumbering Gold.

'There wasn't any girl in the shop after ten to one on that Friday,' said Gold, unhappy at these frequent visits from the law.

'Where is he?' said Baker.

'Out the back with the van.'

A high brick wall made the van park gloomy. Behind it, Wexford knew, was the cemetery. He could see the trees over the top of it. You couldn't get away from that cemetery in Kenbourne Vale; it was the heart and soul of the place.

Gregson had heard them coming. He was leaning against the wall, his arms folded, waiting for them. The pose was defiant, but his face was frightened.

'He doesn't talk, you know,' Howard said conversationally to his uncle as Baker approached the boy. 'I mean, he literally doesn't open his mouth. He told Baker he didn't go out with the girl and where he was on Friday night, and since then he just won't talk.'

'The best defence. I wonder who taught him that?'

'I wish I knew. I only hope his mentor isn't giving lessons to all the villains in Kenbourne.'

Gregson had let his arms fall to his sides because Baker told him to and moved a few inches from the wall. He answered the inspector's questions only with shrugs. In his thin denim jacket he looked cold and pinched and very young.

'We're going to have a talk, my lad,' said Baker. 'Down at the station.'

Gregson shrugged.

At the police station they took him into an interview room. Wexford went upstairs and contemplated his gasworks. The gasometer had deflated quite a lot to reveal behind it a canning factory, a church and a building that was probably Kenbourne town hall. He thought about girls who were fond of romantic names, about babies who didn't look like their parents and then about Peggy Pope and her lover. He came to no conclusions.

His phone rang. Howard's voice said, 'Gregson's scared stiff of us. How about you having a go at him?'

'Why should he talk to me?'

'I don't know, but it can't do any harm.'

It didn't do any good either. Gregson chain-smoked. He made no answers to any of Wexford's questions. Wexford asked him if he knew what sort of a man Harry Slade was, that his word couldn't be relied on (not quite true, this), if he was aware of the implication of the phone call he had received at Mrs Kirby's. Gregson said nothing. It was, in its way, an admirable performance. Real hardened criminals, twice Gregson's age, couldn't have kept it up.

Wexford tried bullying, although it went against the grain with him. He stood over the boy and bawled questions into his ear. Gregson smelt of the sweat of fear but still he didn't speak. His cigarettes were all gone and he held his hands clenched on the table in front of him.

The stuff of martyrs, Wexford thought. In Sir Thomas's day they would have put him to the rack and the thumbscrew. He cooled his voice and went back once more to the telephone call. Who was the girl? He knew there was no girl in the shop at that time, didn't he? At that precise time Loveday Morgan had made a call. The call was to him, wasn't it?

Wexford leant across the table. He fixed his eyes on Gregson, forcing the boy to look at him, and then, shockingly, Gregson spoke. It was the first time Wexford had heard his voice, a thin cockney whine. 'I want a solicitor,' he said.

Wexford went outside, called in D.C. Dinehart, and told Howard what had happened.

'That's bloody marvellous,' said Baker. 'That's all we need.'

'If he wants a solicitor he'll have to have one,' said Howard. 'Someone's been showing him the ropes all right.'

'Mr. Wexford perhaps.' Baker could hardly conceal his rage. 'Telling him his rights, no doubt.'

Taking a leaf out of Gregson's book, Wexford said nothing. They went back into the interview room and Howard asked the boy which solicitor he wanted.

'I haven't got one,' said Gregson. 'You can bring me the phone book.'

14

*If any man had rather bestow this time upon his own
occupation, he is not letted or prohibited.*

IT was half past six before Wexford got away. Howard was
still closeted with a certain Mr de Traynor who smoothly
and sympathetically referred to Gregson as 'my youthful
client here.' Gregson had picked him out of the phone book
because he liked the sound of his name.

There was more than a name to Mr de Traynor. His silky
eyebrows almost disappeared into his silky hair when he heard
that as yet no charges had been made against Gregson, that,
in fact, no one was quite ready to charge him, and he settled
down to teach Howard about the law.

'Am I to understand that my youthful client here has
actually been detained for no less than three hours . . . ?'

Avoiding Baker, Wexford slipped out by a back way he
had discovered which led him into a paved alley. On one side
of it was a building that looked like a section house, on the
other rows of newly-built garages used for housing police cars
and vans. It was all on a much grander scale than anything in
Kingsmarkham, and a few days before it would have had an
oppressive, even deterrent, effect on him. But now neither the
size of the place nor Baker's unjust attitude troubled him much.
Human nature was the same here as in the country, and it was
by studying human nature and patterns of behaviour rather
than relying solely on circumstantial evidence that he had had

his successes in the past. He told himself as he walked briskly in the direction of Kenbourne Lane that he had the edge on Baker, for he had never and would never compose a solution to a mystery and then manipulate facts and human nature to fit it. Pity, though, that he had missed his chance of going to Somerset House.

Rather than rely on finding a bus that would take him to Earls Court, Wexford made for a tube station he had seen from the police car. It wasn't called Kenbourne Vale but Elm Green. Something to do with those famous, long-felled trees about which Dearborn had discoursed? There were no elms now, only a wide grey pavement full of people scurrying towards the station under fluorescent lights, and inside a maze of long tiled passages.

When he came to change at Notting Hill Gate he got into the wrong train. Half an hour had passed before he finally alighted at Earls Court and by then he was fighting claustrophobia, the blood pounding in his head. How did Londoners stick it?

Nevern Gardens turned out to be another of those huge squares, tall houses glaring at each other across rows of parking meters and plane trees with branches like waving threads. He found Lewis Adams on the third floor of one of these houses, in an absurdly narrow, absurdly long, room with a tiny kitchen opening out of it, and he wondered why it was this curious shape until he realised it was a walled-off segment of a huge room, perhaps now divided into five or six shoe boxes like this one.

Adams was eating his evening meal, a Chinese concoction of beansprouts and bamboo shoots and little red bones heaped on a soup plate and balanced on his knees. On the table in front of him was a glass of water, a bottle of soy sauce and a plate of pancakes which resembled chunks of pink foam rubber.

But if his eating arrangements were Bohemian, the room he had shared with Louise Sampson was not. A well-vacuumed red carpet covered the floor, cared-for paperbacks filled the bookshelves, a large television set faced the twin armchairs and the window overlooked the tops of plane trees.

'You'd better ask me questions,' said Adams. 'I don't know what it is you want.' He spoke economically. His voice was cultured and controlled with the tone of a budding barrister or a medical student preparing to sit for triumphant finals. But he looked too young for that, as young as Gregson and not unlike him. Smallish and neat, he had fair-brown hair which stopped short at the lobes of his ears. He would tell exactly what he wanted to tell, no more and no less, Wexford thought. There would be no reiteration here of grandiloquent principles, no juvenile drama.

'Where did you meet her?' he asked.

'She came into the restaurant where I was a waiter.' Adams didn't give a deprecating smile or apologise for his past (perhaps present) humble calling. He finished his beansprouts and set the plate to one side. 'We talked. She said she was sharing with a girl in Battersea, but she wasn't comfortable because they only had one room and the girl had her boy friend there at nights. I asked if she'd like to share with me.' Still without smiling, he added, 'I was finding the rent a bit much.'

'She agreed?'

'The same day. She collected her stuff and moved in that night.'

Wexford was rather shocked. Did they really go on like that these days? 'A bit cold-blooded, wasn't it?'

'Cold-blooded?' Adams hadn't understood and when he did he was more shocked than Wexford had been. His face went cold with disgust. 'You're not suggesting she slept with me, are you? *Are you*?' He shook his head, tapping one finger against his brow. 'I don't understand your generation. You accuse us of being promiscuous and casual and so on, but you're the ones with the unclean minds. I honestly don't care if you believe this or not, but Lulu lived here with me for four months and we were never lovers. Never. I suppose you're going to ask why not. The answer is that these days, whatever happened in your time, you can sleep in the same room

120

as a girl and not want to make love to her because you're not frustrated. No one any longer has the power to force you into an unnatural celibacy, you're free to have the girls you do want. We didn't attract each other, that's all, and we weren't in the position of having to make do with any port in a storm.' He held up one hand. 'I'm not queer. I had girl friends. I went to their places. No doubt Lulu saw her boy friends at theirs.'

'I believe you, Mr Adams.'

At last he smiled. Wexford saw that delivering his little lecture had relaxed him and he wasn't surprised when he said, 'Don't call me that. My name's Lewis. People used to call us Lew and Lulu.'

'Did Lulu work?'

'She had some money of her own, but she worked sometimes. She used to go out cleaning. Why not? You *are* conventional. It's well paid around here and what you get you keep. No cards, no stamps, no tax.'

'What was she like, what sort of a girl?'

'I was fond of her,' said Adams. 'She was quiet and sensible and reserved. I like that. You get sick of the sound and the fury, you know. Her stepfather,' he added, 'was a great guy for sound and fury.'

'He came here?'

'She'd been here four months.' Adams took a drink from the glass of water on his dinner tray. 'She opened the door and when she let him in I heard her give a sort of cry—I was out in the kitchen through there—and say, "Stephen, darling Stephen, I knew you'd come for me one day".' He shook his head disapprovingly both, Wexford thought, at the hysterical utterance itself and at hearing it on his own lips. 'It wasn't like her, losing control. I was shattered.'

'But he'd only come to find out where she was?'

'He explained that. You know all those endless explanations people go in for. I didn't care for him, a big showy man, an extrovert. Lulu didn't say much. She told me afterwards that when she saw him she really believed he wanted her at last

121

and the shock of knowing he didn't for·the second time was too much for her. He thought what you thought, that I was her lover. He made a fuss about that. I didn't deny anything or defend myself. Why should I? Then there was a very nasty scene which is best forgotten and he went.'

'What was the scene about?'

Adams had now adopted a manner rather at odds with his youthful appearance. It was as if the young barrister had become an elderly and successful counsel who, conducting an unsavoury case, reveals because he must for his client's sake the bare facts, while taking pains to omit and make it clear that he is omitting all the nauseating details.

'How can knowing that possibly help you?'

'Anything about Louise might help. I can't make you tell me, but I think you should.'

Adams shrugged. 'I suppose you know your own business best. This stepfather—I don't know his name, I'm afraid, Stephen Something—was telling Lulu in a very tactless way how happy he and her mother were when Lulu said, "You're very fond of children, aren't you, Stephen?" And he said he was and he hoped to have some of his own. Lulu suddenly became rather like a powerhouse. I don't want to dramatise things, but she gave the impression of very strong pressure holding down an irrepressible force.'

Powerhouses, Wexford thought, cauldrons . . . A frightening sort of girl, intimidating as are all those passionate and turbulent creatures with no outlet for their fevers. 'She said something to him?'

'Oh, yes. I said it was nasty. She said, "Not with my mother you won't, Stephen. Surely she didn't forget to tell you she had a hysterectomy when I was fifteen?"' Adams' face creased with distaste. 'I left them then and went out into the kitchen. The stepfather screamed and shouted at her and Lulu did some screaming too. She didn't tell me what they said and a week later she left.'

'Where did she go?'

'She wouldn't tell me. We weren't on very good terms when

we parted. Pity, because we'd always trusted each other. Lulu didn't trust me any more. I'd told her off for shouting at this Stephen. She thought I was sympathising with her parents and that I'd tell them where she was if she told me.'

'You must have some idea,' Wexford protested.

'From various things she said, I think she went to Notting Hill. Possibly to a boy friend.'

'His name?'

'There was someone who used to phone her. Somebody called John. He used to ask for her and say, This is John.'

In the morning he asked to see everything Loveday Morgan had worn on the day of her death, and they showed him bra and tights from a chain store, black shoes, black plastic handbag, lemon acrilan sweater and sage green trouser suit. He saw too the contents of that handbag and every personal article found in her room.

'No cheque book?'

'She wouldn't have had one, sir,' said Sergeant Clements, putting on the indulgent look he kept for this naive old copper who thought every female corpse had been of the landed gentry. 'She hadn't any money, bar her wages.'

'I wonder what's become of the child's birth certificate?'

'With Grandma,' said Clements firmly. 'Grandma's blind or in the laughing house or she'd have come forward by now. Any thing else you want to see, sir?'

'The scarf she was killed with.'

Clements brought it in on a kind of tray.

'She's supposed to have been wearing this?' Wexford queried. 'It's a very expensive scarf. Not for a girl earning twelve pounds a week.'

'They have their funny extravagances, sir. She'd go without her dinners three or four days and then blue a pound on a scarf.'

Slowly Wexford handled the square of silk, exposing the label. 'This is a Gucci scarf, Sergeant. It didn't cost a pound. It cost eight or nine times that.'

Clements' mouth fell open. Who connected with this case, Wexford thought, but Mrs Dearborn would have an expensive silk scarf? Hadn't she been hunting for this very scarf before she went out on Monday afternoon? She hadn't been able to find it because her daughter had borrowed it, without saying anything in the way daughters do, on her last visit to Laysbrook House.

15

*The sage gravity and reverence of the elders should
keep the youngers from wanton licence of words and
behaviour.*

HOWARD was taking part in a top-level conference at Scotland Yard, discussing no doubt what the next move
should be now that Gregson had made his escape under the
protection of the ingenious Mr de Traynor. No matter how
omnipotent Howard might appear to be, Wexford knew he was
in fact answerable always to the head of his Divisional Crime
Squad, a commander who very likely knew nothing of a
country chief inspector's arrival on the scene.

The gasworks loured at him through a veil of drizzle. He
paced up and down, fretting, waiting for Pamela to phone
through and say when Howard would be back. He had to talk
to Howard before going to Laysbrook House, and he half
hoped he wouldn't have to go at all. His wishes in the matter
of Louise Sampson were curiously divided. He liked Mrs
Dearborn and the humane man in him wanted to see her come
out of the mortuary weeping with relief instead of white with
shock. But he was a policeman too, whose pride in his
abilities had recently suffered blows. Considerable experience
and hard work had gone into matching the missing girl with
the dead. He knew his desire was base, but he admitted to
himself that he would feel a thrill of pride if he vindicated
himself in Baker's view and saw Howard's eyes narrow with

admiration. And she had, after all, to be someone's daughter
. . .

He jumped the way Melanie Dearborn jumped when the
phone rang, but instead of Pamela's, the voice was a man's
and one couldn't remember having heard before.

'It's Philip Chell.'

Wexford took a few seconds to remember who this was. 'Oh,
yes, Mr Chell?'

'Ivan said to tell you he's got something for you.'

That bloody *Utopia*, Wexford thought. But it wasn't.

'It's something he's found out. He says, d'you want him to
come to you or will you come here?'

'What's it about?' Wexford asked impatiently.

'Don't know. He wouldn't say.' The voice became aggrieved. 'He never tells me anything.'

'Will tomorrow morning do? About ten at your place?'

'Make it eleven,' said Chell. 'If he knows we've got a
visitor he'll have me up at the crack of dawn.'

Pamela put her head round the door. 'Mr Fortune will be
free at twelve, sir.'

An hour to wait. Why shouldn't he go to Garmisch Terrace
during that hour instead of waiting until tomorrow? Whatever
Teal had to tell him might provide another link between
Loveday and Louise. He took his hand from the mouthpiece
and said, 'How about if I were to . . . ?' but Chell had rang
off.

The front door was open and he walked straight in. For once
the hall was crowded. Chell, in fetching denim and knee-
boots, was leaning against the banisters reading a picture
postcard and giggling with pleasure. Peggy sat on one corner of
the large hall table among newspapers and milk bottles, holding forth shrilly to the Indian and the party-giving girl, while
Lamont, the baby in his arms, stood disconsolately by.

Wexford gave them a general good morning and went up to
Chell, who, when he saw who it was, switched off his preoccupied smile like someone snapping off a light.

126

'Ivan's gone out for the day,' he said. He gave the post-card a last fond look and slipped it into his pocket. 'I can't tell you anything. All I know is Ivan was going through his cuttings when he suddenly said, "My God," and he must get hold of you.'

'What cuttings?'

'He's a designer, isn't he? I thought you knew. Well, people write about him in the papers and when they do he cuts the bit out and pastes it in his book.'

Aware that Peggy had fallen silent and that by now every-one was listening avidly, Wexford said in a lower tone, 'Could we go up and have a look at this book?'

'No, we could *not*. Really, whatever next? Ivan would *kill* me. He was perfectly horrid to me before he went out just because I'd left last night's washing up. I can't help it if I have these frighful migraines, can I?'

The party girl giggled.

'I feel very depressed,' said Chell. 'I'm going to draw out my whole month's allowance and buy some clothes to cheer myself up.' He stuck up his chin and marched out, banging the front door resoundingly behind him.

'All right for some,' said Peggy, passing a dirty hand across her face and leaving black streaks on her beautiful brow. 'Nice to be a kept man, isn't it, Johnny?'

'I look after her, don't I?' Lamont muttered, giving the baby a squeeze to indicate to whom he was referring. 'I've done everything for her practically since she was born.'

'Except when you're down the pub.'

'Three bloody hours at lunchtime! And you go out leaving me stuck with her every evening. I'm going back to bed.' He hoisted the baby on to his shoulder and made for the base-ment stairs, giving Peggy a backward glance which, it seemed to Wexford, contained more of hurt love than resentment.

'Look, Mr What's-your-name,' said Peggy, 'when are you lot going to open up Loveday's room so as we can re-let it? The landlords have lost fourteen quid already and it's keeping them awake at nights.'

'Is there someone wanting to rent it?'

'Yeah, her.' Peggy pointed to the party girl who nodded. 'Funny, isn't it? Big laugh. A guy like you would pay seven quid a week *not* to live in it.'

'It's two pounds a week less than what I'm paying,' said the other girl.

'Well, I'm not discussing the landlords' business in public,' said Peggy huffily. She jumped down from the table and tucked a milk bottle under each arm. 'You'd better come with me down to the hole in the ground.'

Wexford followed her, murmuring vainly that the matter wasn't in his hands. In the basement room Lamont was lying on the bed, staring at the ceiling. Peggy took no notice of him. She began to rummage among letters on the mantelpiece.

'I'm looking for a bit of paper,' she said, 'so you can write down who they have to contact about getting the room back.'

'Will this do?' 'This' was a sheet of paper he had picked up from the top of an untidy pile on the foot of the bed. As he held it out to her he saw that it was an estate agent's specification of a house in Brixton, offered for sale at four thousand, nine hundred and ninety-nine pounds.

'No, it won't do!' said Lamont, rousing himself and seizing the paper which he screwed up and hurled into a sooty cavern behind the electric fire.

Peggy laughed unpleasantly at him. 'You said you were going to chuck that out—God, it must be the weekend before last. Why don't you clear up the place instead of slopping about on the bed all day? It's time you got up, anyway, if that guy's going to phone you about that TV work. Did you give him the number of the Grand Duke?'

Lamont nodded. He slid off the bed, sidled up to Peggy and put his arm round her.

'Oh, you're hopeless,' she said, but she didn't push him away. 'Here,' she said to Wexford, 'you can write the number down on the back of this envelope.'

Wexford wrote down the number of the police station and of

Howard's extension and, glancing at his watch, saw that the hour was up.

The superintendent had spread before him photographs of the carefully restored and made-up face of Loveday Morgan, taken after death. The eyes were blue, the hair light blonde, the mouth and cheeks pink. But to anyone who has seen the dead, this was the modern version of a death mask, a soulless painted shell.

' "Life and these lips have long been separated",' Wexford quoted 'You wouldn't show these to her *mother*?'

'We haven't found a mother to show them to.'

'I have,' said Wexford and he explained.

Howard listened, nodding in slightly hesitant agreement. 'She'd better be brought here,' he said. 'We'll need her to identify the body. It'll be best if you go for her and take Clements and maybe a W.P.C. with you. I think you should go now, Reg.'

'I?' Wexford stared at him. 'You don't expect me to go there and . . . ?'

He felt like Hassan who can just bear the idea of the lovers being tortured to death out of his sight, but revolts in horror when Haroun Al Raschid tells him they must be tortured in his house with him as an onlooker.

Howard was no oriental sadist. He looked distressed, his thin face rather wan. 'Of course, I can't give you orders. You're just my uncle, but . . .'

'But me no buts,' said Wexford, 'and uncle me no uncles. I'll go.'

He phoned her first. He had promised to phone her. A thin hope, a thin dread, made him ask, 'You haven't heard from Louise?' He looked at his watch. Just after one, the time she would hear if she was going to.

'Not a word,' she said.

Break it gently, prepare the ground. 'I think I may . . .' Made cowardly by her anxious gasp, he said, 'There are some people I'd like you to talk to. May I come over straight away?'

'Baker said we'd never identify her,' said Howard. 'This'll shake him. Don't look so miserable, Reg. She has to be someone's child.'

Clements drove. They went through Hyde Park where the daffodils were coming out.

'Bit early, isn't it?' Wexford asked out of a dry throat.

'They do things to the bulbs, sir. Treat 'em so that they bloom before their natural time.' Clements always knew everything, Wexford thought crossly, and made all the facts he imparted sound unpleasant. 'I don't know why they can't leave things alone instead of all this going against nature. The next thing they'll be treating cuckoos and importing them in December.'

In the King's Road all the traffic lights turned red as the car approached them. It made the going slow and by the time Clements turned in under the arch to Laysbrook Place, Wexford felt as sick as he had done thirty years before on the day he took his inspector's exams. The brickwork of Laysbrook House was a pale amber in the sun, it's trees still silver-grey and untouched by the greening mist of spring. But the forsythia was a dazzling gold and the little silvery clusters he had noticed among the snowdrops now showed themselves as bushes of daphne, rose pink bouquets dotted all over the lawn. It was all very quiet, very still. The house basked in the thin diffident sunlight and the air had a fresh scent, free from the fumes of diesel to which Wexford had grown accustomed.

A young, rather smart, cleaning woman let him in and said, 'She told me you were coming. You're to go in and make yourself at home. She's upstairs with the baby, but she'll be down in a tick.' Was this the new char who stole things, who might have—but had not—made off with a Gucci scarf? The police car caught her eye and she gaped. 'What about them?'

'They'll stay there,' said Wexford, and he went into the room where Dearborn had shown him the maps and his wife had opened her heart.

16

*I know how difficult and hardly I myself would have
believed another man telling the same, if I had not
presently seen it with mine own eyes.*

H E didn't sit down but paced about the room, hoping that
she wouldn't keep him waiting for long. And then, suddenly in the midst of his anxiety for her, it occured to him
that once the girl was positively identified, the case would
be solved. Things didn't simply look black for Stephen
Dearborn. Louise Sampson had been murdered and who
could her murderer be but Dearborn, her stepfather?

The motive now. He had better get that clear in his mind.
And there was plenty of motive. Since he had talked to Verity
Bate he had never doubted the sincerity of Louise's love for
Dearborn, but he had supposed that Dearborn had been
speaking the truth when he told Mr Bate that he hadn't
returned it. Perhaps, on the other hand, he *had* originally
been in love with Louise or had at least some strong sensual
feeling towards her, a feeling which had lost some of its force
when he met the mother. Of course, it was the reverse of the
usual pattern, this preference of a man for an older woman
over a young girl, but Wexford didn't find it hard to imagine.
Anyway, a man could love two women at once. Suppose
Dearborn had married the mother because she was more completely to his taste, while retaining the daughter as a mistress
he couldn't bring himself to relinquish? Or their affair could

have started after Dearborn found her at Adams' flat, by which time he might have been growing weary of his wife.

In that case Dearborn was almost certainly the father of her child. Wexford sat down heavily when it occurred to him that the child could be Alexandra. Until now he hadn't thought much about Louise's announcement, reported by Adams, that her mother couldn't have children. After all, Louise had said she was only fifteen at the time. She could have got it wrong and have taken some minor surgery for the far more serious and final operation. If she had been speaking the truth, Melanie Dearborn couldn't be Alexandra's mother. But Dearborn could have brought home his own child—his and Louise's—to be adopted by himself and Louise's mother. And Melanie wouldn't have to know whose it was, only that it was a child whom Dearborn had adopted through a 'third party'. You didn't have to adopt through a society.

Alexandra, an adopted child . . . Or rather, adopted by one of her parents. That would account for the mother's indifference and the father's—the real father's—passionate obsession.

But where was she all this time? Why didn't she come down? He heard her footsteps moving briskly overhead but he heard no other sound. Louise could have threatened Dearborn, especially if he had begun to cool off her, with exposure to her mother of their affair and then of the identity of the child. A very real threat, Wexford thought. Louise hadn't just been young and his mistress, but his stepdaughter as well. Melanie would surely have left him if she had found out. A strong motive for murder.

That was a clever explanation he had come up with for his office number having been found in Louise's handbag. How much more likely, though, that she had it there because she phoned him at work habitually! Perhaps it was he whom she had phoned on February 25th . . . But no, it couldn't be, for on that day, at that time she had phoned her mother.

There was, of course, a good deal more to be worked out. Probably Mrs Dearborn could help him if only she would

132

come down. He felt a return of anguish for her, deepened now by his strong suspicion of her husband's guilt. The footsteps stopped and Alexandra began to cry, but the sounds were those of a baby who is peevish rather than distressed. He looked at his watch and saw that he had been there for nearly a quarter of an hour. Perhaps he should find the cleaning woman and ask her to . . .

The door swung open and Mrs Dearborn walked in. She was more smartly dressed than on the previous occasions when he had seen her, her hair was brushed and lacquered and her face carefully made up. The baby was in her arms.

'Oh, Mr Wexford, I'm terribly sorry to have kept you waiting.' She freed one hand and held it out to him. 'My poor little girl is having such trouble with her teeth. I was trying to get changed and comfort her at the same time. I see you've brought reinforcements,' she said, and joked, 'Don't worry, I'd have come quietly.'

Have come? Did she mean she couldn't come? He wished she didn't look so happy and carefree, cradling the baby and stroking her head with a tenderness he had thought she lacked. 'Mrs. Dearborn,' he began, 'I want you to . . .'

'Sit down, Mr Wexford. You can sit down for a moment, can't you?'

Uneasily he lowered himself on to the edge of one of the mutilated chairs. It is hard enough to break bad news to anyone at any time, but to break it to someone as cheerful and pleased with life as Melanie Dearborn looked now . . . ? 'We really shouldn't delay,' he said. 'The car's waiting and . . .'

'But we don't have to go anywhere. It's *all right*. My daughter phoned me. She phoned me as soon as you rang off.'

His stomach seemed to turn over, the way it sometimes did when he was in a lift, and a faint sweat broke out in the palms of his hands. He couldn't speak. He could only stare stupidly at her. She smiled at him triumphantly, her head a little on one side. Some of her joy at last communicated itself to

Alexandra, who stopped crying, rolled over on to her back on the sofa cushion and gave a crow of laughter.

'Are you sure?' he said, and his voice was a croak. 'Sure it was your daughter?'

'Of course I'm sure! You'll see her if you wait a while. She's coming this afternoon. Isn't it marvellous? Isn't it?'

'Marvellous,' he said.

'The phone rang and I thought it was you, calling back for something or other.' She spoke quickly, chattily, quite unaware of the shock she had given him. 'I picked it up and I heard the pips. As soon as I heard them I *knew*. Then she said, "Hallo, Mummy." Oh, it was wonderful! I tried to get in touch with you but you'd already left. I just sat down and ate an enormous lunch—I haven't been able to eat properly for days—and then I went upstairs and got all dressed up. I don't know why.'

Wexford gave her a stiff, sickly smile. Alexandra laughed at him, kicking her legs in the air.

'Will you stay and see her?'

'No. I don't think anyone would doubt your word on this, Mrs Dearborn. I'll go and tell the sergeant not to wait, and then if you'd just give me a few details . . .'

Clements was treating the policewoman to one of his lectures, waving his hands as he pontificated on change and decay, Utopias and Dystopias, past glory and contemporary decadence. Wexford put his head through the car window.

'Tell Mr Fortune it's no dice. The girl's turned up.'

'Oh, great!' said the policewoman sincerely.

Clements wagged his head up and down with a kind of grim gratification. He started the car. 'She'll have a tale to tell, you can bet on that, and bring home a load of trouble for mother to sort out.'

'Give it a rest, can't you?' Wexford said savagely, knowing he shouldn't speak like that to a man who had been kind to him and hospitable and who liked him, but he hadn't been able to help himself. He saw Clements' face go red and truculent with hurt and then he went back into the house.

Alexandra was chewing voraciously at her teething ring while her mother fetched smoked salmon and a bottle of asti spumante out of her husband's fancy dining refrigerator, setting it all on a tray. Killing the fatted calf, he thought. Thou art ever my daughter and all that I have is thine . . .

'Where had she been? What was all that disappearing act about?'

'She's going to get married. It's this boy, John. I suppose she's been living with him.' Mrs Dearborn sighed. 'They've had their ups and downs, but it sounds as if they really love each other. He's married but separated from his wife—awful, isn't it, to be married and separated before you're twenty-five? He's getting a divorce under the new act. Isa knew that last time she phoned but she wouldn't tell me until he'd got his decree in case something went wrong. That's Isa all over always cautious, always secretive. She sounds so happy now.'

He smiled stiffly. She probably thought he disapproved. Let her. The realisation that he had been hopelessly wrong, the shock of it, was only just beginning to hit him where it hurt. An awful desire to run away had seized him, to run to Victoria and get on a train and go home. He couldn't remember ever having made such a monumental howler before and the memory of how he had talked so eagerly to Howard, had nearly convinced him, made him go hot all over.

And now, as he looked back, he saw that although certain circumstances in the lives of the two girls had seemed alike or coincidental, Loveday had never really matched Louise. He asked himself whether a wealthy girl brought up like Louise would have shown horror when asked to a party or baulked at being taken into a pub; if such a girl would have scuttled off for comfort to a non-denominational church; if Louise, who had been Dearborn's friend before he was her mother's, would have needed to carry his office number in her handbag, a number she must long have known by heart. He knew it was all impossible. Why hadn't he known before? Because he had so desperately wanted to prove his abilities, and in order to do so had sacrificed probability to wild speculation. He had been guilty of the very sin he had laid at Baker's door, that of formulating a theory and forcing the facts to fit it. Fame had been more important to him than truth.

'Good-bye, Mrs Dearborn,' he said, and he added hollowly, 'I'm very glad for you.'

She shook hands with him on the doorstep but she didn't look at him. She was looking past him towards the arch. And she hadn't long to wait. As Wexford crossed Laysbrook Square, he saw the girl coming from the King's Road direction, saw her disappear under the shadows of the arch, a slim fair girl but otherwise quite unlike Howard's photograph of the dead.

Angrily cursing himself for an idiot, he walked for miles about Chelsea. Soon he would have to face Howard. By now Clements would have told him and he would be reflecting how unwise he had been to let family feeling and sentimentality persuade him into seeking his uncle's help. Baker would be told and Baker would shake his head, inwardly derisive.

At last he went home to Theresa Street, hoping there would be no one there, but both women were at home and a third with them, Denise's sister-in-law, who asked after his health, told him he could expect nothing else at his age, and assured him she could get any number of copies of *Utopia* he might desire from her bookshop.

'We all make mistakes, Reg,' said Howard gently when they sat down to dinner. 'And, Reg . . . ? We're not all competing for some sort of national forensics certificate, you know. It's just a job.'

'How many times have I said that, or something very like it, to my own men?' Wexford sighed and managed a grin. 'You can laugh if you like, but last week I really had some sort of idea that I was going to step in and solve the baffling case that eluded the lot of you. An elderly Lord Peter Wimsey. You were going to sit back and gasp in admiration while I expounded.'

'I daresay real life and real police work aren't like that.'
He might have added, Wexford thought, that his uncle had,
however, given them some useful tips. But he hadn't really,
so Howard couldn't. Instead he said almost as generously,
'I'd have felt the same if I'd come down to your manor.'

'It's odd, though, how convinced I was about that girl.'

'And you convinced me, but Baker would never go along
with it. I know you don't like him and I admit he's a peculiar
character, but the fact is he seldom does make mistakes. Even
when his wife went off and there was that business about the
unborn child, he went emotionally to pieces but his work
didn't suffer. If he says Gregson's guilty—and he's got a bee
in his bonnet about it—the probability is Gregson *is* guilty.'

Wexford said rather sourly, 'He doesn't seem to be getting
very far with proving it.'

'He's a lot further than he was. He's breaking up that
Psyche club alibi. Two of the men who were there with Harry
Slade have cracked and admitted they never saw Gregson
after eight o'clock. And another thing. Slade's girl friend—
remember the one he was supposed to be playing Monopoly
with last Saturday?—she's got a record. Baker's having another go at Gregson now without, we hope, the damping presence of Mr de Traynor.'

Wexford took two of his tablets and noticed how far the
level in the bottle had gone down. No one could say he had
failed there, at any rate.

'I don't think I'll come in with you tomorrow, Howard,'
he said. 'We're off on Saturday and there'll be the packing
and...'

'Come off it. Dora will do all that.' Howard surveyed his
uncle's burly figure. 'Besides, the only thing you could pack
is a punch.'

Wexford thought of Lamont. Had he avoided seeking a
further interview with him because he was physically afraid?
Perhaps. Suddenly he realised how deeply his illness had de-
moralised him. Fear of getting tired, fear of getting wet, fear
of being hurt—all these fears had contributed to his failure.

Wasn't it really fear of over-exerting himself that had made him waste the morning at Garmisch Terrace rather than go to Somerset House where a quick examination of records would have prevented today's *faux pas*? Kenbourne Vale police station was no place for him and Howard, for all his kindness, knew it.

'Well, I seem to have time on my hands for once, Reg. May as well catch up on my reading and dip into those Russian short stories my sister-in-law brought round. Curious stuff, but interesting, don't you find? One of these days I'd like your opinion . . .'

Literary chit-chat.

Four short stories and two hours later, Howard got up to answer the phone. Gregson had confessed, Wexford thought. The relentless Baker, Baker with the bee in his bonnet, had finally broken him.

But when Howard came back into the room, he could see from his nephew's face that it wasn't going to be as simple as that.

Howard didn't look at all pleased. 'Gregson's bolted,' he said. 'Baker was having a go at him in that Psyche Club, Gregson apparently doing his customary dumb act, when suddenly he found his fists if not his tongue, clouted Baker one and made a getaway in a stolen car. Baker fell off the bar stool and cut his head open on, of all things, a glass of advocaat.'

'Oh, poor Mr Baker!' said Denise, coming in from the kitchen with a white urn full of African violets.

'You weren't supposed to be listening. Here, let me take that thing, or give it to Reg. It's too heavy for you.'

'Gregson shouldn't take you too long to find,' said Wexford.

'God, no. He'll be under lock and key by morning.'

'Will you have to go over to Kenbourne, darling?' asked Denise, still hugging the urn.

'Not me. I'm going to bed. My days of running round in

squad cars chasing little villains are over. Will you mind that thing?'

Each put out his arms to grasp the urn which looked as if it weighed half a hundredweight. It was partly the idea that Howard had already got hold of it, partly a sudden terror of the effect on him of supporting so heavy a weight, that made Wexford draw back at the last moment. The urn crashed on to the carpet with a ponderous juddering thud, sending earth and broken leaves and pink and mauve petals flying against the walls and the pale hitherto immaculate Wilton.

Denise screamed so loudly that Wexford didn't hear Howard's hollow groan. Muttering apologies—although all apologies were inadequate—falling to his knees among the mess, he tried to scoop earth up in his hands and only made matters worse.

'At least the vase thing isn't broken,' he said stupidly.

'Never mind the bloody vase,' said Howard. 'What about me?' He had collapsed into a chair and was nursing his right foot. 'That landed fair and square on my toes.'

Denise had burst into tears. She sat in the middle of the wreckage and cried.

'I'm terribly sorry,' said Wexford miserably. 'I'd like to ... I mean, is there anything I can ... ?'

'Just leave it,' said Denise, drying her eyes. 'I'll see to it. Leave it to me. You go to bed, Uncle Reg.'

Ever polite, although he was white with pain, Howard said, 'Forget it. You couldn't help it, Reg. You're not fit enough to cope with things like that yet. No wonder you dropped it. God, my foot! I hope nothing's broken.'

He got his shoe off and limped towards the door. Denise fetched a dustpan and brush and began rescuing those of her plants that were still intact while Dora, summoned from upstairs by the uproar, picked grains of soil from the wallpaper.

Watching them disconsolately, Wexford reflected on his nephew's last remarks and upon their double meaning.

17

*You must not forsake the ship in a tempest because
you cannot rule and keep down the winds.*

I N the morning Howard's foot was worse, but he refused to
see a doctor, saying that it was imperative he arrived on
time in Kenbourne Vale.

'But you won't be able to drive, darling.' Denise had
stayed up until the small hours cleaning the carpet and she
had an exhausted air. Transferring her gaze from a large in-
eradicable stain to her husband's swollen instep, she said,
'You can hardly put that foot to the ground.'

'Never mind. I'll phone for a driver.'

'Unless Uncle Reg would . . .'

They looked at Wexford, Howard doubtly, Denise as if she
considered that anyone fit enough to reject yoghurt in favour
of bacon and eggs was quite capable of driving a car through
the London rush hours. Wexford didn't want to go. He had
lost all interest in the Morgan case, and plain cowardice over-
came him when he thought of meeting Baker and Clements,
both of whom would know of his exploded theory. Why had
he ever been so stupid as to go and poke about in the Montfort vault in the first place? Let Howard send for a driver.

He was going to plead a pain in his eye—and for the first
time in days he could feel it aching and pricking again—when
Dora said unexpectedly, 'Of course Reg will take you, dear.
It's the least he can do after dropping that thing on your

140

foot. He can come straight back and have a rest, can't you, darling?'

'Give me the keys,' said Wexford resignedly. 'I hope you realise I've never driven in London traffic.'

But it wasn't as bad as he had feared, and concentrating on being one of the honking, thrusting herd, charging wild beasts which made Kingsmarkham motorists seem like sheep, made him forget his eye and, briefly, that stronger trepidation. They arrived to find Gregson safe in a cell, having been discovered taking refuge at his sister's house in Sunbury. Howard, sure of him now on the grounds of assault on a police officer and of taking and driving away a vehicle without its owner's consent—offences which even Mr de Traynor couldn't dispute—limped off to talk to him. Wexford decided to make his escape and get home before the threatening rain began and he made for that semi-secret exit into the mews. It had occurred to him happily by this time that if Howard's injury was insufficient to keep him from work, Baker's wouldn't be, so he was much disconcerted when, marching confidently down one of the bottle-green caverns, he came face to face with the inspector, his head swathed in bandages.

There was nothing for it but to stop and ask him how he was feeling.'

'I'll survive,' Baker said curtly.

The only polite answer one can make to this churlish response is a muttered, 'I hope so.' Wexford made it, added that he was glad things were no worse and moved on. Baker gave a dry cough.

'Oh, Mr Wexford . . . ? Still got a few days of your holiday left, haven't you?'

This sounded like the first move towards a truce. Wexford's spirits were so low that he was grateful for any show of cordiality. 'Yes, I'm in London till Saturday.'

'You want to try and take in Billingsgate, then. Plenty of red herrings there, and you'll find the wild geese at Smithfield.'

Like a goose himself, Baker cackled at his joke. His laughter with an accompanying patronising pat on the shoulder didn't rob the remark of insult. It simply made it impossible for Wexford to take offence. Immensely pleased with himself, the inspector went into the lift and clanged the doors behind him. Wexford went down the stairs. No point now in avoiding the front entrance.

Suddenly it seemed even more futile to avoid Clements. There, at least, the deference due to rank would forbid any witticisms of the nature Baker had indulged in. Wexford came down the last flight and caught sight of his own reflection in a window which the brick wall behind it had transformed into a huge and gloomy mirror. He saw a big elderly man, a wrinkled man in a wrinkled raincoat, whose face in which some had discerned wisdom and wit, now showed in every line the frustrated petulance of a spoiled child and, at the same time, the bitterness of age. He straightened his shoulders and stopped frowning. What was the matter with him to let a small reverse get him down? And how could he stoop to comfort himself with his rank? Not only must he not avoid Clements, but must seek him out to apologise for his behaviour of the previous day and—this was even more imperative—say good-bye. Had he really thought of quitting Kenbourne Vale for ever without taking a formal leave of the kind sergeant?

The big outer hall was deserted but for the two uniformed men who presided over a long counter and dealt with enquiries. One of them courteously offered to see if the sergeant was in the building, and Wexford sat down in an uncomfortable black leather armchair to wait for him. It was still only ten o'clock. Rain had begun to splash lightly against the arched windows which flanked the entrance. Perhaps the meteorological office had been right in its forecast of a deep depression settling over South-East England. If the weather had been more promising, he might have telephoned Stephen Dearborn and reminded him of the tour he had suggested. It would be doing the man a favour rather than asking for one,

142

and Wexford felt he owed Dearborn something. Not, in this case, an apology—for you cannot apologise to a man for suspecting him of murder—but a friendly gesture to make up for harbouring such absurd and unfounded suspicions. Wexford was well aware of the guilt one can feel for even thinking ill of a man, although those thoughts have never found verbal expression.

He wasn't sure whether it was this reminder of his folly that made him go hot and red in the face or Clements' sudden appearance at his elbow. He rose to his feet, forgetting self-pity and self-recrimination. In a couple of hours Clements would be eating his lunch with his wife and James, his last lunch with James as a probationary father. Or his last lunch with James?

'Sergeant, I want to apologise for the way I spoke to you.'

'That's all right, sir. I'd forgotten all about it.'

Of course he had. He had other things on his mind. Wexford said gently and earnestly, 'Tomorrow's the great day, isn't it?'

As soon as he had spoken he wished he hadn't brought the subject up. Until this moment he had never quite realised the tension under which Clements lived and worked, the strain which daily grew more agonising. It showed now in the mammoth effort he made to keep his face ordinary and civilised and receptive, even stretching his mouth into a rictus smile. Wexford saw that he couldn't speak, that anxiety, invading every corner of his mind and his thoughts, had at last dried up that tide of moralising and censorious criticism. He was empty now of everything but the animal need to hold on to its young.

They stared at each other, Wexford growing embarrassed, the sergeant, all garrulity gone, dumb with panic and the dread of tomorrow. At last he spoke in a thick dry voice.

'I'm taking the morning off. Maybe the whole day.' He paused, swallowed. 'Depends on . . . My wife . . . On what they . . .'

'We shan't meet again, then.' Wexford held out his hand and Clements took it, giving it a hard painful squeeze as if it

143

were a lifeline. 'Good-bye, Sergeant, and all the very best for tomorrow.'

'Good-bye,' said Clements. He dropped Wexford's hand and went out into the rain, not even bothering to turn up his coat collar. A passing car splashed him but he didn't seem to notice. Small incidents such as this, which would once have inspired a diatribe against modern manners, no longer had the power to prick the surface of his mind.

Wexford stood on the steps and watched him go. It was time for him to go too, to leave Kenbourne Vale and Loveday Morgan and forget them if he could. Strange how absorbed he had been in trying to discover who she was, tramping around Fulham, weaving fantasies. Now as he looked back on the past week, he realised that he was no nearer knowing who she was or who had killed her or why than he had been when Howard had found him in the vault. It seemed to him that he had had a few sensible ideas, firm conclusions, which even that howler of his couldn't shake, but they had grown vague now and he had almost forgotten what they were.

Water which had gathered on the blue glass panels of the lamp above his head trickled down and dripped on him. He moved slowly down the steps and as he did so water hit him from another angle. A wave of it splashed against his trouser legs and he glanced up, affronted. The taxi, cause of the offence, had drawn up a few yards from him and directly in front of the police station. Its rear door opened and a vision in a purple silk suit with a white orchid in its buttonhole descended on to the wet pavement.

'What a day for the Honourable Diana's wedding,' said Ivan Teal when he had paid the taxi driver. 'And she such a sunny-natured girl. Where are the flunkeys rushing to meet me with umbrellas?'

'This isn't the Dorchester,' said Wexford.

'Don't I know it! I have some experience of police stations, principally West End Central. Were you on your way to see me?'

'See *you*?' In Wexford's present state of mind, Garmisch Terrace and the case seemed a world away. 'Was I supposed to be seeing you?'

'Of course you were. I told Philip to say ten. He knew I had this wedding at St George's. The bride's gown is one of mine so I must be in at the kill. When you didn't turn up I came to you. The wedding's at half eleven.'

'Oh, that,' said Wexford, recalling how Chell had side-tracked him with his talk of newspaper cuttings. 'It doesn't matter now. Don't you waste your time.'

Teal stared at him. His hair was carefully waved and gusts of Aphrodisia came from it and his suit. 'You mean you've found out who she was?' he said.

Wexford almost asked who. Then he remembered that to some people Loveday Morgan's death was important and he said, 'If you've got some information you'd better see Superintendent Fortune or Inspector Baker.'

'I want to see you.'

'It was never my case. I'm here on holiday and I'm going home on Saturday. You're getting rather wet, you know.'

'This tussore isn't exactly drip-dry,' said Teal, moving under the arch from which the blue lamp hung. 'I wish I'd gone straight to Hanover Square,' he grumbled. 'It's always hell getting a taxi in Kenbourne. Can you see if that one down there has got his light up?'

Wexford didn't bother to look. 'You said you wanted to see the superintendent.'

'You said that. I'm not over-fond of policemen. Remember? You're different. If I can't talk to you I'll be on my way.' Teal flung out a purple silk arm. 'Taxi!' he shouted.

The cab was going the wrong way. It waited for some lights to go green and, in defiance of regulations, began to make a U-turn. Behind it, looming scarlet through the downpour, appeared the bus that went to Chelsea.

'It was nice meeting you,' said Teal, going down the steps. 'Never thought I'd say that to a . . .'

The taxi drew up, the bus went by. 'You'd better come in a

minute,' said Wexford with a sigh. 'I can spare half an hour.'

Teal was never amiable for more than a few minutes.

'I can't spare that long myself,' he said with a return to asperity. 'Really, you're very inconsistent. What a ghastly place! No wonder policemen have a grudge against humanity. What's this? Some sort of annexe to the morgue?'

'An interview room.' Wexford watched him dust the seat of a chair before sitting on it. He supposed he ought to feel flattered. However highly one values one's profession, it is always a compliment to be told that one is better, more human, more sympathetic, less conventional, than the common run. But boredom with the whole business made him almost impervious to flattery.

'Comfy?' he said sarcastically.

'Oh, don't come that!' snapped Teal. 'Not you. You're not one of these flatfeet who think that because one's gay, one's got the mentality of a finicky schoolgirl. I'm going to a wedding and I don't want to muck up my clothes any more than you would.'

Wexford looked at him with positive dislike. 'Well, Mr Teal, what is it you want to tell me?'

'That minister we were talking about—remember? His name is Morgan.'

18

The priests whom they find exceeding vicious livers,
them they excommunicate from having any interest
in divine matters.

IT was like giving up smoking, thought Wexford, who had
given it up with some difficulty years before. The bloody
things made you ill, you resisted them, they even bored you,
but only let someone produce one—or, worse, light it under
your nose—and you were hooked again, yearning, longing to
get back to the old habit. Teal had done that to him, although
he hadn't lighted it yet. Wexford tried to suppress the excitement he felt, the hateful irritating excitement, and said:

'What minister?'

Maddeningly, Teal began to digress. 'Of course it's hind-
sight,' he said, 'but there was something funny about her
voice. I noticed it at the time and yet I didn't, if you know
what I mean. She didn't have any accent.'

'I don't have any accent,' said Wexford rashly.

Teal laughed at that. 'You mean you think you don't. You
can't hear that faint Sussex burr any more than I can hear
the rag-trade camp in my voice unless I listen for it. Just think
about it for a moment. Johnny talks R.A.D.A., Peggy South
London, Phil suppressed cockney with a gay veneer, your
superintendent pure Trinity. One doesn't have to be a Henry
Higgins to sort all that out. Everyone has an accent that he's
got from his parents or his school or his university or the
society he moves in. Loveday didn't have any at all.'

'What's that go to do with some minister?'

'I'm coming to that. I've thought about it a lot. I've asked myself who are these rare creatures that speak unaccented English. One example would be servants of the old school. I should think that when there was a whole servant class they all talked like that—flat, plain English without any inflexion or intonation. Their parents brought them up to it, having been servants themselves and knowing that cockney wouldn't be acceptable in a housemaid. Who else? Children brought up in institutions, maybe. People who spent years of their lives in hospitals and perhaps people who have spent all their lives in closed communities.'

Wexford was growing very impatient. 'Brought up in an institution . . . ?'

'Oh, come *on*. You're the detective. Don't you remember my telling you how she went to the temple of the Children of the Revelation?'

'She can't have been one of them. She worked in a television shop. They don't have television or read newspapers.'

'There you have it, the reason why her parents haven't got in touch. Didn't it occur to you? Anyway, her father couldn't have got in touch. He's that Morgan who was their minister and got put inside. He's in prison.'

There was a dramatic pause. Wexford had thought he could never care about this case again, never experience for a second time the thrill and the dread of the hunter with his quarry in sight. Now he felt the tingle of adrenalin in his blood, a shiver travel up his spine.

'I keep this book of press cuttings,' Teal went on. 'That is, I collect newspapers that have bits about me in them, but often I don't cut the bits out for a year or so and the papers accumulate. Well, a couple of nights ago, having time to kill, I started on my cuttings and on the back of a photograph of one of my gowns there was a story about this Morgan appearing in a magistrates' court.'

'You have the cutting with you?'

'Do me a favour, I'm on my way to a very fashionable wedding. As Wilde says . . .' Here Teal wriggled affectedly— purposely to annoy, Wexford thought—and said in a camp falsetto, 'A well-made dress has no pockets.' He chuckled at the chief inspector's discomfiture. 'Anyway, I stuck it in my book, court proceedings side downwards, of course. You can do some work now.'

'When did these proceedings take place, Mr Teal?' Wexford asked, keeping his temper.

'Last March. He was charged with bigamy, indecent assault on *five* women—the courage the man must have had! —and having had carnal knowledge of a fourteen-year-old girl. I don't know what that means precisely, but I expect you do. He was committed for trial to the Surrey Assizes.' Teal looked at his watch. 'My God, I mustn't be late and find myself in a rear pew. I want to get a good look at the Honourable Diana in all my glory.'

'Mr Teal, you've been very helpful. I'm grateful. There's just one other thing. You said Loveday asked you if Johnny and Peggy were trustworthy. What did she want to entrust to them?'

'To him, you mean. Herself, I suppose, if she was in love with him.'

Wexford looked doubtful. 'A woman of fifty might feel that way, but I don't think a young girl would. I'm asking myself what precious thing she had to entrust to anyone.'

'Then you mûst go on asking yourself, Mr Wexford, because I do have to go now.'

'Yes, of course. Thanks for coming.'

The interview room became a drab little hole again after Teal had gone. Wexford went out into the corridor and began to mount the stairs. It struck him suddenly that he could climb stairs now without getting short of breath.

It was a piece of luck really getting that information from Teal, for passing it on immediately would vindicate him in the eyes of Howard and Baker. Not that he had done anything but listen and that reluctantly. Never mind. He would tell them simply what Teal had told him and leave them to follow it up. Unless . . . Unless he delayed passing it on for half an hour, and used that half-hour to do a little research of his own in the police station library.

If they had one. At the top of the stairs he encountered someone he thought was Sergeant Nolan and asked him. They had. Down one floor, sir, and third door on your right.

In the library he found Pamela and D.C. Dinehart, each occupied with a newspaper file, and wearing on their young faces the serious and absorbed expressions of students in the British Museum. Both looked up to nod and then took no further notice of him. It took him no more than ten minutes to find what he wanted, the proceedings against Morgan in the Assize court.

The *News of the World* had dealt with the case lubriciously, yet with its customary manner of righteous outrage; *The People* had seen in it occasion for a venomous article on corruption among ministers of religion; *The Observer*, its nose in the air had tucked it away under a story about a blackmailed county councillor. For facts and photographs he selected *The Sunday Times* and the *Sunday Express*.

Alexander William Morgan had been separated from his wife for some years before the commission of the offences, he lodging next door to his church in Artois Road, Camberwell, she remaining in the erstwhile matrimonial home in nearby Ivy Street. Apparently, the rift had taken place when Morgan received a call and became shepherd of the Camberwell Temple. He had tried, very gradually, to infuse into the bitter and life-denying creed of the Children of the Revelation a certain liberalism, although, due to the opposition of diehard elders, had got no further than to make a few of them believe that television and radio enjoyed in the privacy of their own homes was no sin.

In sexual matters he had been more successful. Indeed, his success had been startling. A stream of young women had given evidence, including a Miss Hannah Peters whom he had married (gone through a form of marriage was the charge) in a ceremony of his own devising at which he had been both bridegroom and officiating priest. The other girls, even the fourteen-year-old, regarded themselves as his wives under the curious philosophy he had propounded to them. He had treated them affectionately. They said they had expected, as a result of what he had told them and by reason of his relationship with them, to inherit a more blissful form of eternal life than the less favoured Children. It was only when he made advances to older women that his propensities had come to light. Morgan had been sent to prison for three years, still protesting that he was responsible for conferring on these women a peculiar grace.

Wexford noted down the names of all the women witnesses. Then he studied the photographs, but only one of them caught his eye, a picture of the temple itself in Artois Road. He glanced up and, seeing that Pamela had finished her researches, beckoned her over.

'Are you going back to Mr Fortune's office?'

She nodded.

'He has a snapshot of Loveday Morgan . . .'

'Yes, sir, I know the one you mean.'

'I wonder if you mind asking him if he'd have it sent along to me here?'

That was that, then. It was the only way. Howard would, of course, come back with the snapshot himself, note from the newspaper stories that Morgan had two daughters, and the case would pass out of his, Wexford's, hands. He felt rather flat, for he had found her in such an undramatic way.

While her waited for Howard to appear, he looked at the other photographs, round-faced, bespectacled Morgan, forty six years old, a suburban satyr; Morgan with his wife and two fat little girls, either of whom might have been Loveday in childhood; Hannah Peters, plain, smiling, a bride among the handmaidens with an Alice band holding back her frizzy hair.

He smelt Pamela's floral perfume and looked round to find her at his elbow.

'Mr Fortune has gone to court, Mr Wexford, and he's left a message to say he's going straight on to St Biddulph's Hospital to get his foot X-rayed.'

'But you've brought the snapshot,' Wexford said slowly.

'It was on his desk, sir, and since you wanted it, I'm sure he wouldn't . . .'

'Thank you very much, Pamela,' said Wexford.

His hand was trembling oddly as he took it from her and placed it beside the *Sunday Express* photograph of Morgan's temple in Artois Road. Yes, it was as he had thought. The newspaper picture showed the whole church, the snapshot only a corner of it, but in both were the same dusty shrubs nudging a brickwall, the same ridge of coping, and what had seemed in the snapshot to be a wooden post was now revealed as a segment of a door.

There was no girl in the newspaper shot, Morgan, Wexford was sure, had posed the girl—his daughter? one of his 'brides'?—in front of the temple and taken the photograph himself. He returned the snapshot to Pamela and left the library, deep in thought.

What now? Follow Pamela and leave a message for Howard, his reasonable self told him. Or see Baker. The inspector would soon be back from the court. Wexford revolted from the idea of confiding in him and seeing that sharp mouth curl in a will-nothing-teach-the-old-fuddy-duddy expression.

He had been wrong last time. This time he knew he couldn't be. No one would have known of his folly if he hadn't alerted Howard before he had proof. It wouldn't matter if he failed this time, for no one would know except himself. They would think he had gone off on some sightseeing tour of his own, to Smithfield or Billingsgate perhaps, taking Baker's advice.

He could be what retired policemen sometimes become, a private detective. That thought had a bitter taste about it and he put it from him. Not retired, not old, but free to pursue a line of his own, bound to no one. No driver to take him, no sergeant to accompany him, no chief to refer back to. And he wasn't going to withhold vital information for long, for, if he had got nowhere by tonight, he would just tell Howard and leave it at that.

It was just eleven-thirty. The rain fell steadily. Obviously, it was going to be one of those days when the rain never lets up. He had left his umbrella in Theresa Street. With unusual extravagance he bought a new one and then he walked jauntily, like a young man, towards Elm Green tube station.

19

*But if the inhabitants . . . will not dwell with them
to be ordered by their laws, then they drive them out
of those bounds which they have limited and
appointed out for themselves.*

IT was a bit like Kenbourne Vale, the district of South
London that was neither Camberwell nor Kennington but a
dismal area lying between them called Wilman Park. The
resemblance lay in the slummy greyness of the place, the
absence of trees, rather than in the houses, for those in Wilman Park were small and tightly packed in streets standing
at true right angles to each other. Wexford supposed that the
third temple of the Children of the Revelation was probably
situated in a similar district of some industrial city in the
north of England. Strange sects do not abound among the rich
who have their heaven here and need not rely on future bliss.

He found Artois Road which bisected Wilman Park and
walked briskly along it between the puddles, passing women
coming back from the shops before they shut for early closing. They were mothers and daughters mostly, with the
daughter's children shielded from the rain in hooded prams.
He recognised it as the working-class pattern, mother and
daughter going everywhere together, shopping together, not
divided by the girl's marriage. Somewhere here there might be
a mother who walked alone because her daughter had been
divided from her. Or were the Children excluded from such

patterns, as they seemed to be excluded from everything, making their own customs and denying society?

The temple was so small and the rain so torrential that he almost went by without seeing it. He retraced his steps and contemplated it, glad of his umbrella. It was recognisable as the sister, if not the twin, of the one in Garmisch Terrace. The circle of red glass was smaller, the gable shallower, the garden-shed door painted a sticky green, but an identical plaque, signifying the nature of the place, had been cemented into the brickwork which in this case was a plain dull red. The shrubs, against which Loveday had posed, were now a leafless tangle, dripping water on to the pavement.

As in Garmisch Terrace, the temple was the connecting link between two rows of houses, squat mean houses here of yellow brick with stone bays. In one of its immediate neighbours Morgan had been a lodger. In which? Newspapers give the names of streets where defendents and witnesses live, not their house numbers. But it wasn't difficult to guess. One of the houses had daffodils coming into bud in a window box, a television aerial on its roof, red and yellow curtains; the other squatted, its windows blanked out with dark green blinds, behind a tiny front garden whose soil was hidden beneath a layer of concrete.

One of the blinds lifted an inch when he banged on the door —there was no bell, no knocker, only a letter box—but it fell again instantly. The activities of private detectives are limited. They cannot demand entrance or get warrants. He knocked again, and this time there was no movement at the window. He could hear nothing from inside the house, but he sensed hostility as if the people within were ill-wishing him. Strange. Even if they had something to hide, they couldn't know who he was. He might be the gasman, he might be delivering something. A voice behind him made him turn round. A postman with parcels coming out of a red van.

'You won't get in there, mate. They never let no one in.'

'Why not, for God's sake?'

'That's it,' said the postman, grinning. 'For God's sake.

155

They're too religious, see, to talk to the likes of you or me. They call themselves Children of the Revelation. A lot of them live around here, and they won't none of them let no one into their houses.'

'What, not even open their doors?'

'Some do that,' the postman admitted, 'but you can't get inside.'

'Can you tell me where the others live?'

'One lot at 56 and another lot at 92. The 56 lot, they'll *speak* to you, I'll give them that.'

So the refusal to admit him on the part of the occupants of the house next to the temple held no particularly sinister implication. He went to number 56, another grim little house with weeds instead of concrete in its front garden, and the door was answered rather reluctantly by an elderly man in a shiny black suit.

'I'm sorry. I know it's raining, but I can't let you in. What do you want?' His was a flat, cold voice, almost mechanical. Words were necessary for the business of living, Wexford thought, not to grace life, not to be chosen with care for smoothing the path, expressing feelings, pleasing the listener. He remembered what Teal had said.

'I'm writing a book on Christian sects,' he lied unblushingly. 'I wondered if you could give me . . . ?'

In the same dull monotone the man reeled off a list of dates, named the three temples and told Wexford that there were five hundred of the elect on the face of the earth.

'And your Shepherd?' Wexford interrupted him.

'He has a room in the house next to the temple, but they won't open the door to you there.' He gave a sigh as of one who had striven in vain against the temptations of the world. 'They have kept to a purer and straighter way then I. I married *out*.'

'How about number 92?' Wexford began. He got no further for the door was firmly closed in his face. There was nothing for it but to go to Ivy Street, and if that failed, begin a house-to-house in search of the 'brides'.

He had a sandwich in a pub and, feeling almost as guilty as a Child of the Revelation who had opened the door to one of God's rejects, a pint of bitter. Then he phoned Dora to stop her worrying, telling her he was off on a tour with Dearborn and didn't know when he would be home. The rain had slackened slightly. He asked the barman the way to Ivy Street and set off into the back doubles of Artois Road.

The house was a little detached villa with gnomes and an overflowing birdbath in its front garden. It looked shut up. No one answered when he rang the bell and he turned away to come face to face once more with the helpful postman.

'Mrs Morgan's away. Her married daughter's ill and she's gone to look after the son-in-law. Half a tick, while I take this parcel next door.'

Having decided to pump him, Wexford waited impatiently for the postman to return. What he called 'half a tick' became ten minutes' chat with the recipient of the parcel, but at last he came back, whistling cheerfully.

'What about the other daughter?'

'Got a day off from work. I saw her go out half an hour back.'

'I see.' Another disappointment, if you could call finding someone's daughter alive instead of dead a disappointment. 'Did you know Morgan?'

'Not to say know,' said the postman. 'I know *of* him. I used to see him about.'

'Did you ever see him about with a girl?'

The postman laughed. He didn't seem to want to know who Wexford was or why he was asking. 'Morgan was a dark horse,' he said. 'Most of Revelationers didn't know what he was up to till it all came out. Except the girls, that is. One or two of them called themselves Mrs Morgan, had letters addressed to them as Mrs Morgan, as bold as brass.'

'Can you remember which ones?'

'I remember Hannah Peters all right. She was the one as he went through a form of marriage with. That's how his little games came to light. Young Hannah got a letter addressed to

157

Mrs Morgan, her dad got suspicious and then the bomb went up. A lot of other women started complaining. Mind you, his wife had chucked him out years ago but they're not divorced. She says she'll never divorce him. A very vindictive woman is Mrs Morgan and you can't blame her.'

'Can you tell me where Miss Peters lives?'

'Work on a paper, do you?'

'Something like that,' said Wexford.

'I only ask,' said the postman, 'because it seems hard on a feller your age, especially in this weather. Wear the old ones out first, eh?'

Wexford swallowed his humiliation as best he could and managed an unamused grin. The postman gave him the address. 'I daresay she'll be at work now?' he said.

'Not her. The Revelationers don't let their daughters go to work, but I don't reckon you'll see her. They won't let you in.'

But they might open the door. Hannah herself might do that. What he needed now was a piece of luck, one of those near-miracles that had sometimes come his way in the past, clearing and illuminating the path he must follow. And he thought it had happened when, turning into Stockholm Street, he saw the frizzy-haired girl of the newspaper photograph come out of the corner house where the Peters family lived.

She held a letter in her hand which she thrust into the pocket of her long dark raincoat to protect it from the rain, and she paused on the step, darting quick glances about her. Timidly, she came out into the street. It was only a shabby back street where she had probably lived all her life and but for him it was deserted, but she peered about and hesitated as if she were a schoolgirl, separated from her party and lost in a foreign city. Then she walked rapidly towards a pillar box, her head down, keeping custody of her eyes like a nun.

Wexford followed her, and suddenly he felt shy himself. He had an idea, although it was without foundation, that the letter was for Morgan. She started violently when he spoke to her, gasped and put her hand up to cover her mouth.

'Miss Peters, I'm a policeman. I'm only talking to you in

the street because I was afraid I wouldn't be admitted to your home.'

Where did they go to school, these girls? Or did the Revelationers run special schools for their children? Did they never meet outsiders? He wondered if he was the first outsider she had spoken to since she had passed through the terror of the court, an experience which must have been torture to her, enough to shake her reason. Spoken? Was she going to speak now?

She had a plain, unformed face, half-covered still by her hand. No make-up, no rings on her hand. Her body was flat under the stiff heavy coat.

'Miss Peters . . .' Rapidly and rather awkwardly, for she gave him no help, he told her what he wanted and why he was there, accosting her in the rain. He didn't think she was frightened of him, but perhaps she was frightened of God. She scanned the street, her hand now a fist tapping her chin, but before she spoke to him she looked down at her feet. She wouldn't meet his eyes.

'Father would turn me out if he saw me. He was going to turn me out after . . . after . . . Mother made him let me stay.'

The strangest thing in all this strangeness, Wexford thought, was that she should have wanted to stay. But perhaps it wasn't so strange. Hatch out a wild bird, rear it in a cage, and when you set it free it will perish or be destroyed by its fellows. Easing his umbrella over her so that they were both sheltered by it, he began talking to her soothingly, apologising, explaining how important it was for him to know. But all the time he was thinking of the word which lay outside her experience, of the girls like Louise Sampson and Verity Bate who snapped their fingers at their parents, who lived where they liked and with whom they liked, to whom a tyrannical father, wielding real power, was a fictional monster they read about in books written in the distant past. It was almost unbelievable that such opposites as they and Hannah Peters could co-exist in the same city and the same century.

Without looking up, she said, 'I never heard of a girl called Loveday.' She shivered. 'She didn't have to go to the court. What was her real name?'

Wexford shook his head, feeling paralysed by her dull slow voice, her ox-like acceptance of oppression.

'Perhaps she left your congregation in the past twelve months?'

'Mary went away to be a teacher, and Sarah went and Rachel. Edna married out. They all went away.' She didn't speak wistfully but as of some dire enormity. 'My father will punish me if I don't go home now.'

'Their addresses?' he pleaded.

'Oh, no. No, no. Mary was at the court.' It cost her something to say that, he thought. Mary too, had been one of Morgan's brides. She struggled with an emotion no one had ever taught her existed or could be controlled. There were tears on her face or perhaps just rain. 'You must go to the Shepherd,' she said, and ducked out from under the umbrella.

'They won't let me into the house!'

She called back to him something about a prayer meeting that night. Then she ran home through the rain, the caged creature escaping from predators and the humane that would set it free. Back to the cage, the safety of a living death.

Wexford had been shaken by the interview. Hannah Peters bore no physical resemblance to Loveday Morgan, and yet he felt that it was to the latter he had been talking. Here, alive and in a different skin, was the dead girl, the shy, frightened, badly-dressed girl who didn't know how to make friends and was scarcely fit to be employed. At last she had been revealed to him, the cemetery walker, the Bible reader. Teal had known her and had seen her rare, wondering smile; Lamont had sat with her, witness her tortured silences; with a shrug, Dearborn had dismissed her ugly gaucheness. And now he too had seen her, or seen perhaps her ghost.

The street was empty again, the ghost gone. But she had left him a message. He must take the only way open to him now of catching her people outside their prisons.

160

20

*In dim and doubtful light they be gathered together,
and more earnestly fixed on religion and devotion.*

DARKNESS came early after that day of torrents. Sitting
in a lorry driver's retreat, his raincoat steaming in the
red glow of an electric fire, Wexford watched the fluorescent
lamps come on in Artois Road. The wet pavements threw back
scarlet and blue and orange reflections of neon overhead. The
sky was red and vaporous, any stars which might have been
up there quenched by the glare. He wondered when the
prayer meeting would begin. Surely not before seven? Hungry
in spite of tea and a doughnut, he ordered a labourer's meal,
a forbidden sinful meal of sausages and chips and fried eggs.

According to Crocker and Dora and their gloomy disciples,
he ought to have been dead by now, for he had broken all
their rules. He had worked when he should have rested, eaten
saturated fats when he should have fasted, gone out at night,
worried and tóday forgotten all about his pills. Why not break
one more and he hanged for a sheep?

The ultimate forbidden fruit would be to go back into that
pub he had visited at lunchtime and drink spirits. He found it
and had a double Scotch. Far from laying him out, it filled
him with well-being, and he made up his mind then and there
to defy them all. No one but a fool follows a regimen that
debilitates him while moderate indulgence makes him feel
good.

While he had been drinking the rain had stopped. He sniffed

the smell of London after rain, smoky, gaseous, with here and there other scents infiltrating, the odour of frying food and stranger oriental platters, the whiff of a French cigarette. They faded as he walked into the residential depths of Artois Road where the blue-white lamps looked too smart for this hinterland. Another light glowed ahead of him, a round red light like a Cyclops eye, and he saw that he was too late. The prayer meeting had begun. He stood outside the temple and heard the voices of the Children, intoning together sometimes, then one single voice raised in spontaneous praise or perhaps commination. How many hours before they came out? And would they talk to him when they did?

The house where the Shepherd lodged, where Morgan had lodged, looked entirely deserted now, no slits of lights showing at the edges of the blinds. The concrete garden lay under a sheet of water which was black because it had no light to mirror. There were perhaps fifty houses like this one in Wilman Park, vaults for the living. Rachel and Mary and Sarah had gone away . . . He hoped that now they wore scent and false eyelashes and feathers and flowers and sat on steps with their boy friends eating crisps out of paper bags.

Morgan must have met his brides somewhere and not under this severe roof. Did he walk with them, sneak off for clandestine love in the *temple*? Wexford wrinkled his nose in distaste. If he had some neighbour would surely have seen him, perhaps even seen him promenading with the chosen one of the moment.

The house next door showed plenty of light and the curtains weren't even drawn. He rang a bell that chimed, but when she came to admit him his heart sank. She smiled enquiringly. Her eyes were blue and vacant and she supported herself on a white stick.

She was a very old woman, not far off eighty, and she had just enough sight left, he guessed, to make out the shape of him on her doorstep. He didn't want to alarm her, so he explained who he was and why he was there before beginning to

162

retreat. She was no use to him, although he couldn't put it so bluntly. Her blindness disqualified her.

'I was just going to make a cup of tea,' she said. 'Would you like one? My husband was in the force. You'll have heard of him. Wally Lyle.'

Wexford shook his head, then remembered she couldn't see. 'I'm a stranger in these parts,' he said. 'I won't keep you, Mrs Lyle. Perhaps you could just tell me the name of the people next door?'

'Vickers,' she said, and she chuckled. 'You won't get inside there. The only person she ever lets in is the electric meter man. They haven't got no gas.' Her cheerfulness moved him. Here she was, alone, blind, very old, but she could still joke, still find some zest in living. When she said, 'You may as well have that tea. I know how it is on the beat all day,' he agreed on an impulse. She couldn't see that he wasn't in uniform. She wanted a chat about her husband and old times. Why not? He had to pass the time somehow until the temple disgorged its throng.

All the lights were on in the hall and the little rooms. Light must help her, he decided, watching her edge her way to the brighter lamp of the kitchen like a moth. But it was he who finally made the tea and carried their two cups into the front room. All the while she kept close beside him, and when he went to sit by the window, waiting for the temple door to open and send a shaft of light out on to the pavement, she came and sat next to him, hooking her stick over the arm of her chair.

The little pokey living room was crammed with furniture, loaded down with ornaments. He wondered that she could move among all this bric-à-brac without hurting herself or knocking things over, and he recalled his own clumsiness in Howard's house. While she told him anecdotes of her husband's career, he observed the dexterity with which she handled her teacup, and he marvelled.

'How long have you lived here, Mrs Lyle?' he asked gently.

'Forty years. Them Vickerses were here before we come.'

163

'They're quite an elderly couple, then?'

'Not this lot. His mum and dad. I call this one *young* Vickers.' She peered into Wexford's face. 'I daresay he'd be old to you—about fifty he is, but a chip off the old block.'

'And you've never been into their house?'

She liked to talk about the dead Wally Lyle and she returned to him. 'My husband tried to get in there once, years and years ago. Young Vickers and his sister were schoolkids then, and the school sent round this doctor on account of Rebecca—that was the sister—having scarlet fever. They wouldn't have no doctor, you see. Revelationers don't believe in doctors, let their kids die rather than have the doctor.'

'So your husband was called in on account of being a policeman?' Wexford was interested in spite of the irrelevance of all this. 'Did he make them admit the doctor?'

Mrs Lyle laughed shrilly. 'Not likely. He banged and banged in the door till old Vickers come out, and old Vickers cursed him. It made your blood run cold to hear it. My husband said he'd never have nothing to do with them again and he never did.'

'And that was the only contact you ever had with them?'

She looked a little sheepish. 'The only contact *he* did. I never let on to him how I helped Rebecca run away and get married. He'd have given it to me hot and strong, being as he was in the force.'

Rebecca, a girl who had run away . . .

He spoke rather sharply. 'When was that, Mrs Lyle?'

She dashed his faint hope. 'Must be thirty years. It's her brother as lives there now. He got married and had kids and they've all gone now too. God knows where.'

She sighed and fell silent. Wexford watched the dark pavement, growing impatient. Mrs Lyle finished her tea and set the cup down correctly in its saucer. Her blue, filmed eyes were turned on his face now and he sensed that she wanted to make some sort of confession to him.

'What I did,' she said, and her expression was sly, almost naughty, 'I often thought maybe it was against the law, but I

164

never dared ask my husband, never breathed a word about it.'

'What did you do?' Wexford put laughter and encouragement into his voice, for it was no use showing them on his face.

'Won't do no harm telling you after all these years.' She grinned, enjoying herself. 'Rebecca wanted to get married to a fellow she'd met, fellow called Foster who wasn't one of *them*, and her dad he put his foot down and they shut her up in there. Just a prisoner she was, shut up in her bedroom. She used to write notes and throw them to me out of the window. I could see to read in them days. I was all for putting a spoke in the wheel of them Revelationers and I had young Foster in here, jollying him along, and one day when they was all in church we got a ladder and stuck it up at the window and down she come. Like a play it was.'

The orchard walls are high and hard to climb and the place death, considering who thou art, if any of my kinsmen find thee here . . . 'It must have been,' he said.

'I often have a good laugh about it to this day. Mind you, it'd have been better if I'd ever found out what they thought about it but I never did. I'd like to have seen old Vickers' face when he knew the bird had flown. Rebecca got married and she wrote to me, telling me bits of news, but that's stopped now. No good getting letters when you can't read them and you've no one to read them to you, is it?' Mrs Lyle laughed merrily at the doleful situation she had described. 'Vickers—the son, that is—he got married and they had kids but they've all gone off one by one. Couldn't stand it at home. And now there's just the two of them alone in there. Young Vickers—I call him that but he must be all of fifty—he never speaks to me. I reckon he knows what I did for Rebecca. I often have a good laugh when I think of her and that ladder and young Foster like a blessed Romeo. A bit of luck for her that was, catching him. She was nothing to look at and she had a great big mole on the side of her nose . . .'

The temple door must have opened, for a pale stream of

light seeped out across the wet stones and people began to appear on the pavement. Wexford, who had been waiting for this to happen, ignored it and turned to face Mrs Lyle, although he knew she couldn't see him.

'A mole in the side of her nose?'

'Stuck there between her nose and her cheek like.' Mrs Lyle jabbed a finger at her own apple complexion. 'My husband used to say she could have had that seen to, only seeing they didn't believe in doctors . . .'

'Where did she go?'

'South-west Ten her address was. I've got letters about somewhere. You'll have to look for them yourself. But I'll tell you one thing, Rebecca won't get you in that house next door. It'd take one of them bulldozers to do that.'

Wexford stood in the bay window and watched the congregation disperse. The women wore dull fashionless, rather than old-fashioned, coats and hats in black or grey or fawn, the men, even the young men, black suits topped by dark raincoats. Among them, like a crow, moved the Shepherd in his black robe, shaking hands, murmuring farewells until all but two were gone. This pair, evidently a married couple, stood arm-in arm, waiting for him. Then the three of them filed slowly into the house next door. Briefly Wexford caught a glimpse of them mirrored darkly in the pool of water, three strange people crossing the Styx into their own underworld. The front door shut with a slam.

'You looking at young Vickers?' said Mrs Lyle who had the hypersensitivity of the blind. 'I wish my grandson was here to blow him a raspberry. All the kids round here do that, and good luck to them.'

'Better look for those letters now, Mrs Lyle.'

They went upstairs, the old woman leading the way. She took him into her bedroom which had the jumble sale look of rooms occupied by old people and in which they have grown old. Apart from the usual furniture there were work-boxes, wooden and wicker, stacked one on top of the other, trunks under the bed and trunks covered with dust sheets which were themselves piled with old magazines and old albums. Two of those miniature chests of drawers, dear to the hearts of the Victorians, stood on the massive tallboy, and above them on the wall was a what-not, crammed full of letters and papers and little boxes and old pens and jars of hairpins.

'It might be in here,' said Mrs Lyle, 'or it might be in the other rooms.'

Wexford looked into the other rooms. None of them was exactly untidy. Nor were they rooms for people to live in. They were the repositories for the results of sixty years of hoarding, and it was apparent to his practised eye that some crazy filing system had been employed in the days when Mrs Lyle still had her sight.

She seemed to sense that he was taken aback. A note came into her voice that was not quite malice but faintly revengeful. She said, 'You've got a long job.' She meant, 'You can see and I can't, so you get on with it.'

He got on with it, beginning in her bedroom. Perhaps it was the smell of these souvenirs, merely musty to him but evocative to her of the occasions they commemorated, which made her face go strange and dreamy, though not unhappy, her hand shake a little as she touched the cards and photographs he lifted from the drawers. He fetched the old brass bedlamp and put it on the tallboy to give him light, and in its yellow radiance, moted with dust, he explored the archives of Mrs Lyle's long life.

She had been a great correspondent and she had kept every letter, every birthday and Christmas card she had ever received. Some male relative had been a philatelist so she had kept the envelopes too, but the collector had never come for his stamps which had accumulated in their thousands on envelopes and scraps torn from envelopes. The late policeman's love letters were there, bound in ribbon from a wedding cake, pieces of ancient and petrified icing still adhering to it. Every year he had sent her a Valentine. He found five in the tallboy, and then he began on the workboxes, seven more in there.

167

'I never throw anything away,' said Mrs Lyle happily.

He didn't say the cruel thing aloud, but he asked it of himself. Why didn't she? Why did she keep these cards, these cake boxes, these locks of babies' hair, these greetings telegrams and these reams of newspaper cuttings? She was blind; she would never be able to see any of them again. But he knew she kept them for another reason. What matter if she never again read the policeman's writing or looked at his picture and those of her posterity? They were the bricks of her identity, the fabric of the walls which kept it safe and the windows through which, though sightless, it could still look out upon its world. His own identity had been too precariously shaken in recent weeks for him to reproach someone who hoarded and harvested and stored to preserve her own.

And he could see. His eye didn't hurt him at all. Even in this dull and dusty light he could read the spidery writing and distinguish the faces in the cloudy sepia photographs. By now he felt that he could have written Mrs Lyle's biography. It was all here, every day of her life, keeping her alive and a unique personality, waiting to be burned by a grandson when she needed it no longer.

They moved on into the next room. Wexford didn't know what time it was; he was afraid to look at his watch. There must be easier ways of finding Rebecca Foster. If only he could remember where it was that he had seen her for the first time . . .

He wished he had begun in the smallest bedroom, for it was there that he found it. He unstrapped a suitcase, unlocked it, opened it. The case contained only letters, some still in their envelopes, some loose, their sheets scattered and mixed with others. And here it was at last. '36, Biretta St., S.W.10. June 26th, 1954. Dear May, Sorry to hear you are having trouble with your eyes . . .'

'Well, that didn't take too long, did it?' said Mrs Lyle. 'I hope you've put all my things back right, not mixed up. I like to know where they are. If you've done, I'll see you off the premises and then I think I'll get to bed.'

21

*He made the proverb true, which saith: He that
shooteth oft, at last shall hit the mark.*

HIS last day. He didn't think of it as the last day of his
holiday but as his last opportunity to solve this case. And
it was the first time he had really known what it is to be set a
deadline. In the past, of course, at Kingsmarkham, the chief
constable had pressed him and there had sometimes been
threats of calling in the Yard, but no one had ever said, You
have twenty-four hours. After that time has elapsed, the case
will be taken out of your hands. No one was saying it now
except himself.

Howard had ceased to regard him as being involved in it.
Come to that, he had never said, This is your case. Solve it
for me. How could he, in his position? All he had asked for
were his uncle's ideas and his uncle's advice, and with Wexford's failure he had given up asking even that. Not that he
gave any sign of being disappointed, but he pinned his faith
now to Baker and it was of Baker that he had talked the
night before.

Wexford had been too tired to take much of it in, gathering
only that Gregson had been remanded in custody on a charge
of assaulting a police officer. Baker still thought of him as his
prime suspect, but just the same he was pursuing other lines.
The scarf was interesting him at the moment and he was much
concerned about an interview he had had with one of the

169

tenants of Garmisch Terrace. Wexford couldn't summon up energy to ask questions, and Howard too was tired, his foot paining him, and he let his uncle go off to bed, wishing him good night with the optimistic assurance that the case might well be solved before the Wexfords left on the Saturday.

It might well, Wexford reflected on the morning of his last day, but not by Baker.

The women had long given up waiting at the foot of the stairs for him and with regard to breakfast he took pot luck. He felt perfectly well. Yesterday's exercise had taken off more weight while the meals had added none, and even doubtful solicitous Dora had to admit that his holiday had done its good work. It was hard for him to realise that this Friday was just the last day of their holiday for her, a time for packing and going out to buy last-minute gifts. Her only concern was whether or not she had remembered the order for milk to be left on Saturday, and would their little corner shop keep a loaf of bread for her?

'What did you say?' said her husband.

'The bread, Reg. I said I hoped Dixons would keep me a loaf of bread.'

'You said the corner shop . . .' That was where he had seen her! Not, of course, at Dixons down the road from him in Kingsmarkham, but at a little place that might have been its twin opposite a rose-pink house in Fulham. All those hours wasted, rummaging through the storeplace of a life! 'Pity you didn't mention it before,' he said abruptly.

They looked at him as if he were mad, but Denise often did that. 'How are you going to amuse yourself today, Uncle Reg?'

'I shall be all right.'

'Going to see St Thomas for the last time?'

'*Sir* Thomas.' He smiled at her, liking her scented prettiness, glad that he would soon be away from her speckless housekeeping and her dangerous plants. 'Don't you worry about me. I've got things to do. Howard get off all right?'

'Someone came to drive him.'

He waited until they had left the house to buy toys for his grandchildren, and then he walked down past the back way into St Mark and St John, catching sight of a red head by the gates that probably belonged to Verity Bate. She reminded him of his previous failure. He wouldn't fail again, not this time. Everything was falling beautifully into place. He even knew just why Loveday had picked on Belgrade Road and that colourful house opposite the shop as an address to give Peggy Pope. It was straight there that he was going. Why bother with Biretta Street which lay far off his course in the river-bound peninsula that is Chelsea but looks like Wilman Park or Kenbourne Vale?

The shop was ahead of him now, price reductions scrawled on its window, vegetables outside in boxes, a mongrel dog tied up to a lamp standard. He went inside. The shop was full of people, a long queue of women with long shopping lists. Two assistants were serving, a young girl and a woman with a pink wen pushing her nose slightly askew.

There was nothing for it but to wait until the place emptied, if it ever did on a Friday when shoppers stocked up with weekend provisions. He paced up and down the street, time passing with maddening slowness. Years and years ago, when he was young, he had felt like this, arriving too early for a date with a girl, killing time. The cold mist made him shiver and his fingers felt numb. Pity he hadn't thought of putting gloves on. Gloves . . . In all these enquiries of his he mustn't forget the girl with the gloves.

When he went back for the fourth time to the shop door, all but one of the queue had gone and this last one was being served by the girl. His woman, his longed-for date, had gone to the window and was stacking soap packets in a pyramid.

'Mrs Foster?' he said, his throat dry.

She stepped back, surprised, and nodded. The mole, which might once have marred a pretty face, was now only an ugly feature among general worn ugliness. She looked about fifty. Ah, the orchard walls are high and hard to climb . . .

'I'm a police officer. I should like to talk to you.'

When she spoke he heard the voice of a Child of the Revelation, accentless, dull, economical.

'What about?' she said.

'Your niece,' said Wexford. 'Your brother's daughter.'

She didn't argue or expostulate but told the girl to see to the shop and led him into a small room at the rear.

'I've been talking to Mrs Lyle,' he said.

The blood poured into her face and she pressed her ill-kept hands together. It was impossible to imagine her as the young girl, the Juliet, who had climbed down a ladder into her lover's arms. 'Mrs Lyle . . . Does she still live down there? Next door to my brother?'

'She's blind now. She knew nothing, only your address.'

'Blind,' said Mrs Foster. 'Blind. And I'm a widow and Rachel . . .' To his horror she began to cry. She cried as if she were ashamed of her tears, scrubbing them away as they fell. 'The world's all wrong,' she said. 'It ought to be changed.'

'Maybe. Tell me about Rachel.'

'I promised her . . .'

'Your promises mean nothing now, Mrs Foster. Rachel is dead.' He had broken it without preamble but he regretted nothing, for he could tell that her niece had very little to do with her grief. She had been crying for herself, perhaps a little for Mrs Lyle. Who had ever shed a tear for Loveday Morgan?'

'Dead,' she said as she had said 'blind'. 'How, dead?'

He explained and all the time he was speaking her face was stony. 'Now it's your turn,' he said.

'She came to my house in July, last July.' The voice grated on him. It was even, monotonous, without rise or fall. 'My brother turned her out when he found she was expecting. She was small and she didn't eat much and she didn't show till nearly the end. My brother told her to get out.'

He had guessed but he could hardly believe it. In these days? In London in the nineteen seventies? Although she had

172

emancipated herself from her upbringing, Mrs Foster had about her something Victorian, and it was a Victorian situation, chronicled in a thousand novels, that she was describing.

'You can't credit it?' she said. 'You don't know what the Children are. She came to me because there was no one else. She'd never heard of people, societies, that look after girls like her. I'd have thought she was simple if I hadn't been like that myself once.'

'The baby?'

'She hadn't seen a doctor. I told her to go and see one. She wouldn't. She'd never been to a doctor in her life. The Children don't have doctors. She wouldn't go to the Assistance. I kept her. I had this job and two jobs cleaning. What else could I do? One day I got home from work and she'd had the baby all by herself in my bedroom.'

'Without any assistance?'

Mrs. Foster nodded. 'I made her have a doctor then. I sent for my own. He was very angry with me but what could I do? He sent in the midwife every day and I registered the baby in Chelsea, up in the King's Road.'

'Morgan was the father?'

'Yes. She said she was his wife and when he came out of prison they'd be married properly. I knew that wasn't true. He had a wife living. We looked after the baby between us and when she got work, cleaning work, sometimes I'd take it with me or she'd take it with her.'

'And then?'

Mrs Foster hesitated. The girl in the shop called her and she said, 'I'm coming. I'm coming in a minute.' She turned tiredly to Wexford. 'It was adopted. Rachel loved it, but she agreed. She knew it wasn't possible for us to keep it all on our own. We had to work, both of us, and women don't like it if you take a baby with you. But Rachel was no worker, anyway. She wasn't used to it. She was crazy about television. It was new to her, you see. All she wanted was to sit about all day, watching the television with the baby on her lap. She said she'd like to be somewhere where she could watch

173

it all day long. Then the baby went and being in my house without it got her down, so she left and got a room. I never heard from her. I thought maybe my brother had taken her back. All she'd been through hadn't stopped her wanting to be one of the Children . . .' Mrs Foster's voice tailed forlornly away.

'Who adopted the baby? Was it done through a society?'

'I can't tell you that. I promised. Rachel never knew. We thought it best she shouldn't know.'

'I must know.'

'Not through me. I promised.'

'Then I must go to the Children's Department,' said Wexford.

The phone book told him he would find it in Holland Park and he waited for a taxi to take him there. But he knew the answer already, the whole answer, and as he stood at the kerb he began carefully arranging mentally the complete sequence of events from Rachel Vickers' arrival in Biretta Street to her death as Loveday Morgan in Kenbourne Vale cemetery.

Poor Baker. Just for once he was to be cheated of his triumph, forestalled by the old fuddy-duddy from the country. Wexford felt gently amused to think of them all there in Kenbourne, pursuing lines which would lead to dead ends, running off at tangents, clinging obstinately to their need to pin it on a boy van driver. All there at the police station—except Sergeant Clements. And he would be in court, getting his order. Or perhaps, even at this moment, failing to get it?

Howard and Baker were at the Yard. Everyone knew Clements was taking the day off and why he was. Pamela told Wexford she didn't expect the superintendent to put in a further appearance that day.

The snapshot Pamela had found on Howard's desk was no longer there. Someone had taken it or put it away. Instead, Mrs Dearborn's blue scarf lay there, enclosed but not concealed by a case of clear plastic. It had the look of a prewrapped Christmas gift but for the neat official label stuck to the side of the case.

Wexford shrugged, thanked Pamela and went out. To get to Elm Green tube station he made a detour through the cemetery. In the gathering fog the winged victory was ghost-like and the black horses, half-veiled in vapour, seemed to plunge on the air itself without support, without anchorage. Beneath them the royal tombs had lost their solidity as had the still trees, spectres of trees rather, floating, rootless and grey. Water drops, condensed mist, clung to the thready brambles. Obelisks, broken columns, angels with swords, a hunter with two dead lions at his feet . . .

'He who asks questions is a fool.
    He who answers them is a greater fool . . .'

Wexford smiled.

22

The murder being once done, he is in less fear and more hope that the deed shall not be betrayed or known, seeing the party is now dead and rid out of the way, which only might have uttered and disclosed it.

A LAST day well spent. Wexford was a poor typist but he would have been glad of the use of a typewriter now. He had to write the whole thing out on sheet after sheet of Basildon Bond, using Dora's old fountain pen. It was after seven when he finished and then he went downstairs to wait for Howard.

His plan was to give Howard the report after dinner, and he envisaged their discussing it quietly in the study, but his nephew phoned to say he would be delayed and had replaced the receiver before Wexford had a chance to talk to him.

'You ought to go to bed, dear,' Dora said at ten.

'Why? So that I'll be strong enough to sit in the train? I've a good mind to stay up all night.'

He opened the book Denise had at last, in despair over his dilatoriness, fetched him from the library. 'To the Right Honourable and his Very Singular Good Master, Master William Cecil Esquire . . . Ralph Robinson wisheth continuance of good health with daily increase of virtue and honour.' That dedication, with different names substituted, might as well have served as an introduction to his own report as to Sir

Thomas's masterpiece. He had scarcely read the first paragraph when the phone rang again.

'He wants to talk to you, Uncle Reg. I said you were just off to bed.'

Wexford took the phone in a hand that trembled very slightly. 'Howard?'

Howard's voice was hard, a little disdainful. 'If you're on your way to bed it doesn't matter.'

'I'm not. I was waiting up for you.' Now that the time had come, Wexford found himself strangely reluctant, his voice uncertain. 'There are a few points . . . Well, I've written a sort of report . . . Would you care to . . . ? I mean, my conclusions . . .'

'Could be the same as ours,' Howard finished the sentence for him. 'The scarf? Yes, I thought so. Baker and I have just been to see a friend of yours and what we really need now is a little help from you. If you'll hold the line, I'll put Baker on.'

'Howard, wait. I could come over.'

'What, now? To Kenbourne Vale?'

Wexford decided to be firm, not to argue at all. He saw clearly and coldly that he was failing for the second time, but he wouldn't give in without some sort of fight, not let Baker steal his last faint thunder. 'I'll take a taxi,' he said.

The expected wail came from Dora. 'Oh, darling! At this hour?'

'I said I was going to stay up all night.'

What amazed him was that some of the shops were still open at ten minutes to midnight and people were still buying groceries for strange nocturnal feasts. In the launderettes the bluish-white lights were on and the machines continued to turn. His cab took him through North Kensington where the night people walked, chatting desultorily, strolling, as if it were day. In Kingsmarkham anybody still out would be hastening home to bed. Here the sky wore its red, starless glow, above the floating lights, the sleepless city. They came into Kenbourne Lane. The cemetery was like a pitch-black cloud, only visible

177

because its mass was darker than the sky. Wexford felt the muscles of his chest contract as he realised they were nearly there. Soon he would be facing Baker. If only there might be a chance of Howard reading his report first . . .

He had had a foolish feeling that there might be a sort of reception committee awaiting him, but there was no one in the foyer but the officers on duty. And when he tried to treat the place as if it was more familiar with him than he with it, walking casually towards the lift, a sergeant called him back to ask his name and his business.

'Mr Wexford, is it? The superintendent is expecting you, sir.'

That was a little better. His spirits rose higher when he stepped out of the lift and saw Howard standing alone in the corridor outside his office.

'You've been very quick.'

'Howard, I just want to say . . .'

'You want to know about Gregson. I guessed you would and I meant to mention it on the phone. Where d'you think he was on the 25th? Doing that housebreaking job, of all things. The girl who phoned him at Mrs Kirby's was Harry Slade's girl friend to tell him the job was on and give him all the gen. Come on in now, and see Baker. Shall I send down for coffee?'

Wexford didn't answer him. He walked into the office, met Baker's eyes and silently drew his report out of his pocket. The handwritten sheets looked very amateurish, very rustic.

Howard said awkwardly, 'We really only wanted some inside information, Reg. A few questions we had to put to you . . .'

'It's all in there. It won't take you more than ten minutes to read the lot.'

Wexford knew he was being hypersensitive, but a man would have had to be totally without perception not to see that resigned and indulgent glance which passed between Baker and Howard. He sat down, sliding his arms out of his raincoat and letting it fall over the back of the chair. Then he stared at the uncurtained window, the thick red sky and the black

178

bulk of the bottling plant. While Howard phoned to order coffee, Baker cast his eyes over, rather than read, the report.

It was ten pages long. He got to page five and then he said, 'All this stuff about the girl's background, it's very edifying, no doubt, but hardly . . .' He sought for a word. ' . . . Germane to this inquiry,' he said.

'Let me see.' Howard stood behind Baker, reading rapidly. 'You've put in a lot of work here, Reg. Congratulations. You seem to have reached the same conclusions as we have.'

'Taking all the evidence,' said Wexford, 'they are the only possible conclusions.'

Howard gave him a quick look. 'Yes, well . . . Maybe the best thing would be for you to sum up for us, Michael.'

The sheets of blue paper were growing rather crumpled now. Baker folded them and dropped them rather contemptuously on the desk top. But when he spoke it wasn't contemptuously. He cleared his throat and said in the uneasy tone of a man who is unaccustomed to graciousness, 'I owe you a bit of an apology, Mr Wexford. I shouldn't have said what I did about wild goose chases and red herrings and all that. But it did look like a red herring at first, didn't it?'

Wexford smiled. 'It looked like a needless complication.'

'Not needless at all,' Howard said. 'Without it we should never have traced the ownership of the scarf. Here's our coffee. Put it down there, Sergeant, thank you. Well, Michael?'

'For a time,' Baker began, 'we were completely put off the scent by the confusion between Rachel Vickers and Dearborn's own stepdaughter. We neglected to bear in mind the circumstantial evidence and we did not then, of course, know that his daughter Alexandra was not his own child.'

Wexford stirred his coffee, although it was black and sugarless. 'How do you know now?' he interrupted.

'Mrs Dearborn told us herself tonight. She was very frank, very open. When she realised the importance of the inquiry, she told us quite freely that Alexandra—named, she believed, after her natural father—is a child she and her husband had adopted privately. Two adoption societies had refused to consider them on account of their age, and when the opportunity arose just before Christmas for them to take this baby they jumped at it. Dearborn acted very properly. He intended to adopt legally and through the proper channels. As soon as the child was received into his house in late December, he notified the Children's Department and the court of his intention to adopt. Did you want to say something, Mr Wexford?'

'Only that you make it sound very cold. He loves that child passionately.'

'I don't think we should allow our emotions to be involved. Naturally, the whole thing is painful. Let me resume. Mrs Dearborn has never met Rachel Vickers. All she knew about her came from the girl's aunt, her former charwoman, Mrs Foster, and from the guardian *ad litem*.'

'The girl with the gloves,' said Wexford.

Baker took no notice of this. 'The guardian and Mrs Foster knew the girl as Rachel Vickers, never as Loveday Morgan. Until February 14th, Dearborn also only knew the girl by her true name, he had never seen her and supposed everything would be plain sailing. On that day he came home and told his wife that while he had been showing Alexandra some property he intended to buy in Lammas Grove, Rachel Vickers came out of a shop and recognised her child.' Baker paused. 'I must admit I don't quite understand that, a man pointing out houses to a babe in arms, but I daresay it's irrelevant.' He glanced at Wexford and Wexford said nothing. 'According to Mrs Dearborn,' he went on, 'Rachel asked him if she might see Alexandra again and he agreed, though reluctantly, giving her his office phone number. Mrs Dearborn says—and I believe she is speaking the truth—that she knows of no more meetings between Rachel and her husband. As far as she knows, the girl showed no more interest in the child after that.'

'We, however,' put in Howard, 'have been told early in this inquiry that Rachel had an interview at Notbourne Properties sometime after February 14th, and I think we can conclude

180

this interview had nothing to do with an application for a job. What are your views, Reg?'

'Dearborn,' said Wexford slowly, 'wanted to keep the child and Rachel, just as intensely, wanted her back. At that interview in his office she told him she would oppose the granting of his order and he took the highly illegal step of offering her five thousand pounds not to oppose it.'

'How can you possibly know that?'

Wexford shrugged. 'Finish reading my report and you'll know how. Without reading it, you can surely see that this is why Dearborn told his wife no more. He's unscrupulous but Mrs Dearborn isn't. She would never have gone along with him in any scheme to *buy* the child. When did they expect to get the order?'

'On March 24th,' said Baker with a certain triumph. 'If you don't know that, Mr Wexford, I don't see how . . . But let me get on with my ideas of what happened next. Rachel agreed to take the money—some money, we can't say how much—and promised to phone Dearborn to fix a date for this transaction. The date she chose was February 25th and she phoned Dearborn from Garmisch Terrace at one fifteen on that day. They met about an hour later in the cemetery.'

'You've identified the scarf as Mrs Dearborn's?'

'Certainly. That's why we went to see her in the first place. She told us she often wears her husband's sheepskin jacket and probably left the scarf in that jacket pocket. Dearborn met the girl as arranged, but when he was about to part with the money, thought how much easier it would be, how much safer he would be, to keep the money and kill the girl. He would never be sure otherwise that she wouldn't oppose the order just the same. So he strangled her with the scarf and put her body in the Montfort tomb.'

'You helped us again there, Reg,' said Howard. 'It was you who pointed out about its being Leap Year. Dearborn forgot that. He supposed that the last Tuesday of the month had gone by and that the tomb wouldn't be visited until *after* March 24th, by which time he would have his order.'

Wexford reached for his report, fingered it hesitantly and then laid it down again. 'He's confessed all this?' he asked. 'You've talked to him and . . . Have you charged him?'

'He's away from home,' said Baker. 'Up in the north somewhere at some architects' conference.'

'We wanted your *opinion*, Reg,' Howard said rather sharply. 'So much of this is conjecture. As you said yourself it's the only possible conclusion, but we thought you might have something more concrete for us.'

'I said that?'

'Well, surely. I understood you to . . .'

Wexford got up abruptly, pushing back his chair so that it almost fell over. He was suddenly frightened, but not of himself, not any more of failure. 'His wife will get in touch with him!'

'Of course she will. Let her. He's due back tomorrow morning.' Howard looked at his watch. 'This morning, rather. Once he knows he's in danger of not getting that order—his wife will tell him that the court will suspend all action until the matter is cleared up—he'll come hotfoot to us. My God, Reg, she doesn't know we suspect him of murder.'

'But he'll know by now he hasn't a hope in hell of remaining as Alexandra's father?' Wexford gripped the back of the chair. He was shivering. 'Will she have told him that?'

'Unless she's a far more phlegmatic woman than I take her to be, yes.'

He tried to stay calm. He knew his face had grown white, for he could feel the skin shrink and tremble. Baker's face was scornful and sour, Howard's entirely bewildered.

'You wanted my advice. It must be that because you don't want my opinion. My advice to you is to phone Dearborn's hotel now, at once.' Wexford sat down and turned his face to the wall.

'He's in his room,' said Baker, replacing the receiver. 'I don't see the need for all this melodrama. The man's in his room, asleep, but they've gone to check and they'll call us back. I suppose Mr Wexford's idea is they'll find a bundle of clothes under the sheets and the bird flown.'

Wexford didn't comment on that. His hands were clasped tightly together, the knuckles whitened by the strong pressure. He didn't relax them but he relaxed his voice, making conversation for the sake of it. 'What happened about Clements?' he asked, attempting to sound casual.

'He got his order,' Howard said. 'Phoned through to tell us. No difficulty at all.'

'I'll send his wife some flowers,' said Wexford. 'Remind me.' He helped himself to more coffee without bothering to ask permission, but his hand was unsteady and he slopped it on to the desk. Howard didn't say a word.

The phone gave the prefatory click that comes a split second before it rings. Before it rang Wexford had jumped and got the shock over. Three hands went out to the receiver, the other men infected by his dread. It was Howard who lifted it, Howard who said, 'I see. Yes. You've got a doctor? The local police?' He covered the mouthpiece with his hand. His thin face had grown very pale. 'There's a doctor staying in the hotel,' he said. 'He's with Dearborn now.'

'He tried to kill himself,' said Wexford and he said it not as a question but as a statement of fact.

'They think he's dead. They don't know. Some sort of overdose, it sounds like.'

Baker said, attempting a suitable dolefulness, 'Maybe it's the best thing. Horrible, of course, but when you think of the alternative, years inside. In his position I'd take the same way out.'

Howard was talking again, asking sharp questions into the phone. 'What position?' said Wexford. 'You don't still think he did it, do you?'

183

23

*If by none of these means the matter go forward as
they would have it, then they procure occasions of
debate.*

WEXFORD had seen many a dawn in Kingsmarkham, but
never till now a London dawn. He parted the curtains
at Howard's window and watched the indigo sky split
and shred to show between the heavy clouds streaks of
greenish light. A little wind, too slight to set the cemetery trees
in motion, fluttered a flag on the roof of a distant building.
Pigeons had began to coo, to take wing and wheel lazily
against the façades of tower blocks which they, foolish
creatures and slow to learn, still took for the cliffs of southern
Italy from where the Romans had brought them two thousand
years before. The roar of the traffic, half-silenced during the
small dead hours, was rising again to its full daytime volume.

Apart from himself, the office was empty. As the great red
ball of a sun began to rise, thrusting through reddish-black
vapourish folds, the street lamps of Kenbourne Vale went out
gradually. Wexford went across the room and snapped off the
light switch. But no sooner had he found himself in the welcome, restful semi-darkness than the light came on again and
Howard limped into the office with Melanie Dearborn.

Her face was haggard, the eye sockets purple with fatigue
and fear. She wore trousers and a sweater and over them her
husband's sheepskin coat. But for all her pain and her anxiety,

184

she hadn't forgotten her manners. Blinking a little against the light, she came up to Wexford and held out her hand. 'I'm so sorry,' she began, 'that we should meet again like this, that these terrible things . . .'

He shook his head, fetched a chair and helped her into it. Then he met Howard's eyes and Howard gave a tiny, almost imperceptible nod, pursing his lips.

'Your husband . . . ?'

'Is going to recover,' Howard answered for her. 'He's in hospital and he's very tired but he's conscious. He'll be all right.'

'Thank God,' Wexford said sincerely.

She looked up at him and managed a weak watery smile. 'Why was I so stupid as to phone him last night? I got in a panic, you see. I couldn't bear to think of him coming home and perhaps finding Alexandra gone. He told me all he'd done to keep her.'

Wexford sat down and drew his chair close to hers.

'What did he do, Mrs Dearborn?'

'I'm afraid to tell you,' she whispered. 'Because if it comes out . . . they may . . . I mean, they could take Alexandra away and not let us . . .'

Wexford looked at Howard, but Howard didn't move a muscle. 'It will be better to tell us,' he said. 'It's always better to tell the truth. And if the bribe wasn't taken . . .'

There was a discouraging cough from Howard and Melanie Dearborn gave a heavy sigh. She snuggled more deeply inside the coat as if, because it was her husband's and he had worn it, she had near to her a comforting part of himself. 'The bribe was offered,' she said.

'How much?' Howard asked gently but succinctly.

'Five thousand pounds.'

Wexford nodded. 'She was to promise not to oppose the order in exchange for that?'

'She did promise. When she came to my husband's office. Then and there they made an appointment to meet in Kenbourne Vale cemetery on February 25th at two-fifteen.'

'Why did she change her mind?'

'She didn't exactly. According to Stephen, she was a very simple sort of girl. When he and she met that day she began to talk about how she was going to use the money and give it to someone to look after Alexandra while she was out at work. She didn't even have the sense to realise what she was saying. Stephen said, "But you won't have Alexandra. I'm giving you the money so that I can keep her." And then she put her hand over her mouth—you can imagine—and said, "Oh, Mr Dearborn, but I must keep her. She's all I've got in the world and you won't miss the money." She just didn't *see*.'

Wexford nodded but he said nothing. He had seen the girl, or her ghost, her counterpart, her *doppel-gänger*. Both had been brought up in a strict morality, but a morality which leaves out what ordinary human beings call ethics.

'Stephen was—well, appalled,' Mrs Dearborn went on. 'He said he'd give her more, anything she asked. He was prepared to go up to—oh, I don't know—fifty thousand, I expect. But she couldn't imagine that amount of money.'

'He didn't give her anything?'

'Of course he didn't. She was chattering on about how she'd give a thousand to someone to look after Alexandra and keep the four for the future, and he saw it wasn't any good and he just turned away and left her. He was very quiet and moody that night—I thought it was because he was tired of the way I fretted about Louise. By the middle of the next week he was on top of the world again. I know why that was now. He'd realised who the murdered girl was.'

Howard had listened to it all without intervening, but now he said in a steady cool voice, 'If you're going up to see your husband, Mrs Dearborn, we'd better see about transport for you.'

'Thank you. I'm afraid I'm giving everyone a great deal of trouble.' Melanie Dearborn hesitated and then said in a rush, 'What am I to say to him about—about Alexandra?'

'That depends on the outcome of this case and upon the court.'

'But we love her,' she pleaded. 'We can give her a good home. Stephen—he tried to *kill* himself. The bribe wasn't accepted. In the girl's mind it wasn't a bribe at all but a gift, just like the clothes we gave her aunt.'

'Well?' said Wexford to Howard after she had left them, casting over her shoulder a last imploring look.

'The court might, I suppose, see it in that light. But when the evidence given in Dearborn's prosecution . . .'

'What are you going to prosecute him for, Howard? Making a present of money to a poverty-stricken girl, his former servant's niece, so that she could raise a child he was fond of decently? And then withdrawing the offer because the chosen guardians weren't suitable in his eyes?'

'It wasn't like that, Reg, you're being Jesuitical. Dearborn killed her. The scarf was his wife's, in the pocket of that coat which they both wear. He had abundant motive which no one else had. And he had the special knowledge. He put her in a tomb he knew wouldn't be visited until after he had got his adoption order.'

'Knew?' said Wexford. 'He wouldn't have forgotten it was Leap Year. February 29th was his birthday.'

'I don't understand you, Mr Wexford,' said Baker who had just come in and had overheard his last words. 'According to your report you go along with our views entirely.'

'How do you know? You didn't bother to read to the end.'

Howard looked at his uncle, half-smiling as if he understood that this was triumph, this was the end he had asked for and more than Wexford had hoped to attain. He picked up the last two sheets of blue paper and, beckoning Baker to him, read them swiftly. 'We shouldn't be here,' he said when he had finished. 'We should be in Garmisch Terrace.'

'You should,' Wexford retorted. He looked at his watch and yawned. 'I've a train to catch at ten.'

Baker took a step towards him. He didn't hold out this hand or attempt to retract anything or even smile. He said, 'I don't know how Mr Fortune feels, but I'd take it as a personal

187

favour if you'd come with us.' And Wexford understood that this was a frank and full apology.

'There are other trains,' he said, and he put on his coat.

Early morning in Garmisch Terrace, a thin pale sunlight baring the houses in all their dilapidation. Someone had scrawled 'God is dead' on the temple wall, and the Shepherd was in the act of erasing it with a scrubbing brush and a bucket of water. Outside number 22, Peggy Pope, her hair tied up in a scarf, was loading small articles of furniture into a van.

'Going somewhere?' said Wexford.

She shrugged. 'Next week,' she said. 'I thought I owed it to the landlords to give them a week's notice.' Her face, unwashed, unpainted, rather greasy, had a curious spiritual beauty like a young saint's. 'I'm just getting shot of a few of my things.'

Wexford glanced at the driver. It was the Indian tenant. 'Off with him, are you?'

'I'm off *alone*, me and the kid, that is. He's just letting me have a loan of his van. I'm going home to my mother. Nowhere else *to* go, is there?' She thrust a battered record player into the van, wiped her hands on her jeans and went down the area steps. The three policemen followed her.

The stacks of old books were still there, the cumbersome shabby furniture. On the wall a little more paint had peeled away, enlarging the map of that unearthly, Utopian continent. Lamont was in bed, the baby lying restlessly in\the crook of his arm.

Peggy showed none of the outraged propriety that might have been evinced by a respectable housewife under these circumstances. She wasn't a respectable housewife but a wandering girl about to leave her lover. Remembering perhaps how Wexford had once before assisted her in moving heavy objects, she seemed to take his presence as a sign that it was in this role that he had reappeared, and she thrust into his arms a shopping basket full of kitchen utensils. Wexford shook his head at her. He went over to the bed and stared at Lamont who responded first by burying his head in the pillow, then by pulling himself slowly and despairingly into a sitting position.

Howard and Baker came closer to the bed, Peggy watched them. She knew now that something was wrong, that they were not merely here to ask questions. But she said nothing. She was leaving Garmisch Terrace and everything it contained, and perhaps she didn't care.

'Get up, Lamont,' said Baker. 'Get up and get dressed.'

Lamont didn't speak to him. Under the dirty sheet he was naked. His eyes had a naked empty look in them, expressing a total failure, an utter poverty, a lack of love, of possessions, of imagination. Thou art the thing itself, Wexford thought, un-accommodated man is no more than such a poor, bare animal as thou art . . . 'Come along, you know why we are here.'

'I never had the money,' Lamont whispered. He let the sheet drop, took the child in his arms and handed her to Peggy. It was the final renunciation. 'You'll have to look after her now,' he said. 'Just you. I did it for you and her. Would you have stayed if I'd got the money?'

'I don't know,' Peggy said, crying. 'I don't know.'

'I wish,' said Howard tiredly, 'I felt as well as you look. They say a change is as good as a rest, and you haven't had either, but you look fine.'

'I feel fine.' Wexford thought but he didn't say aloud, I'll be glad to get home just the same. 'It's good to be able to read again without feeling you're going to go blind.'

'Which reminds me,' said Howard, 'I've got something for you to read in the train. A parting gift. Pamela went out to the West-End and got it.'

A very handsome copy of *Utopia*, bound in amber calf, tooled in gold. 'So I've got it at last. Thanks very much. If we're going back to Chelsea now, d'you think we could make a detour for me to say good-bye to him?'

'Why not? And in the car, Reg, maybe you'll just clear up a few points for me.'

It was going to be a lovely day, the first really fine day of Wexford's holiday now that his holiday was over. He asked Howard to wind down the window so that he could feel the soft air on his face. 'After I made that first blunder,' he said, 'I realised Dearborn wouldn't have desecrated his cemetery, and then I remembered he'd told me February 29th was his birthday. A man doesn't forget when his own birthday is going to occur, especially when it only really occurs once in every four years. Lamont put her in the Montfort vault because it was outside it that he encountered her—and killed her.'

'What put you on to him in the first place?'

'The way Loveday—I think of her as Loveday, perhaps because she was trying to get out of her darkness into a kind of light—the way she went down to talk to him and wanted to *entrust* something to him. She had nothing to entrust but Alexandra. She approached him and not Peggy partly because she was afraid of Peggy and partly because it was Lamont who mostly cared for his own child.' They entered Hyde Park, a sea of precocious daffodils. Ten thousand saw I at a glance . . . 'She told him she was going to get five thousand pounds, and she must have convinced him in spite of the unlikelihood of it, for he consulted estate agents. I saw a specification he had there for a house costing just under five thousand.'

'She was only going to give him one thousand.'

'I know. I don't suppose he thought of resorting to violence then, but he meant to con the rest out of her.'

'So she phoned Dearborn,' said Howard as they drove past the museums, thronged with tourists this Saturday morning. 'She phoned him at one-fifteen on February 25th to make the appointment.'

'They'd already made it in his office. It was Lamont she phoned. He was in the Grand Duke and he always took his phone calls there. She told him the money was going to be handed over to her in the cemetery that afternoon. He must have waited for her and seen her part from Dearborn, concluding, of course, that she had got the money.'

'Then he waylaid her,' said Howard. 'He asked for his

thousand to start with, but she wouldn't give him even that. She had nothing to give.'

Wexford nodded. 'He desperately wanted to keep Peggy and his child. Nothing was to get in his way now. He strangled her with her own scarf.'

'No, Reg, I can't have that. It was Mrs. Dearborn's scarf.'

'It was once,' said Wexford. 'Dearborn gave it to Loveday's aunt.'

The river was rippling brown and gold, a big brother, dirtier and wider and stronger, of the Kingsbrook. Tonight, Wexford thought, when we've unpacked our bags and the grandchildren have been to get their presents, tonight I'll go down and look at my own river. He got out of the car and walked up to Sir Thomas. This morning the gold cap and the gold chain were almost too dazzling to look at.

Wexford turned to Howard who had limped after him. He tapped his pocket where the new book was. 'More than four hundred years since he wrote that,' he said, 'but I don't know that things have changed all that much for the better, not the way he must have hoped they would. It's a good job he doesn't know. He'd get up off that seat of his and go back to the Tower.'

'Aren't you going to read your new book?' asked Dora when they were in the train, and the outer suburbs, grey streets, red housing estates, white tower blocks, trees like numberless puffs of smoke in the gold mist, flowed past the window.

'In a minute,' said Wexford. 'What have you got there, more presents?'

'I nearly forgot. These two came for you this morning.'

Two parcels, a thick one and a thin one. Who could be sending him parcels? The handwriting on the brown paper wrappings meant nothing. He undid the string in the thin one and a copy of *Utopia* fell out, a paperback version, with a card enclosed, depicting a rabbit in rustic surroundings, and signed with love from Denise's sister-in-law. Wexford snorted.

'Are you all right, darling?' said anxious Dora.

'Of course I'm all right,' Wexford growled. 'Don't start that again.'

The other parcel also contained a book. He wasn't at all surprised to come upon another *Utopia*, second-hand this time but well preserved. The card had a violet border, the name on it printed in gold. 'You forgot this', Wexford read. 'Something to read in the train. You can keep it. One doesn't meet human policemen every day. I.M.T.'

Something to read in the train . . . Tiredness hit him like a physical blow, but he struggled to keep awake, clasping his three new books, staring out of the window. The green country was beginning now, fingers of it groping and inserting themselves into wedges of brick. Soon they would be travelling into the haunch of England, into the swelling downs. Now for *Utopia*, now at last.

Dora bent down and silently picked up the books from the carriage floor. Her husband was asleep.

RUTH RENDELL

SHAKE HANDS
FOR EVER

arrow books

For my aunts, Jenny Waldorff, Laura Winfield, Margot Richards and Phyllis Ridgway, with my love

Chapter 1

The woman standing under the departures board at Victoria station had a flat rectangular body and an iron-hard rectangular face. A hat of fawn-coloured corrugated felt rather like a walnut shell encased her head, her hands were gloved in fawn-coloured cotton, and at her feet was the durable but scarcely used brown leather suitcase she had taken on her honeymoon forty-five years before. Her eyes scanned the scurrying commuters while her mouth grew more and more set, the lips thinning to a hairline crack.

She was waiting for her son. He was one minute late and his unpunctuality had begun to afford her a glowing satisfaction. She was hardly aware of this pleasure and, had she been accused of it, would have denied it, just as she would have denied the delight all failure and backsliding in other people brought her. But it was present as an undefined sense of well-being that was to vanish almost as soon as it had been born and be succeeded on Robert's sudden hasty arrival by her usual ill-temper. He was so nearly on time as to make any remarks about his lateness absurd, so she contented herself with offering her leathery cheek to his lips and saying:

'There you are then.'

'Have you got your ticket?' said Robert Hathall.

She hadn't. She knew that money had been tight with him for the three years of his second marriage, but that was his fault. Paying her share would only encourage him.

'You'd better go and get them,' she said, 'unless you want us to miss the train,' and she held even more tightly to her zipped-up handbag.

He was a long time about it. She noted that the Eastbourne train, stopping at Toxborough, Myringham and Kingsmarkham, was due to depart at six-twelve, and it was five past now. No fully formed uncompromising thought that it would be nice to miss the train entered her mind, any more than she had consciously told herself it would be nice to find her daughter-in-law in tears, the house filthy and no meal cooked, but once more the seeds of pleasurable resentment began germinating. She had looked forward to this weekend with a deep contentment, certain it would go wrong. Nothing would suit her better than that it should begin to go wrong by their arriving late through no fault of hers, and that their lateness should result in a quarrel between Robert and Angela. But all this smouldered silent and unanalysed under her immediate awareness that Robert was making a mess of things again.

Nevertheless, they caught the train. It was crowded and they both had to stand. Mrs Hathall never complained. She would have fainted before citing her age and her varicose veins as reasons why this or that man should give up his seat to her. Stoicism governed her. Instead, she planted her thick body which, buttoned up in a stiff fawn coat, had the appearance of a wardrobe, in such a way as to prevent the passenger in the window seat from moving his legs or reading his newspaper. She had only one thing to say to Robert and that could keep till there were fewer listeners, and she found it hard to suppose he could have anything to say to her. Hadn't they, after all, spent every weekday evening together for the past two months? But people,

2

she had noticed with some puzzlement, were prone to chatter when they had nothing to say. Even her own son was guilty of this. She listened grimly while he went on about the beautiful scenery through which they would soon pass, the amenities of Bury Cottage, and how much Angela was looking forward to seeing her. Mrs Hathall permitted herself a kind of snort at this last, a two-syllabled grunt made somewhere in her glottis that could be roughly interpreted as a laugh. Her lips didn't move. She was reflecting on the one and only time she had met her daughter-in-law, in that room in Earls Court, when Angela had committed the outrage of referring to Eileen as a greedy bitch. Much would have to be done, many amends be made, before that indiscretion could be forgotten. Mrs Hathall remembered how she had marched straight out of that room and down the stairs, resolving never – never under any circumstances – to see Angela again. It only proved how forbearing she was that she was going to Kingsmarkham now.

At Myringham the passenger by the window, his legs numb, staggered out of the train and Mrs Hathall got his seat. Robert, she could tell, was getting nervous. There was nothing surprising in that. He knew very well this Angela couldn't compete with Eileen as cook and housekeeper and he was wondering just how far below his first wife's standards his second would fall. His next words confirmed her conviction that this was troubling his mind.

'Angela's spent the week spring-cleaning the place to make it nice for you.'

Mrs Hathall was shocked that anyone could make such a statement aloud and in front of a carriage full of people. What she would have liked to say was, firstly, that he should keep his voice down and, secondly, that any decent woman kept her house clean at all times. But she contented herself with a 'I'm sure she needn't put herself out for me' and added repressively that it was time he got her suitcase down.

'It's five minutes yet,' said Robert.

She replied by getting heavily to her feet and struggling with the case herself. Robert and another man intervened to help her, the case nearly fell on to the head of a girl with a baby in her arms, and by the time the train drew to a halt at Kingsmarkham, sending them all staggering and clutching each other, the carriage was in a small uproar.

Out on the platform, Mrs Hathall said, 'That could have been avoided if you'd done as you were asked. You always were obstinate.'

She couldn't understand why he didn't retaliate and fight back. He must be more strung-up than she had thought. To goad him further, she said, 'I suppose we're going to have a taxi?'

'Angela's meeting us in the car.'

Then there wasn't much time for her to say what she had to. She pushed her suitcase at him and took hold of his arm in a proprietary manner. It wasn't that she needed his support or his reassurance, but she felt it essential that this daughter-in-law – how galling and disreputable to have two daughters-in-law! – should, in her first glimpse of them, see them consolidated and arm-in-arm.

'Eileen came in this morning,' she said as they gave up their tickets.

He shrugged absently. 'I wonder you two don't live together.'

'That'd make things easy for you. You wouldn't have to keep a roof over her head.' Mrs Hathall tightened her grip on the arm which he had attempted to jerk away. 'She said to give you her love and say why don't you go round one evening while you're in London.'

'You must be joking,' said Robert Hathall, but he

4

said it vaguely and without much rancour. He was scanning the car park.

Pursuing her theme, Mrs Hathall began, 'It's a wicked shame . . .' and then stopped in mid-sentence. A marvellous realization was dawning on her. She knew that car of Robert's, would know it anywhere, he'd had it long enough thanks to the straits that women had brought him to. She too let her sharp eyes rove round the tarmac square, and then she said in a satisfied tone, 'Doesn't look as if she'd put herself out to meet us.'

Robert seemed discomfited. 'The train was a couple of minutes early.'

'It was three minutes late,' said his mother. She sighed happily. Eileen would have been there to meet them all right. Eileen would have been on the platform with a kiss for her mother-in-law and a cheerful promise of the nice tea that awaited them. And her grand-daughter too . . . Mrs Hathall remarked as if to herself but loud enough to be heard, 'Poor little Rosemary.'

It was very unlike Robert, who was his mother's son, to take this sort of aggravation without comment, but again he made none. 'It doesn't matter,' he said. 'It's not all that far.'

'I can walk,' said Mrs Hathall in the stoical tone of one who realizes that there will be worse trials to come and that the first and lightest must be bravely borne. 'I'm quite used to walking.'

Their journey took them up the station approach and Station Road, across Kingsmarkham High Street and along the Stowerton Road. It was a fine September evening, the air aglow with sunset light, the trees heavily foliaged, the gardens bright with the last and finest flowers of summer. But Mrs Hathall, who might have said like the lover in the ballad, 'What are the beauties of nature to me?', disregarded it all.

5

Her wistfulness had given way to certainty. Robert's depression could mean only one thing. This wife of his, this thief, this breaker of a happy marriage, was going to let him down and he knew it.

They turned into Wool Lane, a narrow tree-shaded byway without a pavement. 'That's what I call a nice house,' said Mrs Hathall.

Robert glanced at the detached, between-the-wars villa. 'It's the only one down here apart from ours. A woman called Lake lives there. She's a widow.'

'Pity it's not yours,' said his mother with a wealth of implication. 'Is it much further?'

'Round the next bend. I can't think what's happened to Angela.' He looked at her uneasily. 'I'm sorry about this, Mother. I really am sorry.'

She was so amazed that he should depart from family tradition as actually to apologize for anything, that she could make no answer to this and remained silent until the cottage came into view. A slight disappointment marred her satisfaction, for this was a house, a decent though old house of brown brick with a neat slate roof. 'Is this it?'

He nodded and opened the gate for her. Mrs Hathall observed that the garden was untended, the flower-beds full of weeds and the grass inches high. Under a neglected-looking tree lay a scattering of rotten plums. She said, 'Hmm,' a non-committal noise characteristic of her and signifying that things were turning out the way she expected. He put the key in the front-door lock and the door swung open. 'Come along in, Mother.'

He was certainly upset now. There was no mistaking it. She knew that way he had of compressing his lips while a little muscle worked in his left cheek. And there was a harsh nervous note in his voice as he called out, 'Angela, we're here!'

Mrs Hathall followed him into the living room.

She could hardly believe her eyes. Where were the dirty teacups, finger-marked gin glasses, scattered clothes, crumbs and dust? She planted herself rectangularly on the spotless carpet and turned slowly round, scrutinizing the ceiling for cobwebs, the windows for smears, the ashtrays for that forgotten cigarette end. A strange uncomfortable chill took hold of her. She felt like a champion who, confident of victory, certain of her own superiority, loses the first set to a tyro.

Robert came back and said, 'I can't think where Angela's got to. She's not in the garden. I'll just go into the garage and see if the car's there. Would you like to go on upstairs, Mother? Your bedroom's the big one at the back.'

Having ascertained that the dining-room table wasn't laid and that there was no sign of preparations for a meal in the immaculate kitchen where the rubber gloves and dusting gloves of household labour lay beside the sink, Mrs Hathall mounted the stairs. She ran one finger along the picture rail on the landing. Not a mark, the woodwork might have been newly painted. The bedroom which was to be hers was as exquisitely clean as the rest of the house, the bed turned down to show candy-striped sheets, one dressing-table drawer open and lined with tissue paper. She noted it all but never once, as one revelation followed another, did she allow this evidence of Angela's excellence to mitigate her hatred. It was a pity that her daughter-in-law should have armed herself with this weapon, a pity and that was all. No doubt her other faults, such as this one of not being here to greet her, would more than compensate for this small virtue.

Mrs Hathall went into the bathroom. Polished enamel, clean fluffy towels, guest soap . . . She set her mouth grimly. Money couldn't have been as tight as

7

Robert made out. She told herself only that she resented his deception, not putting even into thought-words that she was confronting a second deprivation, that of not being able to throw their poverty and the reason for it in their faces. She washed her hands and came out on to the landing. The door to the main bedroom was slightly ajar. Mrs Hathall hesitated. But the temptation to take a look inside and perhaps find a tumbled bed, a mess of squalid cosmetics, was too great to resist. She entered the room carefully.

The bed wasn't tumbled but neatly made. On top of the covers lay a girl face-downwards, apparently deeply asleep. Her dark, rather shaggy, hair lay spread over her shoulders and her left arm was flung out. Mrs Hathall said, 'Hmm,' all her warm pleasure welling back unalloyed. Robert's wife was lying asleep, perhaps even drunk. She hadn't bothered to take off her canvas shoes before collapsing there and she was dressed exactly as she had been that day in Earls Court, probably as she always dressed, in shabby faded blue jeans and a red check shirt. Mrs Hathall thought of Eileen's pretty afternoon dresses and short permed hair, of Eileen who would only have slept in the daytime if she had been at death's door, and then she went over to the bed and stared down, frowning. 'Hmm,' she said again, but this time it was a 'Hmm' of admonition, designed to announce her presence and get an immediate shamed response.

There was none. The genuine anger of the person who feels herself unbearably slighted seized Mrs Hathall. She put her hand on her daughter-in-law's shoulder to shake it. But she didn't shake it. The flesh of that neck was icy cold, and as she lifted the veil of hair, she saw a pallid cheek, swollen and bluish.

Most women would have screamed. Mrs Hathall made no sound. Her body became a little more set and cupboard-like as she drew herself upright and placed her thick large hand to her palpitating heart. Many times in her long life she had seen death, her parents', her husband's, uncles', aunts', but she had never before seen what the purplish mark on that neck showed – death by violence. No thought of triumph came to her and no fear. She felt nothing but shock. Heavily, she plodded across the room and began to descend the stairs.

Robert was waiting at the foot of them. In so far as she was capable of love, she loved him, and in going up to him and placing her hand on his arm, she addressed him in a muted reluctant voice, the nearest she could get to tenderness. And she used the only words she knew for breaking this kind of bad news.

'There's been an accident. You'd best go up and see for yourself. It's – it's too late to do anything. Try and take it like a man.'

He stood quite still. He didn't speak.

'She's gone, Robert, your wife's dead.' She repeated the words because he didn't seem to take them in. 'Angela's dead, son.'

A vague uncomfortable feeling came over her that she ought to embrace him, speak some tender word, but she had long ago forgotten how. Besides, she was shaking now and her heart was pumping irregularly. He had neither paled nor flushed. Steadily he walked past her and mounted the stairs. She waited there, impotent, awe-stricken, rubbing her hands together and hunching her shoulders. Then he called out from above in a harsh but calm voice:

'Phone the police, Mother, and tell them what's happened.'

She was glad of something to do, and finding the phone on a low table under a bookshelf, she set her finger to the nine slot in the dial.

Chapter 2

He was a tall man, carrying insufficient weight for
his wide frame. And he had an unhealthy look, his
belly sagging a little, his skin a mottled red. Though
still black, his hair was thinning and dry, and his
features were bold and harsh. He sat in an armchair,
slumped as if he had been injured and then flung
there. By contrast, his mother sat upright, her solid
legs pressed close together, her hands palm-
downwards on her lap, her hard eyes fixed on her
son with more of sternness than sympathy.

Chief Inspector Wexford thought of those Spartan
mothers who preferred seeing their sons brought
home on their shields to knowing they were taken
captive. He wouldn't have been surprised if she had
told this man to pull himself together, but she hadn't
yet uttered a word or made any sign to himself and
Inspector Burden beyond giving them a curt nod
when admitting them to the house. She looked, he
thought, like an old-style prison wardress or mistress
of a workhouse.

From upstairs the footfalls of other policemen
could be heard, passing to and fro. The woman's
body had been photographed where it lay, had been
identified by the widower and removed to the mortuary. But the men still had much to do. The house
was being examined for fingerprints, for the weapon,
for some clue as to how this girl had met her
death. And it was a big house for a cottage, with

10

five good-sized rooms apart from the kitchen and the bathroom. They had been there since eight and now it was nearly midnight.

Wexford, who stood by a table on which lay the dead woman's driving licence, purse and the other contents of her handbag, was examining her passport. It identified her as a British subject, born in Melbourne, Australia, thirty-two years old, occupation housewife, hair dark brown, eyes grey, height five feet five inches, no distinguishing marks. Angela Margaret Hathall. The passport was three years old and had never been used to pass any port. The photograph in it bore about as much resemblance to the dead woman as such photographs usually bear to their subjects.

'Your wife lived alone here during the week, Mr Hathall?' he said, moving away from the table and sitting down.

Hathall nodded. He answered in a low voice not much above a whisper. 'I used to work in Toxborough. When I got a new job in London I couldn't travel up and down. That was in July. I've been living with my mother during the week, coming home for weekends.'

'You and your mother arrived here at seven-thirty, I think?'

'Twenty past,' said Mrs Hathall, speaking for the first time. She had a harsh metallic voice. Under the South London accent lay a hint of North Country origins.

'So you hadn't seen your wife since – when? Last Sunday? Monday?'

'Sunday night,' said Hathall. 'I went to my mother's by train on Sunday night. My – Angela drove me to the station. I – I phoned her every day. I phoned her today. At lunchtime. She was all right.' He made a breath-catching sound like a sob, and his body

11

swayed forward. 'Who – who would have done this? Who would have wanted to kill – *Angela*?'

The words had a stagey ring, a false sound, as if they had been learned from some television play or cliché-ridden thriller. But Wexford knew that grief can sometimes only be expressed in platitudes. We are original in our happy moments. Sorrow has only one voice, one cry.

He answered the question in similarly hackneyed words. 'That's what we have to find out, Mr Hathall. You were at work all day?'

'Marcus Flower, Public Relations Consultants. Half Moon Street. I'm an accountant.' Hathall cleared his throat. 'You can check with them that I was there all day.'

Wexford didn't quite raise his eyebrows. He stroked his chin and looked at the man in silence. Burden's face gave nothing away, but he could tell the inspector was thinking the same thought as his own. And during this silence Hathall, who had uttered this last sentence almost with eagerness, gave a louder sob and buried his face in his hands.

Rigid as stone, Mrs Hathall said, 'Don't give way, son. Bear it like a man.'

But I must feel it like a man ... As the bit from *Macbeth* came into Wexford's mind, he wondered fleetingly why he felt so little sympathy for Hathall, why he wasn't moved. Was he getting the way he'd always sworn he wouldn't get? Was he getting hard and indifferent at last? Or was there really something false in the man's behaviour that gave the lie to these sobs and this abandonment to grief? Probably he was just tired, reading meanings where there was none; probably the woman had picked up a stranger and that stranger had killed her. He waited till Hathall had taken his hands away and raised his face.

'Your car is missing?'

'It was gone from the garage when I got home.'
There were no tears on the hard thin cheeks. Would a
son of that flint-faced woman be capable of squeez-
ing out tears?

'I'll want a description of your car and its number.
Sergeant Martin will get the details from you in a
minute.' Wexford got up. 'The doctor has given you
a sedative, I believe. I suggest you take it and try and
get some sleep. In the morning I should like to talk to
you again, but there's very little more we can do
tonight.'

Mrs Hathall shut the door on them in the manner
of one snapping 'Not today, thanks' at a couple of
hawkers. For a moment or two Wexford stood on the
path, surveying the place. Light from the bedroom
windows showed him a couple of lawns that hadn't
been mown for months and a bare plum tree. The
path was paved but the drive which ran between the
house wall and the right-hand fence was a strip of
concrete.

'Where's this garage he was talking about?'

'Must be round the back,' said Burden. 'There
wasn't room to build a garage on the side.'

They followed the drive round the back of the
cottage. It led them to an asbestos hut with a felt
roof, a building which couldn't be seen from the lane.

'If she went for a drive,' said Wexford, 'and
brought someone back with her, the chances are they
got the car into this garage without a soul seeing
them. They'd have gone into the house by the
kitchen door. We'll be lucky if we find anyone who
saw them.'

In silence they regarded the moonlit empty fields
that mounted towards wooded hills. Here and there,
in the distance, an occasional light twinkled. And as
they walked back towards the road, they were aware
of how isolated the house was, how secluded the

lane. Its high banks, crowned by massive overhanging trees, made it a black tunnel by night, a sylvan unfrequented corridor by day.

'The nearest house,' said Wexford, 'is that place up by the Stowerton Road, and the only other one is Wool Farm. That's a good half-mile down there.' He pointed through the tree tunnel and then he went off to his car. 'We can say goodbye to our weekend,' he said. 'See you first thing in the morning.'

The chief inspector's own home was to the north of Kingsmarkham on the other side of the Kingsbrook. His bedroom light was on and his wife still awake when he let himself in. Dora Wexford was too placid and too sensible to wait up for her husband, but she had been baby-sitting for her elder daughter and had only just got back. He found her sitting up in bed reading, a glass of hot milk beside her, and although he had only parted from her four hours before, he went up to her and kissed her warmly. The kiss was warmer than usual because, happy as his marriage was, contented with his lot as he was, it sometimes took external disaster to bring home to him his good fortune and how much he valued his wife. Another man's wife was dead, had died foully .... He pushed aside squeamishness, his small-hours sensitivity and, starting to undress, asked Dora what she knew of the occupants of Bury Cottage.

'Where's Bury Cottage?'

'In Wool Lane. A man called Hathall lives there. His wife was strangled this afternoon.'

Thirty years of marriage to a policeman hadn't blunted Dora Wexford's sensibilities or coarsened her speech or made her untender, but it was only natural that she could no longer react to such a statement with the average woman's horror.

'Oh, dear,' she said, and conventionally, 'How dreadful! Is it going to be straightforward?'

'Don't know yet.' Her soft calm voice steadied him as it always did. 'Have you ever come across these people?'

'The only person I've ever come across in Wool Lane is that Mrs Lake. She came to the Women's Institute a couple of times, but I think she was too busy in other directions to bother much with that. Very much a one for the men, you know.'

'You don't mean the Women's Institute black-balled her?' said Wexford in mock-horror.

'Don't be so silly, darling. We're not narrow-minded. She's a widow, after all. I can't think why she hasn't married again.'

'Maybe she's like George the Second.'

'Not a bit. She's very pretty. What *do* you mean?'

'He promised his wife on her death-bed that he wouldn't marry again but only take mistresses.' While Dora giggled, Wexford studied his figure in the glass, drawing in the muscles of his belly. In the past year he had lost three stone in weight, thanks to diet, exercise and the terror inspired in him by his doctor, and for the first time in a decade he could regard his own reflection with contentment if not with actual delight. Now he could feel that it had been worth it. The agony of going without everything he liked to eat and drink had been worth while. *Il faut souffrir pour être beau.* If only there was something one could go without, some strenuous game one could play, that would result in remedying hair loss ...

'Come to bed,' said Dora. 'If you don't stop preening yourself, I'll think you're going to take mistresses, and I'm not dead yet.'

Wexford grinned and got into bed. Quite early in his career he had taught himself not to dwell on work during the night, and work had seldom kept him awake or troubled his dreams. But as he switched off the bed lamp and cuddled up to Dora – so much easier and pleasanter now he was thin – he allowed himself a few minutes' reflection on the events of the evening. It could be a straightforward case, it very well could be. Angela Hathall had been young and probably nice to look at. She was childless, and though house-proud, must have found time hanging heavily on her hands during those lonely weekdays and lonely nights. What more likely than that she had picked up some man and brought him back to Bury Cottage? Wexford knew that a woman need not be desperate or a nymphomaniac or on the road to prostitution to do this. She need not even intend infidelity. For women's attitudes to sex, whatever the new thought may hold, are not the same as men's. And though it is broadly true that a man who will pick up an unknown woman is only 'after one thing' and broadly speaking she knows it, she will cling to the generous belief that he wants nothing but conversation and perhaps a kiss. Had this been Angela Hathall's belief? Had she picked up a man in her car, a man who wanted more than that and had strangled her because he couldn't get it? Had he killed her and left her on the bed and then made a getaway in her car?

It could be. Wexford decided he would work along these lines. Turning his thoughts to more pleasant topics, his grandchildren, his recent holiday, he was soon asleep.

Chapter 3

'Mr Hathall,' Wexford said, 'you no doubt have your own ideas as to how this sort of enquiry should be conducted. You will perhaps think my methods unorthodox, but they are my methods and I can assure you they get results. I can't conduct my investigation on circumstantial evidence alone. It's necessary for me to know as much as I can about the persons involved, so if you can answer my questions simply and realistically we shall get on a lot faster. I can assure you I shall ask them from the pure and direct motive of wanting to discover who killed your wife. If you take offence we shall be delayed. If you insist that certain matters concern only your private life and refuse to disclose them, a good deal of precious time may be lost. Do you understand that and will you be co-operative?'

This speech had been occasioned by Hathall's reaction to the first query that Wexford had put to him at nine on the Saturday morning. It had been a simple request for information as to whether Angela had been in the habit of giving lifts to strangers, but Hathall, who seemed refreshed by his night of drugged sleep, had flared at it in a burst of ill-temper.

'What right have you got to impugn my wife's moral character?'

Wexford had said quietly, 'The great majority of people who give lifts to hitch-hikers have no thought

17

in their minds beyond that of being helpful,' and then, when Hathall continued to stare at him with bitter angry eyes, he had delivered his lecture.

The widower made an impatient gesture, shrugging and throwing out his hands. 'In a case like this I should have thought you'd go on fingerprints and – well, that sort of thing. I mean, it's obvious some man got in here and . . . He must have left traces. I've read about how these things are conducted. It's a question of deduction from hairs and footmarks and – well, fingerprints.'

'I've already said I'm sure you have your own ideas as to how an enquiry should be conducted. My methods include those you have put forward. You saw for yourself how thoroughly this house was gone over last night, but we're not magicians, Mr Hathall. We can't find a fingerprint or a hair at midnight and tell you whose it is nine hours later.'

'When will you be able to?'

'That I can't say. Certainly by later today I should have some idea as to whether a stranger entered Bury Cottage yesterday afternoon.'

'A *stranger*? Of course it was a stranger. I could have told you that myself at eight o'clock last night. A pathological killer who got in here, broke in, I daresay, and – and afterwards stole my car. Have you found my car yet?'

Very smoothly and coldly, Wexford said, 'I don't know, Mr Hathall. I am not God, nor have I second sight. I haven't yet even had time to contact my officers. If you'll answer the one question I've put to you, I'll leave you for a while and go and talk to your mother.'

'My mother knows nothing whatever about it. My mother never set foot in this house till last night.'

'My question, Mr Hathall.'

'No, she wasn't in the habit of giving lifts,' Hathall

shouted, his face crimson and distorted. 'She was too shy and nervous even to make friends down here. I was the only person she could trust, and no wonder after what she'd been through. The man who got in here knew that, he knew she was always alone. You want to work on that, get to work on that one. That's my private life, as you call it. I'd only been married three years and I worshipped my wife. But I left her alone all week because I couldn't face the journey up and down and this is what it's come to. She was scared stiff of being alone here. I said it wouldn't be for much longer and to stick it for my sake. Well, it wasn't for much longer, was it?'

He threw his arm over the back of the chair and buried his face in the crook of his elbow, his body shaking. Wexford watched him thoughtfully but said no more. He made his way towards the kitchen where he found Mrs Hathall at the sink, washing breakfast dishes. There was a pair of rubber gloves on the counter but they were dry and Mrs Hathall's bare hands were immersed in the suds. She was the sort of woman, he decided, who would be masochistic about housework, would probably use a brush rather than a vacuum cleaner and aver that washing machines didn't get clothes clean. He saw that instead of an apron she wore a checked tea towel tied round her waist, and this struck him as strange. Obviously she wouldn't have brought an apron with her for a weekend visit, but surely anyone as house-proud as Angela would have possessed several? However, he made no comment on it, but said good morning and asked Mrs Hathall if she would mind answering a few questions while she worked.

'Hmm,' said Mrs Hathall. She rinsed her hands and turned round slowly to dry them on a towel which hung from a rack. 'It's no good asking me. I don't know what she got up to while he was away.'

19

'I understand your daughter-in-law was shy and lonely, kept herself to herself, as you might say.' The noise she made fascinated him. It was part choke, part grunt, with a hint of the death rattle. He assumed it was, in fact, a laugh. 'She didn't impress you in that way?'

'Erotic,' said Mrs Hathall.

'*I beg your pardon?*'

She looked at him with scorn. 'Nervy. More like hysterical.'

'Ah,' said Wexford. This particular malapropism was new to him and he savoured it. 'Why was that, I wonder? Why was she – er, neurotic?'

'I couldn't say. I only saw her once.'

But they had been married for three years . . . 'I'm not sure I understand, Mrs Hathall.'

She shifted her gaze from his face to the window, from the window to the sink, and then she picked up another cloth and began drying the dishes. Her solid board of a body, its back turned to him, was as expressive of discouragement and exclusion as a closed door. She dried every cup and glass and plate and piece of cutlery in silence, scoured the draining board, dried it, hung the cloth up with the concentration of one practising an intricate and hard-learned skill. But at last she was obliged to turn again and confront his seated patient figure.

'I've got the beds to make,' she said.

'Your daughter-in-law has been murdered, Mrs Hathall.'

'I ought to know that. I found her.'

'Yes. How was that exactly?'

'I've already said. I've told it all already.' She opened the broom cupboard, took a brush, a duster, superfluous tools unneeded in that speckless house. 'I've got work to do, if you haven't.'

'Mrs Hathall,' he said softly, 'do you realize that

you will have to appear at the inquest? You're a most important witness. You will be very closely questioned and you will *not be able* to refuse to answer then. I can understand that you have never before come into contact with the law, but I must tell you that there are serious penalties attached to obstructing the police.'

She stared at him sullenly, only a little awed. 'I should never have come here,' she muttered. 'I said I'd never set foot here and I should have stuck to it.'

'Why did you come?'

'Because my son insisted. He wanted things patched up.' She plodded to within a yard of him and stopped. Wexford was reminded of an illustration in a storybook belonging to one of his grandsons, a picture of a cabinet with arms and legs and a surly face. 'I'll tell you one thing,' she said. 'If that Angela was nervy, it was shame that did it. She was ashamed of breaking up his marriage and making him a poor man. And so she should have been, she ruined three people's lives. I'll say that at your inquest. I don't mind telling anyone that.'

'I doubt,' said Wexford, 'if you will be asked. I'm asking you about last night.'

She jerked up her head. Petulantly, she said, 'I'm sure I've nothing to hide. I'm thinking of him, having everything dragged out in the open. She was supposed to meet us at the station last night.' A dry 'Hmm' snapped off the last word.

'But she was dead, Mrs Hathall.'

Ignoring him, she went on shortly and rapidly, 'We got here and he went to look for her. He called out to her. He looked everywhere downstairs and in the garden and in the garage.'

'And upstairs?'

'He didn't go upstairs. He told me to go upstairs and take my things off. I went in their bedroom and

21

there she was. Satisfied? Ask him and see if he can tell you different.' The walking cupboard stumped out of the room and the stairs creaked as it mounted them.

Wexford went back into the room where Hathall was, not moving stealthily but not making much noise either. He had been in the kitchen for about half an hour, and perhaps Hathall believed he had already left the house, for he had made a very rapid recovery from his abandonment to grief, and was standing by the window peering closely at something on the front page of the morning paper. The expression on his lean ruddy face was one of extreme concentration, intense, even calculating, and his hands were quite steady. Wexford gave a slight cough. Hathall didn't jump. He turned round and the anguish which Wexford could have sworn was real again convulsed his face.

'I won't bother you again now, Mr Hathall. I've been thinking about this and I believe it would be much better for you to talk to me in different surroundings. Under the circumstances, these aren't perhaps the best for the sort of talk we must have. Will you come down to the police station at about three, please, and ask for me?'

Hathall nodded. He seemed relieved. 'I'm sorry I lost my temper just now.'

'That's all right. It was natural. Before you come this afternoon, would you have a look through your wife's things and tell me if you think anything is missing?'

'Yes, I'll do that. Your men won't want to go over the place any more?'

'No, all that's over.'

As soon as Wexford reached his own office in Kingsmarkham police station, he looked through the morning papers and found the one Hathall had been

22

scrutinizing, the *Daily Telegraph*. At the foot of the front page, in the stop press, was a paragraph about an inch deep which read: 'Mrs Angela Hathall, 32, was last night found dead at her home in Wool Lane, Kingsmarkham, Sussex. She had been strangled. Police are treating the case as murder.' It was this on which Hathall's eyes had been fixed with such intensity. Wexford pondered for a moment. If his wife had been found murdered, the last thing he would have wanted would be to read about it in the paper. He spoke this thought aloud as Burden came into the room, adding that it didn't do to project one's own feelings on to others, for we can't all be the same.

'Sometimes,' said Burden rather gloomily, 'I think that if everyone was like you and me the world would be a better place.'

'Arrogant devil, you are. Have we got anything from the fingerprint boys yet? Hathall's dead keen on prints. He's one of those people who labour under the misapprehension that we're like foxhounds. Show us a print or a footmark and we put our noses to the ground and follow spoor until we run down our quarry about two hours later.'

Burden snorted. He thrust a sheaf of papers under the chief inspector's nose. 'It's all here,' he said. 'I've had a look and there are points of interest, but the fox isn't going to turn up in two hours or anything like it. Whoever he is, he's far, far away, and you can tell John Peel that one.'

Grinning, Wexford said, 'No sign of that car, I suppose?'

'It'll probably turn up in Glasgow or somewhere in the middle of next week. Martin checked with that company of Hathall's, Marcus Flower. He had a word with his secretary. She's called Linda Kipling and she says Hathall was there all day yesterday.

They both came in at about ten – my God, I should be so lucky! – and apart from an hour and a half off for lunch, Hathall was there till he left at five-thirty.'

'Just because I said he'd been reading about his wife's murder in the paper, I didn't mean I thought he'd done it, you know.' Wexford patted the seat of the chair next to his own and said, 'Sit down, Mike, and tell me what's in that – that ream you've brought me. Condense it. I'll have a look at it myself later.'

The inspector sat down and put on his newly acquired glasses. They were elegant glasses with narrow black frames and they gave Burden the look of a successful barrister. With his large collection of well-tailored suits, his expertly cut fair hair and a figure that needed no dieting to keep it trim, he had never had the air of a detective – a fact which had been to his advantage. His voice was prim and precise, a little more self-conscious than usual, because he wasn't yet accustomed to the glasses which he seemed to regard as changing his whole appearance and indeed his personality.

'The first thing to note, I'd say,' he began, 'is that there weren't nearly as many prints about the house as one would expect. It was an exceptionally well-kept house, everything very clean and well polished. She must have cleaned it very thoroughly indeed because there were hardly any of Hathall's own prints. There was a clear whole handprint on the front door and prints on other doors and the banisters, but those were obviously made after he got home last night. Mrs Hathall senior's prints were on the kitchen counter, the banisters, in the back bedroom, on the bathroom taps and lavatory cistern, on the telephone and, oddly enough, on the picture rail on the landing.'

'Not oddly enough at all,' said Wexford. 'She's the sort of old battleaxe who'd feel along a picture rail to see if her daughter-in-law had dusted it. And if she hadn't, she'd probably write "slut" or something equally provocative in the dust.'

Burden adjusted his glasses, smudged them with his fingertip and rubbed impatiently at them with his shirt cuff. 'Angela's prints were on the back door, the door from the kitchen into the hall, her bedroom door and on various bottles and jars on her dressing table. But they weren't anywhere else. Apparently she wore gloves for doing her housework, and if she took off her gloves to go to the bathroom, she wiped everything afterwards.'

'Sounds bloody obsessional to me. But I suppose some women do go on like that.'

Burden, whose expression conveyed that he rather approved of women who went on like that, said, 'The only other prints in the house were those of one unknown man and one unknown woman. The man's were found only on books and on the inside of a bedroom cupboard door, not Angela's bedroom. There's one single print of this other woman. It too was a whole handprint, the right hand, very clear, showing a small L-shaped scar on the forefinger, and it was found on the edge of the bath.'

'Hmm,' said Wexford, and because the sound reminded him of Mrs Hathall, he changed it to 'Huh'. He paused thoughtfully. 'I don't suppose these prints are on record?'

'Don't know yet. Give them time.'

'No, I mustn't be like Hathall. Is there anything else?'

'Some coarse long dark hairs, three of them, on the bathroom floor. They're not Angela's. Hers were finer. Hers alone were in her hairbrush on the dressing table.'

'Man's or woman's?'

'Impossible to tell. You know how long some

25

blokes wear their hair these days.' Burden touched his own sleek crop and took off his glasses. 'We shan't get anything from the postmortem till tonight.'

'OK. We have to find that car and we have to find someone who saw her go out in it and, let's hope, someone who saw her and her pick-up come back in it – if that's the way it was. We have to find her friends. She must have had *some* friends.'

They went down in the lift and crossed the black and white checkerboard foyer. While Burden paused for a word with the station sergeant, Wexford went up to the swing doors that gave on to the steps and the courtyard. A woman was coming up those steps, walking confidently in the manner of one who has never known rejection. Wexford held the right-hand door open for her, and as she came face to face with him she stopped and looked him full in the eyes.

She wasn't young. Her age couldn't have been far short of fifty, but it was at once apparent that she was one of those rare creatures whom time cannot wither or stale or devitalize. Every fine line on her face seemed the mark of laughter and mischievous wit, but there were few of these around her large bright blue and surprisingly young eyes. She smiled at him, a smile to make a man's heart turn over, and said:

'Good morning. My name is Nancy Lake. I want to see a policeman, the top one, someone very important. Are you important?'

'I daresay I will do,' said Wexford.

She looked him over as no woman had looked him over for twenty years. The smile became musing, delicate eyebrows went up. 'I really think you might,' she said, and stepping inside, 'However, we must be serious. I've come to tell you I think I was the last person to see Angela Hathall alive.'

Chapter 4

When a pretty woman ages, a man's reaction is usually to reflect on how lovely she must once have been. This was not Nancy Lake's effect. There was something very much of the here and now about her. When with her you thought no more of her youth and her coming old age than you think of spring or Christmas when you are enjoying late summer. She was of the season in which they were, a harvest-time woman, who brought to mind grape festivals and ripened fruit and long warm nights. These thoughts came to Wexford much later. As he led her into his office, he was aware only of how extremely pleasing this diversion was in the midst of murder and recalcitrant witnesses and fingerprints and missing cars. Besides, it wasn't exactly a diversion. Happy is the man who can combine pleasure and business . . .

'What a nice room,' she said. Her voice was low and sweet and lively. 'I thought police stations were brown and murky with photographs on the walls of great brutes all wanted for robbing banks.' She glanced with warm approval at his carpet, his yellow chairs, his rosewood desk. 'This is lovely. And what a nice view over all those delicious little roofs. May I sit down?'

Wexford was already holding the chair for her. He was recalling what Dora had said about this woman being 'very much for the men' and added to this statement one of his own: that the men would be very much for her. She was dark. Her hair was abundant and of a rich chestnut brown, probably dyed. But her skin had kept a rose and amber glow, the texture of a peach, and a delicate light seemed to shine from beneath its surface as is sometimes seen in the faces of young girls or children, but which is rarely retained into middle age. The red lips seemed always on the edge of a smile. It was as if she knew some delightful secret which she would almost, but never wholly, divulge. Her dress was just what, in Wexford's opinion, a woman's dress should be, full in the skirt, tight in the waist, of mauve and blue printed cotton, its low neck showing an inch or two of the upper slopes of a full golden bosom. She saw that he was studying her and she seemed to enjoy his scrutiny, basking in it, understanding more thoroughly than he himself what it meant.

He shifted his gaze abruptly. 'You live in the house at the Kingsmarkham end of Wool Lane, I believe?'

'It's called Sunnybank. I always think that sounds like a mental hospital. But my late husband chose the name and I expect he had his reasons.'

Wexford made a determined and eventually successful attempt to look grave. 'Were you a friend of Mrs Hathall's?'

'Oh, *no*.' He thought she was capable of saying she had no women friends, which would have displeased him, but she didn't. 'I only went there for the miracles.'

'The *what*?'

'An in-joke. I'm sorry. I meant the yellow egg plums.'

'Ah, mira*belles*.' This was the second malapropism of his day, but he decided this particular instance was a deliberate mistake. 'You went there yesterday to pick plums?'

'I always do. Every year. I used to when old Mr

28

Somerset lived there, and when the Hathalls came they said I could have them. I make them into jam.'

He had a sudden vision of Nancy Lake standing in a sunfilled kitchen, stirring a pot full of the golden fruit. He smelt the scent of it, saw her face as she dipped in a finger and brought it to those full red lips. The vision threatened to develop into a fantasy. He shook it off. 'When did you go there?'

The roughness in his voice made her eyebrows go up. 'I phoned Angela at nine in the morning and asked if I could go up there and pick them. I'd noticed they were falling. She seemed quite pleased – for her. She wasn't a very gracious person, you know.'

'I don't know. I hope you'll tell me.'

She moved her hands a little, deprecatingly, casually. 'She said to come about half past twelve. I picked the plums and she gave me a cup of coffee. I think she only asked me in to show me how nice the house looked.'

'Why? Didn't it always look nice?'

'Goodness, no. Not that I care, that was her business. I'm not much for housework myself, but Angela's house was usually a bit of a pigsty. Anyway, it was a mess last March which was when I was last in it. She told me she'd cleaned it up to impress Robert's mother.'

Wexford nodded. He had to make an effort of will to continue questioning her in this impersonal way, for she exercised a spell, the magical combination of feminine niceness and strong sexuality. But the effort had to be made. 'Did she tell you she was expecting another caller, Mrs Lake?'

'No, she said she was going out in the car, but she didn't say where.' Nancy Lake leant across the desk rather earnestly, bringing her face to within a foot of his. Her perfume was fruity and warm. 'She asked

29

me in and gave me coffee, but as soon as I'd had one cup she seemed to want to get rid of me. That's what I meant by saying she only wanted to show me how nice the house looked.'

'What time did you leave?'

'Let me see. It would have been just before half past one. But I was only in the house ten minutes. The rest of the time I was picking the miracles.'

The temptation to remain close to that vital, mobile and somehow mischievous face was great, but it had to be resisted. Wexford swivelled his chair round with deliberate casualness, turning to Nancy Lake a stern and businesslike profile. 'You didn't see her leave Bury Cottage or return to it later?'

'No, I went to Myringham. I was in Myringham the whole afternoon and part of the evening.'

For the first time there was something guarded and secretive in her reply, but he made no comment. 'Tell me about Angela Hathall. What sort of person was she?'

'Brusque, tough, ungracious.' She shrugged, as if such failings in woman were beyond her comprehension. 'Perhaps that's why she and Robert got on so well together.'

'Did they? They were a happy couple?'

'Oh, very. They had no eyes for anyone else, as the saying is.' Nancy Lake gave a light laugh. 'All in all to each other, you know. They had no friends, as far as I could tell.'

'I've been given the impression she was shy and nervous.'

'Have you now? I wouldn't say that. I got the idea she was on her own so much because she liked it that way. Of course, they'd been very badly off till he got this new job. She told me they only had fifteen pounds a week to live on after all his outgoings. He was paying alimony or whatever it's called to his

30

first wife.' She paused and smiled. 'People make such messes of their lives, don't they?'

There was a hint of ruefulness in her voice as if she had experience of such messes. He turned round again, for a thought had struck him. 'May I see your right hand, Mrs Lake?'

She gave it to him without question, not laying it on the table but placing it palm-downwards in his. It was almost a lover-like gesture and one that has become typical of the beginning of a relationship between a man and a woman, this covering of hand by hand, a first approach, a show of comfort and trust. Wexford felt its warmth, observed how smooth and tended it was, noted the soft sheen of the nails and the diamond ring which encircled the middle finger. Bemused, he let it rest there a fraction too long.

'If anyone had told me,' she said, her eyes dancing, 'that I should be holding hands with a policeman this morning, I shouldn't have believed them.'

Wexford said stiffly, 'I beg your pardon,' and turned her hand over. No L-shaped scar marred the smooth surface of the tip of her forefinger, and he let the hand drop.

'Is that how you check fingerprints? Goodness, I always thought it was a much more complicated process.'

'It is.' He didn't explain. 'Did Angela Hathall have a woman in to help with the cleaning?'

'Not as far as I know. They couldn't have afforded it.' She was doing her best to conceal her delight at his discomfiture, but he saw her lips twitch and delight won. 'Can I be of any further service to you, Mr Wexford? You wouldn't care to make casts of my footprints, for instance, or take a blood sample?'

'No, thank you. That won't be necessary. But I may want to talk to you again, Mrs Lake.'

31

'I do hope you will.' She got up gracefully and took a few steps towards the window. Wexford, who was obliged to rise when she did, found himself standing close beside her. She had manoeuvred this, he knew she had, but he could only feel flattered. How many years was it since a woman had flirted with him, had wanted to be with him and enjoyed the touch of his hand? Dora had done so, of course, his wife had done so ... As he was drawing himself up, conscious of his new firm figure, he remembered his wife. He remembered that he was not only a policeman but a husband who must be mindful of his marriage vows. But Nancy Lake had laid her hand lightly on his arm, was drawing his attention to the sunshine outside, the cars in the High Street that had begun their long progress to the coast.

'Just the weather for a day by the sea, isn't it?' she said. The remark sounded wistful, like an invitation. 'What a shame you have to work on a Saturday.' What a shame work and convention and prudence prevented him from leading this woman to his car, driving her to some quiet hotel. Champagne and roses, he thought, and that hand once more reaching across a table to lie warmly in his ... 'And the winter will soon be here,' she said.

Surely she couldn't have meant it, couldn't have intended that double meaning? That the winter would soon be there for both of them, the flesh falling, the blood growing cold ... 'I mustn't keep you,' he said, his voice as icy as that coming winter.

She laughed, not at all offended, but she took her hand from his arm and walked towards the door. 'You might at least say it was good of me to come.'

'It was. Very public-spirited. Good morning, Mrs Lake.'

'Good morning, Mr Wexford. You must come to tea quite soon and I'll give you some miracle jam.'

He sent for someone to see her out. Instead of sitting down once more behind his desk, he returned to the window and looked down. And there she was, crossing the courtyard with the assurance of youth, as if the world belonged to her. It didn't occur to him that she would look back and up but she did, suddenly, as if his thoughts had communicated themselves to her and called that swift glance. She waved. Her arm went up straight and she waved her hand. They might have known each other all their lives, so warm and free and intimate was that gesture, having separated after a delightful assignation that was no less sweet because it was customary. He raised his own arm in something like a salute, and then, when she had disappeared among the crowd of Saturday shoppers, he too went down to find Burden and take him off for lunch.

The Carousel Café, opposite the police station, was always crowded at Saturday lunchtime, but at least the juke box was silent. The real noise would start when the kids came in at six. Burden was sitting at the corner table they kept permanently reserved, and when Wexford approached, the proprietor, a meek Italian, came up to him deferentially and with considerable respect.

'My special today for you, Chief Inspector. The liver and bacon I can recommend.'

'All right, Antonio, but none of your reconstituted potato, eh? And no monosodium glutamate.'

Antonio looked puzzled. 'This is not on my menu, Mr Wexford.'

'No, but it's there all right, the secret agent, the alimentary fifth column. I trust you've had no more speedy goings-on of late?'

'Thanks to you, sir, we have not.'

The reference was to an act of mischief performed

a couple of weeks before by one of Antonio's youthful part-time employees. Bored by the sobriety of the clientele, this boy had introduced into the glass tank of orange juice with its floating plastic oranges, one hundred amphetamine tablets, and the result had been a merry near-riot, a hitherto decorous businessman actually dancing on a table top. Wexford, chancing to call in and, on account of his diet, sampling the orange juice himself, had located the source of this almost Saturnalian jollity and, simultaneously, the joker. Recalling all this now, he laughed heartily.

'What's so funny?' said Burden sourly. 'Or has that Mrs Lake been cheering you up?' When Wexford stopped laughing but didn't answer, he said, 'Martin's taken a room in the church hall, a sort of enquiry post and general information pool. The public are being notified in the hope that anyone who may have seen Angela on Friday afternoon will come in and tell us about it. And if she didn't go out, there's a possibility her visitor was seen.'

'She went out,' said Wexford. 'She told Mrs Lake she was going out in the car. I wonder who the lady with the L-shaped scar is, Mike. Not Mrs Lake, and Mrs Lake says Angela didn't have a cleaner or, come to that, any friends.'

'And who's the man who fingers the inside of cupboard doors?'

The arrival of the liver and bacon and Burden's spaghetti Bolognese silenced them for a few minutes. Wexford drank his orange juice, wistfully thinking how much he would enjoy it if this tankful had been 'speeded' up and Burden were suddenly to become merry and uninhibited. But the inspector, eating fastidiously, wore the resigned look of one who has sacrificed his weekend to duty. Deep lines, stretching from nostrils to the corners of his mouth, intensified as he said:

'I was going to take my kids to the seaside.'

Wexford thought of Nancy Lake who would look well in a swimsuit, but he switched off the picture before it developed into a full-colour three-dimensional image. 'Mike, at this stage of a case we usually ask each other if we've noticed anything odd, any discrepancies or downright untruths. Have you noticed anything?'

'Can't say I have, except the lack of prints.'

'She'd spring-cleaned the place to impress the old woman, though I agree it was strange she seems to have wiped everything again before going off on her car jaunt. Mrs Lake had coffee with her at about one, but Mrs Lake's prints aren't anywhere. But there's something else that strikes me as even odder than that, the way Hathall behaved when he got into the house last night.'

Burden pushed away his empty plate, contemplated the menu, and rejecting the idea of a sweet, signalled to Antonio for coffee. 'Was it odd?' he said.

'Hathall and his wife had been married for three years. During that time the old woman had only met her daughter-in-law once, and there had evidently been considerable antagonism between them. This appears to have been something to do with Angela's having broken up Hathall's first marriage. Be that as it may – and I mean to learn more about it – Angela and her mother-in-law seem to have been at loggerheads. Yet there was a kind of *rapprochement*, the old woman had been persuaded to come for the weekend and Angela was preparing to receive her to the extent of titivating the place far beyond her normal standard. Now Angela was supposed to be meeting them at the station, but she didn't turn up. Hathall says she was shy and nervous, Mrs Lake that she was brusque and ungracious. Bearing this in mind, what conclusions would you expect Hathall to have drawn when his wife wasn't at the station?'

'That she'd got cold feet. That she was too frightened to face her mother-in-law.'

'Exactly. But what happened when he got to Bury Cottage? He couldn't find Angela. He looked for her *downstairs* and in the garden. He never went upstairs at all. And yet by then he must have suspected Angela's nervousness and concluded surely that a nervous woman takes refuge not in the garden but in her own bedroom. But instead of looking upstairs for her, *he sent his mother*, the very person he must have believed Angela to be frightened of. This shy and nervous girl to whom he is alleged to be devoted was cowering – he must have thought – in her bedroom, but instead of going up to reassure her and then bring her to confront his mother with him there to support her, he goes off to the garage. That, Mike, is very odd indeed.'

Burden nodded. 'Drink your coffee,' he said. 'You said Hathall was coming in at three. Maybe he'll give you an answer.'

Chapter 5

Although Wexford pretended to study the list of missing articles – a bracelet, a couple of rings and a gilt neck chain – Hathall had brought him, he was really observing the man himself. He had come into the office with head bowed, and now he sat silent, his hands folded in his lap. But the combination of ruddy skin and black hair gives a man an angry look. Hathall, in spite of his grief, looked angry and resentful. His hard craggy features had the appearance of being carved out of roseate granite, his hands were large and red, and even his eyes, though not bloodshot, held a red gleam. Wexford wouldn't have judged him attractive to women, yet he had had two wives. Was it perhaps that certain women, very feminine or nervous or maladjusted women, saw him as a rock to which they might cling, a stronghold where they might find shelter? Possibly that colouring of his indicated passion and tenacity and strength as well as ill-temper.

Wexford placed the list on his desk and, looking up, said, 'What do you think happened yesterday afternoon, Mr Hathall?'

'Are you asking *me* that?'

'Presumably you knew your wife better than anyone else knew her. You'd know who would be likely to call on her or be fetched home by her.'

Hathall frowned, and the frown darkened his whole face. 'I've already said, some man got into the

37

house for the purpose of robbery. He took those things on that list and when my wife interrupted him, he – he killed her. What else could it have been? It's obvious.'

'I don't think so. I believe that whoever came to your house wiped the place clean of a considerable number of fingerprints. A thief wouldn't have needed to do that. He'd have worn gloves. And although he might have struck your wife, he wouldn't have strangled her. Besides, I see here that you value the missing property at less than fifty pounds all told. True, people have been killed for less, but I doubt if any woman has ever been strangled for such a reason.'

When Wexford repeated the word 'strangled', Hathall again bowed his head. 'What alternative is there?' he muttered.

'Tell me who came to your house. What friends or acquaintances called on your wife?'

'We had no friends,' said Hathall. 'When we came here we were more or less on the breadline. You need money to make friends in a place like this. We hadn't got the money to join clubs or give dinner parties or even have people in for drinks. Angela often didn't see a soul from Sunday night till Friday night. And the friends I'd had before I married her – well, my first wife saw to it I'd lost them.' He coughed impatiently and tossed his head in the way his mother had. 'Look, I think I'd better tell you a bit about what Angela and I had been through, and then perhaps you'll see that all this talk of friends calling is arrant nonsense.'

'Perhaps you had, Mr Hathall.'

'It'll be my life history.' Hathall gave a humourless bark of laughter. It was the bitter laugh of the paranoiac. 'I started off as an office boy with a firm of accountants, Craig and Butler, of Gray's Inn Road.

Later on, when I was a clerk there, the senior partner wanted me to be articled and persuaded me to study for the Institute's exams. In the meantime I'd got married and I was buying a house in Croydon on a mortgage, so the extra money was handy.' He looked up with another aggrieved frown. 'I don't think there's ever been a time till now when I've had a reasonable amount of money to live on, and now I've got it it's no good to me.

'My first marriage wasn't happy. My mother may think it was but outsiders don't know. I got married seventeen years ago and two years later I knew I'd made a mistake. But we'd got a daughter by that time, so there wasn't anything I could do about it. I expect I'd have jogged along and made the best of it if I hadn't met Angela at an office party. When I fell in love with her and knew that – well, what I felt for her was returned, I asked my wife for a divorce. Eileen – that's my first wife's name – made hideous scenes. She brought my mother into it and she even brought Rosemary in – a kid of eleven. I can't describe what my life was like and I won't try to.'

'This was five years ago?'

'About five years ago, yes. Eventually I left home and went to live with Angela. She had a room in Earls Court and she was working at the library of the National Archaeologists' League.' Hathall, who had said he couldn't describe what his life had been like, immediately proceeded to do so. 'Eileen set about a – a campaign of persecution. She made scenes at my office and at Angela's place of work. She even came to Earls Court. I begged her for a divorce. Angela had a good job and I was doing all right. I thought I could have afforded it, whatever demands Eileen made. In the end she agreed, but by that time Butler had sacked me on account of Eileen's scenes, sacked me out of hand. It was a piece of outrageous injustice. And, to crown it all, Angela had to leave the library. She was on the verge of a nervous breakdown.

'I got a part-time job as accountant with a firm of toy manufacturers, Kidd and Co., of Toxborough, and Angela and I got a room nearby. We were on our beam ends. Angela couldn't work. The divorce judge awarded Eileen my house and custody of my daughter and a very unfairly large slice out of my very inadequate income. Then we had what looked like a piece of luck at last. Angela has a cousin down here, a man called Mark Somerset, who let us have Bury Cottage. It had been his father's, but of course there wasn't any question of its being rent-free – he didn't take his generosity that far, in spite of being a blood relation. And I can't say he ever did anything else for us. He didn't even befriend Angela, though he must have known how lonely she was.

'Things went on like this for nearly three years. We were literally living on about fifteen pounds a week. I was still paying off the mortgage on a house I haven't set foot in for four years. My mother and my first wife had poisoned my daughter's mind against me. What's the use of a judge giving you reasonable access to a child if the child refuses to come near you? I remember you said you'd want to know about my private life. Well, that was it. Nothing but harassment and persecution. Angela was the one bright spot in it and now – and now she's dead.'

Wexford, who believed that, with certain exceptions, a man only suffers chronic and acute persecution if something masochistic in his psychological make-up seeks persecution, pursed his lips. 'This man Somerset, did he ever come to Bury Cottage?'

'Never. He showed us over the place when he first offered it to us, and after that, apart from a chance meeting in the street in Myringham, we never saw him again. It was as if he'd taken an unreasonable dislike to Angela.'

So many people had disliked or resented her. She sounded, Wexford thought, as inclined to paranoia as her husband. Generally speaking, nice people are not much disliked. And a kind of widespread conspiracy of hatred against them, which Hathall seemed to infer, is never feasible.

'You say this was an unreasonable dislike, Mr Hathall. Was your mother's dislike equally unreasonable?'

'My mother is devoted to Eileen. She's old-fashioned and rigid and she was prejudiced against Angela for what she calls her taking me away from Eileen. It's complete nonsense to say that a woman can steal another woman's husband if he doesn't want to be – well, stolen.'

'They only met once, I believe. Was that meeting not a success?'

'I persuaded my mother to come to Earls Court and meet Angela. I should have known better, but I thought that when she actually got to know her she might get over the feeling she was a kind of scarlet woman. My mother took exception to Angela's clothes – she was wearing those jeans and that red shirt – and when she said something uncomplimentary about Eileen my mother walked straight out of the house.'

Hathall's face had grown even redder at the memory. Wexford said, 'So they weren't on speaking terms for the whole of your second marriage?'

'My mother refused to visit us or have us come to her. She saw me, of course. I tell you frankly, I'd have liked to cut myself off from her entirely but I felt I had a duty towards her.'

Wexford always took such assertions of virtue with a grain of salt. He couldn't help wondering if

41

old Mrs Hathall, who must have been nearly seventy, had some savings to leave.

'What brought about the idea of the reunion you planned for this weekend?'

'When I landed this job with Marcus Flower – at, incidentally, double the salary I'd been getting from Kidd's – I decided to spend my week nights at my mother's place. She lives in Balham, so it wasn't too far for me to go into Victoria. Angela and I were looking for a flat to buy in London, so it wouldn't have gone on for too long. But, as usual with me, disaster hit me. However, as I was saying, I'd spent every week night at my mother's since July and I'd had a chance to talk to her about Angela and how much I'd like them to be on good terms. It took eight weeks of persuasion, but she did at last agree to come here for a weekend. Angela was very nervous at the whole idea. Of course she was as anxious for my mother to like her as I was, but she was very apprehensive. She scrubbed the whole place from top to bottom so that my mother couldn't find any fault there. I shall never know now whether it would have worked out.'

'Now, Mr Hathall, when you got to the station last night and your wife wasn't there to meet you as had been arranged, what was your reaction?'

'I don't follow you,' said Hathall shortly.

'What did you feel? Alarmed? Annoyed? Or just disappointed?'

Hathall hesitated. 'I certainly wasn't annoyed,' he said. 'I suppose I thought it was an unfortunate start to the weekend. I assumed Angela had been too nervous to come, after all.'

'I see. And when you reached the house, what did you do?'

'I don't know what all this is leading up to, but I suppose there's some purpose behind it.' Again

Hathall gave that impatient toss of the head. 'I called out to Angela. When she didn't answer, I looked for her in the dining room and in the kitchen. She wasn't there, so I went out into the garden. Then I told my mother to go upstairs while I looked to see if the car was in the garage.'

'You thought perhaps that you on foot and your wife in the car might have missed each other?'

'I don't know what I thought. I just naturally looked everywhere for her.'

'But not upstairs, Mr Hathall?' said Wexford quietly.

'Not at first. I would have done.'

'Wasn't it likely that of all places in the house a nervous woman, afraid to meet her mother-in-law, would have been, the first was her own bedroom? But you didn't go there first, as might have been expected. You went to the garage and sent your mother upstairs.'

Hathall, who might have blustered, who might have told Wexford to state plainly what he was getting at, said instead in a rather stiff and awkward tone, 'We can't always account for our actions.'

'I disagree. I think we can if we look honestly into our motives.'

'Well, I suppose I thought if she hadn't answered my call, she couldn't be in the house. Yes, I did think that. I thought she must have set off in the car and we'd missed each other because she'd gone some other way round.'

But some other way round would have meant driving a mile down Wool Lane to its junction with the Pomfret to Myringham road, then following this road to Pomfret or Stowerton before doubling back to Kingsmarkham station, a journey of five miles at least instead of a half-mile trip. But Wexford said no more about it. Another factor in the man's behaviour had suddenly struck him, and he wanted to be alone to think about it, to work out whether it was significant or merely the result of a quirk in his character.

As Hathall rose to go, he said, 'May I ask you something now?'

'By all means.'

But Hathall seemed to hesitate, as if still to postpone some burning question or to conceal it under another of less moment. 'Have you had anything from the – well, the pathologist yet?'

'Not yet, Mr Hathall.'

The red rock face tightened. 'These fingerprints. Have you got something from them yet? Isn't there some clue there?'

'Very little, as far as we can tell.'

'It seems a slow process to me. But I know nothing about it. You'll keep me informed, will you?'

He had spoken hectoringly, like a company chairman addressing a junior executive. 'Once an arrest has been made,' said Wexford, 'you may be sure you won't be left in the dark.'

'That's all very well, but neither will any newspaper reader. I should like to know about this . . .' He bit off the sentence as if he had been tending towards an end it might have been unwise to approach. 'I should like to know about this pathologist's report.'

'I will call on you tomorrow, Mr Hathall,' said Wexford. 'In the meantime, try to keep calm and rest as much as you can.'

Hathall left the office, bowing his head as he went. Wexford couldn't escape the notion that he had bowed it to impress the young detective constable who had shown him out. Yet the man's grief seemed real. But grief, as Wexford knew, is much easier to simulate than happiness. It demands little more than a subdued voice, the occasional outburst of righteous anger, the reiteration of one's pain. A man like Hathall, who believed the world owed him a living and who suffered from a persecution complex, would have no difficulty in intensifying his normal attitude.

But why had he shown no sign of shock? Why, above all, had he never shown that stunned disbelief which is the first characteristic reaction of one whose wife or husband or child has met with a violent death? Wexford thought back over the three conversations he had had with Hathall, but he wasn't able to recall a single instance of disbelief in awful reality. And he recalled similar situations, bereaved husbands who had interrupted his questions with cries that it couldn't be true, widows who had exclaimed that it couldn't be happening to them, that it was a dream from which they must soon awaken. Disbelief temporarily crowds out grief. Sometimes whole days pass before the fact can be realized, let alone accepted. Hathall had realized and accepted at once. It seemed to Wexford, as he sat musing and awaiting the postmortem results, that he had accepted even before he let himself in at his own front door.

'So she was strangled with a gilt necklace,' said Burden. 'It must have been a pretty tough one.'

Looking up from the report, Wexford said, 'It could be the one on Hathall's list. It says here a gilt ligature. Some shreds of gilding were found embedded in her skin. No tissue from her killer found under her fingernails, so there was presumably no struggle. Time of death, between one-thirty and three-thirty. Well, we know it wasn't one-thirty because that was when Mrs Lake left her. She seems to have been a healthy woman, she wasn't pregnant, and there was no sexual assault.' He gave Burden a condensed version of what Robert Hathall had told

45

him. 'The whole thing's beginning to look peculiar now, isn't it?'

'You mean you've got it into your head that Hathall had some sort of guilty knowledge?'

'I know he didn't kill her. He couldn't have done. When she died he was at this Marcus Flower place with Linda Whatsit and God knows how many other people. And I don't see any motive there. He seems to have been fond of her, if no one else was. But why didn't he go upstairs last night, why isn't he stunned with shock, and why does he get so worked-up about fingerprints?'

'The killer must have hung around after the deed was done to wipe off prints, you know. He must have touched things in the bedroom and the other rooms, and then forgotten what he *had* touched, so that he had to do a big clean-up job to be on the safe side. Otherwise Angela's and Mrs Lake's prints would have been in the living room. Doesn't that argue a lack of premeditation?'

'Probably. And I think you're right. I don't for a moment believe Angela was so fanatical or so frightened of her mother-in-law that she polished the living room after Mrs Lake had gone as well as before she came.'

'It's a funny thing, though, that he went to all that trouble, yet still left prints on the inside of a door to a cupboard in a spare room, a cupboard that was apparently never used.'

'If he did, Mike,' said Wexford, 'if he did. I think we're going to find that those prints belong to a Mr Mark Somerset, the owner of Bury Cottage. We'll find out just where in Myringham he lives and then we'd better get over to see him.'

Chapter 6

Myringham, where the University of the South is situated, lies about fifteen miles from Kingsmarkham. It boasts a museum, a motte and bailey castle and one of the best-preserved remains of a Roman villa in Britain. And although a new centre has grown up between the university buildings and the railway station, a place of tower blocks and shopping precincts and multi-storey car parks, all this red brick and concrete has been kept well away from the old town which stands, unspoilt, on the banks of the Kingsbrook.

Here there are narrow lanes and winding by-streets that call to the mind of the visitor the paintings of Jacob Vrel. The houses are very old, some – of brown brick and worm-eaten grey-brown timber – built before the Wars of the Roses, or even, it is said, before Agincourt. Not all of them have owner-occupiers or steady tenants, for some have fallen into such disrepair, such dismal decay, that their owners cannot afford to put them in order. Squatters have taken possession of them, secure in their ancient right from police interference, safe from eviction because their 'landlords' are prevented by law from demolishing their property and by lack of money from repairing it.

But these form only a small colony of the Old Town. Mark Somerset lived in the smarter part, in one of the old houses by the river. In the days when

England was Catholic it had been a priest's house and in one of the walls of its garden was a narrow and beautiful stained-glass window, for this was also a wall of St Luke's Church. The Myringham Catholics had a new church now in the new town, and the presbytery was a modern house. But here where the brown walls clustered about the church and the mill, the fifteenth century still lingered.

There was nothing fifteenth century about Mark Somerset. An athletic-looking man in his fifties, he wore neat black jeans and a tee-shirt, and Wexford detected his age only by the lines about his bright blue eyes and the veining of his strong hands. The man's belly was flat, his chest well muscled, and he had had the good fortune to keep his hair which, having once been golden, was now silver-gilt.

'Ah, the fuzz,' he said, his smile and pleasant tone robbing the greeting of rudeness. 'I thought you'd turn up.'

'Shouldn't we have turned up, Mr Somerset?'

'Don't know. That's for you to decide. Come in, but be as quiet as you can in the hall, will you? My wife only came out of hospital this morning and she's just managed to get off to sleep.'

'Nothing serious, I hope?' said Burden fatuously – and unnecessarily, in Wexford's view.

Somerset smiled. It was a smile of sad experience, of endurance, tinged very slightly with contempt. He spoke in a near-whisper. 'She's been an invalid for years. But you haven't come to talk about that. Shall we go in here?'

The room had a beamed ceiling and panelled walls. A pair of glass doors, a later but pleasing addition, were open to a small paved garden backed by the riverside trees, and the foliage of these trees looked like black lace against the amber flare of the

48

setting sun. Beside these doors was a low table on which was a bottle of hock in an ice-bucket.

'I'm a sports coach at the university,' said Somerset. 'Saturday night's the only time I allow myself a drink. Will you have some wine?'

The two policemen accepted and Somerset fetched three glasses from a cabinet. The Liebfraumilch had the delicate quality peculiar to some kinds of hock, that of tasting like liquid flowers. It was ice-cold, scented, dry.

'This is very kind of you, Mr Somerset,' said Wexford. 'You're disarming me. I hardly like to ask you now if we may take your fingerprints.'

Somerset laughed. 'You can take my fingerprints with pleasure. I suppose you've found the prints of some unknown mystery man at Bury Cottage, have you? They're probably mine, though I haven't been in the place for three years. They can't be my father's. I had the whole place redecorated after he died.' He spread out his strong work-broadened hands with a kind of bold innocence.

'I understand you didn't get on with your cousin?'

'Well, now,' said Somerset, 'rather than let you interrogate me and probably put to me a lot of time-wasting questions, wouldn't it be better if I told you what I know about my cousin and gave you a sort of history of our relationship? Then you can ask me what you like afterwards.'

Wexford said, 'That's exactly what we want.'

'Good.' Somerset had the good teacher's succinct crisp manner. 'You wouldn't want me to have any squeamishness about not speaking ill of the dead, would you? Not that I have much ill to speak of Angela. I was sorry for her. I thought she was feeble, and I don't much care for feeble people. I first met her about five years ago. She'd come to this country from Australia and I'd never seen her before. But she

49

was my cousin all right, the daughter of my father's dead brother, so you needn't get any ideas she might have been an impostor.'

'You have been reading too many detective stories, Mr Somerset.'

'Maybe.' Somerset grinned and went on, 'She looked me up because I and my father were the only relatives she had in this country, and she was lonely in London. Or so she said. I think she was on the look-out for any pickings there might be for her. She was a greedy girl, poor Angela. She hadn't met Robert at that time. When she did she stopped coming out here and I didn't hear from her again until they were about to get married and hadn't anywhere to live. I'd written to her to tell her of my father's death – to which, by the way, she didn't reply – and she wanted to know if I'd let her and Robert have Bury Cottage.

'Well, I'd been meaning to sell it, but I couldn't get the price I wanted, so I agreed and let it to Angela and Robert for five pounds a week.'

'A very low rent, Mr Somerset,' said Wexford, interrupting him. 'You could have got at least twice that.'

Somerset shrugged. Without asking them he re-filled their glasses. 'Apparently, they were very badly off, and she was my cousin. I have some silly old-fashioned ideas about blood being thicker than water, Mr Wexford, and I can't shake them off. I didn't in the least mind letting them have the place furnished at what was little more than a nominal rent. What I did mind was when Angela sent me her electricity bill for me to pay.'

'You'd made no agreement about that, of course?'

'Of course not. I asked her to come over here and we'd talk about it. Well, she came and spun me the old sob story I'd heard from her before about their poverty, her nerves and her unhappy adolescence with her mother who wouldn't let her go to university. I suggested that if money was so tight with them she should get a job. She was a qualified librarian and she could easily have got a library job at Kingsmarkham or Stowerton. She pleaded her mental breakdown, but she seemed perfectly healthy to me. I think she was just lazy. Anyway, she flounced out of the house, telling me I was mean, and I didn't see either her or Robert again until about eighteen months ago. On that occasion they didn't see me. I was out with a friend in Pomfret and I saw Robert and Angela through the windows of a restaurant. It was a very expensive restaurant and they seemed to be doing themselves proud, so I came to the conclusion they were doing a good deal better financially.

'We actually *met* again only once more. That was last April. We ran into each other in Myringham in that monstrosity the planners are pleased to call a shopping precinct. They were loaded down with stuff they'd bought, but they seemed depressed in spite of the fact that Robert had got himself this new job. Perhaps they were only embarrassed at coming face to face with me. I never saw Angela again. She wrote to me about a month ago to say that they'd want to leave the cottage as soon as they'd got a place in London, and that that would probably be in the New Year.'

'Were they a happy couple?' Burden asked when Somerset had finished.

'Very, as far as I could tell.' Somerset got up to close the glass doors as the sunset light faded and a little wind rose. 'They had so much in common. Should I be very mean-spirited if I said that what they had in common were paranoia, greed and a general idea that the world owed them a living? I'm sorry she's dead, I'm sorry to hear of anyone dying like that, but I can't say I liked her. Men can be gauche and tough as they please, but I like a little grace in a woman, don't you? I don't want to be fanciful, but I sometimes thought Robert and Angela got on so well because they were united in graceless-ness against the world.'

'You've been very helpful, Mr Somerset,' said Wexford more as a matter of form than with sincerity. Somerset had told him much he didn't know, but had he told him anything that mattered? 'You won't take it amiss, I'm sure, if I ask you what you were doing yesterday afternoon.'

He could have sworn the man hesitated. It was as if he had already thought up how he must answer, but still had to brace himself to give that answer. 'I was here alone. I took the afternoon off to get things ready for my wife's coming home. I'm afraid I was quite alone and I didn't see anyone, so I can't give you confirmation.'

'Very well,' said Wexford. 'That can't be helped. I don't suppose you have any idea as to what friends your cousin had?'

'None at all. According to her, she had no friends. Everyone she'd ever known but Robert had been cruel to her, she said, so making friends was just to invite more cruelty.' Somerset drained his glass. 'Have some more wine?'

'No, thank you. We've taken enough of your Saturday-night ration as it is.'

Somerset gave them his pleasant frank smile. 'I'll see you to the door.'

As they came out into the hall, a querulous voice sounded from upstairs: 'Marky, Marky, where are you?'

Somerset winced, perhaps only at the ugly dimin-utive. But blood is thicker than water, and a man and

52

his wife are one. He went to the foot of the stairs, called out that he was just coming, and opened the front door. Wexford and Burden said good night quickly, for the voice from above had risen to a thin petulant wail.

In the morning Wexford returned as he had promised to Bury Cottage. He had news, some of which had only just reached him, for Robert Hathall, but he had no intention of telling the widower what he most wanted to know.

Mrs Hathall let him in and said her son was still asleep. She showed him into the living room and told him to wait there, but she offered him neither tea nor coffee. She was the kind of woman, he decided, who had probably seldom if ever in her life dispensed refreshment to anyone but members of her own family. They were a strange guarded lot, these Hathalls, whose isolationism apparently infected the people they married, for when he asked Mrs Hathall if Angela's predecessor had ever been to the cottage, she said:

'Eileen wouldn't have lowered herself. She keeps herself to herself.'

'And Rosemary, your grand-daughter?'

'Rosemary came once, and once was enough. Anyway, she's too busy with her schoolwork to go out and about.'

'Will you give me Mrs Eileen Hathall's address, please?'

Mrs Hathall's face grew as red as her son's, as red as the wrinkled skin on a turkey's neck. 'No, I won't! You've no business with Eileen. Find it out for yourself.' She banged the door on him and he was left alone.

It was the first time he had ever been alone there, so he used the waiting time to survey the room. The furniture, which he had supposed to be Angela's and had therefore credited her with taste, was in fact Somerset's, the lifelong collection perhaps of Somerset's father. It was the prettiest kind of late-Victorian with some earlier pieces, spindle-legged chairs, an elegant small oval table. By the window was a red and white Venetian glass oil-lamp that had never been converted to electricity. A glass-fronted bookcase contained, for the most part, the kind of works an old man would have collected and loved: a complete set of Kipling bound in red leather, some H. G. Wells, Gosse's *Father and Son*, a little of Ruskin and a lot of Trollope. But on the top shelf, where previously perhaps had stood an ornament, were the Hathalls' own books. There were half a dozen thrillers in paperback, two or three works of 'pop' archaeology, a couple of novels which had aroused controversy over their sexual content when they had been published, and two handsomely jacketed imposing tomes.

Wexford took down the first of these. It was a volume of colour prints of ancient Egyptian jewellery, contained scarcely any text apart from the captions beneath the pictures, and bore inside its front cover a plate which proclaimed it as the property of the library of the National Archaeologists' League. Stolen, of course, by Angela. But books, like umbrellas, pens and boxes of matches, belong in a category of objects the stealing of which is a very venial offence, and Wexford thought little of it. He replaced the book and took out the last one on the shelf. Its title was *Of Men and Angels, A Study of Ancient British Tongues*, and when he opened it he saw that it was a very learned work with chapters on the origins of Welsh, Erse, Scottish Gaelic and Cornish and their common Celtic source. Its price was nearly six pounds, and he wondered that anyone as poor as the Hathalls had claimed to have been should have spent so much on something which was surely as far above their heads as it was above his own.

He was still holding the book when Hathall came into the room. He saw the man's eyes go warily to it, then look sharply away.

'I didn't know you were a student of Celtic languages, Mr Hathall,' he said pleasantly.

'It was Angela's. I don't know where it came from, but she'd had it for ages.'

'Strange, since it was only published this year. But no matter. I thought you'd like to know that your car has been found. It had been abandoned in London, in a side street near Wood Green station. Are you familiar with the district?'

'I've never been there.' Hathall's gaze kept returning, with a kind of reluctant fascination or perhaps apprehensively, to the book Wexford still kept hold of. And for this very reason Wexford determined to keep hold of it and not to remove the finger which he had slipped at random between its pages as if to keep a place. 'When can I have it back?'

'In two or three days. When we've had a good look at it.'

'Examined it for those famous fingerprints you're always on about, I suppose?'

'Am I, Mr Hathall? I? Aren't you rather projecting on to me what you think I ought to feel?' Wexford looked blandly at him. No, he wouldn't gratify the man's curiosity, though it was hard to tell now what Hathall most longed for. A revelation of what the fingerprints had disclosed? Or for that book to be laid down casually as of no account? 'My present feeling is that you should stop worrying about investigations which only we can make. Your mind may be eased a little when I tell you your wife hadn't been sexually assaulted.' He waited for some sign of relief, but only saw those eyes with their red glint dart once more to the book. And there was no response when he said as he prepared to leave, 'Your wife died very quickly, in perhaps no more than fifteen seconds. It's possible that she scarcely knew what was happening to her.'

Getting up, he eased his finger from the pages of the book and slipped the jacket flap in where it had been. 'You won't mind if I borrow this for a few days, will you?' he said, and Hathall shrugged but still said nothing at all.

Chapter 7

The inquest took place on Tuesday morning, and a verdict was returned of murder by person or persons unknown. Afterwards, as Wexford was crossing the courtyard between the coroner's court and the police station, he saw Nancy Lake go up to Robert Hathall and his mother. She began to speak to Hathall, to condole with him perhaps or offer him a lift home to Wool Lane in her car. Hathall snapped something short and sharp at her, took his mother's arm and walked off rapidly, leaving Nancy standing there, one hand up to her lips. Wexford watched this little pantomime, which had taken place out of earshot, and was nearing the car-park exit when a car drew up alongside him and a sweet vibrant voice said:

'Are you very very busy, Chief Inspector?'

'Why do you ask, Mrs Lake?'

'Not because I have any fascinating clues to give you.' She put her hand out of the window and beckoned to him. It was a mischievous and seductive gesture. He found it irresistible and he went up to her and bent down. 'The fact is,' she said, 'that I have a table for two booked at the Peacock in Pomfret and my escort has most churlishly stood me up. Would you think it very forward of me if I asked you to lunch with me instead?'

He was staggered. There was no doubt now that this rich, pretty and entirely charming woman was making advances to him – *him!* It was forward all right, it was almost unprecedented. She looked at him calmly, the corners of her mouth tilted, her eyes shining.

But it wouldn't do. Along whatever paths of fantasy his imagination might lead him, into whatever picture galleries of erotica, it wouldn't do. Once though, when he was young and without ties or prestige or pressures, it could have been a different story. And in those days he had taken such offers or made them without much appreciation and with little awareness of their delight. Ah, to be a little bit younger and know what one knows now ... !

'But I also have a table booked for lunch,' he said, 'at the Carousel Café.'

'You won't cancel that and be my guest?'

'Mrs Lake, I am, as you said, very very busy. Would you think *me* forward if I said you would distract me from my business?'

She laughed, but it wasn't a laugh of merriment, and her eyes had ceased to dance. 'It's something, I suppose, to be a distraction,' she said. 'You make me wonder if I've ever been anything but a – distraction. Good-bye.'

He went quickly away and up in the lift to his office, wondering if he had been a fool, if such a chance would ever come to him again. He attached no special significance to her words, neither to ponder on them nor to try and interpret them, for he couldn't think of her intellectually. In his mind, her face went with him, so seductive, so hopeful, then so downcast because he had refused her invitation. He tried to thrust this image away and concentrate on what was before him, the dry and technical report on the examination of Robert Hathall's car, but it kept returning, and with it her entrancing voice, reduced now to a cajoling whisper.

Not that there was much in the report to get

excited about. The car had been found parked in a street near Alexandra Park, and the discovery had been made by a constable on the beat. It was empty but for a couple of maps and a ball-point pen on the dashboard shelf, and inside and out it had been wiped clean. The only prints were those of Robert Hathall, found on the underside of the boot and bonnet lids, and the only hairs two of Angela's on the driving seat.

He sent for Sergeant Martin, but got nothing encouraging from him. No one claiming to be a friend of Angela's had come forward, and nobody, apparently, had seen her go out or return home on Friday afternoon. Burden was out, making enquiries – for the second or third time – among the workers at Wool Farm, so Wexford went alone to the Carousel Café for a solitary lunch.

It was early, not much past midday, and the café was still half-empty. He had been sitting at his corner table for perhaps five minutes and had ordered Antonio's speciality of the day, roast lamb, when he felt a light touch that was almost a caress on his shoulder. Wexford had had too many shocks in his life to jump. He turned round slowly and said with a cool note in his voice that he didn't feel, 'This is an unexpected pleasure.'

Nancy Lake sat down opposite him. She made the place look squalid. Her cream silk suit, her chestnut silk hair, her diamonds and her smile threw into sordid relief Antonio's Woolworth cutlery and the tomato-shaped plastic sauce container.

'The mountain,' she said, 'wouldn't come to Mahomet.'

He grinned. It was pointless to pretend he wasn't delighted to see her. 'Ah, you should have seen me a year ago,' he said. 'Then I *was* a mountain. What will you eat? The roast lamb will be bad, but better than the pie.'

'I don't want to eat anything. I'll just have coffee. Aren't you flattered that I didn't come for the food?'

He was. Eyeing the heaped plate which Antonio set before him, he said, 'It's not much of a compliment, though. Coffee only for the lady, please.' Were her attractions enhanced, he asked himself, by Antonio's obvious admiration of them? She was aware of it all, he could see that, and in her awareness, her experienced acceptance of her powers, lay one of the few signs of her age.

She was silent for a few moments while he ate, and he noticed that her expression was one of rueful repose. But suddenly, as he was preparing to ask her why Robert Hathall had repulsed her so violently that morning, she looked up and said:

'I'm sad, Mr Wexford. Things aren't going well for me.'

He was very surprised. 'Do you want to tell me about it?' How strange that their intimacy had advanced so far that he could ask her that . . .

'I don't know,' she said. 'No, I don't think so. One gets conditioned into habits of secrecy and discretion, even if one doesn't personally see much point in them.'

'That's true. Or can be true in certain circumstances.' The circumstances Dora had referred to?

Yet she was on the brink of telling him. Perhaps it was only the arrival of her coffee and Antonio's admiring flutterings that deterred her. She gave a little shrug, but instead of the small-talk that he expected, she said something that astonished him. It was so surprising and so intensely spoken that he pushed away his plate and stared at her.

'Is it very wrong, d'you think, to want someone to die?'

'Not,' he said, puzzled, 'if that wish remains just a wish. Most of us wish that sometimes, and most of us, fortunately, let I dare not wait upon I would.'

'Like the poor cat in the adage?'

He was delighted that she had capped his quotation. 'Is this – er, enemy of yours connected with these habits of secrecy and discretion?'

She nodded. 'But I shouldn't have brought it up. It was silly of me. I'm very lucky really, only it gets hard sometimes, alternating between being a queen and a – distraction. I shall get my crown back, this year, next year, sometime. I shall never abdicate. Goodness, all this mystery! And you're much too clever not to have guessed what I'm on about, aren't you?' He didn't reply to that one. 'Let's change the subject,' she said.

So they changed the subject. Afterwards, when she had left him and he found himself standing, bemused, in the High Street, he could hardly have said what they had talked about, only that it had been pleasant, too pleasant, and had left him with most unpleasant feelings of guilt. But he would see her no more. If necessary, he would eat his lunch in the police canteen, he would avoid her, he would never again be alone with her, even in a restaurant. It was as if he had committed adultery, had confessed it, and been told to 'avoid the occasion'. But he had committed nothing, not even himself. He had only talked and listened.

Had what he had listened to helped him? Perhaps. All that circumlocution, those hints at an enemy, at secrecy and discretion, that had been a pointer. Hathall, he knew, would admit nothing, would have had his ego boosted by the coroner's sympathy. Yet, knowing all this, he nevertheless set off along the High Street towards Wool Lane. He had no idea that it was to be his last visit to Bury Cottage, and that,

61

although he would see Hathall again, it was to be more than a year before they exchanged another word.

Wexford had forgotten all about the book of Celtic languages, hadn't, in fact, bothered to glance at it again, but it was with a request for its immediate return that Hathall greeted him.

'I'll have it sent over to you tomorrow,' he said.

Hathall looked relieved. 'There's also the matter of my car. I need my car.'

'You can have that tomorrow as well.'

The sour old woman was evidently in the kitchen, closeted behind a shut door. She had maintained the house in the immaculate condition in which her dead daughter-in-law had left it, but the touch of an alien and tasteless hand was already apparent. On old Mr Somerset's oval table stood a vase of plastic flowers. What impulse, festive or funereal, had prompted Mrs Hathall to buy them and place them there? *Plastic* flowers, thought Wexford, in the season of mellow fruitfulness when real flowers filled the gardens and the hedgerows and the florists' shops.

Hathall didn't ask him to sit down and he didn't sit down himself. He stood with one elbow resting on the mantelpiece, his fist pressed into his hard red cheek.

'So you didn't find anything incriminating in my car?'

'I didn't say that, Mr Hathall.'

'Well, did you?'

'As a matter of fact, no. Whoever killed your wife was very clever. I don't know that I've ever come across anyone in this sort of situation who covered his tracks so expertly.' Wexford piled it on, letting a note of grudging admiration creep into his voice. Hathall listened impassively. And if gratified was too strong a word to use to describe his expression, satisfied wasn't. The fist uncurled and relaxed, and he leant back against the fireplace with something like arrogance. 'He seems to have worn gloves to drive your car,' Wexford said, 'and to have given it a wash as well, for good measure. Apparently, he wasn't seen to park the car, and no one was seen driving it on Friday. At the moment, we really have very few leads to go on.'

'Will – will you find any more?' He was eager to know, but as anxious to disguise his eagerness.

'It's early days yet, Mr Hathall. Who knows?' Perhaps it was cruel to play with the man. Does the end ever justify the means? And Wexford didn't know what end he was aiming for, or where next to grab in this game of hide-and-seek in a dark room. 'I can tell you that we found the fingerprints of a man, other than your own, in this house.'

'Are they on – what d'you call it? – record?'

'They proved to be those of Mr Mark Somerset.'

'Ah, well ...' Suddenly Hathall looked more genial than Wexford had ever seen him. Perhaps only an inhibition as to touching prevented him from stepping forward to pat the chief inspector on the back. 'I'm sorry,' he said. 'I'm not myself at the moment. I should have asked you to sit down. So the only prints you found were those of Mr Somerset, were they? Dear Cousin Mark, our tight-fisted landlord.'

'I didn't say that, Mr Hathall.'

'Well, and mine and – and Angela's, of course.'

'Of course. But apart from those, we found a whole handprint of a woman in your bathroom. It's the print of her right hand, and on the tip of the forefinger is an L-shaped scar.'

Wexford had expected a reaction. But he believed Hathall to be so well under control that he had thought that reaction would show itself only as fresh indignation. He would expostulate perhaps, ask why the police hadn't followed this evidence up, or with a shrug of impatience suggest that this was the handprint of some friend of his wife's whose existence, in his grief, he had forgotten to mention. Never had he supposed, feeling his way in the dark as he was, that his words would have had such a cataclysmic effect.

For Hathall froze where he stood. Life seemed driven out of him. It was as if he had suddenly been stricken with a pain so great that it had paralysed him or forced him to hold himself still for the protection of his heart and his whole nervous system. And yet he said nothing, he made no sound. His self-control *was* magnificent. But his body, his physical self, was triumphing over his mental processes. It was as strong an example of matter over mind as Wexford had ever seen. The shock had come to Hathall at last. The stunning, with its attendant disbelief and terror and realization of what the future must now be, which should have bludgeoned him when he first saw his wife's body, was taking effect five days later. He was pole-axed by it.

Wexford was excited but he behaved very casually. 'Perhaps you can throw some light on whose this handprint may be?'

Hathall drew in his breath. He seemed to have a very real need of oxygen. Slowly he shook his head.

'No idea at all, Mr Hathall?'

The head-shaking went on. It was robot-like, automatic, as if running on some dreadful cerebral clockwork, and Wexford had the notion that Hathall would have to take his head in both hands and grasp it to stop that slow mechanical movement.

'A clear handprint on the side of your bath. An L-shaped scar on the right forefinger. We shall, of course, take it as a lead for our main line of enquiry.'

Hathall jerked up his chin. A spasm ran through his body. He forced a thin constricted voice through stiff lips. 'On the bath, you said?'

'On the bath. I'm right, aren't I, in thinking you can guess whose it may be?'

'I haven't,' Hathall said tremulously and weakly, 'the faintest idea.' His skin had taken on a mottled pallor, but now the blood returned to it and pulsed in the veins on his forehead. The worst of the shock was over. It had been replaced by – what? Not anger, not indignation. Sorrow, Wexford thought, surprised. He was overcome at this late stage by real sorrow . . .

Wexford felt no impulse to be merciful. He said relentlessly, 'I've noticed how anxious you've been right through my enquiries to know what we've deduced from fingerprints. In fact, I've never known a bereaved husband to take quite such a keen interest in forensics. Therefore, I can't help feeling you expected a certain print to be found. If that's so and we've found it, I must tell you that you'll be obstructing this enquiry if you keep what may be vital information to yourself.'

'Don't threaten me!' Though the words were sharp, the voice that spoke them was feeble and the huffiness in the tone pathetically assumed. 'Don't think you can persecute me.'

'I should rather advise *you* to think over what I've said, and then, if you are wise, you'll make a frank disclosure to us of what I'm sure you know.'

But even as he spoke, looking into the man's miserable, shocked eyes, he knew that any such disclosure would be far from wise. For whatever alibi the man might have, whatever love for her and devotion to her he might profess, he had killed his wife. And as he left the room, making his own way out of the house, he imagined Robert Hathall collapsing into a chair, breathing shallowly, feeling his racing heart, gathering his resources for very survival.

The revelation that they had found a woman's handprint had done this to him. Therefore, he knew who that woman was. He had been anxious about fingerprints because all the time he had dreaded she might have left this evidence behind. But his reaction hadn't been that of a man who merely suspects something or fears the confirmation of a fact he has guessed at. It had been the reaction of someone who fears for his own liberty and peace, the liberty and peace too of another, and, above all, that he and that other might not now have that liberty and peace together.

Chapter 8

His discovery had driven from Wexford's mind memories of that lunchtime interlude. But when he walked into his own house soon after four they returned to him, discoloured by guilt. And if he hadn't spent that hour in Nancy Lake's company, or if it had been less enjoyable, he might not now have given Dora such a hearty kiss or asked her what he did ask her.

'How would you like to go up to London for a couple of days?'

'You mean you have to go?'

Wexford nodded.

'And you can't bear to be parted from me?' Wexford felt himself blushing. Why did she have to be so perceptive? It was almost as if she read his thoughts. But if she had been less perceptive, would he have married her? 'I'd love to, darling,' she said blandly. 'When?'

'If Howard and Denise will have us, as soon as you can pack a bag.' He grinned, knowing the quantity of clothes she would want to take with her for even two days with his fashionable niece. 'Like – ten minutes?'

'Give me an hour,' said Dora.

'OK. I'll phone Denise.'

Chief Superintendent Howard Fortune, the head of Kenbourne Vale CID, was the son of Wexford's dead sister. For years Wexford had been in awe of him, his awe mixed with envy of this nephew, so aptly named, into whose lap so many good things had fallen, apparently without effort on his part, a first-class honours degree, a house in Chelsea, marriage to a beautiful fashion model, rapid promotion until his rank far surpassed his uncle's. And these two had taken on in his eyes the hard gloss of jet-set people, entering, although he hardly knew them, into that category of rich relations who will despise us from a distance and snub us if we make overtures to them. With misgivings he had gone to stay with them to convalesce after an illness, and his misgivings had turned out to be groundless, the silly suspicions that are born only of a grudge. For Howard and Denise had been kind and hospitable and unassuming, and when he had helped Howard solve a Kenbourne Vale murder case – solved it himself, Howard said – he had felt he was vindicated and a friendship established.

Just how firm that friendship was to be had been shown by the Fortunes' enjoyment of family Christmases at Wexford's house, by the new *rapport* between uncle and nephew, and revealed itself again in the greeting the chief inspector and his wife got as their taxi brought them to the house in Teresa Street. It was just after seven and one of Denise's elaborate dinners was almost ready.

'But you've got so thin, Uncle Reg,' she said as she kissed him. 'Here was I, counting calories for you, and now it looks as if it was all labour in vain. You look quite handsome.'

'Thank you, my dear. I must confess my weight loss has removed one of my principal fears of London.'

'And what would that be?'

'That *was* that I'd get myself inside one of those automatic ticket things on the Underground – you know, the kind with the snapping jaws – and be unable to get out.'

Denise laughed and took them into the living room. Since that first visit, Wexford had got over his fear of knocking over Denise's flower arrangements and conquered his awe of her fragile china ornaments and the pastel satin upholstery he was sure he would ruin with coffee stains. The abundance of everything, the smooth-running splendours and the air of gracious living, no longer intimidated him. He could sit with ease on a chair in one of those little circles of chairs and a silk sofa that reminded him of photographs of royal palace interiors. He could laugh about the tropical central heating, or as now when it wasn't on, comment on its summer counterpart, the newly installed air conditioning.

'He reminds me,' he said, 'of that description of Scott's of the Lady Rowena's apartments. "The rich hangings shook to the night blast . . . the flame of the torches streamed sideways into the air like the unfurled pennon of a chieftain." Only, in your case, it's house plants that stream and not flames.'

They had an in-joke about their exchange of quotations, for at one time Wexford had used them to assert his intellectual equality, and Howard had replied, or so his uncle believed, to keep discreetly off the subject of their shared occupation.

'Literary chit-chat, Reg?' said Howard, smiling.

'To break the ice only – and you'll get real ice on your flower vases if you keep that going, Denise. No, I want to talk to you about why I've come up here, but that'll keep till after dinner.'

'And I thought you'd come up here to see me!' said Denise.

'So I have, my dear, but another young woman is interesting me a good deal more at present.'

'What's she got that I haven't got?'

Wexford took her hand and, pretending to scrutinize it, said, 'An L-shaped scar on her forefinger.'

When Wexford was in London he always hoped people would take him for a Londoner. To sustain this illusion, he took certain measures such as remaining in his seat until the tube train had actually come to a halt at his destination instead of leaping up nervously thirty seconds beforehand as is the habit of non-Londoners. And he refrained from enquiring of other passengers if the train he was in was actually going to the place announced by the confusing indicator. As a result, he had once found himself in Uxbridge instead of Harrow-on-the-Hill. But there is no easy way of getting from the western reaches of Chelsea to the West End by Tube, so Wexford boarded the number 14 bus, an old friend.

Instead of one person, Marcus Flower turned out to be two, Jason Marcus and Stephen Flower, the former looking like a long-haired and youthful Ronald Colman and the latter a short-haired and superannuated Mick Jagger. Wexford refused a cup of the black coffee they were drinking – apparently as a hangover remedy – and said he had really come to talk to Linda Kipling. Marcus and Flower went off into a double act of innuendo at this, declaring that Miss Kipling was far better worth seeing than they, that no one ever came there except to look at the girls, and then, falling simultaneously grave, said almost in unison how frightfully sorry they had been to hear of 'poor old Bob's loss' about which they had been 'absolutely cut up'.

Wexford was then conducted by Marcus through a series of offices that were strangely lush and stark at the same time, rooms where the furniture was made of steel and leather and set against extravagant velvet drapes and high-pile carpets. On the walls were abstract paintings of the splashed ketchup and copulating spiders *genre*, and on low tables magazine pornography so soft as to be gently blancmange-like in texture and kind. The secretaries, three of them, were all together in a blue velvet room, the one who had received him, a red-headed one, and Linda Kipling. Two others, said Linda, were in one case at the hairdresser's and in the other at a wedding. It was that sort of place.

She led him into an empty office where she sat down on the kind of black leather and metal bench you find in airport lounges. She had the look of a dummy in the window of a very expensive dress shop, realistic but not real, as if made of high-quality plastic. Contemplating her fingernails, which were green, she told him that Robert Hathall had phoned his wife every day at lunchtime since he had been with them, either calling her himself or asking her to put the call through for him. This she had thought 'terribly sweet', though now, of course, it was 'terribly tragic'.

'You'd say he was very happily married, would you, Miss Kipling? Talked about his wife a lot, kept her photograph on his desk, that sort of thing?'

'He did have her photograph, but Liz said it was frightfully bourgeois, doing things like that, so he put it away. I wouldn't know if he was happy. He was never very *lively*, not like Jason and Steve and some of the other blokes.'

'What was he like last Friday?'

'The same as usual. *Just* the same. I've told that to a policeman already. I don't know what's the good of saying the same thing over and over again. He was just the same as usual. He got in a bit before ten and he was in here all the morning working out the details of a sort of scheme for private hospital treatment for those of the staff who wanted it.

Insurance, you know.' Linda looked her contempt for those executives who couldn't afford to pay for their own private treatment. 'He phoned his wife a bit before one and then he went out to lunch in a pub with Jason. They weren't gone long. I know he was back here by half past two. He dictated three letters to me.' She seemed aggrieved at the memory, as if this had been an unfairly demanding task. 'And he went off at five-thirty to meet his mother and take her off to wherever he lives, somewhere in Sussex.'

'Did he ever get phone calls here from women or a woman?'

'His wife never phoned *him*.' His meaning sank in and she stared at him. She was one of those people who are so narrow and who have imaginations so limited that hints at anything unexpected in the field of sex or social conduct or the emotions throw them into fits of nervous giggles. She giggled now. 'A girl-friend, d'you mean? Nobody like that phoned him. No one ever phoned him.'

'Was he attracted by any of the girls here?'

She looked astonished and edged slightly away. 'The girls *here*?'

'Well, there are five girls here, Miss Kipling, and if the three of you I've seen are anything to go by, you're not exactly repulsive. Did Mr Hathall have a special friendship with any girl here?'

The green fingernails fluttered. 'Do you mean a relationship? D'you mean, was he *sleeping* with anyone?'

'If you like to put it that way. After all, he was a lonely man, temporarily separated from his wife. I suppose you were all here on Friday afternoon, none of you out having her hair done or at a wedding?'

'Of course we were all here! And as to Bob Hathall having a relationship with any of us, you might care to know that June and Liz are married, Clare's

72

engaged to Jason and Suzanne is Lord Carthew's daughter.'

'Does that exempt her from sleeping with a man?'

'It exempts her from sleeping with someone of Bob Hathall's – er, kind. And that goes for all of us. We mayn't be "exactly repulsive", as you put it, but we haven't come down to that!'

Wexford said good morning to her and walked out, feeling rather sorry he had paid her even that one grudging compliment. In Piccadilly, he went into a call-box and dialled the number of Craig and Butler, Accountants, of Gray's Inn Road. Mr Butler, he was told, was at present engaged, but would be happy to see him at three o'clock that afternoon. How should he spend the intervening time? Although he had discovered Mrs Eileen Hathall's address, Croydon was too far distant to sandwich in a visit there between now and three. Why not find out a little more about Angela herself and get some background to this marriage that everyone said was happy but which had ended in murder? He leafed through the directory and found it: The National Archaeologists' League Library, 17 Trident Place, Knightsbridge SW7. Briskly, he walked up to the Tube station in Piccadilly Circus.

Trident Place wasn't easy to find. Although he had consulted his *A to Z Guide* in the privacy of the call-box, he found he had to look at it again in full view of sophisticated Londoners. As he was telling himself he was an old fool to be so self-conscious, he was rewarded by the sight of Sloane Street from which, according to the guide, Trident Place debouched.

It was a wide street of four-storey mid-Victorian houses, all smart and well kept. Number seven had a pair of heavy glass doors, framed in mahogany, through which Wexford went into a hall hung with monochrome photographs of amphorae and with portraits of gloomy-looking unearthers of the past, and thence through another door into the library itself. The atmosphere was that of all such places, utterly quiet, scholarly, redolent of books, ancient and modern. There were very few people about. A member was busy with one of the huge leather-bound catalogues, another was signing for the books he had taken out. Two girls and a young man were occupied in a quiet and studious way behind the polished oak counter, and it was one of these girls who came out and took Wexford upstairs, past more portraits, more photographs, past the sepulchrally silent reading room, to the office of the chief librarian, Miss Marie Marcovitch.

Miss Marcovitch was a little elderly woman, presumably of Central European Jewish origin. She spoke fluent academic English with a slight accent. As unlike Linda Kipling as one woman can be unlike another, she asked him to sit down and showed no surprise that he had come to question her about a murder case, although she had not at first connected the girl who used to work for her with the dead woman.

'She left here, of course, before her marriage,' said Wexford. 'How would you describe her, as tough and ungracious, or nervous and shy?'

'Well, she was quiet. I could put it like this – but, no, the poor girl is dead.' After her small hesitation, Miss Marcovitch went on hastily, 'I really don't know what I can tell you about her. She was quite ordinary.'

'I should like you to tell me everything you know.'

'A tall order, even though she *was* ordinary. She came to work here about five years ago. It's not the usual practice of the library to employ people without university degrees, but Angela was a qualified librarian and she had some knowledge of

74

archaeology. She'd no practical experience, but neither, for that matter, have I.'

The bookish atmosphere had reminded Wexford of a book he still had in his possession. 'Was she interested in Celtic languages?'

Miss Marcovitch looked surprised. 'Not that I know of.'

'Never mind. Please go on.'

'I hardly know how to go on, Chief Inspector. Angela did her work quite satisfactorily, though she was absent rather a lot on vague medical grounds. She was bad about money ...' Again Wexford noticed the hesitation. 'I mean, she couldn't manage on her salary and she used to complain that it was inadequate. I gathered she borrowed small sums from other members of the staff, but that was no business of mine.'

'I believe she worked here for some months before she met Mr Hathall?'

'I'm not at all sure when she did meet Mr Hathall. First of all she was friendly with a Mr Craig who used to be on our staff but who has since left. Indeed, all the members of our staff from that time have left except myself. I'm afraid I never met Mr Hathall.'

'But you did meet the first Mrs Hathall?'

The librarian pursed her lips and folded her small shrivelled hands in her lap. 'This seems very much like scandalmongering,' she said primly.

'So much of my work is, Miss Marcovitch.'

'Well ...' She gave a sudden unexpected smile, bright and almost naughty. 'In for a penny, in for a pound, eh? I did meet the first Mrs Hathall. I happened to be in the library itself when she came in. You'll have noticed that this is a very quiet place. Voices aren't raised and movements aren't swift, an atmosphere which suits members and staff alike. I must confess to having been very angry indeed when this woman burst into the library, rushed up to where Angela was behind the counter and began to rant and rave at her. It was impossible for members not to realize that she was reproaching Angela for what she called stealing her husband. I asked Mr Craig to get rid of the woman as quietly as he could, and then I took Angela upstairs with me. When she calmed down I told her that, although her private affairs were no business of mine, such a thing mustn't be allowed to occur again.'

'It didn't occur again?'

'No, but Angela's work began to suffer. She was the kind that goes to pieces easily under strain. I was sorry for her, but not otherwise sorry, when she said she'd have to give up her job on her doctor's advice.'

The librarian finished speaking, seemed to have said everything she had to say and was on her feet. But Wexford, instead of getting up, said in a dry voice, 'In for a pound, Miss Marcovitch?'

She coloured and gave a little embarrassed laugh. 'How perspicacious of you, Chief Inspector! Yes, there is one more thing. I suppose you noticed my hesitations. I've never told anyone about this, but – well, I will tell you.' She sat down again, and her manner became more pedantic. 'In view of the fact that the library members pay a large subscription – twenty-five pounds annually – and are by their nature careful of books, we charge no fines should they keep books beyond the allotted period of one month. Naturally, however, we don't publicize this, and many new members have been pleasantly surprised to find that, on returning books they have kept for perhaps two or three months, no charge is made.

'About three and a half years ago, a little while after Angela had left us, I happened to be helping out at the returns counter when a member handed to me three books that I saw were six weeks overdue. I should have made no comment on this had the member not produced one pound eighty, which he assured me was the proper fine for overdue books, ten pence per week per book. When I told him no fines were ever exacted in this library, he said he'd only been a member for a year and had only once before kept books longer than a month. On that occasion the "young lady" had asked him for one pound twenty, and he hadn't protested, thinking it to be reasonable.

'Of course I made enquiries among the staff who all appeared perfectly innocent, but the two girls told me that other members had recently also tried to get them to accept fines for overdue books, which they had refused and had given an explanation of our rules.'

'You think Angela Hathall was responsible?' Wexford asked.

'Who else could have been? But she had gone, no very great harm was done, and I didn't relish raising this matter at a meeting of the trustees which might have led to trouble and perhaps to a prosecution with members called as witnesses and so on. Besides, the girl had been under a strain and it was a very small fraud. I doubt if she made more than ten pounds out of it at the most.'

Chapter 9

A very small fraud ... Wexford hadn't expected to encounter fraud at all, and it was probably irrelevant. But the shadowy figure of Angela Hathall had now, like a shape looming out of fog, begun to take more definite outlines. A paranoid personality with a tendency to hypochondria; intelligent but unable to persevere at a steady job; her mental state easily overthrown by adversity; financially unstable and not above making extra money by fraudulent means. How, then, had she managed on the fifteen pounds a week which was all she and her husband had had to live on for a period of nearly three years?

He left the library and took the Tube to Chancery Lane. Craig and Butler, Accountants, had their offices on the third floor of an old building near the Royal Free Hospital. He noted the place, had a salad and orange juice lunch in a café, and at one minute to three was shown up into the office of the senior partner, William Butler. The room was as old-fashioned and nearly as quiet as the library, and Mr Butler as wizened as Miss Marcovitch. But he wore a jolly smile, the atmosphere was of business rather than scholarship, and the only portrait a highly coloured oil of an elderly man in evening dress.

'My former partner, Mr Craig,' said William Butler.

'It would be his son, I imagine, who introduced Robert and Angela Hathall?'

'His nephew. Paul Craig, the son, has been my partner since his father's retirement. It's Jonathan Craig who used to work at the archaeologists' place.'

'I believe the introduction took place at an office party here?'

The old man gave a sharp scratchy little chuckle. 'A party *here*? Where would we put the food and drink, not to mention the guests? They'd be reminded of their income tax and get gloomy and depressed. No, that party was at Mr Craig's own home in Finchley on his retirement from the firm after forty-five years.'

'You met Angela Hathall there?'

'It was the only time I did meet her. Nice-looking creature, though with a bit of that Shetland pony look so many of them have nowadays. Wearing trousers too. Personally, I think a woman should put on a skirt to go to a party. Bob Hathall was very smitten with her from the first, you could see that.'

'That can't have pleased Mr Jonathan Craig.'

Again Mr Butler gave his fiddle-string squawk. 'He wasn't serious about *her*. Got married since, as a matter of fact. His wife's nothing to look at but loaded, my dear fellow, pots of it. This Angela wouldn't have gone down at all well with the family, they're not easy-going like me. Mind you, even I took a bit of a dim view when she went up to Paul and said what a lovely job he'd got, just the thing for knowing how to fiddle one's tax. Saying that to an accountant's like telling a doctor he's lucky to be able to get hold of heroin.' And Mr Butler chortled merrily. 'I met the first Mrs Hathall too, you know,' he said. 'She was a lively one. We had quite a scene, what with her banging about trying to get to Bob, and Bob locking himself up in his office. What a voice she's got when she's roused! Another time she sat on the stairs all day waiting for Bob to come out.

He locked himself up again and never went out all night. God knows when she went home. The next day she turned up again and screamed at me to make him go back to her and their daughter. Fine set-out that was. I'll never forget it.'

'As a result,' said Wexford, 'you gave him the sack.'

'I never did! Is that what he says?'

Wexford nodded.

'God damn it! Bob Hathall always was a liar. I'll tell you what happened, and you can believe it or not, as you like. I had him in here after all that set-out and told him he'd better manage his private affairs a bit better. We had a bit of an argument and the upshot was he flew into a rage and said he was leaving. I tried to dissuade him. He'd come to us as an office boy and done all his training here. I told him that if he was getting a divorce he'd need all the money he could lay his hands on and there'd be a rise for him in the New Year. But he wouldn't listen, kept saying everyone was against him and this Angela. So he left and got himself some tin-pot part-time job, and serve him right.'

Recalling Angela's fraud and her remark to Paul Craig, and telling himself that birds of a feather flock together, Wexford asked Mr Butler if Robert Hathall had ever done anything which could be construed even mildly as on the shady side of the law. Mr Butler looked shocked.

'Certainly not. I've said he wasn't always strictly truthful, but otherwise he was honest.'

'Susceptible to women, would you say?'

William Butler gave another squawk and shook his head vehemently. 'He was fifteen when he first came here, and even in those days he was walking out with that first wife of his. They were engaged for God knows how many years. I tell you, Bob was so narrow and downright repressed, he didn't know there were other women on the face of the earth. We'd got a pretty typist in here, and for all the notice he took, she might have been a type*writer*. No, that was why he went overboard for that Angela, went daft about her like some silly romantic schoolboy. He woke up, the scales fell from his eyes. It's often the way. Those late developers are always the worst.'

'So perhaps, having awakened, he began looking around some more?'

'Perhaps he did, but I can't help you there. You thinking he might have done away with that Angela?'

'I shouldn't care to commit myself on that, Mr Butler,' said Wexford as he took his leave.

'No. Silly question, eh? I thought he was going to murder that other one, I can tell you. That's just where she had her sit-in, the step you're on now. I'll never forget it, never as long as I live.'

Howard Fortune was a tall thin man, skeletally thin in spite of his enormous appetite. He had the Wexford family's pale hair, the colour of faded brown paper, and the light grey-blue eyes, small and sharp. In spite of the difference in their figures, he had always resembled his uncle, and now that Wexford had lost so much weight, that resemblance was heightened. Sitting opposite each other in Howard's study, they might have been father and son, for, likeness apart, Wexford was now able to talk to his nephew as familiarly as he talked to Burden, and Howard to respond without the delicacy and self-conscious tact of former days.

Their wives were out. Having spent the day shopping, they had adjourned to a theatre, and uncle and nephew had eaten their dinner alone. Now, while Howard drank brandy and he contented himself with a glass of white wine, Wexford enlarged on the theory he had put forward the night before.

'As far as I see it,' he said, 'the only way to account for Hathall's horror – and it was horror, Howard – when I told him about the handprint, is that he arranged the killing of Angela with the help of a woman accomplice.'

'With whom he was having a love affair?'

'Presumably. That would be the motive.'

'A thin motive these days, isn't it? Divorce is fairly easy and there were no children to consider.'

'You've missed the point.' Wexford spoke with a sharpness that would once have been impossible. 'Even with this new job of his, he couldn't have afforded two discarded wives. He's just the sort of man who'd think himself almost justified in killing if killing was going to rid him of further persecution.'

'So this girl-friend of his came to the cottage in the afternoon . . .'

'Or was fetched by Angela.'

'I can't see that part, Reg.'

'A neighbour, a woman called Lake, says Angela told her she was going out.' Wexford sipped his drink to cover the slight confusion even the mention of Nancy Lake's name caused in him. 'I have to bear that in mind.'

'Well, maybe. The girl killed Angela by strangling her with a gilt necklace which hasn't been found, then wiped the place clean of her own prints but left one on the side of the bath. Is that the idea?'

'That's the idea. Then she drove Robert Hathall's car to London, where she abandoned it in Wood Green. I may go there tomorrow, but I haven't much hope. The chances are she lives as far from Wood Green as possible.'

'And then you'll go to this toy factory place in – what's it called? – Toxborough? I can't understand why you're leaving it till last. He worked there, after all, from the time of his marriage till last July.'

'And that's the very reason why,' said Wexford. 'It's just possible he knew this woman *before* he met Angela, or met her when his marriage was three years old. But there's no doubt he was deeply in love with Angela – everyone admits that – so is it likely he'd have begun a new relationship during the earliest part of his marriage?'

'No, I see that. Does it have to be someone he'd met at work? Why not a friend he'd met socially or the wife of a friend?'

'Because he doesn't seem to have had any friends, and that's not so difficult to understand. In his first marriage, the way I picture it, he and his wife would have been friendly with other married couples. But you know how it goes, Howard. In these cases, a married couple's friends are their neighbours or her woman friends and their husbands. Isn't it probable that at the time of the divorce all these people would have rallied round Eileen Hathall? In other words, they'd remain her friends and desert him.'

'This unknown woman could be someone he'd picked up in the street or got talking to by chance in a pub. Have you thought of that?'

'Of course. If it's so, my chances of finding her are thin.'

'Well, Wood Green for you tomorrow. I'm taking the day off myself. I have to speak at a dinner at Brighton in the evening and I thought of taking a leisurely drive down, but maybe I'll come up to darkest Ally Pally with you first.'

The phone ringing cut short Wexford's thanks at this offer. Howard picked up the receiver and his first words, spoken cordially but without much familiarity, told his uncle that the caller was someone he knew socially but not very well. Then the phone was passed to him and he heard Burden's voice.

'Good news first,' said the inspector, 'if you can call it good,' and he told Wexford that at last someone had come forward to say he had seen Hathall's car driven into the drive of Bury Cottage at five past three on the previous Friday afternoon. But he had seen only the driver whom he described as a dark-haired young woman wearing some sort of red checked shirt or blouse. That she had had a passenger he was sure, and almost sure it had been a woman, but he was able to fill in no more details. He had been cycling along Wool Lane in the direction of Wool Farm and had therefore been on the left-hand side of the road, the side which would naturally give him a view of the car's driver but not necessarily of the other occupant. The car had stopped since he had the right of way, and he had assumed, because its right-hand indicator was flashing, that it was about to turn into the cottage drive.

'Why didn't this cyclist guy come forward before?'

'He was on holiday down here, he and his bicycle,' said Burden, 'and he says he never saw a paper till today.'

'Some people,' Wexford growled, 'live like bloody chrysalises. If that's the good news, what's the bad?'

'It may not be bad, I wouldn't know. But the chief constable's been in here after you, and he wants to see you at three sharp tomorrow afternoon.'

'That puts paid to our Wood Green visit,' said Wexford thoughtfully to his nephew, and he told him what Burden had said. 'I'll have to go back and try and take in Croydon or Toxborough on my way. I shan't have time for both.'

'Look, Reg, why don't I drive you to Croydon and then to Kingsmarkham via Toxborough? I'd still have three or four hours before I need to be in Brighton.'

'Be a bit of a drag for you, won't it?'

'On the contrary. I don't mind telling you I'm very keen to take a look at this virago, the first Mrs Hathall. You come back with me and Dora can stay on. I know Denise wants her to be here on Friday for some party or other she's going to.'

And Dora, who came in ten minutes later, needed no encouragement to remain in London till the Sunday.

'But will you be all right on your own?'

'I'll be all right. I hope you will. Personally, I should think you'll perish with the cold in this bloody awful air-conditioning.'

'I have my subcutaneous fat, darling, to keep me warm.'

'Unlike you, Uncle Reg,' said Denise who, coming in, had heard the last sentence. 'All yours has melted away quite beautifully. I suppose it really *is* all diet? I was reading in a book the other day that men who have a succession of love affairs keep their figures because a man unconsciously draws in his stomach muscles every time he pays court to a new woman.'

'So now we know what to think,' said Dora.

But Wexford, who had at that moment drawn his in consciously, wasn't brought to the blush which would have been his reaction the day before. He was wondering what he was to think of his summons by the chief constable, and making a disagreeable guess at the answer.

Chapter 10

The house which Robert Hathall had bought at the time of his first marriage was one of those semi-detached villas which sprang up during the thirties in their thousands, in their tens of thousands. It had a bay window in the front living room, a gable over the front bedroom window, and a decorative wooden canopy, of the kind sometimes seen sheltering the platforms of provincial railway stations, over the front door. There were about four hundred others exactly like it in the street, a wide thoroughfare along which traffic streamed to the south.

'This house,' said Howard, 'was built for about six hundred pounds. Hathall would have paid around four thousand for it, I should think. When did he get married?'

'Seventeen years ago.'

'Four thousand would be right. And now it would fetch eighteen.'

'Only he can't sell it,' said Wexford. 'I daresay he could have done with eighteen thousand pounds.' They got out of the car and went up to the front door.

She had none of the outward signs of a virago. She was about forty, short, high-coloured, her stout stocky figure crammed into a tight green dress, and she was one of those women who have been roses and are now cabbages. Ghostly shades of the rose showed in the pretty fat-obscured features, the skin

86

which was still good, and the gingery hair that had once been blonde. She took them into the room with the bay window. Its furnishings lacked the charm of those at Bury Cottage, but it was just as clean. There was something oppressive about its neatness and the absence of any single object not totally conventional. Wexford looked in vain for some article, a hand-embroidered cushion maybe, an original drawing or a growing plant, that might express the personalities of the woman and the girl who lived here. But there was nothing, not a book, not a magazine even, no paraphernalia of a hobby. It was like a Times Furnishing window display before the shop assistant has added those touches that will give it an air of home. Apart from a framed photograph, the only picture was that reproduction of a Spanish gypsy with a black hat on her curls and a rose between her teeth, which Wexford had seen on a hundred lounge-bar walls. And even this stereotyped picture had more life about it than the rest of the room, the gypsy's mouth seeming to curl a little more disdain-fully as she surveyed the sterile surroundings in which she was doomed to spend her time.

Although it was mid-morning and Eileen Hathall had been forewarned of their coming, she offered them nothing to drink. Her mother-in-law's ways had either rubbed off on her or else her own lack of hospitality had been one of the traits which so endeared the old woman to her. But that Mrs Hathall senior had been deluded in other respects soon showed. Far from keeping 'herself to herself', Eileen was ready to be bitterly expansive about her private life.

At first, however, she was subdued. Wexford began by asking her how she had spent the previous Friday, and she replied in a quiet reasonable voice that she had been at her father's in Balham, remaining there till the evening because her daughter had been on a day trip to France, sponsored by her school, from which she hadn't returned until nearly midnight. She gave Wexford her widowed father's address which Howard, who knew London well, remarked was in the next street to where Mrs Hathall senior lived. That did it. Eileen's colour rose and her eyes smouldered with the resentment which was now perhaps the mainspring of her life.

'We grew up together, Bob and me. We went to the same school and there wasn't a day went by we didn't see each other. After we got married we were never apart for a single night till that woman came and stole him from me.'

Wexford, who held to the belief that it is impossible for an outsider to break up a secure and happy marriage, made no comment. He had often wondered too at the attitude of mind that regards people as things and marriage partners as objects which can be stolen like television sets or pearl necklaces.

'When did you last see your former husband, Mrs Hathall?'

'I haven't seen him for three and a half years.'

'But I suppose, although you have custody, he has reasonable access to Rosemary?'

Her face had grown bitter, a canker eating the blown rose. 'He was allowed to see her every other Sunday. I used to send her round to his mum and he'd fetch her from there and take her out for the day.'

'But you didn't see him yourself on these occasions?'

She looked down, perhaps to hide her humiliation. 'He said he wouldn't come if I was going to be there.'

'You said "used", Mrs Hathall. D'you mean this meeting between father and daughter has ceased?'

'Well, she's nearly grown-up, isn't she? She's old enough to have a mind of her own. Me and Bob's mum, we've always got on well, she's been like another mother to me. Rosemary could see the way we thought about it – I mean, she was old enough to understand what I'd suffered from her dad, and it's only natural she was resentful.' The virago was appearing and the tone of voice which Mr Butler had said would always remain in his memory. 'She took against him. She thought it was wicked what he'd done.'

'So she stopped seeing him?'

'She didn't *want* to see him. She said she'd got better things to do with her Sundays, we thought she was quite right. Only once she went to that cottage place and when she came back she was in an awful state, tears and sobbing and I don't know what. And I don't wonder. Can you imagine a father actually letting his little girl see him kiss another woman? That's what happened. When the time came for him to bring Rosemary back, she saw him put his arms round that woman and kiss her. And it wasn't one of your ordinary kisses. Like what you'd see on the TV, Rosemary said, but I won't go into details, though I was disgusted, I can tell you. The upshot of it was that Rosemary can't stand her dad, and I don't blame her. I just hope it won't do something to her mentality the way these psychological people say it does.'

The red flush on her skin was high now and her eyes flashed. And now, as her bosom rose and she tossed her head, she had something in common with the gypsy on the wall.

'*He* didn't like it. He begged her to see him, wrote her letters and God knows what. Sent her presents and wanted to take her away on holiday. Him as said he hadn't got a penny to bless himself with. Fought tooth and nail he did to try and stop me getting this house and a bit of his money to live on. Oh, he's got money enough when he likes to spend it, money to spend on anyone but me.'

Howard had been looking at that single framed photograph and now he asked if it was of Rosemary.

'Yes, that's my Rosemary.' Still breathless from her outpouring of invective, Eileen spoke in gasps. 'That was taken six months ago.'

The two policemen looked at the portrait of a rather plain heavy-faced girl who wore a small gold cross hanging against her blouse, whose lank dark hair fell to her shoulders, and who bore a marked resemblance to her paternal grandmother. Wexford, who felt unable to tell an outright lie and say the girl was pretty, asked what she was going to do when she left school. This was a good move, for it had a calming effect on Eileen whose bitterness gave way, though only briefly, to pride.

'Go on to college. All her teachers say she's got it in her and I wouldn't stand in her way. It's not as if she's got to go out and earn money. Bob'll have plenty to spare *now*. I've told her I don't care if she goes on training till she's twenty-five. I'm going to get Bob's mum to ask him to give Rosemary a car for her eighteenth birthday. After all, that's like being twenty-one nowadays, isn't it? My brother's been teaching her to drive and she'll take her test the minute she's seventeen. It's his duty to give her a car. Just because he's ruined my life, that's no reason why he should ruin hers, is it?'

Wexford put out his hand to her as they left. She gave him hers rather reluctantly, but her reluctance was perhaps only part and parcel of that ungraciousness which seemed to be a feature of all the Hathalls and all their connections. Staring down, he held it just long enough to make sure there was no scar on the relevant finger.

'Let us be thankful for our wives,' said Howard devoutly when they were back in the car and driving southwards. 'He didn't kill Angela to go back to that one, at any rate.'

'Did you notice she didn't once mention Angela's death? Not even to say she wasn't sorry she was dead? I've never come across a family so nourished on hatred.' Wexford thought suddenly of his own two daughters who loved him, and on whose education he had spent money freely and happily because they loved him and he loved them. 'It must be bloody awful to have to support someone you hate and buy presents for someone who's been taught to hate you,' he said.

'Indeed it must. And where did the money come from for those presents and that projected holiday, Reg? Not out of fifteen pounds a week.'

By a quarter to twelve they were in Toxborough. Wexford's appointment at Kidd's factory was for half past, so they had a quick lunch in a pub on the outskirts before finding the industrial site. The factory, a large white concrete box, was the source of those children's toys which he had often seen on television commercials and which were marketed under the name of Kidd's Kits for Kids. The manager, a Mr Aveney, told him they had three hundred workers on the payroll, most of them women with part-time jobs. Their white-collar staff was small, consisting of himself, the personnel manager, the part-time accountant, Hathall's successor, his own secretary, two typists and a switchboard girl.

'You want to know what female office staff we had here when Mr Hathall was with us. I gathered that from what you said on the phone and I've done my best to make you a list of names and addresses. But the way they change and change about is ridiculous, Chief Inspector. Girls are crazy to change their jobs every few months these days. There isn't anyone in the office now who was here when Mr Hathall was here, and he's only been gone ten weeks. Not girls, that is. The personnel manager's been with us for five years, but his office is down in the works and I don't think they ever met.'

'Can you remember if he was particularly friendly with any girl?'

'I can remember he wasn't,' said Mr Aveney. 'He was crazy about that wife of his, the one who got herself killed. I never heard a man go on about a woman the way he went on about her. She was Marilyn Monroe and the Shah-ess of Persia and the Virgin Mary all rolled in one as far as he was concerned.'

But Wexford was tired of hearing about Robert Hathall's uxoriousness. He glanced at the list, formidably long, and there were the names, the sort of names they all seemed to have these days, Junes and Janes and Susans and Lindas and Julies. They had all lived in and around Toxborough and not one of them had stayed at Kidd's more than six months. He had a horrible prevision of weeks of work while half a dozen men scoured the Home Counties for this Jane, this Julie, this Susan, and then he put the list in his briefcase.

'Your friend said he'd like to have a look round the works, so if you'd care to, we'll go down and find him.'

They found Howard in the custody of a Julie who was leading him between benches where women in overalls and with turbans round their heads were peeling the casts from plastic dolls. The factory was airy and pleasant, apart from the smell of cellulose, and from a couple of speakers came the seductive voice of Engelbert Humperdinck imploring his listeners to release him and let him love again.

'A bit of a dead loss that,' said Wexford when they had said good-bye to Mr Aveney. 'I thought it would be. Still, you'll be in plenty of time for your dinner date. It's no more than half an hour from here to Kingsmarkham. And I shall be in time to get myself promptly hauled over the coals. Would you like me to direct you round the back doubles so that we can miss the traffic and I can show you one or two points of interest?'

Howard said he would, so his uncle instructed him how to find the Myringham Road. They went through the centre of the town and past that shopping precinct whose ugliness had so offended Mark Somerset and where he had met the Hathalls on their shopping spree.

'Follow the signs for Pomfret rather than Kingsmarkham, and then I'll direct you into Kingsmarkham via Wool Lane.'

Obediently, Howard followed the signs and within ten minutes they were in country lanes. Here was unspoilt country, the soft Sussex of undulating hills topped with tree rings, of acres of fir forest and little brown-roofed farms nestling in woody hollows. The harvest was in, and where the wheat had been cut the fields were a pale blond, shining like sheets of silver gilt in the sun.

'When I'm out here,' said Howard, 'I feel the truth of what Orwell said about every man knowing in his heart that the loveliest thing to do in the world is to spend a fine day in the country. And when I'm in London I agree with Charles Lamb.'

'D'you mean preferring to see a theatre queue than all the flocks of silly sheep on Epsom Downs?'

Howard laughed and nodded. 'I take it I'm to avoid that turn that says Sewingbury?'

'You want the right turn for Kingsmarkham, coming up in about a mile. It's a little side road and eventually it becomes Wool Lane. I think Angela must have come along here in the car with her passenger last Friday. But where did she come *from*?'

Howard took the turn. They passed Wool Farm and saw the sign Wool Lane, at which the road became a narrow tunnel. If they had met another car, its driver or Howard would have had to pull right up on to the bank to allow the other's passage, but they met no cars. Motorists avoided the narrow perilous lane and few strangers took it for a through road at all.

'Bury Cottage,' Wexford said.

Howard slowed slightly. As he did so, Robert Hathall came round from the side of the house with a pair of garden shears in his hands. He didn't look up, but began chopping the heads off Michaelmas daisies. Wexford wondered if his mother had nagged him into this unaccustomed task.

'That's him,' he said. 'Did you get a look?'

'Enough to identify him again,' said Howard, 'though I don't suppose I shall have to.'

They parted at the police station. The chief constable's Rover was already parked on the forecourt. He was early for his appointment but so was Wexford. There was no need to rush up breathless and penitent, so he took his time about it, walking in almost casually to where the carpet and the coals awaited him.

'I can guess what it's about, sir. Hathall's been complaining.'

'That you can guess,' said Charles Griswold, 'only makes it worse.' He frowned and drew himself up to his full height which was a good deal more than Wexford's own six feet. The chief constable bore an uncanny likeness to the late General de Gaulle, whose initials he shared, and he must have been aware of it. A chance of nature may account for a physical resemblance to a famous man. Only knowledge of that resemblance, the continual reminders of it from friends and enemies, can account for similarities of the one personality to the other. Griswold was in the habit of speaking of Mid-Sussex, his area, in much the same tones as the dead statesman had spoken of *La France*. 'He's sent me a very strongly worded letter of complaint. Says you've been trying to trap him, using unorthodox methods. Sprang something about a fingerprint on him and then walked out of the house without waiting for his answer. Have you got any grounds for thinking he killed his wife?'

'Not with his own hands, sir. He was in his London office at the time.'

'Then what the hell are you playing at? I am proud of Mid-Sussex. My life's work has been devoted to Mid-Sussex. I was proud of the rectitude of my officers in Mid-Sussex, confident that their conduct might not only be beyond reproach but seen to be beyond reproach.' Griswold sighed heavily. In a moment, Wexford thought, he would be saying, '*L'état, c'est moi*.' 'Why are you harassing this man? Persecuting is what he calls it.'

'Persecuting,' said Wexford, 'is what he always calls it.'

'And that means?'

'He's paranoid, sir.'

'Don't give me that headshrinkers' jargon, Reg. Have you got one single piece of concrete evidence against this chap?'

'No. Only my personal and very strong feeling that he killed his wife.'

'Feeling? Feeling? We hear a damn sight too much about feelings these days and at your age you ought to bloody know better. What d'you mean then, that he had an accomplice? Have you got a *feeling* who this accomplice might be? Have you got any evidence about *him*?'

What could he say but 'No, sir, I haven't'? He added more firmly, 'May I see his letter?'

'No, you mayn't,' Griswold snapped. 'I've told you what's in it. Be thankful I'm sparing you his uncomplimentary remarks about your manners and your tactics. He says you've stolen a book of his.'

'For Christ's sake ... You don't believe that?'

'Well, no, Reg, I don't. But have it sent back to him and fast. And lay off him pronto, d'you get that?'

'Lay off him?' said Wexford aghast. 'I have to talk to him. There's no other line of investigation I can pursue.'

'I said lay off him. That's an order. I won't have any more of it. I will not have the reputation of Mid-Sussex sacrificed to your *feelings*.'

Chapter 11

It was this which marked the end of Wexford's official investigation into the death of Angela Hathall.

Later, when he looked back, he was aware that three twenty-one on the afternoon of Thursday, 2 October, was the moment when all hope of solving her murder in a straightforward above-board way died. But at the time he didn't know that. He felt only grievance and anger, and he resigned himself to the delays and irritations which must ensue if Hathall couldn't be directly pursued. He still thought ways were open to him of discovering the identity of the woman without arousing fresh annoyance in Hathall. He could delegate. Burden and Martin could make approaches of a more tactful nature. Men could be put on the trail of those girls on Aveney's list. In a roundabout way it could be done. Hathall had betrayed himself, Hathall was guilty – therefore, the crime could ultimately be brought home to Hathall.

But he was disheartened. On his way back to Kingsmarkham he had considered phoning Nancy Lake, taking advantage – to put it into plain words – of Dora's absence, but even an innocent dinner with her, envisaged now, lost the savour the prospect of it had had. He didn't get in touch with her. He didn't phone Howard. He spent the lonely weekend of a grass widower, fulminating to himself about

Hathall's good luck and about his own folly in being careless in his handling of an irritable and prickly personality.

Of Men and Angels was sent back, accompanied by a printed card on which Wexford had written a polite note regretting having kept it so long. No response came from Hathall, who must, the chief inspector thought, have been rubbing his hands with glee.

On Monday morning he went back to Kidd's factory at Toxborough.

Mr Aveney seemed pleased to see him – those who cannot be incriminated usually take a virtuous pleasure in their involvement in police enquiries – but he couldn't offer much help. 'Other women Mr Hathall might have met here?' he asked.

'I was thinking about sales reps. After all, it's children's toys you make.'

'The sales reps all work from our London office. There's only one woman among them and he never met her. What about those girls' names I gave you? No luck?'

Wexford shook his head. 'Not so far.'

'You won't. There's nothing there. That only leaves the cleaners. We've got one cleaning woman who's been here since we started up, but she's sixty-two. Of course she has a couple of girls working with her, but they're always changing like the rest of our staff. I suppose I *could* give you another list of names. I never see them and Mr Hathall wouldn't have. They've finished before we come in. The only one I can recall offhand I remember because she was so honest. She stayed behind one morning to hand me a pound note she'd found under someone's desk.'

'Don't bother with the list, Mr Aveney,' said Wexford. 'There's obviously nothing there.'

'You've got Hathall-itis,' said Burden as the second week after Angela's death came to an end.

'Sounds like bad breath.'

'I've never known you so – well, I was going to say pigheaded. You haven't got a scrap of evidence that Hathall so much as took another woman out, let alone conspired with her to do murder.'

'That handprint,' said Wexford obstinately, 'and those long dark hairs and that woman seen with Angela in the car.'

'He *thought* it was a woman. How many times have you and I seen someone across the street and not been able to make up our minds whether it was a boy or a girl? You always say the Adam's apple is the one sure distinguishing mark. Does a cyclist glancing into a car notice if the passenger's got an Adam's apple? We've followed up all the girls on that list, bar the one that's in the United States and the one who was in hospital on the nineteenth. Most of them could hardly remember who Hathall is.'

'What's your idea then? How do you account for that print on the bath?'

'I'll tell you. It was a bloke killed Angela. She was lonely and she picked him up like you said at first. He strangled her – by accident maybe – while he was trying to get the necklace off her. Why should he leave prints? Why should he touch anything in the house – except Angela? If he did, there wouldn't have been many and he could have wiped them off. The woman who left the print, she's not even involved. She was a passer-by, a motorist, who called and asked to use the phone ...'

'And the loo?'

'Why not? These things happen. A similar thing happened in my own home yesterday. My daughter was in on her own and a young fellow who'd walked from Stowerton because he couldn't hitch a lift, came and asked for a drink of water. She let him in – I had something to say about that, as you can imagine – and she let him use the bathroom too. Luckily, he was OK and no harm was done. But why shouldn't something like that have happened at Bury Cottage? The woman hasn't come forward because she doesn't even know the name of the house she called at or the name of the woman who let her in. Her prints aren't on the phone or anywhere else because Angela was still cleaning the place when she called. Isn't that more reasonable than this conspiracy idea that hasn't the slightest foundation?'

Griswold liked the theory. And Wexford found himself in charge of an enquiry based on a postulation he couldn't for a moment believe in. He was obliged to give his support to a nation-wide hue and cry aimed at locating an amnesiac female motorist and a thief who killed by chance for a valueless necklace. Neither were found, neither took more definite shape than the vague outlines Burden had invented for them, but Griswold and Burden and the newspapers talked about them as if they existed. And Robert Hathall, Wexford learned at second-hand, had made a series of helpful suggestions as to one fresh lead after another. The chief constable couldn't understand – so the grass roots had it – what had given rise to the idea that the man suffered from a persecution complex or was bad-tempered. Nothing could have been more cooperative than his attitude once Wexford was removed from direct contact with him.

Wexford thought he would soon grow sick of the whole thing. The weeks dragged on and there were no new developments. At first it is maddening to have one's certain knowledge discounted and derided. Then, as fresh interests and fresh work enter, it becomes merely annoying; lastly, a bore.

Wexford would have been very happy to have regarded Robert Hathall as a bore. After all, no one solves every murder case. Dozens have always, and always will have, eluded solution. Right should, of course, be done and justice hold sway, but the human element makes this impossible. Some must get away and Hathall was evidently going to be one of them. He ought by now to have been relegated to the ranks of the bores, for he wasn't an interesting man but essentially an irritating humourless bore. Yet Wexford couldn't think of him as such. In himself, he might be tedious but what he had done was not. Wexford wanted to know why he had done it and how and with what help and by what means. And above all he felt a righteous indignation that a man might kill his wife and bring his mother to find her body and yet be regarded by the powers-that-be as *co-operative*.

He mustn't let this thing develop into an obsession. He reminded himself that he was a reasonable, level-headed man, a policeman with a job to do, not an executioner impelled to the hunt by some political mission or holy cause. Perhaps it was those months of starving himself that had robbed him of his steadiness, his equanimity. But only a fool would gain a good figure at the price of an unbalanced mind. Reminding himself of this excellent maxim, he kept cool when Burden told him Hathall was about to give up his tenancy of Bury Cottage, and replied with sarcasm rather than explosively.

'I suppose I'm to be allowed to know where he's going?'

Burden had been considered by Griswold as having a nice line in tact and had therefore, throughout the autumn, been the link with Hathall. The Mid-Sussex envoy was what Wexford called him, adding that he imagined 'our man' in Wool Lane would be in possession of such top-level secrets.

'He's staying with his mother in Balham for the time being and he talks of getting a flat in Hampstead.'

'The vendor will cheat him,' said Wexford bitterly, 'the train service will be appalling. He'll be made to pay an extortionate rent for his garage and someone's going to put up a tower block that'll spoil his view of the Heath. All in all, he'll be very happy.'

'I don't know why you make him out such a masochist.'

'I make him out a murderer,'

'Hathall didn't murder his wife,' said Burden. 'He's just got an unfortunate manner that got in your hair.'

'An unfortunate manner! Why not be blunt about it and say he has fits? He's allergic to fingerprints. Mention you've found one on his bath and he has an epileptic seizure.'

'You'd hardly call that evidence, would you?' said Burden rather coldly, and he put on his glasses for no better reason, Wexford thought, than to peer censoriously through them at his superior officer.

But the idea of Hathall's departing and beginning the new life he had planned for himself and done murder to achieve was a disturbing one. That it had been allowed to happen was almost entirely due to his own mishandling of the investigation. He had spoilt things by being tough with and rude to the kind of man who would never respond to such treatment. And now there was nothing more he could do because Hathall's person was sacrosanct and every clue to the unknown woman's identity locked up in his sacrosanct mind. Was there any point in learning Hathall's new address? If he wasn't permitted to talk to him in Kingsmarkham, what hope had he of breaching his London privacy? For a long time personal pride stopped him asking Burden for news of Hathall, and Burden offered none until one day in spring, when they were lunching together at the Carousel. The inspector dropped Hathall's new address casually into their conversation, prefacing his remark with a 'by the by', as if he were speaking of some slight acquaintance of theirs, a man in whom neither could have more than a passing interest.

'So now he tells me,' said Wexford to the tomato-shaped sauce bottle.

'There doesn't seem to be any reason why you shouldn't know.'

'Got it okayed by the Home Secretary first, did you?'

Having the address didn't really help matters and its location meant very little to Wexford. He was prepared to drop the subject there and then, knowing as he did that discussing Hathall with Burden only made them both feel awkward. Strangely enough, it was Burden who pursued it. Perhaps he hadn't cared for that crack about the Home Secretary or, more likely, disliked the idea of the significance that might attach to his announcement if he left it islanded.

'I've always thought,' he said, 'though I haven't said so before, that there was one major drawback to your theory. If Hathall had had an accomplice with that scar on her finger, he'd have insisted she wear gloves. Because if she left only one print, he'd never be able to live with her or marry her or even see her again. And you say he killed Angela in order to do that. So he can't have. It's simple when you think about it.'

Wexford didn't say anything. He betrayed no excitement. But that night when he got home he

103

studied his map of London, made a phone call and spent some time poring over his latest bank statement.

The Fortunes had come to stay for the weekend. Uncle and nephew walked down Wool Lane and paused outside the cottage which hadn't yet been relet. The 'miracle' tree was laden with white blossom, and behind the house young lambs were pastured on the hillside whose peak was crowned by a ring of trees.

'Hathall doesn't prefer the flocks of silly sheep either,' said Wexford, recalling a conversation they had had near this spot. 'He's taken himself as far from Epsom Downs as can be, yet he's a South Londoner. West Hampstead is where he's living. Dartmeet Avenue. D'you know it?'

'I know where it is. Between the Finchley Road and West End Lane. Why did he pick Hampstead?'

'Just because it's as far as possible from South London where his mother and his ex-wife and his daughter are.' Wexford pulled down a branch of plum blossom to his face and smelt its faint honey scent. 'Or that's what I think.' The branch sprang back, scattering petals on the grass. Musingly, he said, 'He appears to lead a celibate life. The only woman he's been seen with is his mother.'

Howard seemed intrigued. 'You mean you have a – a watcher?'

'He's not much of a spy,' Wexford admitted, 'but he was the best and safest I could find. As a matter of fact, he's the brother of an old customer of mine, a chap called Monkey Matthews. The brother's name is Ginge, so-called on account of his hair. He lives in Kilburn.'

Howard laughed, but sympathetically. 'What does this Ginge do? Tail him?'

'Not exactly. But he keeps an eye. I give him a remuneration. Out of my own pocket, naturally.'

'I didn't realize you were that serious.'

'I don't know when I was ever so serious about a thing like this in my whole career.'

They turned away. A little wind had sprung up and it was growing chilly. Howard gave a backward glance at the hedge tunnel which was already greening and thickening, and said quietly, 'What is it you hope for, Reg?'

His uncle didn't reply at once. They had passed the isolated villa where Nancy Lake's car stood on the garage drive, before he spoke. He had been deep in thought, so silent and preoccupied that Howard had perhaps thought he had forgotten the question or had no answer to it. But now as they came to the Stowerton Road, he said, 'For a long time I wondered why Hathall was so horrified – and that's an understatement – when I told him about the print. Because he didn't want the woman discovered, of course. But it wasn't just fear he showed. It was something more like a terrible sorrow he showed – when he'd recovered a bit, that is. And I came to the conclusion that his reaction was what it was because he'd had Angela killed expressly so that he could be with that woman. And now he knew he'd never dare see her again.

'And then he reflected. He wrote that letter of protest to Griswold to clear the field of me because he knew I knew. But it might still be possible for him to get away with it and have what he wanted, a life with that woman. Not as he'd planned it. Not a flit to London, then after a few weeks a friendship with a girl, the lonely widower seeking consolation with a new woman friend whom, as time went by, he could marry. Not that – now. Even though he'd pulled the wool over Griswold's eyes, he wouldn't dare try that one on. The handprint had been found and however much we might seem to be ignoring him, he couldn't hope to go in for a public courtship and then marriage with a woman whose hand would betray her. Betray her to anyone, Howard, not just to an expert.'

'So what can he do?'

'He has two alternatives,' said Wexford crisply. 'He and the woman may have agreed to part. Presumably, even if one is madly in love, liberty is preferable to the indulgence of love. Yes, they could have parted.'

'"Shake hands for ever, cancel all our vows"?'

'The next bit is even more appropriate.

"And if we meet at any time again,
Be it not seen in either of our brows
That we one jot of former love retain."

'Or,' Wexford went on, 'they could have decided – let's say grandiloquently that their passion decided for them, love was bigger than both of them – to have gone on meeting clandestinely. Not to live together, never to meet in public, but to carry on as if each of them had a jealous suspicious spouse.'

'What, go on like that indefinitely?'

'Maybe. Until it wears itself out or until they find some other solution. But I think that's what they're doing, Howard. If it isn't so, why has he picked North-west London where no one knows him as a place to live? Why not south of the river where his mother is and his daughter? Or somewhere near his work. He's earning a good salary now. He could just as well have got himself a place in Central London. He's hidden himself away so that he can sneak out in the evenings to be with *her*.

'I'm going to try and find her,' Wexford said thoughtfully. 'It'll cost me some money and take up my spare time, but I mean to have a go.'

Chapter 12

In describing Ginge Matthews as not much of a spy, Wexford had rather underrated him. The miserable resources at his disposal made him bitter. He was perpetually irritated by Ginge's unwillingness to use the phone. Ginge was proud of his literary style which was culled from the witness-box manner of thick-headed and very junior police constables whose periphrasis he had overheard from the dock. In Ginge's reports his quarry never went anywhere, but always proceeded; his home was his domicile and, rather than going home, he withdrew or retired there. But in honesty and in fairness to Ginge, Wexford had to admit that, although he had learnt nothing of the elusive woman during these past months, he had learnt a good deal about Hathall's manner of life.

According to Ginge, the house where he had his flat was a big three-storeyed place and – reading between the lines – of Edwardian vintage. Hathall had no garage but left his car parked in the street. From meanness or the impossibility of finding a garage to rent? Wexford didn't know and Ginge couldn't tell him. Hathall left for work at nine in the morning and either walked or caught a bus from West End Green to West Hampstead Tube station where he took the Bakerloo Line train to (presumably) Piccadilly. He reached home again soon after six, and on several occasions Ginge, lurking in a phone box opposite number 62 Dartmeet Avenue, had seen him go out again in his car. Ginge always knew when he was at home in the evenings because then a light showed in the second floor bay window. He had never seen him accompanied by anyone except his mother – from his description it could only be old Mrs Hathall – whom he had brought to his flat by car one Saturday afternoon. Mother and son had had words, a harsh low-voiced quarrel on the pavement before they even got to the front door.

Ginge had no car. He had no job either, but the small amount of money Wexford could afford to give him didn't make it worth his while to spend more than one evening and perhaps one Saturday or Sunday afternoon a week watching Robert Hathall. It could easily have happened that Hathall brought his girl home on one or two of the other six evenings. And yet Wexford clung to hope. One day, sometime . . . He dreamed at night of Hathall, not very often, possibly once a fortnight, and in these dreams he saw him with the dark-haired girl with the scarred finger, or else alone as he had been when he had stood by the fireplace in Bury Cottage, paralysed with fear and realization and – yes, with grief.

'On the afternoon of Saturday, June 15th inst., at 3.5 p.m., the party was seen to proceed from his domicile at 62 Dartmeet Avenue to West End Lane where he made purchases at a supermarket . . .' Wexford cursed. They were nearly all like that. And what proof had he that Ginge had even been there 'on the afternoon of Saturday, June 15th inst.'? Naturally, Ginge would say he had been there when there was a quid in it for every tailing session. July came and August, and Hathall, if Ginge was to be trusted, led a simple regular life, going to work, coming home, shopping on Saturdays, sometimes taking an evening drive. If Ginge could be trusted . . .

That he could be, up to a point, was proved in September just before the anniversary of Angela's death. 'There is reason to believe', wrote Ginge, 'that the party has disposed of his motor vehicle, it having disappeared from its customary parking places. On the evening of Thursday, September 10th inst., having arrived home from his place of business at 6.10 p.m., he proceeded at 6.50 from his domicile and boarded the number 28 bus at West End Green NW6.'

Was there anything in it? Wexford didn't think so. On his salary Hathall could easily afford to run a car, but he might have got rid of it only because of the increasing difficulty of on-street parking. Still, it was a good thing from his point of view. Hathall could now be followed.

Wexford never wrote to Ginge. It was too risky. The little red-headed spy might not be above blackmail, and if any letters should fall into the hands of Griswold . . . . He sent his wages in notes in a plain envelope, and when he had to talk to him, which, on account of the paucity of news, happened rarely, he could always get him between twelve and one at a Kilburn public house called the Countess of Castlemaine.

'Follow him?' said Ginge nervously. 'What, on that bleeding 28?'

'I don't see why not. He's never seen you, has he?'

'Maybe he has. How should I know? It's not easy following a bloke on a bleeding bus.' Ginge's conversational manner was markedly different from his literary style, particularly as to his use of adjectives. 'If he goes up top, say, and I go inside, or vicey-versy . . .'

'Why does there have to be any vicey-versy?' said Wexford. 'You sit in the seat behind him and stick close. Right?'

Ginge didn't seem to think it was right at all, but he agreed rather dubiously to try it. Whether or not he had tried it, Wexford wasn't told, for Ginge's next report made no reference to buses. Yet the more he studied it with its magistrates' court circumlocutions, the more interested he was by it. 'Being in the neighbourhood of Dartmeet Avenue NW6, at 3 p.m. on the 26th inst., I took it upon myself to investigate the party's place of domicile. During a conversation with the landlord, during which I represented myself as an official of the local rating authority, I enquired as to the number of apartments and was informed that only single rooms were to let in the establishment . . .'

Rather enterprising of Ginge, was Wexford's first thought, though he had probably only assumed this role to impress his employer and hope he would forget about the more dangerous exercise of tailing Hathall on a bus. But that wasn't important. What astonished the chief inspector was that Hathall was a tenant rather than an owner-occupier and, moreover, the tenant of a room rather than a flat. Strange, very strange. He could have afforded to buy a flat on a mortgage. Why hadn't he? Because he didn't intend to be permanently domiciled (as Ginge would put it) in London? Or because he had other uses for his income? Both maybe. But Wexford seized upon this as the most peculiar circumstance he had yet discovered in Hathall's present life. Even with rents in London as extortionate as they were, he could hardly be paying more than fifteen pounds a week at the most for a room, yet, after deductions, he must be drawing sixty. Wexford had no confidant but Howard, and it was to Howard, on the phone, that he talked about it.

'You're thinking he could be supporting someone else?'

'I am,' said Wexford.

'Say fifteen a week for himself and fifteen for her on accommodation . . .? And if she's not working he has to keep her as well.'

'Christ, you don't know how good it is for me to hear someone talk about her as a real person, as "she". You believe she exists, don't you?'

'It wasn't a ghost made that print, Reg. It wasn't ectoplasm. She exists.'

In Kingsmarkham they had given up. They had stopped searching. Griswold had told the newspapers some rubbish – in Wexford's phrase – about the case not being closed, but it *was* closed. His statement was only face-saving. Mark Somerset had let Bury Cottage to a couple of young Americans, teachers of political economy at the University of the South. The front garden was tidied up and they talked of having the back garden landscaped at their own expense. One day the plums hung heavily on the tree, the next it was stripped. Wexford never found out if Nancy Lake had had them and made them into 'miracle' jam, for he had never seen Nancy since the day he was told to lay off Hathall.

Nothing came from Ginge for a fortnight. At last Wexford phoned him at the Countess of Castlemaine to be told that on his watching evenings Hathall had remained at home. He would, however, watch again that night and on the Saturday afternoon. On Monday his report came. Hathall had done his usual shopping on Saturday, but on the previous evening had walked down to the bus stop at West End Green at seven o'clock. Ginge had followed him, but being intimidated ('made cautious' was his expression) by Hathall's suspicious backward glances, hadn't pursued him on to the 28 bus which his quarry had caught at ten past seven. Wexford hurled the sheet of paper into the wastepaper basket. That was all he needed, for Hathall to get wise to Ginge.

Another week went by. Wexford was on the point of throwing Ginge's next communication away unopened. He felt he couldn't face another account of Hathall's Saturday shopping activities. But he did open the letter. And there, of couse, was the usual nonsense about the supermarket visit. There too, appended casually as if it were of no importance, a throwaway line to fill up, was a note that after his shopping Hathall had called at a travel agency.

'The place he went to is called Sudamerica Tours, Howard. Ginge didn't dare follow him in, lily-livered idiot that he is.'

Howard's voice sounded thin and dry. 'You're thinking what I'm thinking.'

'Of course. Some place where we've no extradition treaty. He's been reading about train robbers and that gave him the idea. Bloody newspapers do more harm than good.'

'But, my God, Reg, he must be dead scared if he's prepared to throw up his job and flit to Brazil or somewhere. What's he going to do there? How will he live?'

'As birds do, nephew. God knows. Look, Howard, could you do something for me? Could you get on to Marcus Flower and try and find out if they're sending him abroad? I daren't.'

'Well, I dare,' said Howard. 'But if they were, wouldn't they be arranging the whole thing and paying for it?'

'They wouldn't pay and arrange for his girl, would they?'

'I'll do my best and call you back this evening.'

Was that why Hathall had been living so economi-cally? In order to save up his accomplice's fare? He would have to have a job there waiting for him, Wexford thought, or else be very desperate to get to safety. In that case, the money for two air fares would have to be found. In the *Kingsmarkham Courier*, which had been placed on his desk that morning, he remembered seeing an advertisement for trips to Rio de Janeiro. He fished it out from under a pile of papers and looked at the back page. There it was, the return fare priced at just over three hundred and fifty pounds. Add a bit more for two single fares, and Hathall's saving could be accounted for . . .

He was about to discard the newspaper when a name in the deaths column caught his eye. Somerset. 'On October 15th, at Church House, Old Myringham, Gwendolen Mary Somerset, beloved wife of Mark Somerset. Funeral St Luke's Church October 22nd. No flowers, please, but donations to Stowerton Home for Incurables.' So the demanding and querulous wife had died at last. The *beloved* wife? Perhaps she had been, or perhaps this was the usual hypocrisy, so stale, hackneyed and automatic a formula as to be hardly hypocrisy any more. Wexford smiled drily and then forgot about it. He went home early – the town was quiet and crimeless – and waited for Howard's telephone call.

The phone rang at seven, but it was his younger daughter, Sheila. She and her mother chatted for about twenty minutes, and after that the phone didn't ring again. Wexford waited till about half past ten and then he dialled Howard's number.

'He's bloody well out,' he said crossly to his wife. 'I call that the limit.'

'Why shouldn't he go out in the evening? I'm sure he works hard enough.'

'Don't I work? I don't go gallivanting about in the evenings when I've promised to phone people.'

113

'No, and if you did perhaps your blood pressure wouldn't rage the way it's doing at this moment,' said Dora.

At eleven he tried to get Howard again, but again there was no reply and he went off to bed in a peevish frame of mind. It wasn't surprising that he had another of those obsessive Hathall dreams. He was at an airport. The great jet aircraft was ready to take off and the doors had been closed, but they opened again as he watched and there appeared at the head of the steps, like a royal couple waving graciously to the well-wishing crowd, Hathall and a woman. The woman raised her right hand in a gesture of farewell and he saw the L-shaped scar burning red, an angry cicatrice – L for love, for loss, for leave-taking. But before he could rush up the steps as he had begun to do, the stairs themselves melted away, the couple retreated, and the aircraft sailed up, up into the ice-blue winter sky.

Why is it that as you get older you tend to wake up at five and are unable to get off to sleep again? Something to do with the blood sugar level being low? Or the coming of dawn exerting an atavistic pull? Wexford knew further sleep would elude him, so he got up at half past six and made his own breakfast. He didn't like the idea of phoning Howard before eight, and by a quarter to he was so fidgety and restless that he took a cup of tea in to Dora and went off to work. By now, of course, Howard would have left for Kenbourne Vale. He began to feel bitterly injured, and those old feelings he used to have about Howard reasserted themselves. True, he had listened sympathetically to all his uncle's ramblings about this case, but what was he really thinking? That this was an elderly man's fantasy? Country bumpkin rubbish? It seemed likely that he had only played along to humour him and had deferred that call to Marcus Flower until he could spare the time from his more important metropolitan business. He probably hadn't made it yet. Still, it was no use getting paranoid in Hathall style. He must humble himself, phone Kenbourne Vale and ask again.

This he did at nine-thirty. Howard hadn't yet come in, and he found himself involved in a gossipy chat with Sergeant Clements, an old friend from days when they had worked together on the Kenbourne Vale cemetery murder. Wexford was too kind a man to cut the sergeant short after he had discovered that Howard was delayed at some top-level conference, and resigned himself to hearing all about Clements' adopted son, prospective adopted daughter, and new maisonette. A message would be left for the chief superintendent, Clements said at last, but he wasn't expected in till twelve.

The call finally came at ten past.

'I tried to get you at home before I left,' said Howard, 'but Dora said you'd gone. I haven't had a moment since, Reg.'

There was a note of barely suppressed excitement in his nephew's voice. Maybe he'd been promoted again, Wexford thought, and he said not very warmly, 'You did say you'd phone last night.'

'So I did. At seven. But your line was engaged. I couldn't after that. Denise and I went to the pictures.'

It was the tone of amusement – no, of glee – that did it. Forgetting all about rank, Wexford exploded. 'Charming,' he snapped. 'I hope the people in the row behind you chattered the whole way through and the people in front had it off on the seats and the people in the circle dropped orange peel on you. What about my chap? What about my South America thing?'

'Oh, that,' said Howard, and Wexford could have

sworn he heard a yawn. 'He's leaving Marcus Flower, he's resigned. I couldn't get any more.'

'Thanks a lot. And that's all?'

Howard was laughing now. 'Oh, Reg,' he said, 'it's wicked to keep you in suspense, but you were so ripe for it. You're such an irascible old devil, I couldn't resist.' He controlled his laughter and suddenly his voice became solemn, measured. 'That is by no means all,' he said. 'I've seen him.'

'You *what*? D'you mean you've talked to Hathall?'

'No, I've *seen* him. Not alone. With a woman. I've seen him with a woman, Reg.'

'Oh, my God,' said Wexford softly. 'The Lord hath delivered him into mine hands.'

Chapter 13

'I wouldn't be so sure of that,' said Howard. 'Not yet. But I'll tell you about it, shall I? Funny, isn't it, the way I said I didn't suppose I'd ever have to identify him? But I did identify him last night. Listen, and I'll tell you how it was.'

On the previous evening, Howard had attempted to call his uncle at seven but the line had been engaged. Since he had nothing but negative news for him, he decided to try again in the morning as he was pressed for time. He and Denise were to dine in the West End before going on to the nine o'clock showing of a film at the Curzon Cinema, and Howard had parked his car near the junction of Curzon Street and Half Moon Street. Having a few minutes to spare, he had been drawn by curiosity to have a look at the exterior of the offices he had phoned during the day, and he and Denise were approaching the Marcus Flower building when he saw a man and a woman coming towards it from the opposite direction. The man was Robert Hathall.

At the plate-glass window they paused and looked inside, surveying velvet drapery and wall-to-wall Wilton and marble staircase. Hathall seemed to be pointing out to his companion the glossy splendours of the place where he worked. The woman was of medium height, good-looking but not startlingly so, with very short blonde hair. Howard thought she was in her late twenties or early thirties.

'Could the hair have been a wig?' Wexford asked.

'No, but it could have been dyed. Naturally, I didn't see her hand. They were talking to each other in what I thought was an affectionate way and after a bit they walked off down towards Piccadilly. And, incidentally, I didn't enjoy the picture. Under the circumstances, I couldn't concentrate.'

'They haven't shaken hands for ever, Howard. They haven't cancelled all their vows. It's as I thought, and now it can only be a matter of time before we find her.'

The following day was his day of rest, his day off. The ten-thirty train from Kingsmarkham got him to Victoria just before half past eleven and by noon he was in Kilburn. What quirk of romantic imagination had prompted the naming of this squalid Victorian public house after Charles the Second's principal mistress, Wexford couldn't fathom. It stood in a turning off the Edgware Road and it had the air of a gone-to-seed nineteenth-century gin palace. Ginge Matthews was sitting on a stool at the bar in earnest and apparently aggrieved conversation with the Irish barman. When he saw Wexford his eyes widened – or, rather, one eye widened. The other was half-closed and sunk in purple swelling.

'Take your drink over to the corner,' said Wexford. 'I'll join you in a minute. May I have a glass of dry white wine, please?'

Ginge didn't look like his brother or talk like him and he certainly didn't smoke like him, but nevertheless they had something in common apart from their partiality for petty crime. Perhaps one of their parents had been possessed of a dynamic personality, or there might even have been something exceptionally vital in their genes. Whatever it was, it made Wexford say that the Matthews brothers were just like other people only more so. Both were inclined to do things to excess. Monkey smoked sixty king-sized cigarettes a day. Ginge didn't smoke at all but drank, when he could afford it, a concoction of pernod and Guinness.

Ginge hadn't spoken to Monkey for fifteen years and Monkey hadn't spoken to him. They had fallen out as the result of the bungling mess they had made of an attempt to break into a Kingsmarkham furrier's. Ginge had gone to prison and Monkey had not – most unfairly, as Ginge had reasonably thought – and when he came out, the younger brother had taken himself off to London where he had married a widow who owned her own house and a bit of money. Ginge had soon spent the money and she, perhaps in revenge, had presented him with five children. He didn't, therefore, enquire after his brother whom he blamed for many of his misfortunes, but remarked bitterly to Wexford when he joined him at a corner table:

'See my eye?'

'Of course I see it. What the hell have you done to yourself? Walked into your wife's fist?'

'Very funny. I'll tell you who done it. That bleeding Hathall. Last night when I was following him down to the 28 stop.'

'For Christ's sake!' said Wexford, aghast. 'You mean he's on to you?'

'Thanks for the sympathy.' Ginge's small round face flushed nearly as red as his hair. 'Course he was bound to spot me sooner or later on account of my bleeding hair. He hadn't got no cause to turn round and poke me in the bleeding eye, though, had he?'

'Is that what he did?'

'I'm telling you. Cut me, he did. The wife said I looked like Henry Cooper. It wasn't so bleeding funny, I can tell you.'

119

Wearily, Wexford said, 'Could you stop the bleeding?'

'It stopped in time, naturally, it did. But it isn't healed up yet and you can see the bleeding . . .'

'Oh, *God*. I mean stop saying "bleeding" every other word. It's putting me off my drink. Look, Ginge, I'm sorry about your eye, but there's no great harm done. Obviously, you'll have to be a damn sight more careful. For instance, you could try wearing a hat . . .'

'I'm not going back there again, Mr Wexford.'

'Never mind that now. Let me buy you another of those what-d'you-call-'ems. What *do* you call them?'

'You ask for a half of draught Guinness with a double pernod in.' Ginge added proudly and more cheerfully, 'I don't know what *they* call 'em but I call 'em Demon Kings.'

The stuff smelt dreadful. Wexford fetched himself another glass of white wine and Ginge said, 'You won't get very fat on that.'

'That's the idea. Now tell me where this 28 bus goes.'

Ginge took a swig of his Demon King and said with extreme rapidity, 'Golders Green, Child's Hill, Fortune Green, West End Lane, West Hampstead Station, Quex Road, Kilburn High Road . . .'

'For God's sake! I don't know any of those places, they don't mean a thing to me. Where does it end up?'

'Wandsworth Bridge.'

Disappointed at this disclosure yet pleased for once to be at an advantage in the face of so much sophisticated knowledge, Wexford said, 'He's only going to see his mother in Balham. That's near Balham.'

'Not where that bus goes isn't. Look, Mr Wexford,' said Ginge with patient indulgence, 'you don't know

London, you've said so yourself. I've lived here fifteen years and I can tell you nobody as wasn't out of his bleeding twist would go to Balham that way. He'd go to West Hampstead Tube and change on to the Northern at Waterloo or the Elephant. Stands to reason he would.'

'Then he's dropping off somewhere along the route. Ginge, will you do one more thing for me? Is there a pub near this bus stop where you've seen him catch the 28?'

'Oppo-sight,' said Ginge warily.

'We'll give him a week. If he doesn't complain about you during the next week – oh, all right, I know you think you're the one with grounds for complaint – but if he doesn't we'll know he either thinks you're a potential mugger . . .'

'Thanks very much.'

'. . . and doesn't connect you with me,' Wexford went on, ignoring the interruption, 'or else he's too scared at this stage to draw attention to himself. But, beginning next Monday, I want you to station yourself in that pub by six-thirty every night for a week. Just note how often he catches that bus. Will you do that? I don't want you to follow him and you won't be running any risk.'

'That's what you lot always say,' said Ginge. 'You want to remember he's already done some poor bleeder in. Who's going to see after my bleeding wife and kids if he gets throttling me with his bleeding gold chains?'

'The same as look after them now,' said Wexford silkily. 'The Social Security.'

'What a nasty tongue you've got.' For once Ginge sounded exactly like his brother, and briefly he looked like him as a greedy gleam appeared in his good eye. 'What's in it for me if I do?'

'A pound a day,' said Wexford, 'and as many of

those – er, bleeding Demon Kings as you can get down you.'

Wexford waited anxiously for another summons from the chief constable, but none came, and by the end of the week he knew that Hathall wasn't going to complain. That, as he had told Ginge, didn't necessarily mean any more than that Hathall thought the man who was following him intended to attack him and had taken the law into his own hands. What was certain, though, was that whatever came out of Ginge's pub observations, he couldn't use the little red-headed man again. And it wasn't going to be much use finding out how often Hathall caught that bus if he could set no one to catch it with him.

Things were very quiet in Kingsmarkham. Nobody would object if he were to take the fortnight's holiday that was owing to him. People who take their summer holidays in November are always popular with colleagues. It all depended on Ginge. If it turned out that Hathall caught that bus regularly, why shouldn't he take his holiday and try to follow that bus by car? It would be difficult in the London traffic, which always intimidated him, but not all that difficult out of the rush hours. And ten to one, a hundred to one, Hathall wouldn't spot him. Nobody on a bus looks at people in cars. Nobody on a bus can *see* the driver of a pursuing car. If only he knew when Hathall was leaving Marcus Flower and when he meant to leave the country ...

But all this was driven out of his head by an event he couldn't have anticipated. He had been certain the weapon would never be found, that it was at the bottom of the Thames or tossed on to some local authority rubbish dump. When the young teacher of political science phoned him to say that a necklace had been found by the men excavating the garden of

Bury Cottage and that her landlord, Mr Somerset, had advised her to inform the police, his first thought was that now he could overcome Griswold's scruples, now he could confront Hathall. He had himself driven down Wool Lane – observing on the way the For Sale board outside Nancy Lake's house – and then he walked into the waste land, the area of opencast mining, which had been Hathall's back garden. A load of Westmorland stone made a mountain range in one corner and a mechanical digger stood by the garage. Would Griswold say he should have had this garden dug over? When you're searching for a weapon, you don't dig up a garden that looks just like a bit of field without an exposed, freshly dug bit of earth in the whole of it. There hadn't been even a minuscule break in the long rank grass last September twelvemonth. They had raked over every inch of it. How then had Hathall or his accomplice managed to bury the necklace and restore earth and grass without its being detected?

The teacher, Mrs Snyder, told him.

'There was a kind of cavity under here. A septic pit, would you call it? I guess Mr Somerset said something about a pit.'

'A cesspit or septic tank,' said Wexford. 'The main drainage came through to this part of Kingsmarkham about twenty years ago, but before that there'd have been a cesspit.'

'For heaven's sake! Why didn't they have it taken out?' said Mrs Snyder with the wonderment of a native of a richer and more hygiene-conscious country. 'Well, this necklace was in it, whatever it's called. That thing ...' She pointed to the digger, '... smashed it open. Or so the workmen said. I didn't look personally. I don't want to seem to criticize your country, Captain, but a thing like that! A cess tank!'

Extremely amused by his new title which made

123

him feel like a naval officer, Wexford said he quite understood that primitive methods of sewage disposal weren't pleasant to contemplate, and where was the necklace?

'I washed it and put it in the kitchen closet. I washed it in antiseptic.'

That hardly mattered now. It wouldn't, after its long immersion, bear prints, if it had ever done so. But the appearance of the necklace surprised him. It wasn't, as had been believed, composed of links, but was a solid collar of grey metal from which almost all the gilding had disappeared, and it was in the shape of a snake twisted into a circle, the snake's head passing, when the necklace was fastened, through a slot above its tail. Now he could see the answer to something that had long puzzled him. This was no chain that might snap when strained but a perfect strangler's weapon. All Hathall's accomplice had had to do was stand behind her victim, grasp the snake's head and pull . . .

But how could it have got into the disused cesspit? The metal cover, for use when the pit was emptied, had been buried under a layer of earth and so overgrown with grass that Wexford's men hadn't even guessed it might be there. He phoned Mark Somerset.

'I think I can tell you how it got there,' said Somerset. 'When the main drainage came through, my father, for the sake of economy, only had what's called the "black water" linked on to it. The "grey water" – that is, the waste from the bath, the hand basin and the kitchen sink – went on passing into the cesspit. Bury Cottage is on a bit of a slope, so he knew it wouldn't flood but would just soak away.'

'D'you mean someone could have simply dropped the thing down the sink plughole?'

'I don't see why not. If "someone" ran the taps hard, it'd get washed down.'

'Thank you, Mr Somerset. That's very helpful. By the way, I'd like to – er, express my sympathy for you in the loss of your wife.'

Was it his imagination, or did Somerset sound for the first time ill-at-ease? 'Well, yes, thanks,' he muttered and he rang off abruptly.

When he had had the necklace examined by laboratory experts, he asked for an appointment with the chief constable. This was granted for the following Friday afternoon and by two o'clock on that day he was in Griswold's own house, a tarted-up, unfarm-like farmhouse in a village called Millerton between Myringham and Sewingbury. It was known as Hightrees Farm but Wexford privately called it Millerton-*Les-Deux-Eglises*.

'What makes you think this is the weapon?' were Griswold's opening words.

'I feel it's the only type of necklace which could have been used, sir. A chain would have snapped. The lab boys say the gilt which remains on it is similar to the specimens of gilding taken from Angela Hathall's neck. Of course they can't be sure.'

'But I suppose they've got a "feeling"? Have you got any reason to believe that necklace hadn't been there for twenty years?'

Wexford knew better than to mention his feelings again. 'No, but I might have if I could talk to Hathall.'

'He wasn't there when she was killed,' said Griswold, his mouth turning down and his eyes growing hard.

'His girl-friend was.'

'Where? When? I am supposed to be the chief constable of Mid-Sussex where this murder was committed. Why am I not told if the identity of some female accomplice has been discovered?'

'I haven't exactly ...'

'Reg,' said Griswold in a voice that had begun to tremble with anger, 'have you got any more evidence of Robert Hathall's complicity in this than you had fourteen months ago? Have you got one concrete piece of evidence? I asked you that before and I'm asking you again. *Have you?*'

Wexford hesitated. He couldn't reveal that he had had Hathall followed, still less that Chief Superintendent Howard Fortune, his own nephew, had seen him with a woman. What evidence of homicide lay in Hathall's economy or the sale of his car? What guilt was evinced by the man's living in North-west London or his having been seen to catch a London bus? There was the South American thing, of course ... Grimly, Wexford faced just what that amounted to. Nothing. As far as he could prove, Hathall had been offered no job in South America, hadn't even bought a brochure about South America, let alone an air ticket. He had merely been seen to go into a travel agency, and seen by a man with a criminal record.

'No, sir.'

'Then the situation is unchanged. Totally unchanged. Remember that.'

Chapter 14

Ginge had done as he was told, and on Friday, 8 November, a report arrived from him stating that he had been at his observation post in the pub each evening and on two of those evenings, the Monday and the Wednesday, Hathall had appeared at West End Green just before seven and had caught the 28 bus. That, at any rate, was something. There should have been another report on the Monday. Instead, the unheard-of happened and Ginge phoned. He was phoning from a call-box and he had, he told Wexford, plenty of two and ten pence pieces, and he knew a gentleman like the chief inspector would reimburse him.

'Give me the number and I'll call you myself.' For God's sake, how much of this was he supposed to stand out of his own pocket? Let the ratepayers fork out. Ginge picked up the receiver before the bell had rung twice. 'It has to be good, Ginge, to get you to the phone.'

'I reckon it's bleeding good,' said Ginge cockily. 'I seen him with a bird, that's what.'

The same climactic exultation is never reached twice. Wexford had heard those words – or words having the same meaning – before, and this time he didn't go off into flights about the Lord delivering Hathall into his hands. Instead he asked when and where.

'You know all that about me stationing myself in

that pub and watching the bleeding bus stop? Well, I thought to myself there was no harm doing it again Sunday.' Make sure he got seven days' worth of cash and Demon Kings, thought Wexford. 'So I was in there Sunday dinnertime – that is, yesterday like – when I seen him. About one it was and pissing down with rain. He'd got a mac on and his umbrella up. He didn't stop to catch no bus but went right on walking down West End Lane. Well, I never give a bleeding thought to following him. I seen him go by and that was all. But I'd got to thinking I'd better be off to my own dinner – on account of the wife likes it on the table one-thirty sharp – so down I goes to the station.'

'Which station?'

'Wes' Haamsted Stesh'n,' said Ginge with a very lifelike imitation of a West Indian bus conductor. He chortled at his own wit. 'When I get there I'm putting a five-pee bit in the machine, on account of its being only one stop to Kilburn, when I see the party standing by the bleeding barrier. He'd got his back to me, thank Gawd, so I nips over to the bookstall and has a look at the girlie mags of what they've got a very choice selection. Well, bearing in mind my duty to you, Mr Wexford, I see my train come in but I don't run down the bleeding steps to catch it. I wait. And up the steps comes about twenty people. I never dared turn round, not wanting my other eye poked, but when I think the coast's clear, I has a bit of a shufty and he'd gone.

'I nips back into West End Lane like a shot and the rain's coming down like stair rods. But up ahead, on his way home, is bleeding Hathall with this bird. Walking very close, they was, under his bleeding umbrella, and the bird's wearing one of them see-through plastic macs with the hood up. I couldn't see no more of her, barring she was wearing a long skirt all trailing in the bleeding wet. So I went off home then and got a bleeding mouthful from the wife for being late for my dinner.'

'Virtue is its own reward, Ginge.'

'I don't know about that,' said Ginge, 'but you'll be wanting to know what my wages and the Demon Kings came to, and the bill's fifteen pound sixty-three. Terrible, the cost of bleeding living, isn't it?'

It wouldn't be necessary, Wexford decided as he put the phone down, to think any longer of ways and means of following a man on a bus. For this man had taken this bus only as far as West Hampstead station, had walked instead this Sunday because he had an umbrella and umbrellas are always a problem on buses. It must be possible now to catch Hathall and his woman together and follow them to Dartmeet Avenue.

'I've got a fortnight's holiday owing to me,' he said to his wife.

'You've got about three months' holiday owing to you with what's mounted up over the years.'

'I'm going to take a bit of it now. Next week, say.'

'What, in November? Then we'll have to go somewhere warm. They say Malta's very nice in November.'

'Chelsea's very nice in November too, and that's where we're going.'

The first thing to do on the first day of his 'holiday' was to familiarize himself with a so far unknown bit of London's geography. Friday, 22 November, was a fine sunny day, June in appearance if January in temperature. How better to get to West Hampstead than on the 28 bus? Howard had told him that its route passed across the King's Road on its way to Wandsworth Bridge, so it wasn't a long walk from Teresa Street to the nearest stop. The bus went up through Fulham into West Kensington, an area he remembered from the time he had helped Howard on that former case, and he noticed to his satisfaction certain familiar landmarks. But soon he was in unknown territory and very varied and vast territory it was. The immense size of London always surprised him. He had had no inkling when he had interrupted Ginge's recitation of the stops on this route of how long the list would have been. Naively, he had supposed that Ginge would have named no more than two or three further places before the terminus, whereas in fact there would have been a dozen. As the conductor sang out, 'Church Street', 'Notting Hill Gate', 'Pembridge Road', he felt a growing relief that Hathall had merely caught the bus to West Hampstead station.

This station was reached at last after about three-quarters of an hour. The bus went on over a bridge above railway lines and past two more stations on the opposite side, West End Lane and another West Hampstead on some suburban line. It had been climbing ever since it left Kilburn and it went on climbing up narrow winding West End Lane till it reached West End Green. Wexford got off. The air was fresh here, not only fresh in comparison to that of Chelsea, but nearly as diesel-free as in Kingsmarkham. Surreptitiously, he consulted his guide. Dartmeet Avenue lay about a quarter of a mile to the east, and he was a little puzzled by this. Surely Hathall could have walked to West Hampstead station in five minutes and walked by the back doubles. Why catch a bus? Still, Ginge had seen him do it. Maybe he merely disliked walking.

Wexford found Dartmeet Avenue with ease. It was a hilly street like most of the streets round here and lined with fine tall houses built mostly of red brick, but some had been modernized and faced with stucco, their sash windows replaced by sheets of plain plate glass. Tall trees, now almost leafless, towered above roofs and pointed gables, and there were mature unpollarded trees growing in the pavements. Number 62 had a front garden that was all shrubbery and weeds. Three black plastic dust-bins with 62 painted on their sides in whitewash stood in the side entrance. Wexford noted the phone-box where Ginge had kept his vigils and decided which of the bay windows must be Hathall's. Could anything be gained by calling on the landlord? He concluded that nothing could. The man would be bound to tell Hathall someone had been enquiring about him, would describe that someone, and then the fat would be in the fire. He turned away and walked slowly back to West End Green, looking about him as he did so for such nooks, crannies and convenient trees as might afford him shelter if he dared tail Hathall himself. Night closed in early now, the evenings were long and dark, and in a car . . .

The 28 bus sailed down Fortune Green Road as he reached the stop. It was a good frequent service. Wexford wondered, as he settled himself behind the driver, if Robert Hathall had ever sat on that very seat and looked out through this window upon the three stations and the radiating railway lines. Such ruminations verged on the obsessional, though, and that he must avoid. But it was impossible to refrain from wondering afresh why Hathall had caught the bus at all just to reach this point. The woman, when she came to Hathall's home, came by train. Perhaps Hathall didn't like the Tube train, got sick of travelling to work by Tube, so that when he went to her home, he preferred the relaxation of a bus ride.

It took about ten minutes to get to Kilburn. Ginge, who was as sure to be found in the Countess of

Castlemaine at noon as the sun is to rise at daybreak or the sound of thunder to follow the sight of lightning, was hunched on his bar stool. He was nursing a half of bitter but when he saw his patron he pushed the tankard away from him, the way a man leaves his spoon in his half-consumed soup when his steak arrives. Wexford ordered a Demon King by name and without description of its ingredients. The barman understood.

'He's got you on your toes, this bleeder, hasn't he?' Ginge moved to an alcove table. 'Always popping up to the Smoke, you are. You don't want to let it get on top of you. Once let a thing like that get a hold on you and you could end up in a bleeding bin.'

'Don't be so daft,' said Wexford, whose own wife had said much the same thing to him that morning, though in more refined terms. 'It won't be for much longer, anyway. This coming week ought to see an end of it. Now what I want you to do . . .'

'It won't be for *no* longer, Mr Wexford.' Ginge spoke with a kind of shrinking determination. 'You put me on this to spot him with a bird and I've spotted him with a bird. The rest's up to you.'

'Ginge,' Wexford began cajolingly, 'just to watch the station next week while I watch the house.'

'No,' said Ginge.

'You're a coward.'

'Cowardness,' said Ginge, exhibiting his usual difficulty in making his command of the spoken language match up to his mastery of the written, 'don't come into it.' He hesitated and said with what might have been modesty or shame, 'I've got a job.'

Wexford almost gasped. 'A *job*?' In former days this monosyllable had exclusively been employed by Ginge and his brother to denote a criminal exercise. 'You mean you've got paid work?'

'Not me. Not exactly.' Ginge contemplated his

Demon King rather sadly and, lifting his glass, he sipped from it delicately and with a kind of nostalgia. *Sit transit gloria mundi* or it had been good while it lasted. 'The wife has. Bleeding barmaid. Evenings and Sunday dinnertimes.' He looked slightly embarrassed. 'Don't know what's got into her.'

'What I don't know is why it stops you working for me.'

'Anyone'd think,' said Ginge, 'you'd never had no bleeding family of your own. Someone's got to stay home and mind the kids, haven't they?'

Wexford managed to delay his outburst of mirth until he was out on the pavement. Laughter did him good, cleansing him of the feverish baulked feeling Ginge's refusal to cooperate further had at first brought him. He could manage on his own now, he thought as once more he boarded the 28 bus, and manage for the future in his car. From his car he could watch West Hampstead station on Sunday. With luck, Hathall would meet the woman there as he had done on the previous Sunday, and once the woman was found, what would it matter that Hathall knew he had been followed? Who would reproach him for breaking the rules when his disobedience had resulted in that success?

But Hathall didn't meet the woman on Sunday, and as the week wore on Wexford wondered at the man's elusiveness. He stationed himself in Dartmeet Avenue every evening but he never saw Hathall and he only once saw evidence of occupancy of the room with the bay window. On the Monday, the Tuesday and the Wednesday he was there before six and he saw three people enter the house between six and seven. No sign of Hathall. For some reason, the traffic was particularly heavy on the Thursday evening. It was six-fifteen before he got to Dartmeet Avenue. Rain was falling steadily and the long hilly street was black and glittering with here and there on its surface the gilt glare of reflected lamplight. The place was deserted but for a cat which snaked from between the dustbins and vanished through a fissure in the garden wall. A light was on in a downstairs room and a feebler glow showed through the fanlight above the front door. Hathall's window was dark, but as Wexford put on the handbrake and switched off the ignition, the bay window suddenly became a brilliant yellow cube. Hathall was in, had arrived home perhaps a minute before Wexford's own arrival. For a few seconds the window blazed, then curtains were drawn across it by an invisible hand until all that could be seen were thin perpendicular lines of light like phosphorescent threads gleaming on the dim wet façade.

The excitement this sight had kindled in him cooled as an hour, two hours, went by and Hathall didn't appear. At half past nine a little elderly man emerged, routed out the cat from among the sodden weeds and carried it back into the house. As the front door closed on him, the light that rimmed Hathall's curtains went out. That alerted Wexford and he started to move the car to a less conspicuous position, but the front door remained closed, the window remained dark, and he realized that Hathall had retired early to bed.

Having brought Dora to London for a holiday, he remembered his duty to her and squired her about the West End shopping centres in the daytime. But Denise was so much more adept at doing this than he that on the Friday he deserted his wife and his nephew's wife for a less attractive woman who was no longer a wife at all.

The first thing he saw when he came to Eileen Hathall's house was her ex-husband's car parked on the garage drive, the car which Ginge said had long ago been sold. Had Ginge made a mistake about that? He drove on till he came to a call-box where he phoned Marcus Flower. Yes, Mr Hathall was in, said the voice of a Jane or a Julie or a Linda. If he would just hold the line ... Instead of holding the line, he put the receiver back and within five minutes he was in Eileen Hathall's arid living room, sitting on a cushionless chair under the Spanish gypsy.

'He gave his car to Rosemary,' she said in answer to his question. 'She sees him sometimes at her gran's, and when she said she'd passed her test he gave her his car. He won't need it where he's going, will he?'

'Where is he going, Mrs Hathall?'

'Brazil.' She spat out the rough r and the sibilant as if the word were not the name of a country but of some loathsome reptile. Wexford felt a chill, a sudden anticipation that something bad was coming. It came. 'He's all fixed up,' she said, 'to go the day before Christmas Eve.'

In less than a month ...

'Has he got a job there?' he said steadily.

'A very good position with a firm of international accountants.' There was something pathetic about the pride she took in saying it. The man hated her, had humiliated her, would probably never see her again, yet for all that, she was bitterly proud of what he had achieved. 'You wouldn't believe the money he's getting. He told Rosemary and she told me. They're paying me from London, deducting what I get before it goes to him. He'll still have thousands and thousands a year to live on. And they're paying his fare, fixing it all up, got a house there waiting for him. He hasn't had to do a thing.'

Should he tell her Hathall wouldn't be going alone, wouldn't live in that house alone? She had grown stouter in the past year, her thick body – all bulges where there should be none – stuffed into salmon-pink wool. And she was permanently flushed as if she ran an endless race. Perhaps she did. A race to keep up with her daughter, keep pace with rage and leave the quiet dullness of misery behind. While he was hesitating, she said, 'Why d'you want to know? You think he killed that woman, don't you?'

'Do *you*?' he said boldly.

If she had been struck across the face her skin couldn't have crimsoned more deeply. It looked like flogged skin about to split and bleed. 'I wish he had!' she said on a harsh gasp, and she put up her hand, not to cover her eyes as he had at first thought, but her trembling mouth.

He drove back to London, to a fruitless Friday night vigil, an empty Saturday, a Sunday that might – just might – bring him what he desired.

1 December, and once more pouring with rain. But this was no bad thing. It would clear the streets and make the chance of Hathall's peering into a suspicious-looking car less likely. By half past twelve he had parked as nearly opposite the station as he dared, for it wasn't only the chance of being spotted by Hathall that worried him, but also the risk of obstructing this narrow bottleneck. Rain drummed hard on the car roof, streamed down the gutter between the kerb and the yellow painted line. But this rain was so heavy that, as it washed over the windscreen, it didn't obscure his view but had only a distorting effect as if there were a fault in the glass. He could see the station entrance quite clearly and about a hundred yards of West End Lane where it humped over the railway lines. Trains rattled unseen

beneath him, 159 and 28 buses climbed and descended the hill. There were few people about and yet it seemed as if a whole population were travelling, proceeding from unknown homes to unknown destinations through the wet pallid gloom of this winter Sunday. The hands of the dashboard clock crawled slowly through and past the third quarter after twelve.

By now he was so used to waiting, resigned to sitting on watch like a man who stalked some wary cunning animal, that he felt a jolt of shock which was almost disbelief when at ten to one he saw Hathall's figure in the distance. The glass played tricks with him. He was like someone in a hall of mirrors, first a skeletal giant, then a fat dwarf, but a single sweep of the windscreen wipers brought him suddenly into clear focus. His umbrella up, he was walking swiftly towards the station – fortunately, on the opposite side of the road. He passed the car without turning his head, and outside the station he stopped, snapped the umbrella shut and open, shut, open and shut, to shake off the water drops. Then he disappeared into the entrance.

Wexford was in a dilemma. Was he meeting someone or travelling himself? In daylight, even in this rain, he dared not leave the car. A red train scuttled under the road and came to a stop. He held his breath. The first people to get off the train began to come out on to the pavement. One man put a newspaper over his head and ran, a little knot of women fluttered, struggling with umbrellas that wouldn't open. Three opened simultaneously, a red one, a blue one and an orange pagoda, blossoming suddenly in the greyness like flowers. When they had lifted and danced off, what their brilliant circles had hidden was revealed – a couple with their backs to the street, a couple who stood close together but not touching each other while the man opened a black umbrella and enclosed them under its canopy.

She wore blue jeans and over them a white raincoat, the hood of which was up. Wexford hadn't been able to catch a glimpse of her face. They had set off as if they meant to walk it, but a taxi came splashing down with its For Hire light glowing orange like a cigarette end. Hathall hailed it and it bore them off northwards. Please God, thought Wexford, let it take them home and not to some restaurant. He knew he hadn't a hope of tailing a London taxi-driver, and the cab had vanished before he was out into West End Lane and off.

And the journey up the hill was maddeningly slow. He was bogged down behind a 159 bus – a bus that wasn't red but painted all over with an advertisement for Dinky Toys which reminded him of Kidd's at Toxborough – and nearly ten minutes had passed before he drew up in front of the house in Dartmeet Avenue. The taxi had gone, but Hathall's light was on. Of course he'd have to put the light on at midday on such a day as this. Wondering with interest rather than fear if Hathall would hit him too, he went up the path and examined the bells. There were no names by the bell-pushes, just floor numbers. He pressed the first-floor bell and waited. It was possible Hathall wouldn't come down, would just refuse to answer it. In that case, he'd find someone else to let him in and he'd hammer on Hathall's room door.

This turned out to be unnecessary. Above his head the window opened and, stepping back, he looked up into Hathall's face. For a moment neither of them spoke. The rain dashed between them and they stared at each other through it while a variety of emotions crossed Hathall's features – astonishment, anger, cautiousness, but not, Wexford thought, fear. And all were succeeded by what looked strangely like satisfaction. But before he could speculate as to what this might mean, Hathall said coldly:

'I'll come down and let you in.'

Within fifteen seconds he had done so. He closed the door quietly, saying nothing, and pointed to the stairs. Wexford had never seen him so calm and suave. He seemed entirely relaxed. He looked younger and he looked triumphant.

'I should like you to introduce me to the lady you brought here in a taxi.'

Hathall didn't demur. He didn't speak. As they went up the stairs Wexford thought, has he hidden her? Sent her to some bathroom or up on to the top floor? His room door was on the latch and he pushed it open, allowing the chief inspector to precede him. Wexford walked in. The first thing he saw was her raincoat, spread out to dry over a chair back.

At first he didn't see her. The room was very small, no more than twelve feet by ten, and furnished as such places always are. There was a wardrobe that looked as if it had been manufactured round about the time of the Battle of Mons, a narrow bed with an Indian cotton cover, some wooden-armed chairs that are euphemistically known as 'fireside', and pictures that had doubtless been painted by some relative of the landlord's. The light came from a dust-coated plastic sphere suspended from the pock-marked ceiling.

A canvas screen, canvas-coloured and hideous, shut off one corner of the room. Behind it, presumably, was a sink, for when Hathall gave a cautionary cough, she pushed it aside and came out, drying her hands on a tea towel. It wasn't a pretty face, just a very young one, heavy-featured, tough and confident. Thick black hair fell to her shoulders and her eyebrows were heavy and black like a man's. She wore a teeshirt with a cardigan over it, Wexford had seen that face somewhere before, and he was wondering where when Hathall said:

'This is the "lady" you wanted to meet.' His triumph had changed to frank amusement and he was almost laughing. 'May I present my daughter, Rosemary?'

Chapter 15

It was a long time since Wexford had experienced such an anticlimax. Coping with awkward situations wasn't usually a problem with him, but the shock of what Hathall had just said – combined with his realization that his own disobedience was now known – stunned him into silence. The girl didn't speak either after she had said a curt hello, but retreated behind the screen where she could be heard filling a kettle.

Hathall, who had been so withdrawn and aloof when Wexford first arrived, seemed to be getting the maximum possible enjoyment from his adversary's dismay. 'What's this visit in aid of?' he asked. 'Just looking up old acquaintances?'

In for a penny, in for a pound, thought Wexford, echoing Miss Marcovitch. 'I understand you're going to Brazil,' he said. 'Alone?'

'Can one go alone? There'll be about three hundred other people in the aircraft.' Wexford smarted under that one and Hathall saw him smart. 'I hoped Rosemary might go with me, but her school is here. Perhaps she'll join me in a few years' time.'

That fetched the girl out. She picked up her raincoat, hung it on a hanger and said, 'I haven't even been to Europe yet. I'm not burying myself in Brazil.'

Hathall shrugged at this typical sample of his

family's ungraciousness, and said as brusquely, 'Satisfied?'

'I have to be, don't I, Mr Hathall?'

Was it his daughter's presence that kept his anger in check? He was almost mild, only a trace of his usual resentful querulousness sounding in his voice when he said, 'Well, if you'll excuse us, Rosemary and I have to get ourselves some lunch which isn't the easiest thing in the world in this little hole. I'll see you out.'

He closed the door instead of leaving it on the latch. It was dark and quiet on the landing. Wexford waited for the explosion of rage but it didn't come, and he was conscious only of the man's eyes. They were the same height and their eyes met on a level. Briefly, Hathall's showed white and staring around hard black irises in which that curious red spark glittered. They were at the head of the steep flight of stairs, and as Wexford turned to descend them, he was aware of a movement behind him, of Hathall's splayed hand rising. He grasped the banister and swung down a couple of steps. Then he made himself walk down slowly and steadily. Hathall didn't move, but when Wexford reached the bottom and looked back, he saw the raised hand lifted higher and the fingers closed in a solemn and somehow portentous gesture of farewell.

'He was going to push me down those stairs,' Wexford said to Howard. 'And I wouldn't have had much redress. He could have said I'd forced my way into his room. God, what a mess I've made of things! He's bound to put in another of his complaints and I could lose my job.'

'Not without a pretty full enquiry, and I don't think Hathall would want to appear at any enquiry.' Howard threw the Sunday paper he had been reading on to the floor and turned his thin bony face, his ice-blue penetrating eyes, towards his uncle. 'It wasn't his daughter all the time, Reg.'

'Wasn't it? I know you saw this woman with short fair hair, but can you be sure it was Hathall you saw her with?'

'I'm sure.'

'You saw him once,' Wexford persisted. 'You saw him twenty yards off for about ten seconds from a car *you were driving*. If you had to go into court and swear that the man you saw outside Marcus Flower was the same man you saw in the garden of Bury Cottage, would you swear? If a man's life depended on it, would you?'

'Capital punishment is no longer with us, Reg.'

'No, and neither you nor I – unlike many of our calling – would wish to see it back. But if it were with us, then would you?'

Howard hesitated. Wexford saw that hesitation and he felt tiredness creep through his body like a depressant drug. Even a shred of doubt could dispel what little hope he now had left.

At last, 'No, I wouldn't,' Howard said flatly.

'I see.'

'Wait a minute, Reg. I'm not sure nowadays if I could ever swear to a man's identity if my swearing to it might lead to his death. You're pressing me too hard. But I'm sure beyond a reasonable doubt, and I'll still say to you, yes, I saw Robert Hathall. I saw him outside the offices of Marcus Flower in Half Moon Street with a fair-haired woman.'

Wexford sighed. What difference did it make, after all? By his own blundering of that day he had put an end to all hope of following Hathall. Howard mistook his silence for doubt and said, 'If he isn't with her, where does he go all those evenings he's out? Where did he go on that bus?'

'Oh, I still believe he's with her. The daughter just

goes there sometimes on Sundays. But what good does that do me? I can't follow him on a bus. He'll be looking for me now.'

'He'll think, you know, that seeing him with his daughter will put you off.'

'Maybe. Maybe he'll get reckless. So what? I can't conceal myself in a doorway and leap on a bus after him. Either the bus would go before I got on or he'd turn round and see me. Even if I got on without his seeing me . . .'

'Then someone else must do it,' said Howard firmly.

'Easy to say. My chief constable says no, and you won't cross swords with my chief constable by letting me have one of your blokes.'

'That's true, I won't.'

'Then we may as well give over talking about it. I'll go back to Kingsmarkham and face the music – a bloody great symphony in Griswold sharp major – and Hathall can go to the sunny tropics.'

Howard got up and laid a hand on his shoulder. 'I will do it,' he said.

The awe had gone long ago, giving way to love and comradeship. But that 'I will do it', spoken so lightly and pleasantly, brought back all the old humiliation and envy and awareness of the other's advantages. Wexford felt a hot dark flush suffuse his face. '*You?*' he said roughly, 'you yourself? You must be joking. You take rank over me, remember?'

'Don't be such a snob. What if I do? I'd like to do it. It'd be fun. I haven't done anything like that for years and years.'

'Would you really do that for me, Howard? What about your own work?'

'If I'm the god you make me out to be, don't you think I have some say in the hours I work? Of course

I shan't be able to do it every night. There'll be the usual crises that come up from time to time and I'll have to stay late. But Kenbourne Vale won't degenerate into a sort of twentieth-century Bridewell just because I pop up to West Hampstead every so often.'

So on the following evening Chief Superintendent Howard Fortune left his office at a quarter to six and was at West End Green on the hour. He waited until half past seven. When his quarry didn't come, he made his way along Dartmeet Avenue and observed that there was no light on in the window his uncle had told him was Hathall's.

'I wonder if he's going to her straight from work?'

'Let's hope he's not going to make a habit of that. It'll be almost impossible to follow him in the rush hour. When does he give up this job of his?'

'God knows,' said Wexford, 'but he leaves for Brazil in precisely three weeks.'

One of those crises at which he had hinted prevented Howard from tailing Hathall on the following night, but he was free on the Wednesday and, changing his tactics, he got to Half Moon Street by five o'clock. An hour later, in Teresa Street, he told his uncle what had happened.

'The first person to come out of Marcus Flower was a seedy-looking guy with a toothbrush moustache. He had a girl with him and they went off in a Jaguar.'

'That'd be Jason Marcus and his betrothed,' said Wexford.

'Then two more girls and then – Hathall. I *was* right, Reg. It's the same man.'

'I shouldn't have doubted you.'

Howard shrugged. 'He got into the Tube and I lost him. But he wasn't going home. I know that.'

'How can you know?'

'If he'd been going home he'd have walked to

Green Park station, gone one stop on the Piccadilly Line to Piccadilly Circus or on the Victoria Line to Oxford Circus and changed on to the Bakerloo. He'd have walked south. But he walked north, and at first I thought he was going to get a bus home. But he went to Bond Street station. You'd never go to Bond Street if you meant to go to North-west London. Bond Street's only on the Central Line until the Fleet Line opens.'

'And the Central Line goes where?'

'Due east and due west. I followed him into the station but – well, you've seen our rush hours, Reg. I was a good dozen people behind him in the ticket queue. The thing was I had to be so damn careful he didn't get a look at me. He went down the escalator to the westbound platform – and I lost him.' Howard said apologetically, 'There were about five hundred people on the platform. I got stuck and I couldn't move. But it's proved one thing. D'you see what I mean?'

'I think so. We have to find where the west-bound Central Line route crosses the 28 bus route, and somewhere in that area lives our unknown woman.'

'I can tell you where that is straight off. The west-bound Central Line route goes Bond Street, Marble Arch, Lancaster Gate, Queensway, Notting Hill Gate, Holland Park, Shepherd's Bush, and so on. The south-bound 28 route goes Golders Green, West Hampstead, Kilburn, Kilburn Park, Great Western Road, Pembridge Road, Notting Hill Gate, Church Street, on through Kensington and Fulham to here and ultimately to Wandsworth. So it has to be Notting Hill. She lives, along with half the roving population of London, somewhere in Notting Hill. Small progress, but better than nothing. Have you made any?'

Wexford, on tenterhooks for two days, had

phoned Burden, expecting to hear that Griswold was out for his blood. But nothing was further from the truth. The chief constable had been 'buzzing around' Kingsmarkham, as Burden put it, tearing between there and Myringham where there was some consternation over a missing woman. But he had been in an excellent frame of mind, had asked where Wexford had gone for his holiday, and on being told London ('For the theatres and museums, you know, sir,' Burden had said) had asked facetiously why the chief inspector hadn't sent him a picture postcard of New Scotland Yard.

'Then Hathall hasn't complained,' said Howard thoughtfully.

'Doesn't look like it. If I were to be optimistic, I'd say he thinks it safer not to draw attention to himself.'

But it was 3 December . . . Twenty days to go. Dora had dragged her husband round the stores, doing the last of her Christmas shopping. He had carried her parcels, agreed that this was just the thing for Sheila and that was exactly what Sylvia's elder boy wanted, but all the time he was thinking, twenty days, twenty days . . . This year Christmas for him would be the season of Robert Hathall's getaway.

Howard seemed to read his thoughts. He was eating one of those enormous meals he consumed without putting on a pound. Taking a second helping of *charlotte russe*, he said, 'If only we could get him on something.'

'What d'you mean?'

'I don't know. Some little thing you could hold him on that would stop him leaving the country. Like shoplifting, say, or travelling on the Tube without a ticket.'

'He seems to be an honest man,' said Wexford bitterly, 'if you can call a murderer honest.'

His nephew scraped the dessert bowl. 'I suppose he *is* honest?'

'As far as I know, he is. Mr Butler would have told me if there's been a smell of dishonesty about him.'

'I daresay. Hathall was all right for money in those days. But he wasn't all right for money when he got married to Angela, was he? Yet, in spite of their having only fifteen pounds a week to live on, they started doing all right. You told me Somerset had seen them on a shopping spree and then dining at some expensive place. Where did that money come from, Reg?'

Pouring himself a glass of Chablis, Wexford said, 'I've wondered about that. But I've never come to any conclusion. It didn't seem relevant.'

'Everything's relevant in a murder case.'

'True.' Wexford was too grateful to his nephew to react huffily at this small admonition. 'I suppose I reckoned that if a man's always been honest he doesn't suddenly become dishonest in middle age.'

'That depends on the man. This man suddenly became an unfaithful husband in middle age. In fact, although he'd been monogamous since puberty, he seems to have turned into a positive womanizer in middle age. And he became a murderer. I don't suppose you're saying he killed anyone before, are you?' Howard pushed away his plate and started on the gruyère. 'There's one factor in all this I don't think you've taken into sufficient account. One personality.'

'Angela?'

'Angela. It was when he met her that he changed. Some would say she'd corrupted him. This is an outside chance – a very way-out idea altogether – but Angela had been up to a little fraud on her own, one you know about, possibly others you don't. Suppose she encouraged him into some sort of dishonesty?'

148

'Your saying that reminds me of something Mr Butler said. He said he overheard Angela tell his partner, Paul Craig, that he was in a good position to fiddle his income tax.'

'There you are then. They must have got that money from somewhere. It didn't grow on trees like the "miracle" plums.'

'There hasn't been a hint of anything,' said Wexford. 'It would have to be at Kidd's. Aveney didn't drop so much as a hint.'

'But you weren't asking him about money. You were asking him about women.' Howard got up from the table and pushed aside his chair. 'Let's go and join the ladies. If I were you I'd take a little trip to Toxborough tomorrow.'

Chapter 16

The rectangular white box set on green lawns, the screen of saplings, leafless and pathetic in December, and inside, the warm cellulose smell and the turbanned women painting dolls to the theme music from *Doctor Zhivago*. Mr Aveney conducted Wexford through the workshops to the office of the personnel manager, talking the while in a shocked and rather indignant way.

'Cooking the books? We've never had anything like that here.'

'I'm not saying you have, Mr Aveney. I'm working in the dark,' said Wexford. 'Have you ever heard of the old pay-roll fiddle?'

'Well, yes, I *have*. It used to be done a lot in the forces. No one'd get away with it here.'

'Let's see, shall we?'

The personnel manager, a vague young man with fair bristly hair, was introduced as John Oldbury. His office was very untidy and he seemed somewhat distraught as if he had been caught in the middle of searching for something he knew he would never find. 'Messing about with the wages, d'you mean?' he said.

'Suppose you tell me how you work with the accountant to manage the pay-roll.'

Oldbury looked distractedly at Aveney, and Aveney nodded, giving an infinitesimal shrug. The personnel manager sat down heavily and pushed his fingers through his unruly hair. 'I'm not very good at explaining things,' he began. 'But I'll try. It's like this: when we get a new worker I sort of tell the accountant details about her and he works them out for her wages. No, I'll have to be more explicit. Say we take on a – well, we'll call her Joan Smith, Mrs Joan Smith.' Oldbury, thought Wexford, was as unimaginative as he was inarticulate. 'I tell the accountant her name and her address – say ...'

Seeing his total defeat, Wexford said, 'Twenty-four Gordon Road, Toxborough.'

'Oh, fine!' The personnel manager beamed his admiration. 'I tell him Mrs Joan Smith, of whatever-it-is Gordon Road, Toxborough ...'

'Tell him by what means? Phone? A chit?'

'Well, either. Of course I keep a record. I haven't,' said Oldbury unnecessarily, 'got a very good memory. I tell him her name and her address and when she's starting and her hours and whatever, and he feeds all that into the computer and Bob's your uncle. And after that I do it every week for her overtime and – and whatever.'

'And when she leaves you tell him that too?'

'Oh, sure.'

'They're always leaving. Chop and change, it's everlasting,' said Aveney.

'They're all paid in weekly wage packets?'

'Not all,' said Oldbury. 'You see, some of our ladies don't use their wages for – well, housekeeping. Their husbands are the – what's the word?'

'Breadwinners?'

'Ah, fine. Breadwinners. The ladies – some of them – keep their wages for holidays and sort of improving their homes and just saving up, I suppose.'

'Yes, I see. But so what?'

'Well,' said Oldbury triumphantly, '*they* don't get wage packets. Their wages are paid into a bank

151

account – more likely the Post Office or a Trustee Savings Bank.'

'And if they are, you tell that to the accountant and he feeds it into his computer?'

'He does, yes.' Oldbury smiled delightedly at the realization he had made himself so clear. 'You're absolutely right. Quick thinking, if I may say so.'

'Not at all,' said Wexford, slightly stupefied by the man's zany charm. 'So the accountant could simply invent a woman and feed a fictitious name and address into the computer? Her wages would go into a bank account which the accountant – or, rather, his female accomplice – could draw on when they chose?'

'That,' said Oldbury severely, 'would be fraud.'

'It would indeed. But, since you keep records, we can easily verify if such a fraud has ever been committed.'

'Of course we can.' The personnel manager beamed again and trotted over to a filing cabinet whose open drawers were stuffed with crumpled documents. 'Nothing easier. We keep records for a whole year after one of our ladies has left us.'

A whole year ... And Hathall had left them eighteen months before. Aveney took him back through the factory where the workers were now being lulled (or stimulated) by the voice of Tom Jones. 'John Oldbury,' he said defensively, 'has got a very good psychology degree and he's marvellous with people.'

'I'm sure. You've both been very good. I apologize for taking up so much of your time.'

The interview had neither proved nor disproved Howard's theory. But since there were no records, what could be done? If the enquiry wasn't a clandestine one, if he had men at his disposal, he could send them round the local Trustee Savings Banks. But it was, and he hadn't. Yet he could see so clearly now how such a thing could have been done; the idea coming in the first place from Angela; the female accomplice brought in to impersonate the women Hathall had invented, and to draw money from the accounts. And then – yes, Hathall growing too fond of his henchwoman so that Angela became jealous. If he was right, everything was explainable, the deliberately contrived solitude of the Hathalls, their cloistral life, the money that enabled them to dine out and Hathall to buy presents for his daughter. And they would all have been in it together – until Angela realized the woman was more than an accomplice to her husband, more than a useful collector of revenues ... What had she done? Broken up the affair and threatened that if it started again, she'd shop them both? That would have meant the end of Hathall's career. That would put paid to his job at Marcus Flower or any future accountancy job. So they had murdered her. They had killed Angela to be together, and knowing Kidd's kept records for only one year, to be safe for ever from the risk of discovery ...

Wexford drove slowly down the drive between the flat green lawns, and at the gateway to the main industrial estate road met another car coming in. Its driver was a uniformed police officer and its other occupant Chief Inspector Jack 'Brock' Lovat, a small snub-nosed man who wore small gold-rimmed glasses. The car slowed and Lovat wound his window down.

'What are you doing here?' Wexford asked.

'My job,' said Lovat simply.

His nickname derived from the fact that he kept three badgers, rescued from the diggers before badger-digging became an offence, in his back garden. And Wexford knew of old that it was useless questioning the head of Myringham CID about anything but this hobby of his. On that subject he was fulsome and enthusiastic. On all others – though he did his work in exemplary fashion – he was almost mute. You got a 'yes' or a 'no' out of him unless you were prepared to talk about setts and plantigrade quadrupeds.

'Since there are no badgers here,' Wexford said sarcastically, 'except possibly clockwork ones, I'll just ask this. Is your visit connected in any way with a man called Robert Hathall?'

'No,' said Lovat. Smiling closely, he waved his hand and told the driver to move on.

But for its new industries, Toxborough would by now have dwindled to a semi-deserted village with an elderly population. Industry had brought life, commerce, roads, ugliness, a community centre, a sports ground and a council estate. This last was traversed by a broad thoroughfare called Maynnot Way, where the concrete stilts of street lamps replaced the trees, and which had been named after the only old house that remained in it, Maynnot Hall. Wexford, who hadn't been this way for ten years when the concrete and the brick had first begun to spread across Toxborough's green fields, knew that somewhere, not too far from here, was a Trustee Savings Bank. At the second junction he turned left into Queen Elizabeth Avenue, and there it was, sandwiched between a betting shop and a place that sold cash-and-carry carpets.

The manager was a stiff pompous man who reacted sharply to Wexford's questions.

'Let you look at our books? Not without a warrant.'

'All right. But tell me this. If payments stop being made into an account and it's left empty or nearly empty, do you write to the holder and ask him or her if they want it closed?'

'We gave up the practice. If someone's only got fifteen pence in an account he's not going to waste money on a stamp saying he wants the account closed. Nor is he going to spend five pence on a bus fare to collect it. Right?'

'Would you check for me if any accounts held by women have had no payments made into them or withdrawals made from them since – well, last April or May twelvemonth? And if there are any, would you communicate with the holders?'

'Not,' said the manager firmly, 'unless this is an official police matter. I haven't got the staff.'

Neither, thought Wexford as he left the bank, had he. No staff, no funds, no encouragement; and still nothing but his own 'feelings' with which to convince Griswold that this was worth pursuing. Kidd's had a pay-roll, Hathall could have helped himself to money from it by the means of accounts held by fictitious women. Come to that, Kingsmarkham police station had a petty cash box and he, Wexford, could have helped himself out of it. There was about as much ground for suspicion in the latter case as in the former, and that was how the chief constable would see it.

'Another dead end,' he said to his nephew that night. 'But I understand how it all happened now. The Hathalls and the other woman work their fraud for a couple of years. The share-out of the loot takes place at Bury Cottage. Then Hathall gets his new job and there's no longer any need for the pay-roll fiddle. The other woman should fade out of the picture, but she doesn't because Hathall has fallen for her and wants to go on seeing her. You can imagine Angela's fury. It was *her* idea, she planned it, and it's led to this. She tells Hathall to give her up or she'll blow the whole thing, but Hathall can't. He pretends he has and all seems well between him and Angela, to the extent of Angela asking her mother-in-law to stay and cleaning up the cottage to impress her. In the afternoon Angela fetches her rival, perhaps to wind up the whole thing finally. The other woman strangles her as arranged, but leaves that print on the bath.'

'Admirable,' said Howard. 'I'm sure you're right.'

'And much good it does me. I may as well go home tomorrow. You're coming to us for Christmas?'

Howard patted his shoulder as he had done on the day he promised his vigilance. 'Christmas is a fortnight off. I'll keep on watching every free evening I get.'

At any rate, there was no summons from Griswold awaiting him. And nothing much had happened in Kingsmarkham during his absence. The home of the chairman of the rural council had been broken into. Six colour sets had been stolen from the television rental company in the High Street. Burden's son had been accepted by Reading University, subject to satisfactory A Levels. And Nancy Lake's house had been sold for a cool twenty-five thousand pounds. Some said she was moving to London, others that she was going abroad. Sergeant Martin had decorated the police station foyer with paper chains and mobiles of flying angels which the chief constable had ordered removed forthwith as they detracted from the dignity of Mid-Sussex.

'Funny thing Hathall didn't complain, wasn't it?'

'Lucky for you he didn't.' At ease now in his new glasses, Burden looked more severe and puritanical than ever. With a rather exasperated indrawing of breath, he said, 'You must give that up, you know.'

'Must? Little man, little man, *must* is not a word to

be addressed to chief inspectors. Time was when you used to call me "sir".'

'And it was you asked me to stop. Remember?'

Wexford laughed. 'Let's go over to the Carousel and have a spot of lunch, and I'll tell you all about what I *must* give up.'

Antonio was delighted to see him back and offered him the speciality of the day – *moussaka*.

'I thought that was Greek.'

'The Greeks,' said Antonio, flinging out his hands, 'got it from us.'

'A reversal of the usual process. How interesting. I may as well have it, Antonio. And steak pie, which you got from *us*, for Mr Burden. Have I got thinner, Mike?'

'You're wasting away.'

'I haven't had a decent meal for a fortnight, what with chasing after that damned Hathall.' Wexford told him about it while they ate. 'Now do you believe?'

'Oh, I don't know. It's mostly in your head, isn't it? My daughter was telling me something the other day she got from school. About Galileo, it was. They made him recant what he'd said about the earth moving round the sun but he wouldn't give it up, and on his death-bed his last words were, "It does move".'

'I've heard it. What are you trying to prove? He was right. The earth does go round the sun. And on *my* death-bed I'll say, "He did do it".' Wexford sighed. It was useless, may as well change the subject ... 'I saw old Brock last week. He was as close as ever. Did he find his missing girl?'

'He's digging up Myringham Old Town for her.'

'As missing as that, is she?'

Burden gave Wexford's *moussaka* a suspicious look and a suspicious sniff, and attacked his own steak pie. 'He's pretty sure she's dead and he's arrested her husband.'

'What, for murder?'

'No, not without the body. The bloke's got a record and he's holding him on a shop-breaking charge.'

'Christ!' Wexford exploded. 'Some people have all the luck.'

His eyes met Burden's, and the inspector gave him the kind of look we level at our friends when we begin to doubt their mental equilibrium. And Wexford said no more, breaking the silence only to ask after young John Burden's successes and prospects. But when they rose to go and a beaming Antonio had been congratulated on the cooking, 'When I retire or die, Antonio,' Wexford said, 'will you name a dish after me?'

The Italian crossed himself. 'Not to speak of such things, but yes, sure I will. *Lasagne* Wexford?'

'*Lasagne Galileo*.' Wexford laughed at the other's puzzlement. 'It sounds more Latin,' he said.

The High Street shops had their windows filled with glitter, and the great cedar outside the Dragon pub had orange and green and scarlet and blue light bulbs in its branches. In the toyshop window a *papier mâché* and cotton wool Santa Claus nodded and smiled and gyrated at an audience of small children who pressed their noses to the glass.

'Twelve more shopping days to Christmas,' said Burden. 'Oh, shut up,' Wexford snapped.

Chapter 17

A grey mist hung over the river, curtaining its opposite bank, shrouding the willows in veils of vapour, making colourless the hills and the leafless woods so that they appeared like a landscape in an out-of-focus monochrome photograph. On this side, the houses of the Old Town slept in the freezing mist, all their windows closed against it, their garden trees utterly still. The only motion was that of water drops falling gently and very slowly from threadlike branches. It was bitterly cold. As Wexford walked down past St Luke's and Church House, it seemed wonderful to him that up there beyond those layers of cloud, miles of icy mist, must be a bright though distant sun. A few more days to the shortest day, the longest night. A few more days to the solstice when the sun would have moved to its extremest limit from this part of the earth. Or as he should put it, he thought, recalling Burden's snippet of pop education from the day before, when the ground on which he stood would have moved to its extremest limit from the sun . . .

He saw the police cars and police vans in River Lane before he saw any of the men who had driven them there or any signs of their purpose. They were parked all along the lane, fronting the row of almost derelict houses whose owners had abandoned them and left them to be inhabited intermittently by the desperate homeless. Here and there, where the glass or even the frame of an ancient window had collapsed and gone, the cavity was patched with plastic sheeting. Against other windows hung bedspreads, sacks, rags, torn and soaking brown paper. But there were no squatters here now. Winter and the damp rising from the river had driven them to find other quarters, and the old houses, immeasurably more beautiful even now than any modern terrace, waited in the sour cold for new occupants or new purchasers. They were old but they were also very nearly immortal. No one might destroy them. All that could become of them was a slow disintegration into extreme decay.

An alley led between broken brick walls to the gardens which lay behind them, gardens which had become repositories of rubbish, rat-infested, and which sloped down to the river bank. Wexford made his way down this alley to a point where the wall had caved in, leaving a gap. A young police sergeant, standing just inside and holding a spade in his hand, barred his way and said, 'Sorry, sir. No one's allowed in here.'

'Don't you know me, Hutton?'

The sergeant looked again and, taken aback, said, 'It's Mr Wexford, isn't it? I beg your pardon, sir.'

Wexford said that was quite all right, and where was Chief Inspector Lovat to be found?

'Down where they're digging, sir. On the right-hand side at the bottom.'

'They're digging for this woman's body?'

'Mrs Morag Grey. She and her husband squatted here for a bit the summer before last. Mr Lovat thinks the husband may have buried her in this garden.'

'They lived *here*?' Wexford looked up at the sagging gable, shored up with a baulk of timber. The leprous split plaster had scaled off in places, showing the bundles of wattle the house had been built of four hundred years before. A gaping doorway revealed interior walls which, slimy and running with water, were like those of a cave that the sea invades daily.

'It wouldn't be so bad in summer,' said Hutton by way of apology, 'and they weren't here for more than a couple of months.'

A great tangle of bushes, mud-spattered, under which lay empty cans and sodden newspaper, cut off the end of the garden. Wexford pushed his way through them into a waste land. Four men were digging, and digging more than the three spits deep which is the gardener's rule. Mountains of earth, scattered with chalk splinters, were piled against the river wall. Lovat was sitting on this wall, his coat collar turned up, a thin damp cigarette stuck to his lower lip, watching them inscrutably.

'What makes you think she's here?'

'Got to be somewhere.' Lovat showed no surprise at his arrival but spread another sheet of newspaper on the wall for him to sit down. 'Nasty day,' he said.

'You think the husband killed her?' Wexford knew it was useless asking questions. You had to make statements and wait for Lovat to agree with them or refute them. 'You've got him on a shop-breaking charge. But you've got no body, just a missing woman. Someone must have made you take that seriously, and not Grey himself.'

'Her mother,' said Lovat.

'I see. Everyone thought she'd gone to her mother, and her mother thought she was elsewhere, but she didn't answer mother's letters. Grey's got a record, maybe living with another woman. Told a lot of lies. Am I right?'

'Yes.'

Wexford thought he had done his duty. It was a

pity he knew so little about badgers, was even less interested in them than he was in the Grey affair. The icy mist was seeping through his clothes to his spine, chilling his whole body. 'Brock,' he said, 'will you do me a favour?'

Most people when asked that question reply that it all depends on what the favour is. But Lovat had virtues to offset his taciturnity. He took another crumpled cigarette from a damp and crumpled packet. 'Yes,' he said simply.

'You know that guy Hathall I'm always on about? I think he worked a pay-roll fiddle while he was with Kidd's at Toxborough. That's why I was there when we met the other day. But I've no authority to act. I'm pretty sure it was like this . . .' Wexford told him what he was pretty sure it was like. 'Would you get someone along to those trustee savings banks and see if you can smell out any false accounts? And quick, Brock, because I've only got ten days.'

Lovat didn't ask why he only had ten days. He wiped his spectacles which the fog had misted and readjusted them on his red snub nose. Without looking at Wexford or showing the least interest, he fixed his eyes on the men and said, 'One way and another I've had a lot to do with digging in my time.'

Wexford made no response. Just at the moment he couldn't summon up much enthusiasm for a League-Against-Cruel-Sports homily. Nor did he repeat his request, which would only have annoyed Lovat, but sat silent in the damp cold listening to the sounds the spades made when they struck chalk, and the soft slump of earth lifted and slung heavily aside. Cans, waterlogged cartons, were lumped on to the growing heaps, to be followed by unearthed rose bushes, their roots scorpion-like and matted with wet soil. Was there a body under there? At any moment a spade might reveal, not a clod of ancient mortar or another mass of brown root, but a white and rotting human hand.

The mist was thickening over the almost stagnant water. Lovat threw his cigarette end into an oil-scummed puddle. 'Will do,' he said.

It was a relief to get away from the river and its miasma – the miasma that had once been thought of as a breeder of disease – and up into the fashionable part of the Old Town where he had parked his car. He was wiping its misted windscreen when he saw Nancy Lake, and he would have wondered what she was doing there had she not, at that moment, turned into a little baker's shop, famous for its home-baked bread and cakes. More than a year had passed since he had last seen her, and he had almost forgotten the sensation he had felt then, the catching of breath, the faint tremor in the heart. He felt it now as he saw the glass door close on her, the shop's warm orange glow receive her.

Although he was shivering now, his breath like smoke on the cold haze, he waited there for her on the kerb. And when she came out she rewarded him with one of her rich sweet smiles. 'Mr Wexford! There are policemen everywhere down here, but I didn't expect to see you.'

'I'm a policeman too. May I give you a lift back to Kingsmarkham?'

'Thank you, I'm not going back just now.' She wore a chinchilla coat that sparkled with fine drops. The cold which pinched other faces had coloured hers and brightened her eyes. 'But I'll come and sit in your car with you for five minutes, shall I?'

Someone, he thought, ought to invent a way of heating a car while the engine was switched off. But she didn't seem to feel the cold. She leaned towards him with the eagerness and the vitality of a young woman. 'Shall we share a cream cake?'

He shook his head. 'Bad for my figure, I'm afraid.'

'But you've got a lovely figure!'

Knowing that he shouldn't, that this was inviting a renewal of flirtation, he looked into those shining eyes and said, 'You are always saying things to me that no woman has said for half a lifetime.'

She laughed. 'Not always. How can it be "always" when I never see you?' She began to eat a cake. It was the kind of cake no one should attempt to eat without a plate, a fork and a napkin. She managed it with her bare fingers remarkably well, her small red tongue retrieving flecks of cream from her lips. 'I've sold my house,' she said. 'I'm moving out the day before Christmas Eve.'

The day before Christmas Eve . . . 'They say that you're going abroad.'

'Do they? They've been saying things about me round here for twenty years and most of it has been a distortion of the truth. Do they say that my dream has come true at last?' She finished her cake, licked her fingers delicately. 'Now I must go. Once – Oh, it seems years ago – I asked you to come and have tea with me.'

'So you did,' he said.

'Will you come? Say – next Friday?' When he nodded, she said, 'And we'll have the last of the miracle jam.'

'I wish you'd tell me why you call it that.'

'I will, I will . . .' He held the car door open for her and she took the hand he held out. 'I'll tell you the story of my life. All shall be made clear. Till Friday, then.'

'Till Friday.' It was absurd, this feeling of excitement. You're old, he told himself sternly. She wants to give you plum jam and tell you the story of her life, that's all you're fit for now. And he watched her walk away until her grey fur had melted into the river mist and was gone.

'I can't follow him on the Tube, Reg. I've tried three times, but each night the crowds get worse with the pre-Christmas rush.'

'I can imagine,' said Wexford, who felt he never wanted to hear the word 'Christmas' again. He was more aware of the season's festive pressures than he had ever been in the past. Was Christmas more christmassy this year than usual? Or was it simply that he saw every card which flopped on to his front door mat, every hint of the coming celebrations, as a threat of failure? There was a bitter irony in the fact that this year they were going to fill the house with more people than ever before, both his daughters, his son-in-law, his two grandsons, Howard and Denise, Burden and his children. And Dora had already begun to put up the decorations. He had to hunch in his chair, the phone on his knees, to avoid prickling his face on the great bunch of holly that hung above his desk. 'That seems to be that then, doesn't it?' he said. 'Give it up, finish. Something may come out of the pay-roll thing. It's my last hope.'

Howard's voice sounded indignant. 'I didn't mean I want to give it up. I only meant I can't do it that way.'

'What other way is there?'

'Why shouldn't I try to tail him from the other end?'

'The other end?'

'Last night after I'd lost him on the Tube, I went up to Dartmeet Avenue. You see, I'd reckoned he may stay all night with her some nights, but he doesn't always stay there. If he did, there'd be no point in his having a place of his own. And he didn't stay last night, Reg. He came home on the last 28 bus. So I thought, why shouldn't I also get on that last bus?'

'I must be getting thick in my old age,' said Wexford, 'but I don't see how that helps.'

'This is how. He'll get on at the stop nearest to her place, won't he? And once I find it I can wait at it the next night from five-thirty onwards. If he comes by bus I can follow him, if he comes by Tube it'll be harder, but there's still a good chance.'

Kilburn Park, Great Western Road, Pembridge Road, Church Street ... Wexford sighed. 'There are dozens of stops,' he said.

'Not in Notting Hill, there aren't. And it has to be Notting Hill, remember. The last 28 bus crosses Notting Hill Gate at ten to eleven. Tomorrow night I'll be waiting for it in Church Street. I've got six more weekday evenings, Reg, six more watching nights to Christmas.'

'You shall have the breast of the turkey,' said his uncle, 'and the fifty-pence piece from the pudding.'

As he put the phone down, the doorbell rang and he heard the thin reedy voices of young carol singers.

'God rest you merry, gentlemen,
Let nothing you dismay ...'

Chapter 18

The Monday of the week before Christmas passed and the Tuesday came and there was nothing from Lovat. Very likely he was too busy with the Morag Grey case to make much effort. Her body hadn't been found, and her husband, remanded in custody for a week, was due to appear in court again solely on the shop-breaking charge. Wexford phoned Myringham police station on Tuesday afternoon. It was Mr Lovat's day off, Sergeant Hutton told him, and he wouldn't be found at home as he was attending something called the convention of the Society of Friends of the British Badger.

No word came from Howard. It wasn't awe that stopped Wexford phoning him. You don't harass someone who is doing you the enormous favour of giving up all his free time to gratify your obsession, pursue your chimera. You leave him alone and wait. *Chimera*: Monster, bogy, thing of fanciful conception. That was how the dictionary defined it, Wexford discovered, looking the word up in the solitude of his office. Thing of fanciful conception ... Hathall was flesh and blood all right, but the woman? Only Howard had ever seen her, and Howard wasn't prepared to swear that Hathall – the monster, the bogy – had been her companion. Let nothing you dismay, Wexford told himself. Someone had made that handprint, someone had left those coarse dark hairs on Angela's bedroom floor.

And even if his chances of ever laying hands on her were now remote, growing more remote with each day that passed, he would still want to know how it had been done, fill in those gaps that still remained. He'd want to know where Hathall had met her. In the street, in a pub, as Howard had once suggested? Or had she originally been a friend of Angela's from those early London days before Hathall had been introduced to his second wife at that Finchley party? Surely she must have lived in the vicinity of Toxborough or Myringham if hers had been the job of making withdrawals from those accounts. Or had that task been shared between her and Angela? Hathall had worked only part-time at Kidd's. On his days off, Angela might have used the car to collect.

Then there was the book on Celtic languages, another strange 'exhibit' in the case he hadn't even begun to account for. Celtic languages had some, not remote, connection with archaeology, but Angela had shown no interest in them while working at the library of the National Archaeologists' League. If the book wasn't relevant, why had Hathall been so upset by the sight of it in his, Wexford's, hands?

But whatever he might deduce from the repeated examination of these facts, from carefully listing apparently unconnected pieces of information and trying to establish a link, the really important thing, the securing of Hathall before he left the country, depended now on finding evidence of that fraud. Putting those puzzle pieces together and making a picture of his chimera could wait until it was too late and Hathall was gone. That, he thought bitterly, would make an occupation for the long evenings of the New Year. And when he had still heard nothing from Lovat by Wednesday morning, he drove to Myringham to catch him in his own office, getting there by ten o'clock. Mr Lovat, he was told, was in court and wasn't expected back before lunch.

Wexford pushed his way through the crowds in Myringham's shopping precinct, climbing concrete steps, ascending and descending escalators – the whole lot strung with twinkling fairy lights in the shape of yellow and red daisies – and made his way into the magistrates' court. The public gallery was almost empty. He slid into a seat, looked round for Lovat, and spotted him sitting at the front almost under the Bench.

A pale-faced gangling man of about thirty was in the dock – according to the solicitor appearing for him, one Richard George Grey, of no fixed abode. Ah, the husband of Morag. No wonder Lovat looked so anxious. But it didn't take long for Wexford to gather that the shop-breaking charge against Grey was based on very fragile evidence. The police, obviously, wanted a committal which it didn't look as if they would get. Grey's solicitor, youthful, suave and polished, was doing his best for his client, an effort that made Lovat's mouth turn down. With rare *schadenfreude*, Wexford found himself hoping Grey would get off. Why should he be the lucky one, able to hold a man until he had got enough evidence against him to charge him with the murder of his wife?

'And so you will appreciate, Your Worships, that my client has suffered from a series of grave misfortunes. Although he is not obliged to divulge to you any previous convictions, he wishes to do so, aware, no doubt, of how trivial you will find his one sole conviction to be. And of what does this single conviction consist? That, Your Worships, of being placed on probation for being found on enclosed premises at the tender age of seventeen.'

Wexford shifted along to allow for the entry of two

elderly women with shopping bags. Their expressions were avid and they seemed to make themselves at home. This entertainment, he thought, was free, matutinal, and the real nitty-gritty stuff of life, three advantages it had over the cinema. Savouring Lovat's discomfiture, he listened as the solicitor went on.

'Apart from this, what do his *criminal proclivities* amount to? Oh, it is true that when he found himself destitute and without a roof over his head, he was driven to take refuge in a derelict house for which its rightful owner had no use and which was classified as *unfit for human habitation*. But this, as Your Worships are aware, is no crime. It is not even, as the law has stood for six hundred years, trespass. It is true too that he was dismissed by his previous employer for – he frankly admits, though no charge was brought – appropriating from this employer the negligible sum of two pounds fifty. As a result, he was obliged to leave his flat or tied cottage in Maynnot Hall, Toxborough, and as an even more serious result was deserted by his wife on the ground that she refused to live with a man whose honesty was not beyond reproach. This lady, whose whereabouts are not known and whose desertion has caused my client intense distress, seems to have something in common with the Myringham police, in particular that of hitting a man when he is down . . .'

There was a good deal more in the same vein. Wexford would have found it less boring, he thought, if he had heard more of the concrete evidence and less of this airy-fairy-pleading. But the evidence must have been thin and the identification of Grey shaky, for the magistrates returned after three minutes to dismiss the case. Lovat got up in disgust and Wexford rose to follow him. His elderly neighbours moved their shopping bags under protest, there was a press of people outside the court – a crowd of witnesses appearing for a grievous bodily harm case – and by the time he got through, Lovat was off in his car and not in the direction of the police station.

Well, he was fifteen miles north of Kingsmarkham, fifteen miles nearer London. Why waste those miles? Why not go on northwards for a last word with Eileen Hathall? Things could hardly be worse than they were. There was room only for improvement. And how would he feel if she were to tell him Hathall's emigration had been postponed, that he was staying a week, a fortnight, longer in London?

As he passed through Toxborough, the road taking him along Maynnot Way, a memory twitched at the back of his mind. Richard and Morag Grey had lived here once, had been servants presumably at Maynnot Hall – but it wasn't that. Yet it had something to do with what the young solicitor had said. Concentratedly, he reviewed the case, what he had come to think of as Hathall country, a landscape with figures. So many places and so many figures . . . Of all the personalities he had encountered or heard spoken of, one had been hinted at by that solicitor in his dramatic address to the Bench. But no name had been mentioned except Grey's . . . Yes, his wife. The lost woman, that was it. 'Deserted by his wife on the ground that she refused to live with a man whose honesty was not beyond reproach.' But what did it remind him of? Way back in Hathall country, a year ago perhaps, or months or weeks, someone somewhere had spoken to him of a woman with a peculiar regard for honesty. The trouble was that he hadn't the slightest recollection of who that someone had been.

No effort of memory was required to identify Eileen Hathall's lunch guest. Wexford hadn't seen old Mrs Hathall for fifteen months and he was somewhat aghast to find her there. The ex-wife wouldn't tell the ex-husband of his call, but the mother would very likely tell the son. Never mind. It no longer mattered. Hathall was leaving the country in five days' time. A man who is fleeing his native land for ever has no time for petty revenges and needless precautions.

And it seemed that Mrs Hathall, who was sitting at the table drinking an after-lunch cup of tea, was under a lucky misapprehension as to the cause of his visit. This tiresome policeman had called at a house where she was before; he was calling at a house where she was again. On each previous occasion he had wanted her son, therefore – 'You won't find him here,' she said in that gruff voice with its North Country undercurrent. 'He's busy getting himself ready for going abroad.'

Eileen met his questioning glance. 'He came here last night and said good-bye,' she said. Her voice sounded calm, almost complacent. And looking from one woman to the other, Wexford realized what had happened to them. Hathall, while living in England, had been to each of them a source of chronic bitterness, breeding in the mother a perpetual need to nag and harass, in the ex-wife resentment and humiliation. Hathall gone, Hathall so far away that he might as well be dead, would leave them at peace. Eileen would take on the status almost of a widow, and the old woman would have a ready-made respectable reason – her grand-daughter's English education – as to why her son and daughter-in-law were parted.

'He's going on Monday?' he said.

Old Mrs Hathall nodded with a certain smugness. 'Don't suppose we shall ever set eyes on him again.' She finished her tea, got up and began to clear the table. The minute you finished a meal you cleared

172

the remains of it away. That was the rule. Wexford saw her lift the lid from the teapot and contemplate its contents with an air of irritation as if she regretted the wicked waste of throwing away half a pint of tea. And she indicated to Eileen with a little dumb show that there was more if she wanted it. Eileen shook her head and Mrs Hathall bore the pot away. That Wexford might have drunk it, might at least have been given the chance to refuse it, didn't seem to cross their minds. Eileen waited till her mother-in-law had left the room.

'I'm well rid of him,' she said. 'He'd no call to come here, I'm sure. I'd done without him for five years and I can do without him for the rest of my life. As far as I'm concerned, it's good riddance.'

It was as he had supposed. She was now able to pretend to herself that she had sent him away, that now Angela was gone she could have accompanied him to Brazil herself had she so chosen. 'Mum and me,' she said, surveying the bare room, unadorned by a single bunch of holly or paper streamer, 'Mum and me'll have a quiet Christmas by ourselves. Rosemary's going to her French pen-friend tomorrow and she won't be back till her school term starts. We'll be nice and quiet on our own.'

He almost shivered. The affinity between these women frightened him. Had Eileen married Hathall because he could bring her the mother she wanted? Had Mrs Hathall chosen Eileen for him because this was the daughter she needed?

'Mum's thinking of coming to live here with me,' she said as the old woman came plodding back. 'When Rosemary goes off to college, that is. No point in keeping up two homes, is there?'

A warmer, a more affectionate, woman might have reacted by smiling her gratification or by linking an arm with this ideal daughter-in-law. Mrs Hathall's small cold eyes flickered their approval over the barren room, resting briefly on Eileen's puffy face and crimped hair, while her mouth, rigid and down-turned, showed something like disappointment that she had no fault to find. 'Come along then, Eileen,' she said. 'We've got them dishes to do.'

They left Wexford to find his own way out. As he came from under the canopy that reminded him of a provincial railway station, the car that had been Hathall's turned into the drive, Rosemary at the wheel. The face that was an intelligent version of her grandmother's registered recognition but no polite expression of greeting, no smile.

'I hear you're going to France for Christmas?'

She switched off the engine but otherwise she didn't move.

'I remember your saying once before that you'd never been out of England.'

'That's right.'

'Not even on a day trip to France with your school, Miss Hathall?'

'Oh, that,' she said with icy calm. 'That was the day Angela got herself strangled.' She made a quick chilling gesture of running one finger across her throat. 'I told my mother I was going with school. I didn't. I went out with a boy instead. Satisfied?'

'Not quite. You can drive, you've been able to drive for eighteen months. You disliked Angela and seem fond of your father . . .'

She interrupted him harshly. 'Fond of *him*? I can't stand the sight of any of them. My mother's a vegetable and the old woman's a cow. You don't know – no one knows – what they put me through, pulling me this way and that between them.' The words were heated but her voice didn't rise. 'I'm going to get away this year and none of them'll ever see me again for dust. Those two can live here together and one day they'll just die and no one'll find them for months.' Her hand went up to push a lock of coarse dark hair from her face, and he saw her fingertip, rosy red and quite smooth. 'Satisfied?' she said again.

'I am now.'

'Me kill Angela?' She gave a throaty laugh. 'There's others I'd kill first, I can tell you. Did you really think I'd killed her?'

'Not really,' said Wexford, 'but I'm sure you could have if you'd wanted to.'

He was rather pleased with this parting shot and thought of a few more *esprits d'escalier* as he drove off. It had only once before been his lot to confound a Hathall. He might, of course, have asked her if she had ever known a woman with a scarred fingertip, but it went against the grain with him to ask a daughter to betray her father, even such a daughter and such a father. He wasn't a medieval inquisitor or the pillar of a Fascist state.

Back at the police station he phoned Lovat who, naturally, was out and not expected to reappear till the following day. Howard wouldn't phone. If he had watched last night he had watched in vain, for Hathall had been making his farewells at Croydon.

Dora was icing the Christmas cake, placing in the centre of the white frosted circle a painted plaster Santa Claus and surrounding it with plaster robins, ornaments which came out each year from their silver paper wrappings and which had first been bought when Wexford's elder daughter was a baby.

'There! Doesn't it look nice?'

'Lovely,' said Wexford gloomily.

Dora said with calculated callousness, 'I shall be glad when that man's gone to wherever he's going and you're your normal self again.' She covered the cake and rinsed her hands. 'By the way, d'you remember once asking me about a woman called Lake? The one you said reminded you of George the Second?'

'I didn't say that,' said Wexford uneasily.

'Something like that. Well, I thought you might be interested to know she's getting married. To a man called Somerset. His wife died a couple of months ago. I imagine something has been going on there for years, but they kept it very dark. Quite a mystery. He can't have made any death-bed promises about only taking mistresses, can he? Oh, darling, I do wish you'd show a bit of interest sometimes and not look so perpetually fed up!'

Chapter 19

Thursday was his day off. Not that he would take a day off as he meant to run Lovat to earth – a fine metaphor, he thought, to use in connection with a protector of wildlife – but there was no reason for early rising. He had gone to sleep thinking what an old fool he was to suppose Nancy Lake fancied him when she was going to marry Somerset, and when morning came he was deep in a Hathall dream. This time it was totally nonsensical with Hathall and his woman embarking on to a flying 28 bus, and the phone ringing by his bed jerked him out of it at eight o'clock.

'I thought I'd get you before I left for work,' said Howard's voice. 'I've found the bus stop, Reg.'

That was more alerting than the alarm bell of the phone. 'Tell,' he said.

'I saw him leave Marcus Flower at five-thirty, and when he went up to Bond Street station I knew he'd be going to her. I had to go back to my own manor for a couple of hours, but I got down to the New King's Road by half past ten. God, it was easy. The whole exercise worked out better than I dared hope.

'I was sitting on one of the front seats downstairs, the nearside by the window. He wasn't at the stop at the top of Church Street or the next one just after Notting Hill Gate station. I knew if he was going to get on it would have to be soon and then, lo and behold, there he was all on his own at a request stop half-way up Pembridge Road. He went upstairs. I stayed on the bus and saw him get off at West End Green, and then,' Howard ended triumphantly, 'I went on to Golders Green and came home in a cab.'

'Howard, you are my only ally.'

'Well, you know what Chesterton said about that. I'll be at that bus stop from five-thirty onwards tonight and then we'll see.'

Wexford put on his dressing gown and went downstairs to find what Chesterton had said. 'There are no words to express the abyss between isolation and having one ally. It may be conceded to the mathematicians that four is twice two. But two is not twice one; two is two thousand times one . . .' He felt considerably cheered. Maybe he had no force of men at his disposal but he had Howard, the resolute, the infinitely reliable, the invincible, and together they were two thousand. Two thousand and one with Lovat. He must bath and dress and get over to Myringham right away.

The head of Myringham CID was in, and with him Sergeant Hutton.

'Not a bad day,' said Lovat, peering through his funny little spectacles at the uniformly white, dull, sun-free sky.

Wexford thought it best to say nothing about Richard Grey. 'Did you get to work on that pay-roll thing?'

Lovat nodded very slowly and profoundly, but it was the sergeant who was appointed spokesman. 'We found one or two accounts which looked suspicious, sir. Three, to be precise. One was in the Trustee Savings Bank at Toxborough, one at Passingham St John and one here. All had had regular payments made into them by Kidd and Co., and in all cases the payments and withdrawals ceased in March or April of last year. The one in Myringham was in the name of a woman whose address turned

178

out to be a sort of boarding house-cum-hotel. The people there don't remember her and we haven't been able to trace her. The one at Passingham turned out to be valid, all above board. The woman there worked at Kidd's, left in the March and just didn't bother to take the last thirty pee out of her account.'

'And the Toxborough account?'

'That's the difficulty, sir. It's in the name of a Mrs Mary Lewis and the address is a Toxborough address, but the house is shut up and the people evidently away. The neighbours say they're called Kingsbury not Lewis, but they've taken in lodgers over the years and one of them could have been a Lewis. We just have to wait till the Kingsburys come back.'

'Do these neighbours know when they're coming back?'

'No,' said Lovat.

Does anyone ever go away the week before Christmas and not stay away till after Christmas? Wexford thought it unlikely. His day off stretched before him emptily. A year ago he had resolved to be patient, but the time had come when he was counting the hours rather than the days to Hathall's departure. Four days. Ninety-six hours. And that, he thought, must be the only instance when a large number sounds pitifully smaller than a small number. Ninety-six hours. Five thousand, seven hundred and sixty minutes. Nothing. It would be gone in the twinkling of an eye . . .

And the frustrating thing was that he had to waste those hours, those thousands of minutes, for there was nothing left for him personally to do. He could only go home and help Dora hang up more paper chains, arrange more coy bunches of mistletoe, plant the Christmas tree in its tub, speculate with her as to whether the turkey was small enough to lie on an oven shelf or big enough instead to be suspended by strings from the oven roof. And on Friday when only seventy-two hours remained (four thousand three hundred and twenty minutes) he went with Burden up to the police station canteen for the special Christmas dinner. He even put on a paper hat and pulled a cracker with Policewoman Polly Davis.

Ahead of him was his tea date with Nancy Lake. He nearly phoned her to cancel it, but he didn't do this, telling himself there were still one or two questions she could answer for him and that this was as good a way as any of using up some of those four thousand-odd minutes. By four o'clock he was in Wool Lane, not thinking about her at all, thinking how, eight months before, he had walked there with Howard, full of hope and energy and determination.

'We've been lovers for nineteen years,' she said. 'I'd been married for five and I'd come to live here with my husband, and one day when I was walking in the lane I met Mark. He was in his father's garden, picking plums. We knew its proper name, but we called it a miracle tree because it was a miracle for us.'

'The jam,' said Wexford, 'is very good.'

'Have some more.' She smiled at him across the table. The room where they were sitting was as bare as Eileen Hathall's and there were no Christmas decorations. But it wasn't barren or sterile or cold. He could see signs everywhere of the removal of a picture, a mirror, an ornament, and looking at her, listening to her, he could imagine the beauty and the character of those furnishings that were packed now, ready to be taken to her new home. The dark blue velvet curtains still hung at the french window, and she had drawn them to shut out the early mid-winter dusk. They made for her a sombre night sky background, and she glowed against them, her face a little flushed, the old diamond on her finger and the new diamond beside it, sparking rainbow fire from the light of the lamp at her side. 'Do you know,' she said suddenly, 'what it's like to be in love and have nowhere to go to make love?'

'I know it – vicariously.'

'We managed as best we could. My husband found out and then Mark couldn't come to Wool Lane any more. We'd tried not seeing each other and sometimes we kept it up for months, but it never worked.'

'Why didn't you marry? Neither of you had children.'

She took his empty cup and re-filled it. As she passed it to him, her fingers just brushed his and he felt himself grow hot with something that was almost anger. As if it wasn't bad enough, he thought, her being there and looking like that without all this sex talk as well. 'My husband died,' she said. 'We were going to marry. Then Mark's wife got ill and he couldn't leave her. It was impossible.'

He couldn't keep the sneering note out of his voice. 'So you remained faithful to each other and lived in hopes?'

'No, there were others – for me.' She looked at him steadily, and he found himself unable to return that look. 'Mark knew, and if he minded he never blamed me. How could he? I told you once, I felt like a distraction, something to – to divert him when he could be spared from his wife's bedside.'

'Was it she you meant when you asked me if it was wrong to wish for someone's death?'

'Of course. Who else? Did you think – did you think I was speaking of *Angela*?' Her gravity went and she was smiling again. 'Oh, my dear . . . ! Shall I tell you something else? Two years ago when I was very bored and very lonely because Gwen Somerset was home from hospital and wouldn't let Mark out

181

of her sight, I – I made advances to Robert Hathall. There's confession for you! And he wouldn't have me. He turned me down. I am not accustomed,' she said with mock pomposity, 'to being turned down.'

'I suppose not. Do you think I'm blind,' he said rather savagely, 'or a complete fool?'

'Just unapproachable. If you've finished, shall we go into the other room? It's more comfortable. I haven't yet stripped it of every vestige of me.'

His questions were answered, and there was no need now to ask where she had been when Angela died or where Somerset had been, or probe any of those mysteries about her and Somerset, which were mysteries no more. He might as well say good-bye and go, he thought, as he crossed the hall behind her and followed her into a warmer room of soft textures and deep rich colours, and where there seemed no hard surfaces, but only silk melting into velvet and velvet into brocade. Before she could close the door, he held out his hand to her, meaning to begin a little speech of thanks and farewell. But she took his hand in both of hers.

'I shall be gone on Monday,' she said, looking up into his face. 'The new people are moving in. We shan't meet again. I would promise you that, if you like.'

Up till then he had doubted her intentions towards him. There was no room for doubt now.

'Why should you think I want to be the last fling for a woman who is going to her first love?'

'Isn't it a compliment?'

He said, 'I'm an old man, and an old man who is taken in by compliments is pathetic.'

She flushed a little. 'I shall soon be an old woman. We could be pathetic together.' A rueful laugh shook her voice. 'Don't go yet. We can – talk. We've never really talked yet.'

'We have done nothing but talk,' said Wexford, but

he didn't go. He let her lead him to the sofa and sit beside him and talk to him about Somerset and Somerset's wife and the nineteen years of secrecy and deception. Her hand rested in his, and as he relaxed and listened to her, he remembered the first time he had held it and what she had said when he had kept hold of it a fraction too long. At last she got up. He also rose and put that hand to his lips. 'I wish you happy,' he said. 'I hope you're going to be very happy.'

'I'm a little afraid, you know, of how it will be after so long. Do you understand what I mean?'

'Of course.' He spoke gently, all savagery gone, and when she asked him to have a drink with her, he said, 'I'll drink *to* you and to your happiness.'

She put her arms round his neck and kissed him. The kiss was impulsive, light, over before he could respond to her or resist her. She was gone from the room for some minutes, more minutes than were needful to fetch drinks and glasses. He heard the sound of her footsteps overhead, and he guessed how she would be when she came back. So he had to decide what he should do, whether to go or stay. Gather ye rosebuds, roses, other men's flowers, while ye may? Or be an old man, dreaming dreams and being mindful of one's marriage vows?

The whole of his recent life seemed to him a long series of failures, of cowardice and caution. And yet the whole of his recent life had also been bent towards doing what he believed to be right and just. Perhaps, in the end, it came to the same thing.

At last he went out into the hall. He called her name, 'Nancy!', using that name for the first and only time, and when he moved to the foot of the stairs, he saw her at the head of them. The light there was soft and kind, unnecessarily kind, and she was as he had known she would be, as he had seen her in his fantasies – only better than that, better than his expectations.

He looked up at her in wondering appreciation, looked for long silent minutes. But by then he had made up his mind.

Only the unwise dwell on what is past with regret for rejected opportunity or nostalgia for chosen delight. He regretted nothing, for he had only done what any man of sense would have done in his position. His decision had been reached during those moments while she had been away from the room and he had stuck to that decision, confident he was acting according to his own standards and what was right for him. But he was astonished to find it was so late when he let himself into his own house, nearly eight o'clock. And at the recalling of his mind to time's passing, he was back to counting the minutes, back to calculating that only about three and a half thousand of them remained. Nancy's face faded, the warmth of her vanished. He marched into the kitchen where Dora was making yet another batch of mince pies and said rather brusquely, 'Has Howard phoned?'

She looked up. He had forgotten – he was always forgetting – how astute she was. 'He wouldn't phone at this time, would he? It's last thing at night or first thing in the morning with him.'

'Yes, I know. But I'm strung up about this thing.'

'Indeed you are. You forgot to kiss me.'

So he kissed her, and the immediate past was switched off. No regrets, he reminded himself, no nostalgia, no introspection. And he took a mince pie and bit into the hot crisp crust.

'You'll get fat and gross and revolting.'

'Perhaps,' said Wexford thoughtfully, 'that wouldn't be such a bad thing – in moderation, of course.'

184

Chapter 20

Sheila Wexford, the chief inspector's actress daughter, arrived on Saturday morning. It was good to see her in the flesh, her father said, instead of two-dimensionally and monotonally in her television serial. She pranced about the house, arranging the cards more artistically and singing that she was dreaming of a white Christmas. It seemed, however, that it was going to be a foggy one. The long-range weather forecast had said it would be, and now the weather signs themselves fulfilled this prediction as a white morning mist shrouded the sun at noon and by evening was dense and yellowish.

The shortest day of the year. The Winter Solstice. It was arctic in light as well as in temperature, the fog closing out daylight at three and heralding seventeen hours of darkness. Along the streets lighted Christmas trees showed only as an amber blur in windows. God rest you merry, gentlemen, let nothing you dismay ... Seventeen hours of darkness, thirty-six hours to go.

Howard had promised to phone and did so at ten. Hathall had been indoors alone at 62 Dartmeet Avenue since three. Howard was in the call-box opposite the house, but now he was going home. His six watching nights to Christmas were over – today's had been a bonus vigil, undertaken because he couldn't bear to be beaten and he was going home.

'I'll watch him tomorrow, Reg, for the last time.'

'Is there any point?'

'I shall feel I've done the job as thoroughly as it can be done.'

Hathall had been alone most of the day. Did that mean he had sent the woman on ahead of him? Wexford went to bed early and lay awake thinking of Christmas, thinking of himself and Howard retired to a quiet corner and holding their last inquest over what had happened, what else they could have done, what might have happened if on 2 October a year ago Griswold hadn't issued his ban.

On Sunday morning the fog began to lift. The vague hope Wexford had entertained that fog might force Hathall to postpone his departure faded as the sun appeared strong and bright by midday. He listened to the radio news but no airports were closed and no flights cancelled. And as the evening began with a bright sunset and a clear frosty sky – as if winter was already dying with the passing of the solstice – he knew he must resign himself to Hathall's escape. It was all over.

But though he could teach himself to avoid introspection where Nancy Lake was concerned, he couldn't help dwelling with regret and bitterness over the long period during which he and Robert Hathall had been adversaries. Things might have been very different if only he had guessed at that payroll fraud – if fraud there was – before. He should have known too that an angry paranoiac with much at stake wouldn't react passively to his clumsy probing and what that probing implied. But it was all over now and he would never know who the woman was. Sadly he thought of other questions that must remain unanswered. What was the reason for the presence in Bury Cottage of the Celtic languages book? Why had Hathall, who in middle life had come to enjoy sexual variety, repulsed such a woman as Nancy Lake? Why had his accomplice, in most ways so thorough and careful, left her handprint on, of all places, the side of the bath? And why had Angela, anxious to please her mother-in-law, desperate for a reconciliation, worn on the day of her visit the very clothes which had helped turn her mother-in-law against her?

It didn't cross his mind that, at this late stage, Howard would have any further success. Hathall's habit was to stay at home on Sundays, entertaining his mother or his daughter. And even though he had already said good-bye to them, there seemed no reason to suppose he would change his ways to the extent of going to Notting Hill and her, when they were leaving together on the following day. So when he lifted the receiver at eleven that Sunday night and heard the familiar voice, a little tired now and a little irritable, he thought at first Howard was phoning only to say at what time he and Denise would arrive on Christmas Eve. And when he understood the true reason for the call, that at last when it was too late, Howard was on the brink of accomplishing his task, he felt the sick despair of a man who doesn't want hope to come in and threaten his resignation.

'You saw her?' he said dully. 'You actually saw her?'

'I know how you're feeling, Reg, but I have to tell you. I couldn't keep it to myself. I saw him. I saw her. I saw them together. And I lost them.'

'Oh, *God*'. My God, it's more than I can take.'

'Don't kill the messenger, Reg,' Howard said gently. 'Don't do a Cleopatra on me. I that do bring the news made not the match.'

'I'm not angry with you. How could I be after all you've done? I'm angry with – fate, I suppose. Tell me what happened.'

'I started watching the house in Dartmeet Avenue after lunch. I didn't know whether Hathall was in or not until I saw him come out and put a great sackful of rubbish into one of those dustbins. He was having a clear-out, packing, I expect, and throwing out what he didn't want. I sat there in the car, and I nearly went home when I saw his light go on at half past four.

'Maybe it would have been better if I had gone home. At least I couldn't have raised your hopes. He came out of the house at six, Reg, and walked down to West End Green. I followed him in the car and parked in Mill Lane – that's the street that runs westwards off Fortune Green Road. We both waited for about five minutes. The 28 bus didn't come and he got into a taxi instead.'

'You followed it?' said Wexford, admiration for a moment overcoming his bitterness.

'It's easier to follow a taxi than a bus. Buses keep stopping. Following a taxi in London on a Sunday night is a different matter from trying to do it by day in the rush hours. Anyway, the driver took more or less the same route as the bus. It dropped Hathall outside a pub in Pembridge Road.'

'Near that stop where you saw him get on the bus before?'

'Quite near, yes. I've been to that bus stop and the streets round about it every night this week, Reg. But he must have used the back street to get to her from Notting Hill Gate station. I never saw him once.'

'You went into this pub after him?'

'It's called the Rosy Cross and it was very crowded. He bought two drinks, gin for himself and pernod for her, although she hadn't come in yet. He managed to find two seats in a corner and he put his coat on one of them to keep it. Most of the time the crowd blocked my view of him, but I could see that glass of yellow pernod waiting on the table for her to come and drink it.

'Hathall was early or she was ten minutes late. I didn't know she'd come in till I saw a hand go round that yellow glass and the glass lifted up out of my sight. I moved then and pushed through the crowd to get a better look. It was the same woman I saw him with outside Marcus Flower, a pretty woman in her early thirties with dyed blonde cropped hair. No, don't ask. I didn't see her hand. I was too close for safety as it was. I think Hathall recognized me. God, he'd have to be blind not to by now, even with the care I've taken.

'They drank their drinks quite quickly and pushed their way out. She must live quite near there, but where she lives I can't tell you. It doesn't matter now, anyway. I saw them walking away when I came out and I was going to follow them on foot. A taxi came and they got into it. Hathall didn't even wait to tell the driver where he wanted to go. He just got in and must have given his instructions afterwards. He wasn't going to run the risk of being followed, and I couldn't follow them. The taxi went off up Pembridge Road and I lost them. I lost them and went home.

'The last of Robert Hathall, Reg. It was good while it lasted. I really thought – well, never mind. You were right all along the line and that, I'm afraid, must be your consolation.'

Wexford said good night to his nephew and that he would see him on Christmas Eve. An aircraft sounded overhead, coming out of Gatwick. He stood by his bedroom window and watched its white and red lights like meteors crossing the clear starlit sky. Just a few more hours and Hathall would be on such an aircraft. First thing in the morning? Or an afternoon flight? Or would he and she be going by night? He found he knew very little about extradition. It hadn't come in his way to know about it. And things had taken such strange turns lately that a country would probably bargain, would want concessions or some sort of exchange before releasing a foreign national. Besides, though you might get an extradition order if you had irrefutable evidence of murder, surely you wouldn't on a fraud charge. Deception, the charge would be, he thought, deception under Section 15 of the Theft Act of 1968. It suddenly seemed fantastic to contemplate putting all that political machinery in motion to fetch a man out of Brazil for helping himself to the funds of a plastic doll factory.

He thought of Crippen being apprehended in mid-Atlantic by a wireless message, of train robbers caught after long periods of freedom in the distant South, of films he had seen in which some criminal, at ease now and believing himself secure, felt the heavy hand of the law descend on his shoulder as he sat drinking wine in a sunny pavement café. It wasn't his world. He couldn't see himself, even in a minor capacity, taking part in exotic drama. Instead he saw Hathall flying away to freedom, to the life he had planned and had done murder to get, while in a week or two perhaps Brock Lovat was obliged to admit defeat because he had found no fraud or theft or deception but only a few vague hints of something underhand which Hathall might have been called to account for – if only Hathall had been there to answer.

The day had come.

Waking early, Wexford thought of Hathall waking early too. He had seen Howard the night before, had suspected he was still being followed, so wouldn't have dared spend the night with the woman or have her spend the night with him. Now he was washing at the sink in that nasty little room, taking a suit from the Battle of Mons wardrobe, shaving before packing his razor into the small hand-case he would take with him in the aircraft. Wexford could see the red granite face, more heavily flushed from its contact with the razor's edge, the thinning black hair slicked back with a wet comb. Now Hathall would be taking a last look at the ten by twelve cell which had been his home for nine months, and thinking with happy anticipation of the home that was to be his; now across to the call-box, at mid-winter daybreak, to check his flight with the airport and harangue the girl who spoke to him for not being prompt enough or efficient or considerate enough; now, lastly, a call to *her*, wherever she was, in the labyrinth of Notting Hill. No, perhaps one more call. To the taxi rank or car-hire place for the car that would take him and his luggage away for ever . . .

Stop it, he told himself severely. Leave it. No more of this. This way madness – or at least an obsessional neurosis – lies. Christmas is coming, go to work, forget him. He took Dora a cup of tea and went to work.

In his office he went through the morning mail and stuck a few Christmas cards around. There was one from Nancy Lake, which he looked at thoughtfully for a moment or two before putting it inside his desk. No less than five calendars had come, including one of the glossy nudes *genre*, the offering of a local garage. It brought to mind Ginge at West Hampstead station, the offices of Marcus Flower . . . Was he going crazy? What was happening to him when he let erotica bring to mind a murder hunt? Stop it. From his selection he chose a handsome and immensely dull calendar, twelve colour plates of Sussex scenes, and pinned it on to the wall next to the district map. The gift of a grateful garage he put into a new envelope, marked it *For Your Eyes Only* and had it sent down to Burden's office. That would set the prim inspector fulminating against current moral standards and divert his, Wexford's, mind from that bloody, unspeakable, triumphant, God-damned crook and fugitive, Robert Hathall.

Then he turned his attention to the matters that were at present concerning Kingsmarkham police. Five women in the town and two from outlying villages had complained of obscene telephone calls. The only extraordinary thing about that was that their caller had also been a woman. Wexford smiled a little to note the odd corners of life into which Women's Liberation was infiltrating. He smiled more grimly and with exasperation at Sergeant Martin's attempt to make an issue out of the activities of four small boys who had tied a length of string from a lamp-post to a garden wall in an effort to trip up passers-by. Why did they waste his time with this rubbish? Yet sometimes it is better to have one's time wasted than spent on hankering ever and ever after a vain thing . . .

His internal phone was bleeping. He lifted the receiver, expecting the voice of a self-righteous and indignant Burden.

'Chief Inspector Lovat to see you, sir. Shall I show him up?'

Chapter 21

Lovat came in slowly, and with him his inevitable interpreter, his *fidus Achates*, Sergeant Hutton.

'Lovely day.'

'Be damned to the day,' said Wexford in a throaty voice because his heart and his blood pressure were behaving very strangely. 'Never mind the day. I wish it would bloody well snow, I wish ...'

Hutton said quietly, 'If we might just sit down a while, sir? Mr Lovat has something to tell you which he thinks will interest you greatly. And since it was you put him on to it, it seemed only a matter of courtesy ...'

'Sit down, do as you like, have a calendar, take one each. I know why you've come. But just tell me one thing. Can you get a man extradited for what you've found out? Because if you can't, you've had it. Hathall's going to Brazil today, and ten to one he's gone already.'

'Dear me,' said Lovat placidly.

Wexford nearly put his head in his hands. 'Well, can you?' he shouted.

'I'd better tell you what Mr Lovat *has* found, sir. We called at the home of Mr and Mrs Kingsbury again last night. They'd just returned. They'd been on a visit to their married daughter who was having a baby. No Mrs Mary Lewis has never lodged with them and they have never had any connection with Kidd and Co. Moreover, on making further enquiries

193

at the boarding house Mr Lovat told you about, he could discover no evidence at all of the existence of the other so-called account holder.'

'So you've had a warrant sworn for Hathall's arrest?'

'Mr Lovat would like to talk to Robert Hathall, sir,' said Hutton cautiously. 'I'm sure you'll agree we need a little more to go on. Apart from the – er, courtesy of the matter, we called on you for Hathall's present address.'

'His present address,' Wexford snapped, 'is probably about five miles up in the air above Madeira or wherever that damned plane flies.'

'Unfortunate,' said Lovat, shaking his head.

'Maybe he hasn't left, sir. If we could phone him?'

'I daresay you could if he had a phone and if he hasn't left.' Wexford looked in some despair at the clock. It was ten-thirty. 'Frankly, I don't know what to do. The only thing I can suggest is that we all get out to Millerton-*les-deux* – er, Hightrees Farm, and lay all this before the chief constable.'

'Good idea,' said Lovat. 'Many a fine night I've spent watching the badger setts there.'

Wexford could have kicked him.

He never knew what prompted him to ask the question. There was no sixth sense about it. Perhaps it was just that he thought he should have the facts of this fraud as straight in his mind as they were in Hutton's. But he did ask it, and afterwards he thanked God he had asked it then on the country lane drive to Millerton.

'The addresses of the account holders, sir? One was in the name of Mrs Dorothy Carter of Ascot House, Myringham – that's the boarding house place – and the other of Mrs Mary Lewis at 19 Maynnot Way, Toxborough.'

'Did you say Maynnot Way?' Wexford asked in a voice that sounded far away and unlike his own.

'That's right. It runs from the industrial estate to . . .'

'I know where it runs to, sergeant. I also know who lived at Maynnot Hall in the middle of Maynnot Way.' He felt a constriction in his throat. 'Brock,' he said, 'what were you doing at Kidd's that day I met you at the gates?'

Lovat looked at Hutton and Hutton said, 'Mr Lovat was pursuing his enquiries in connection with the disappearance of Morag Grey, sir. Morag Grey worked as a cleaner at Kidd's for a short while when her husband was gardener at the hall. Naturally, we explored every way open to us.'

'You haven't explored Maynnot Way enough.' Wexford almost gasped at the enormity of his discovery. His chimera, he thought, his thing of fanciful conception. 'Your Morag Grey isn't buried in anyone's garden. She's Robert Hathall's woman, she's going off to Brazil with him. My God, I can see it all . . . !' If only he had Howard beside him to explain all this to instead of the phlegmatic Lovat and this open-mouthed sergeant. 'Listen,' he said. 'This Grey woman was Hathall's accomplice in the fraud. He met her when they both worked at Kidd's, and she and his wife had the job of making withdrawals from those accounts. No doubt, she thought up the name and address of Mrs Mary Lewis because she knew Maynnot Way and knew the Kingsburys let rooms. Hathall fell for her and she murdered Hathall's wife. She isn't dead, Brock, she's been living in London as Hathall's mistress ever since . . . When did she disappear?'

'As far as we know, in August or September of last year, sir,' said the sergeant, and he brought the car to a halt on the gravel outside Hightrees Farm.

195

For the sake of the reputation of Mid-Sussex, it would be most unfortunate for Hathall to escape. This, to Wexford's amazement, was the opinion of Charles Griswold. And he saw a faint flush of unease colour the statesman-like face as the chief constable was forced to admit the theory was tenable.

'This is a little more than "feeling", I think, Reg,' he said, and it was he personally who phoned London Airport.

Wexford and Lovat and Hutton had to wait a long time before he came back. And when he did it was to say that Robert Hathall and a woman travelling as Mrs Hathall were on the passenger list of a flight leaving for Rio de Janeiro at twelve forty-five. The airport police would be instructed to hold them both on a charge of deception under the Theft Act, and a warrant had better be sworn at once.

'She must be travelling on his passport.'

'Or on Angela's,' Wexford said. 'He's still got it. I remember looking at it, but it was left with him in Bury Cottage.'

'No need to be bitter, Reg. Better late than never.'

'It happens, sir,' said Wexford very politely but with an edge to his voice, 'to be twenty to twelve now. I just hope we're in time.'

'Oh, he won't get out now,' Griswold said on a breezy note. 'They'll stop him at the airport where you can take yourselves forthwith. Forthwith, Reg. And tomorrow morning you can come over for a Christmas drink and tell me all about it.'

They went back to Kingsmarkham to pick up Burden. The inspector was in the foyer, peering through his glasses at the envelope he brandished, and angrily enquiring of a puzzled station sergeant who had had the effrontery to send him pornography for his exclusive perusal.

'Hathall?' he said when Wexford explained. 'You don't mean it. You're joking.'

'Get in the car, Mike, and I'll tell you on the way. No, Sergeant Hutton will tell *us* on the way. What have you got there? Art studies? Now I see why you needed glasses.'

Burden gave a snort of rage and was about to launch into a long explanation of his innocence, but Wexford cut him short. He didn't need diversions now. He had been waiting for this day, this moment, for fifteen months, and he could have shouted his triumph at the crisp blue air, the spring-like sun. They left in two cars. The first contained Lovat and his driver and Polly Davis, the second Wexford, Burden and Sergeant Hutton with their driver.

'I want to know everything you can tell me about Morag Grey.'

'She was – well, is – a Scot, sir. From the north-west of Scotland, Ullapool. But there's not much work up there and she came south and went into service. She met Grey seven or eight years ago and married him and they got that job at Maynnot Hall.'

'What, he did the garden and she cleaned the place?'

'That's right. I don't quite know why as she seems to have been a cut above that sort of thing. According to her mother and – more to the point – according to her employer at the hall, she'd had a reasonable sort of education and was quite bright. Her mother says Grey had dragged her down.'

'How old is she and what does she look like?'

'She'd be about thirty-two now, sir. Thin, dark-haired, nothing special. She did some of the house-work at the hall and did outside cleaning jobs as well. One of those was at Kidd's, in last March twelvemonth, but she only stayed two or three weeks. Then Grey got the sack for taking a couple of quid from his employer's wife's handbag. They had to leave their flat and go and squat in Myringham Old Town. But soon after that Morag turned him out. Grey says she found out the reason for their getting the push and wouldn't go on living with a thief. A likely story, I'm sure you'll agree, sir. But he insisted on it, despite the fact that he went straight from her to another woman who had a room about a mile away on the other side of Myringham.'

'It doesn't,' said Wexford thoughtfully, 'seem a likely story under the circumstances.'

'He says he spent the money he pinched on a present for her, a gilt snake necklace . . .'

'Ah.'

'Which may be true but doesn't prove much.'

'I wouldn't say that, Sergeant. What happened to her when she was left on her own?'

'We know very little about that. Squatters don't really have neighbours, they're an itinerant population. She had a series of cleaning jobs up until August and then she went on Social Security. All we know is that Morag told a woman in that row of houses that she'd got a good job in the offing and would be moving away. What that job was and where she was going we never found out. No one saw her after the middle of September. Grey came back around Christmas and took away what possessions she'd left behind.'

'Didn't you say it was her mother who started the hue and cry?'

'Morag had been a regular correspondent, and when her mother got no answers to her letters she wrote to Grey. He found the letters when he went back at Christmas and at last he wrote back with some cock-and-bull story about thinking his wife had gone to Scotland. Mother had never trusted Richard Grey and she went to the police. She came down here and we had to get an interpreter in on account of – believe it or not – her speaking only Gaelic.'

Wexford, who at that moment felt, like the White Queen, that he could have believed six impossible things before breakfast, said, 'Does Morag also – er, have the Gaelic?'

'Yes, sir, she does. She's bilingual.'

With a sigh Wexford sank back against the upholstery. There were a few loose ends to be tied, a few small instances of the unaccountable to be accounted for, but otherwise . . . He closed his eyes. The car was going very slowly. Vaguely he wondered, but without looking, if they were running into heavy traffic as they approached London. It didn't matter. Hathall would have been stopped by now, detained in some little side room of the airport. Even if he hadn't been told why he wasn't allowed to fly, he would know. He would know it was all over. The car was almost stopping. Wexford opened his eyes and seized Burden's arm. He wound down the window.

'See,' he said, pointing to the ground that now slid past at a snail's pace. 'It does move. And that . . .' his arm went upwards, skywards, '. . . that doesn't.'

'What doesn't?' said Burden. 'There's nothing to see. Look for yourself. We're fogbound.'

Chapter 22

It was nearly four o'clock before they reached the airport. All aircraft were grounded, and Christmas holiday travellers filled the lounges while queues formed at enquiry desks. The fog was all-enveloping, fluffy like aerated snow, dense earthbound clouds of it, a white gas that set people coughing and covering their faces.

Hathall wasn't there.

The fog had begun to come down at Heathrow at eleven-thirty, but it had affected other parts of London earlier than that. Had he been among the hundreds who had phoned the airport from fog-bound outer suburbs to enquire if their flights would leave? There was no way of knowing. Wexford walked slowly and painstakingly through the lounges, from bar to restaurant, out on to the observation terraces, looking into every face, tired faces, indignant faces, bored faces. Hathall wasn't there.

'According to the weather forecast,' said Burden, 'the fog'll lift by evening.'

'And according to the long-range, it's going to be a white Christmas, a white fog Christmas. You and Polly stay here, Mike. Get on to the chief constable and fix it so that we have every exit watched, not just Heathrow.'

So Burden and Polly remained while Wexford and

Lovat and Hutton began the long drive to Hampstead. It was very slow going. Streams of traffic, bound for the M1, blocked all the north-west roads as the fog, made tawny by the yellow overhead lights, cast a blinding pall over the city. The landmarks on the route, which by now were all too familiar, had lost their sharp outlines and become amorphous. The winding hills of Hampstead lay under a smoky shroud and the great trees of Hampstead loomed like black clouds before being swallowed up in paler vapour. They crawled into Dartmeet Avenue at ten minutes to seven and pulled up outside number 62. The house was in darkness, every window tight shut and dead black. The dustbins were dewed where the fog had condensed on them. Their lids were scattered, and a cat darted out from under one of them, a chicken bone in its mouth. As Wexford got out of the car, the fog caught at his throat. He thought of another foggy day in Myringham Old Town, of men digging in vain for a body that had never been there. He thought of how his whole pursuit of Hathall had been befogged by doubt and confusion and obstruction, and then he went up to the front door and rang the landlord's bell.

He had rung it twice more before a light showed through the pane of glass above the lintel. At last the door was opened by the same little elderly man Wexford had once before seen come out and fetch his cat. He was smoking a thin cigar and he showed neither surprise nor interest when the chief inspector said who he was and showed him his warrant card.

'Mr Hathall left last night,' he said.

'Last night?'

'That's right. To tell you the truth, I didn't expect him to go till this morning. He'd paid his rent up to tonight. But he got hold of me in a bit of a hurry last night and said he'd decided to go, so it wasn't for me to argue, was it?'

The hall was icy cold, in spite of the oil heater which stood at the foot of the stairs, and the place reeked of burning oil and cigar smoke. Lovat rubbed his hands together, then held them out over the guttering blue and yellow flames.

'Mr Hathall came back here about eight last night in a taxi,' said the landlord. 'I was out in the front garden, calling my cat. He came up to me and said he wanted to vacate his room there and then.'

'How did he seem?' Wexford said urgently. 'Worried? Upset?'

'Nothing out of the way. He was never what you'd call a pleasant chap. Always grumbling about something. We went up to his room for me to take the inventory. I always insist on that before I give them back their deposits. D'you want to go up now? There's nothing to see, but you can if you want.'

Wexford nodded and they mounted the stairs. The hall and the landing were lit by the kind of lights that go off automatically after two minutes, and they went off now before Hathall's door was reached. In the pitch dark the landlord cursed, fumbling for his keys and for the light switch. And Wexford, his nerves tautening again, let out a grunt of shock when something snaked along the banister rail and jumped for the landlord's shoulder. It was, of course, only the cat. The light went on, the key was found, and the door opened.

The room was stuffy and musty as well as cold. Wexford saw Hutton's lip curl as he glanced at the First World War wardrobe, the fireside chairs and the ugly paintings, as he thought no doubt of an inventory being taken of this Junk City rubbish. Thin blankets lay untidily folded on the bare mattress beside a bundle of nickel knives and forks secured with a rubber band, a whistling kettle with a string-bound handle and a plaster vase that still bore on its base the price ticket indicating that it had cost thirty-five pence.

The cat ran along the mantelpiece and leapt on to the screen. 'I knew there was something fishy about him, mind you,' said the landlord.

'How? What gave you that idea?'

He favoured Wexford with a rather contemptuous smile. 'I've seen you before, for one thing. I can spot a copper a mile off. And there was always folks watching him. I don't miss much, though I don't say much either. I spotted the little fellow with the ginger hair – made me laugh when he came here and said he was from the council – and the tall thin one that was always in a car.'

'Then you'll know,' Wexford said, swallowing his humiliation, 'why he was watched.'

'Not me. He never did nothing but come and go and have his mother to tea and grouse about the rent.'

'He never had a woman come here? A woman with short fair hair?'

'Not him. His mother and his daughter, that's all. That's who he told me they were, and I reckon it was true seeing they was the spitting image of him. Come on, puss, let's get back where it's warm.'

Turning wearily away, standing on the spot where Hathall had been on the point of flinging him down those stairs, Wexford said, 'You gave him back his deposit and he left. What time was that?'

'About nine.' The landing light went off again and again the landlord flicked the switch, muttering under his breath while the cat purred on his shoulder. 'He was going abroad somewhere, he said. There were a lot of labels on his cases but I didn't

203

look close. I like to see what they're doing, you know, keep an eye till they're off the premises. He went over the road and made a phone call and then a taxi came and took him off.'

They went down into the smelly hall. The light went off and this time the landlord didn't switch it on. He closed the door on them quickly to keep out the fog.

'He could have gone last night,' said Wexford to Lovat. 'He could have crossed to Paris or Brussels or Amsterdam and flown from there.'

'But why should he?' Hutton objected. 'Why should he think we're on to him after all this time?'

Wexford didn't want to tell them, at this stage, about Howard's involvement or Howard's encounter with Hathall on the previous evening. But it had come sharply into his mind up in that cold deserted room. Hathall had seen Howard at about seven, had recognized this man who was tailing him, and soon after had given him the slip. The taxi he had got into had dropped the girl off and taken him back to Dartmeet Avenue where he had settled with his landlord, taken his luggage and gone. Gone where? Back to her first and then...? Wexford shrugged unhappily and went across the road to the call-box.

Burden's voice told him the airport was still fogbound. The place was swarming with disappointed stranded would-be travellers, and swarming by now with anxious police. Hathall hadn't appeared. If he had phoned, along with hundreds of other callers, he hadn't given his name.

'But he knows we're on to him,' said Burden.

'What d'you mean?'

'D'you remember a chap called Aveney? Manager of Kidd's?'

'Of course I remember. What the hell is this?'

'He got a phone call from Hathall at his home at

nine last night. Hathall wanted to know – asked in a roundabout way, mind you – if we'd been asking questions about him. And Aveney, the fool, said not about his wife, that was all over, but only looking into the books in case there was something fishy about the pay-roll.'

'How do we know all this?' Wexford asked dully.

'Aveney had second thoughts, wondered if he ought to have told him anything, though he knew our enquiries had come to nothing. Apparently, he tried to get hold of you this morning and when he couldn't he at last contacted Mr Griswold.'

That, then, was the phone call Hathall had made from the call-box in Dartmeet Avenue, this very call-box, after leaving the landlord and before getting into that taxi. That, coupled with his recognition of Howard, would have been enough to frighten the wits out of him. Wexford went back across the road and got into the car where Lovat was smoking one of his nasty little damp cigarettes.

'I think the fog's thinning, sir,' said Hutton.

'Maybe. What time is it?'

'Ten to eight. What do we do now? Get back to the airport or try and find Morag Grey's place?'

With patient sarcasm, Wexford said, 'I have been trying to do that for nine months, Sergeant, the normal period of gestation, and I've brought forth nothing. Maybe you think you can do better in a couple of hours.'

'We could at least go back through Notting Hill, sir, instead of taking the quicker way by the North Circular.'

'Oh, do as you like,' Wexford snapped, and he flung himself into the corner as far as possible from Lovat and his cigarette which smelt as bad as the landlord's cigar. Badgers! Country coppers, he thought unfairly. Fools who couldn't make a simple charge like shop-breaking stick. What did Hutton think Notting Hill was? A village like Passingham St John where everyone knew everyone else and would be all agog and raring to gossip because a neighbour had gone off to foreign parts?

They followed the 28 bus route. West End Lane, Quex Road, Kilburn High Road, Kilburn Park ... The fog was decreasing, moving now, lying here in dense patches, there shivering and thinning into streaks. And Christmas colours began to glitter through it, garish paper banners in windows, sharp little starry lights that winked on and off. Shirland Road, Great Western Road, Pembridge Villas, Pembridge Road ...

One of these, Wexford thought, sitting up, must be the bus stop where Howard had seen Hathall board the 28. Streets debouched everywhere, streets that led into other streets, into squares, into a vast multitudinously peopled hinterland. Let Hutton make what he could of ...

'Stop the car, will you?' he said quickly.

Pink light streamed across the roadway from the glazed doors of a public house. Wexford had seen its sign and remembered. The Rosy Cross. If they had been regular customers, if they had often met there, the licensee or a barman might recall them. Perhaps they had met there again last night before leaving or had gone back just to say good-bye. At least he would know. This way he might know for sure.

The interior was an inferno of light and noise and smoke. The crowd was of a density and a conviviality usually only reached much later in the evening, but this was Christmas, the night before the Eve. Not only was every table occupied and every bar stool and place by the bar, but every square foot of floor space too where people stood packed, pressed against each other, their cigarettes sending spirals of smoke to mingle with the blue pall that hung between gently swaying paper chains and smarting screwed-up eyes. Wexford pushed his way to the bar. Two barmen and a girl were working it, serving drinks feverishly, wiping down the counter, slopping dirty glasses into a steaming sink.

'And the next?' called the older of the barmen, the licensee maybe. His face was red, his forehead gleaming with sweat and his grey hair plastered against it in wet curls. 'What's for you, sir?'

Wexford said, 'Police. I'm looking for a tall black-haired man, about forty-five, and a younger blonde woman.' His elbow was jostled and he felt a trickle of beer run down his wrist. 'They were in here last night. The name is . . .'

'They don't give their names. There were about five hundred people in here last night.'

'I've reason to think they came in here regularly.'

The barman shrugged. 'I have to attend to my customers. Can you wait ten minutes?'

But Wexford thought he had waited long enough. Let it pass into other hands, he could do no more. Struggling through the press of people, he made again for the door, bemused by the colours and the lights and the smoke and the heady reek of liquor. There seemed to be coloured shapes everywhere, the circles of red and purple balloons, the shining translucent cones of liqueur bottles, the squares of stained window glass. His head swimming, he realized he hadn't eaten all day. Red and purple circles, orange and blue paper spheres, here a green glass square, there a bright yellow rectangle . . .

A bright yellow rectangle. His head cleared. He steadied and stilled himself. Jammed between a man in a leather coat and a girl in a fur coat, he looked through a tiny space that wasn't cluttered by skirts and legs and chair legs and handbags, looked through the blue acrid smoke at that yellow rectangle which was liquid in a tall glass, and saw it raised by a hand and carried out of his sight.

Pernod. Not a popular drink in England. Ginge had drunk it mixed with Guinness as a Demon King. And one other, she that he sought, his chimera, his thing of fanciful conception, drank it diluted and yellowed by water. He moved slowly, pushing his way towards that corner table where she was, but he could get only within three yards of her. There were too many people. But now there was a space clear enough at eye level for him to see her, and he looked long and long, staring greedily as a man in love stares at the woman whose coming he has awaited for months on end.

She had a pretty face, tired and wan. Her eyes were smarting from the smoke and her cropped blonde hair showed half an inch of dark at the roots. She was alone, but the chair beside her was covered by a folded coat, a man's coat, and stacked against the wall behind her, piled at her feet and walling her in, were half a dozen suitcases. She lifted her glass again and sipped from it, not looking at him at all, but darting quick nervous glances towards a heavy mahogany door marked *Telephone and Toilets*. But Wexford lingered, looking his fill at his chimera made flesh, until hats and hair and faces converged and cut off his view.

He opened the mahogany door and slipped into a passage. Two more doors faced him, and at the end of the passage was a glass kiosk. Hathall was bent over the phone inside it, his back to Wexford. Phoning the airport, Wexford thought, phoning to see if his flight's on now the fog is lifting. He stepped into the men's lavatory, pulling the door to, waiting till he heard Hathall's footsteps pass along the passage.

The mahogany door swung and clicked shut. Wexford let a minute go by and then he too went back into the bar. The cases were gone, the yellow glass empty. Thrusting people aside, ignoring expostulation, he gained the street door and flung it open. Hathall and the woman were on the pavement edge, surrounded by their cases, waiting to hail a taxi.

Wexford flashed a glance at the car, caught Hutton's eye and raised his hand sharply, beckoning. Three of the car's doors opened simultaneously and the three policemen it had contained were on their feet, bounced on to the wet stone as if on springs. And then Hathall understood. He swung round to face them, his arm enclosing the woman in a protective but useless hold. The colour went out of his face, and in the light of the misted yellow lamps the jutting jaw, the sharp nose and the high forehead were greenish with terror and the final failure of his hopes. Wexford went up to him.

The woman said, 'We should have left last night, Bob,' and when he heard her accent, made strong by fear, he knew. He knew for sure. But he couldn't find his voice and, standing silent, he left it to Lovat to approach her and begin the words of the caution and the charge.

'Morag Grey . . .'

She brought her knuckles to her trembling lips, and Wexford saw the small L-shaped scar on her forefinger as he had seen it in his dreams.

209

Chapter 23

Christmas Eve.

They had all arrived and Wexford's house was full. Upstairs, the two little grandsons were in bed. In the kitchen Dora was again examining that turkey, consulting Denise this time as to the all-important question of whether to hang it up or lay it on the oven shelf. In the living room Sheila and her sister were dressing the tree while Burden's teenage children subjected the record player, which had to be in good order for the following day, to a rather inexpert servicing. Burden had taken Wexford's son-in-law down to the Dragon for a drink.

'The dining room for us then,' said Wexford to his nephew. The table was already laid for Christmas dinner, already decorated with a handsome centrepiece. And the fire was laid too, as sacrosanct as the table, but Wexford put a match to the sticks. 'I shall get into trouble about that,' he said, 'but I don't care. I don't care about anything now I've found her, now *you*,' he added generously, 'and I have found her.'

'It was little or nothing I did,' said Howard. 'I never even found where she was living. Presumably, you know now?'

'In Pembridge Road itself,' said Wexford. 'He only had that miserable room but he paid the rent of a whole flat for her. No doubt, he loves her, though the last thing I want is to be sentimental about him.' He took a new bottle of whisky from the sideboard, poured a glass for Howard and then, recklessly, one for himself. 'Shall I tell you about it?'

'Is there much left to tell? Mike Burden's already filled me in on the identity of the woman, this Morag Grey. I tried to stop him. I knew you'd want to tell me yourself.'

'Mike Burden,' said his uncle as the fire began to crackle and blaze, 'had today off. I haven't seen him since I left him at London Airport yesterday afternoon. He hasn't filled you in, he doesn't know, unless – is it in the evening papers? The special court, I mean?'

'It wasn't in the early editions.'

'Then there is much left to tell.' Wexford drew the curtains against the fog which had returned in the afternoon. 'What did Mike say?'

'That it happened more or less the way you guessed, the three of them in the pay-roll fraud. Wasn't it that way?'

'My theory,' Wexford said, 'left far too many loopholes.' He pulled his armchair closer to the fire. 'Good to relax, isn't it? Aren't you glad you haven't got to get your tailing gear on and go off up to West End Green?'

'I'll say it again, I did very little. But at least I don't deserve to be kept in suspense.'

'True, and I won't keep you in it. There was a pay-roll fraud all right. Hathall set up at least two fictitious accounts, and maybe more, soon after he joined Kidd's. He was pulling in a minimum of an extra thirty pounds a week for two years. But Morag Grey wasn't in on it. She wouldn't have helped anyone swindle a company. She was an honest woman. She was so honest she didn't even keep a pound note she found on an office floor, and so upright she wouldn't stay married to a man who'd stolen two pounds fifty. She couldn't have been in on it, still less have planned and collected from the Mary Lewis account because Hathall didn't meet her till the March. She was only at Kidd's for a couple of weeks and that was three months before Hathall left.'

'But Hathall was in love with her, surely? You said so yourself. And what other motive . . .?'

'Hathall was in love with his wife. Oh, I know we decided he'd acquired amorous tastes, but what real evidence did we have of that?' With a slight self-consciousness too well covered for Howard to detect, Wexford said, 'If he was so susceptible, why did he reject the advances of a certain very attractive neighbour of his? Why did he give everyone who knew him the impression of being an obsessively devoted husband?'

'You tell me,' Howard grinned. 'You'll be saying in a minute that Morag Grey didn't kill Angela Hathall.'

'That's right. She didn't. Angela Hathall killed Morag Grey.'

A wail rose from the record player in the next room. Small feet scuttled across the floor above and there was a violent crash from the kitchen. The noise drowned Howard's low exclamation.

'I was pretty surprised myself,' Wexford went on casually. 'I suppose I guessed when I found out yesterday about Morag Grey being so honest and only being at Kidd's for such a short while. Then when we arrested them and I heard her Australian accent I knew.'

Howard shook his head slowly in astonishment and wonder rather than disbelief. 'But the identification, Reg? How could he hope to get away with it?'

'He did get away with it for fifteen months. You see, the secretive isolated life they led in order to make the pay-roll scheme work was in their favour when they planned this murder. It wouldn't have done for Angela to get well known in case she was recognized as not being Mrs Lewis or Mrs Carter when she went to make withdrawals from those accounts. Hardly a soul knew her even by sight. Mrs Lake did, of course, and so did her cousin, Mark Somerset, but who on earth would have called on them to identify the body? The natural person was Angela's husband. And just in case there was any doubt, he took his mother with him, taking care she should see the body first. Angela had dressed Morag in her own clothes, those very clothes she was wearing on the only previous occasion her mother-in-law had seen her. That was a fine piece of psychology, Howard, thought up, I'm sure, by Angela who planned all the intricacies of this business. It was old Mrs Hathall who phoned us, old Mrs Hathall who put doubt out of court by telling us her daughter-in-law had been found dead in Bury Cottage.

'Angela started cleaning the place weeks ahead to clean off *her own fingerprints*. No wonder she had rubber gloves and dusting gloves. It wouldn't have been too difficult a task, seeing she was alone all week without Hathall there to leave his own prints about. And if we queried such extreme cleanliness, what better reason for it than that she was getting the cottage perfect for old Mrs Hathall's visit?'

'Then the handprint and the L-shaped scar were hers?'

'Of course.' Wexford drank his whisky slowly, making it last. 'The prints we thought were hers were Morag's. The hair in the brush we thought was hers was Morag's. She must have brushed the dead girl's hair – nasty, that. The coarser dark hairs were Angela's. She didn't have to clean the car in the

213

garage or at Wood Green. She could have cleaned it at any time she chose in the previous week.'

'But why did she leave that one print?'

'I think I can guess at that. On the morning of the day Morag died, Angela was up early getting on with her cleaning. She was cleaning the bathroom, had perhaps taken off her rubber gloves and was about to put on the others to polish the floor, when the phone rang. Mrs Lake rang to ask if she could come over and pick the miracle plums. And Angela, naturally nervous, steadied herself with her bare hand on the side of the bath when she got up to answer the phone.

'Morag Grey spoke, and doubtless read, Gaelic. Hathall must have known that. So Angela found out her address – they would have been keeping a close eye on her – and wrote to her, or more probably called on her, to ask if she would give her some assistance into the research she was doing into Celtic languages. Morag, a domestic servant, can only have been flattered. And she was poor too, she needed money. This, I think, was the good job she spoke of to her neighbour, and she gave up her cleaning work at this time, going on to the Social Security until Angela was ready for her to start.'

'But didn't she know Angela?'

'Why should she? Angela would have given her a false name, and I see no reason why she should have known Hathall's address. On the nineteenth of September Angela drove over to Myringham Old Town, collected her and drove her to Bury Cottage for a discussion on their future work. She took Morag upstairs to wash or go to the loo or comb her hair. And there she strangled her, Howard, with her own gilt snake necklace.

'After that it was simple. Dress Morag in the red shirt and the jeans, imprint a few mobile objects with

214

her fingerprints, brush her hair. Gloves on, take the car down that tunnel of a lane, away to London. Stay a night or two in an hotel till she could find a room, wait for time to go by till Hathall could join her.'

'But why, Reg? Why kill her?'

'She was an honest woman and she found out what Hathall was up to. She was no fool, Howard, but rather one of those people who have potential but lack drive. Both her former employer and her mother said she was a cut above the kind of work she was doing. Her feckless husband dragged her down. Who knows? Maybe she would have had the ability to advise a *genuine* etymologist on demotic Gaelic, and maybe she thought this was her chance, now she was rid of Grey, to better herself. Angela Hathall, when you come to think of it, is a very good psychologist.'

'I see all that,' said Howard, 'but how did Morag find out about the pay-roll fraud?'

'That,' Wexford said frankly, 'I don't know – yet. I'd guess Hathall stayed late one evening while she was working there, and I'd guess she overheard a phone conversation he had with Angela on that occasion. Perhaps Angela had suggested a false address to him and he called her to check up he'd got it right before he fed it into the computer. Don't forget Angela was the mainspring behind all this. You couldn't have been more right when you said she'd influenced and corrupted him. Hathall is just the sort of man to think of a cleaner as no more than a piece of furniture. But even if he'd spoken guardedly, that name, Mrs Mary Lewis, and that address, 19 Maynnot Way, would have alerted Morag. It was just down the road from where she and her husband lived and she knew no Mary Lewis lived there. And if, after that call, Hathall immediately began to feed the computer . . .'

'She blackmailed him?'

'I doubt it. She was an honest woman. But she'd have queried it, on the spot perhaps. Maybe she merely told him she'd overheard what he'd said and there was no Mary Lewis there, and if he'd seemed flustered – my God, you should see him when he's flustered! – she could have asked more and more questions until she had some hazy idea of what was actually going on.'

'They killed her for *that*?'

Wexford nodded. 'To you and me it seems a wretched motive. But to them? They would ever after have been in a panic of fear, for if Hathall's swindle were uncovered he'd lose his job, lose his new job at Marcus Flower, never get another job in the one field he was trained for. You have to remember what a paranoid pair they were. They expected to be persecuted and hounded, they suspected even the innocent and harmless of having a down on them.'

'You weren't innocent and harmless, Reg,' said Howard quietly.

'No, and perhaps I'm the only person who has ever truly persecuted Robert Hathall.' Wexford raised his almost empty glass. 'Happy Christmas,' he said. 'I shan't let Hathall's loss of liberty cloud the season for me. If anyone deserves to lose it, he does. Shall we join the others? I think I heard Mike come in with my son-in-law.'

The tree had been dressed. Sheila was jiving with John Burden to the thumping cacophony that issued from the record player. Having restored a sleepy little boy to his bed for the third time, Sylvia was wrapping the last of the presents, one of Kidd's Kits for Kids, a paint-box, a geographical globe, a picture book, a toy car. Wexford put an arm round his wife and an arm round Pat Burden and kissed them under the mistletoe. Laughing, he put his hand out to the globe and spun it. Three times it circled on its axis before Burden saw the point, and then he said:

'It does move. You were right. He did do it.'

'Well, you were right too,' said Wexford. 'He didn't murder his wife.' Seeing Burden's look of incredulity, he added, 'And now I suppose I shall have to tell the story all over again.'